dangerous
LOVE

*IN THE END, THERE WAS NOTHING
MORE DANGEROUS THAN LOVE.*

KRIS BUTLER

DARK CONFESSIONS SERIES
BOOK FOUR

Dangerous Love
Dark Confessions Book Four
Kris Butler

First Edition: June 2022
Published by: Incognito Scribe Productions LLC
Kris Butler

Proofreading: © 2022 by Owlsome Author Services
Formatting: © 2022 Incognito Scribe Productions
Cover Design: © 2021 by The Pretty Little Design Co.

❊ Created with Vellum

dangerous LOVE

IN THE END, THERE WAS NOTHING
MORE DANGEROUS THAN LOVE.

KRIS BUTLER

CONTENTS

BLURB

In the end, there was nothing more dangerous than love.

"Atticus was all in, and well, I guess I was all in with the mafia."

If you'd asked me six months ago if this was what my life would look like, I would've politely told you that you were insane.

But now, the mafia, or the men in it, had become my world, and I was learning to embrace the darkness I'd long ignored.

When an enemy rose from the grave and took people from my life, I realized I could no longer play it safe. Always being underestimated meant I was ready to show Dayton Mascro just what a therapist could do. He was about to learn why there was nothing more dangerous than love.

This was the fight of my life. I just had to believe in myself long enough to win.

FOREWORD

This is the 4th book in the series. This is a why choose novel, meaning the main female character doesn't have to choose between love interests. This is a dark contemporary mafia romance, medium burn with a slow build harem. The characters are adults with most being 30 and above. This is an adult romance and intended for readers 18+ due to language and content. This series does contain an MM relationship.

This series deals with killing bad guys, death, depression, child loss, kidnapping, torture, and suicidal thoughts. While these things are dealt with care, please take care of yourself and do not read if triggering for you. While Loren is a therapist, this is fiction and should be treated as such.

Love is love.
However you find it, with whoever you find it, it's valid.
Create your own family and hold onto them with all your got.

PROLOGUE

DAYTON

Leaning against the railing of my new arena, I observed the men below as they carried in the shipment. The bustle made me grin, the success of my takeover coming to fruition. The games I'd managed to play, the cons I'd pulled off successfully, filled me with triumph. It had been more fun than I'd originally imagined watching them all scurry about, trying to figure out my next move, not even knowing who was pulling their strings. It was my greatest symphony.

"Sir, your guest has arrived," a guard said, dipping his head in fearful reverence as it should be.

My son was a fool for thinking things could be different. Corruption worked because people were, at their core, corrupt. They needed someone to mold them into little worker bees, giving them a purpose. I didn't want them to respect me—for respect brought nothing but cold nights and empty bellies. No, fear was the proper way to rule.

Sighing, I stepped away from watching my empire and headed to the dreadful office in the back. Darren had decorated it in blacks and reds when he'd been under the false impression he was in charge. Ah, how nice it was for my son to take care of him for me. Though, I couldn't allow him to stay in FBI custody for too long. Darren knew too much, and for that, he'd need to be taken care of in the end, but at least he was out of the way for now.

Stepping into the cold space, I looked at my guest, observing every inch of him. He held my stare as I walked closer, showing more courage than most men twice his age. The guard Darren had flipped stood against the wall, shifting his weight. I pulled out my gun, not even hesitating as I put a bullet between his eyes. The boy jumped but didn't make a sound. The body slid to the ground in a heap, his lifeless eyes staring back at me. I couldn't risk him growing a conscience and letting Atticus know where we were. He'd already struggled to bring me the kid; only threatening his parents and disabled sister seemed to keep him in line. Too bad I'd killed them, too.

"I have nothing to tell you," the kid said, his voice even.

"I have nothing to ask you, kid. You're leverage, nothing more, nothing less."

"I'm not scared of you."

I stared, assessing. He believed what he was saying, holding my stare as I peered down at him.

"You should be." Taking the gun, I smacked it across his forehead, pistol-whipping him. His eyes rolled back, and he slumped forward.

"There, now I can get some work done." Picking up the phone, I hit a number and waited for them to pick up. "Send someone to clean up a body." I hung up before they could respond, not needing an answer. Here, you either jumped when I asked, or you were taken to the curb in a body bag. There wasn't any in-between with me.

Sitting back on my throne, I kicked my feet up on the desk, the shiny leather winking back at me. When I thought about all the steps that had led me here, I wasn't sure which was my favorite.

Stealing Shayna from my brother and friends.
Raping my brother's side piece and letting him believe he was a father.
Killing my wife and brother.
Letting Atticus think he'd killed me.
Playing with the pretty therapist.
Tricking Darren into thinking that we were partners.
Kidnapping the kid who everyone seemed to care about.

The most satisfying had to be my ruse over Atticus. It hadn't started as a way to deceive him but to test his loyalties. When he went against me with his sister, not seeing my vision for the Mascros, I knew I needed to act.

I'd kept Benny's bones handy in case I ever needed them, and thankfully, I'd found the perfect opportunity for their use. Finally, my brother had been worth his weight in bones.

Every single step had been anticipated, and I'd lured Atticus into the trap with ease. The only thing I hadn't expected was for him to actually shoot me. It almost made me question following through, thinking that maybe there was something worth cultivating in him.

But in the end, I stayed the course, following through with the subterfuge, and escaped through the drainage system. Seth had been waiting for me on the other end and hid me away while I mended. When he got himself killed, I had to find a new spy, but Joel proved to be more loyal to Atticus than my son would ever know.

Too bad he got himself imprisoned as well.

By then, it didn't matter. There were enough defectors ready to leave Atticus and join the new family. My family.

The door opening broke my musing, and I nodded toward the corner where the traitor guard lay. The two men got to work, and I left, nodding to the guard to stay and watch them.

It was time I sent my son his final gift. A wide grin spread across my face, and I wished I could be there to see his.

Buckle up, Son. Daddy's back, and this time, I planned to

win. There wouldn't be anything left of your precious life when I was through.

I'd make sure of that.

ONE

LOREN

The air felt colder, and yet the sun hotter as it beat down on me. I stood in the damp grass, my heels sinking into the ground as I stared at the mahogany casket. It gleamed in the sunlight, and something about that felt disrespectful. Why did it have to look so pristine? Death shouldn't be so shiny.

An arm brushed against me, and I opened my hand, hoping whoever was next to me would take the offering. I couldn't look away, worried it would be over if I did. I wasn't ready for it to be over.

I knew he was dead, but I hadn't accepted it yet. I couldn't.

How did one prepare for this?

It was impossible. This was impossible. I shouldn't be here.

Anger replaced the overwhelming bleakness, bringing me back to life. I could deal with the anger. If I focused on it, then I wouldn't spiral out of control, falling so far into my pit of despair I wouldn't return.

Dayton was responsible for this. I knew it.

An arm wrapped around me from the other side, and I leaned into their body. The smell of clean cotton filled my nostrils, and I knew Monroe stood there. It was comforting feeling him, reminding something inside me that whispered it would be different this time. I could say goodbye without breaking apart.

I wasn't alone. In fact, I was loved beyond anything I'd ever imagined possible.

But this would be hard.

Sucking in a breath, my hand tightened on the one I held, needing to feel their strength as I clung to it.

Guests mingled, but I ignored them all. They weren't important. Only one person here shared my grief, and he wasn't allowed to openly show it.

Tears fell down my cheek, making my sight blurry. I didn't try to stop them. They needed to fall.

"It's time, Loren." I didn't know who said it, but I nodded, letting them lead me up to the casket. Someone handed me a white rose, and I placed it delicately on top. It looked right there. He deserved something pure at his funeral. Taking a minute, I set my hand on the casket, wanting to feel his presence one last time.

I hadn't gotten to say goodbye, his text the last words I'd ever heard from him. We'd opted for a closed casket, the fire having caused extensive damage. I'd been shielded from it, my men taking care of all the tasks for me. Again, I couldn't deny the difference between this funeral and the last.

There I'd been alone, but here I was surrounded by love. It was a gift to grieve openly without having to put a mask on.

"Dry your tears, Loren! You're embarrassing yourself," my mother scoffed, pushing me aside as she laid her own flower. The rage I'd barely been able to contain rose up, and I found a target to unleash it on.

"What are you even doing here, Mother? Dad left you and was finally living his truth. Marcus should be the one up here, not you. You're nothing more than a power-hungry cow. Do us all a favor and leave. No one wants you here, especially Dad."

"How dare you, you ungrateful, spoiled whore!" Her words came out as angry barbs, the spit flying as she threw them at me. For once in my life, they didn't land, her thoughts about my character not holding any value. "Your father's to blame for this. He spoiled you. If he hadn't been out sleeping with men, then maybe you wouldn't have become such a disgrace. I tried, I really did. You and your father deserve whatever you get." She leaned close, whispering her words, so they weren't overheard. "You have nothing now. No case, no witness. *Nothing.* And with his death, I no longer need you. I won, sweetie. Your father finally did something good for me."

Without hesitation, I raised my hand, slapping her across the face. The crowd gasped, but I ignored them all. "Don't you ever speak of him that way! You're so wrong, Jacqueline. It was you who was never worthy of *us*. Take your money, you're gonna need it for a good lawyer. Because don't doubt for one second that I'm not still coming for you. You're far from innocent, and Dad wasn't the only witness I had. If I find you had something to do with his death, there won't be anyone who'd be able to find you. Remember that, *sweetie*."

She gaped at me, her eyes landing on my hand, shock sitting there. I stepped back, straightening the sleeves of my black blazer. I wiped my hand on my side, not wanting her taint to linger on my skin. Ignoring her look of outrage, I placed my palm back on the casket, saying my goodbyes.

"Thank you for showing me the man you truly were in the end. I wish we'd had more time. Our second chance was stolen from us, but I'll never forget the sacrifice you made. Thank you, Dad."

One final tear rolled down my cheek, and I leaned over, kissing the shiny wood. It was warm against my lips, the sun having heated it. The tear fell onto the surface, marking my love for my father forever. I stepped back, walking over to the man sitting in the front row who I'd wished I'd gotten to know more.

"Marcus." I clasped his hands, holding them tight.

"Loren, your father was so proud of you. I'm going to

miss him." He began to tear up, the words hard for him to say.

"Me too. If you'd like, I'd love to get to know you better, as the man my father loved?"

He smiled, nodding. "I'd like that a lot."

"Maybe, together we can share the grief, and it won't feel so scary. Do you have my number?"

He shook his head, and I looked over my shoulder. Nicco stood there, my phone in his hand. I smiled at his attentiveness. Kissing his cheek, I turned back to Marcus. "Give him yours, and I'll be in touch. I need to say hello to a few other guests. If Jacqueline gives you any trouble, just let one of the men with me know. I tried to bar her from attending, but as his wife, she had a legal right to be present according to the funeral home." I gritted my teeth at the information.

He squeezed my hand, and I leaned forward, kissing his cheek. He smelled of peppermints, and it instantly reminded me of my father. The tears I'd been able to swallow dared to return, but I stepped away, needing to focus on something else.

The hollow part of my soul needed a break from grieving my father's death and Jude's kidnapping. I knew I wasn't alone, but I needed to feel whole for a second instead of the broken pieces I'd become.

Strong Loren was capable and sure of herself. I liked feeling that way. I refused to think of the what-ifs, not wanting to play that game, afraid if I thought it, then it would come into existence. Instead, I focused on positive thoughts, knowing that Jude was strong and there was an ending where he returned to us.

While I was the only one grieving the loss of my father, we were all struggling with Jude being gone. He'd touched us all, changing our lives in the brief time we'd had with him.

It wasn't enough time. We needed him, and he needed us. We were the misfit penguin club, which didn't work without him.

"Lore, do you need anything?" I felt Atticus touch my elbow, pulling me into him. He wrapped his arms around me from behind, his head falling on the crook of my neck.

"Just needed a moment where I didn't feel so fucking sad." I turned, wrapping my arms around his neck. "Please, tell me you have something."

"I've heard from Nat. She's made her first contact with the O'Sullivans. Topher and Malek are scouting the Masked Kingpin. So far, the intel Malek's provided seems accurate, but we can't take into account my father not changing it when he left. I don't want you to get your hopes up, but they're planning on going in tonight. It could be the end of the beginning."

"It's something. Thank you for telling me." I leaned up, touching his lips to mine. I didn't deepen it, only needing to feel his against mine to be reassured. I pulled back, laying my head on his chest. The small modicum of strength I'd had a moment ago fled me. "I'm so tired," I admitted. I knew he'd understand. I wasn't just physically exhausted, but I was tired of this fight.

"I know Bellezza, I know. It's okay to rest and let someone else take over for a while. Didn't you say that once?"

"Mmm, if it sounds smart, then probably." I smiled into his jacket, loving the way his hands felt on my body.

"Then definitely you." Chuckling, I pulled back, grateful for the slight reprieve.

"Thank you, Attie. I love you. You gave me my dad back, even if only briefly. That's something I'll never be able to repay you for."

"Don't you get it, Bellezza? You don't have to. You fill my life with so much more just by being in it. I don't need anything else."

"You sound pretty smitten for a badass mafia boss," I whispered, pulling the lapels of his suit.

"What can I say? It only took a sassy therapist to show me what I'd been missing out on. Are you ready to go?"

I sighed, looking around. Most of the guests were gone, only showing for appearance, not caring one way or another about my father. "Yeah. I want to watch them lower him, though. I need it, I think."

He nodded once over my head, leading me over to the casket. My mother was long gone, only Marcus remained. Taking his hand, I held it as we both watched a man who hadn't gotten enough time to show the world what he was made of. The caretaker looked up once he'd lowered him all the way, the spinning wheel making a loud sound.

"I'll give you a few moments." He stood, stepping away. I saw Sax give him an envelope off to the side, and I knew they were making sure my father's grave got extra attention. It was a weirdly sweet gesture.

"Do you want to say anything?" I asked Marcus. He looked anxious, put on the spot, and I knew I needed to do this for him. Closing my eyes, I took a deep breath, finding the words to say out loud.

"I'll miss you, Dad. Thank you for showing me who you really were at the end. I wish we'd gotten more time, but I'm glad we had the few moments we did. I won't stop our fight. Your death won't be meaningless. I love you."

Using some of the things I'd said to him privately, it felt important to make my last words the same as he'd given me. Opening my eyes, I turned to Marcus, hoping he'd feel more comfortable now.

"That was beautiful, Loren. I know he'd wish he'd had more time too. I look forward to meeting Jude. Your father spoke highly of him."

I ignored the statement, not wanting to fall apart at the thought of Jude being gone. "Please, give me a call, okay?" He nodded, and I hugged him quickly. "Be safe, and stay as long as you need."

"Thank you."

I stepped back, not looking at the casket, wanting to remember it as I had when I said goodbye. Five dangerous men in suits stepped up next to me, and together, we made our way to the limo. I imagined our group looked menacing, and for once, I felt it. Power radiated through us, and we weren't something to dismiss.

Focusing on the plan for tonight, I tucked my grief away, pulling the rage back out, ready to take on a murdering psychopath.

Dayton thought he was the smartest person, moving us around like little game pieces. He'd underestimated me, though, not taking into account my mama bear nature or the fact I was now Lady of the fucking Manor.

It was time I introduced him to Mrs. Mascro.

TWO

LOREN

The ring felt odd on my hand as I twirled it around; the diamond sitting there felt like a foreign object now. I'd only been wearing it for a few days, but I'd somehow already picked up a nervous habit of twisting it around. My husband picked up my hand, placing it in his, stopping my movement.

"It will work, Lore."

I turned, taking in Atticus' solemn expression, and nodded. The past week had felt like a blur, and I honestly couldn't remember all the steps we'd taken to end up here.

One moment it felt like everything was falling apart around me, and the next, I was saying "I do" in front of a judge in the middle of the night.

When Atticus had told me his plan to make me Mrs. Mascro, I'd balked at the idea. How could I marry him when I loved five men? I wouldn't do that to them. Plus,

I wasn't sure I wanted to do that whole married life thing again after the first disaster.

Been there, done that, and it wasn't all that great the first time. The fact my ex-husband had recently shot me only sealed the decision to stay far away from the commitment.

So how had I become Mrs. Mascro?

Simple. He'd asked, telling me it was the best way to take down Dayton and rescue Jude. When he put it like that, I couldn't argue. Because he was right.

Dayton didn't understand the concept of sacrifice or love. The only thing that man understood was the power he gained from fear. So to consider that his son could be more powerful through love, well, it didn't even occur to him. He was too much of a narcissist to know what unconditional love felt like. It was his weakness, and it was how we'd win in the end.

I saw that now. Between the truth and the lies lay the darkest confession that whispered to us in the middle of the night, vowing to grant us our heart's desire if we were only brave enough to take it.

Love.

It was the one thing Dayton lacked, and it would be the one thing we could use to destroy him. And it all started with me becoming a Mafia Queen.

Sax squeezed my leg from the other side, and I looked down, grabbing his hand. The shiny metal on his finger contrasted with the rough calluses of his hand, the weathered and beaten skin he'd used to smack plenty of men around with. But it was there, reminding me that I hadn't had to choose in the end.

Because I wasn't just Mrs. Mascro, but Mrs. Mascro-Wessex-Young-Miller. Yeah, I'd married them all. And despite being worried and sad at the moment, I knew one day soon, we'd celebrate it properly, and I looked forward to the day we could share our happiness with our friends.

But for now, we had a purpose, and that was to rescue my son.

"Have you heard anything from Beau or Malek?" I asked.

Sax shook his head, pulling his phone out of his pocket. I looked across the seat to Wells, Monroe, and Nicco observing me. Wells and Monroe were holding hands, similar bands on their fingers, but I didn't miss the way Nicco's leg pressed into Wells' or how he tried to pretend he wasn't pressing back. I smiled at them, hoping they'd quit the dance and do something about the tension I'd felt between them since the greenhouse.

"Anything from Imogen?" I asked, just needing to know my kids were safe. Monroe was the one to answer this time.

"She texted that Levi, Lily, and Olivia made Lego houses, and they were going to bake some cookies with Cami and Mama Hart." He smiled at me, and I relaxed, knowing they were safe.

"Good. I'm glad they're not too focused on Jude." I knew Imogen had to be struggling, but she'd taken it upon herself to be strong for the little ones. Atticus had moved everyone into the manor house and doubled security. He'd had Pixel go over it to make sure it was impenetrable. It felt nice having all the people I cared about close for once. Now, to just get Jude back with us.

"Do you think he got the message?" Nicco asked, looking at his brother.

"Yes." Atticus didn't say anything more, but he didn't need to. We'd made a public display of strength at my father's funeral, wanting to show Dayton we weren't afraid. I knew he'd had my father killed. I wasn't sure if it was meant to be someone else or if my father had been the target all along. Either way, his strike had hit, and I wouldn't forget it.

The car settled back into silence, no one knowing what else to say as we drove back to the manor. Today had been a long day, and it was only getting started. Part two of our plan would go into place tonight. Closing my eyes, I laid my head on Atticus' shoulder, just wanting to close my eyes for a moment.

GENTLE ROCKING WOKE ME, and I realized I was being carried in Sax's arms. I burrowed into his chest more, not wanting to face reality yet. "It's okay, Spitfire. I got you."

"She awake?" I heard one of the men ask.

"No. Just stirring," Sax said, shielding me.

"I'm worried about her," was whispered, and I wasn't sure by whom.

"We all are," Atticus said, not hiding his voice. "But she'll pull through it. She's strong."

"I'm not saying she isn't," Wells hissed, no longer being quiet. "I can be worried about her and not mean she's weak, man."

"I think you're all missing the point," Monroe piped in, and I wanted to wake up and be more aware, so I could be a fly on the wall for this conversation. I bet the facial expressions would be amazing, but the fog of sleep kept me from being fully awake as I wavered in and out of consciousness.

"Oh, Goldie, what's that?" Atticus asked, hitting something that made a beeping sound.

"We all care for her. We're all committed to her now. We need to quit the dominance dance and just remember that when we're with Loren, it's not a mafia boss and his subjects, but five men who love one woman and are finding a way to make it work. We're a family now, and we have dependents. That's important to her, and we're never going to get anywhere if we're always arguing or trying to measure our dicks."

"I don't need to measure. I know mine's the biggest," Sax said, his voice smug. I felt a slap to his arm, and a body move closer. The smell of leather and ginger told me it was Nicco.

"Sunshine was using a metaphor. And it doesn't matter the size. Mine's the most decorative."

"Ew, just stop," Atticus hissed, and I could imagine he was waving his hands to make them. "Listen, I tolerate you three for her, but it doesn't mean I want to know about your dicks. Especially my little brother's."

"Ah, bro, are we having a moment?"

I giggled, the fog clearing the more they talked around me. I peeked open my eyes to find Sax smirking down at me, and Nicco shoved his head in, winking.

"Hey, Beautiful. Tell them mine's the prettiest."

I shook my head, smiling at him. I wasn't falling into that trap. I tapped Sax's arm, and he sat me down on my feet, and I could see we were in the conference room, the TV on, showing some video playback.

"Any news?" I asked, realizing it was of the Masked Kingpin.

"No. I was just checking the feeds. They're not going to move in until later." I nodded, some of the excitement spilling out of me.

"Oh, okay." I rubbed my hands on my dress, realizing I was still in the black garb from the funeral. "I think I'll check on the kids and change. I need to be out of this."

"Care for some company?" Monroe asked.

I nodded, relaxing at the realization I wouldn't have to do it alone. He smiled, walking over to me and wrapping his arm around me. He looked over his shoulder when we got to the door, stopping.

"Try not to kill one another, and if you do have a dick measuring contest, Wells honey, be sure to get pictures for later."

The four men in the room stared back in shock as Monroe pulled me the rest of the way out of the room. I didn't make it more than a few feet before bending over, laughing hysterically.

"Thanks, I needed that," I said a few minutes later, wiping the tears from my eyes. "You surprise me every day, Monroe."

"Good." He stepped forward, took my face between his hands, and kissed me. "I know they get off on calling me good guy names like I'm a golden retriever or pure sunshine, but I don't care. They can call me whatever they want because I get to be with you at the end of the day."

"You're the sweetest, you know?" I pecked his lips, smiling at him. "Come on, let's check on the kids."

He linked his fingers with mine, and we walked to the side of the manor the kids were holed up in. The instant we neared, we could hear their laughter. We stepped into the game room and instantly ducked as a nerf gun dart flew over where we stood. The kids stopped, looking around, unsure if they should keep going or were in trouble.

Topher raised his hands in apology, a smile on his face. "Sorry, ma'am."

I nodded, accepting it as I looked around. They'd turned the game room into an obstacle course. There were pillows and blanket forts, hideaways, and jump spots spread out. I spotted Cami under one with Lily, and Imogen and Levi behind a couch. I looked across the room, finally spotting Lark and Seb hiding with Olivia. She was quiet, but she'd been warming up to the younger kids more. I wanted to get to know her and Seb and Lark, but life hadn't allowed time for it yet. I was glad they were all here, though.

"What are you guys playing? It looks fun."

Levi decided to brave it, stepping forward from his hiding spot as he went into an explanation only an eight-year-old could give. "So, it's like the floor is lava, but with nerf guns, and obstacles, and teams, and you have to run and not touch the floor, but also don't get hit." He beamed, out of breath, and I shook my head, only catching about half of it.

"Sounds fun," I said when he kept staring at me. Monroe chuckled behind me, and I nudged him with my elbow. "Well, we're home, and I just wanted to say hi. I'm going to change my clothes. I'm guessing dinner will be soon. Um, just don't break anything?" I grimaced, not used to being the parent. Monroe squeezed my hand, stepping forward.

"Ten more minutes, and then everyone needs to wash up for dinner. This room needs to return to how it was before you entered. Understand?"

"Yes," chorused out, the adults laughing but knowing they'd be the ones to pay if it wasn't followed.

He pulled me away from the kids, and I let him lead me to my room. It felt weird to say that now, but I couldn't deny I lived here any longer. I spent the majority of my time here. My men were here, and now so was my life. It made sense. There were a few things left in my apartment for now, but all of my clothes and possessions that meant something to Jude and me had been moved. Monroe and Wells had done the same, and we all had our own space on a floor.

"Levi seems to be adjusting," I said, wanting to fill the empty space.

"Yeah, he is. I keep waiting for him to ask about seeing his mom, but so far, he hasn't. I don't know if it's because he's too distracted by all the new things or he doesn't actually miss her. I hope I made the right call, and he doesn't hate me someday."

I turned, taking his arms in mine. "Hey, none of that. You did what you had to. I didn't know how to make that decision for you at the time, but I can see you made the right choice now. With Jude," I swallowed, the words not willing to leave my mouth, "I can see that I'd do anything to keep him safe. So, I get it. I don't begrudge you the choice you had to make, and I know it wasn't out of spite. You're not that person. So, yes, if Levi were to ever learn the truth, he'd forgive you. Has there been any word yet on her?"

He shook his head, his shoulders relaxing. "Kenneth has officially reported her missing. A warrant was also issued when she didn't show up for her mandated court hearing. So, it's only a matter of time."

"One less problem to worry about. Speaking of exes," I said, sighing as I rubbed my forehead. "Shit, we need to figure something out with Brian soon. We can't keep him locked up forever."

"I don't know. I think Atticus could," Monroe laughed, pulling me back toward the direction of my room. As I changed and got dressed for our plans tonight, I had to keep focused on what was ahead.

If everything went according to plan, Jude would be back with us tonight. I didn't know what condition he'd be in, but I had to pray that he'd be okay. My brain wouldn't let me consider any other outcome.

I was worried if he wasn't, that nothing of me would survive, and my darkness would take over, wiping all traces of light from me.

It wasn't a situation I wanted to test. Jude needed to be safe, for all of our sakes.

THREE

SAX

I shifted in the chair I'd squeezed into; the creaking blaring around me in the van. Atticus wouldn't let me or Nicco enter the Masked Kingpin, too afraid our emotions would cloud our judgment, but I'd refused to not be part of it. So, we'd been relegated to the van on monitor duty with Pixel. It sucked, and I was this close to throwing open the doors and storming the place.

Okay, maybe Atticus had a point, but I didn't have to like it.

"Looks like Stocke wasn't lying," Nicco said, pointing at the screen. We watched as they stepped through a hidden door, pulling the black caps on their heads down further to cover their faces. They wore Delgado security uniforms, hoping to blend right in with the enemy.

"Presto, bango," Pixel cheered, hitting a button. The screen showed a looped video, but when I looked at our screen, I could see our guys moving, giving them video cover.

"Nice going, kid," I grunted. I'd finally pieced together the joke she'd played on me by calling me Oscar the Grouch, so now I made it my life's mission to remind her how young she was. It was juvenile, but I had fun doing it. She stuck out her tongue, not caring, and I wondered if maybe I was the one being suckered here.

"Do you think he's here?" I whispered to Nicco, the fear this was all a waste of time rising up.

He shrugged, his eyes glued to the screen. "It makes the most sense. The only other place would be the mansion, and we know every inch of it, so it would be harder for him to hide someone there. I'm hopeful."

"How do you do it?" I asked, curious. "Sometimes it feels like the world is crashing around us, and you just smile more."

Nicco turned, looking at me this time. "I never had to be scared because you and Mas were always watching over me. It made me believe that you guys could conquer anything. I don't doubt you two. You allowed me to live a life of relative safety, shielding me from a lot of the horrors. I knew as long as you two were around, then it would work out somehow." He shrugged, and I sat back, struck dumb by his words. It almost felt like he'd hit me with them; the meaning was so profound.

I cleared my throat, shaking my head a little. "Wow, um, I never realized you saw me that way."

"You never asked." He shrugged his shoulder, turning back in the chair, but stopped, looking back. "For what it's worth, you gave me the freedom to hope, and I know that came at a sacrifice to you, so thank you. But you're not alone in carrying the burdens of this family anymore. In fact, we've kind of grown, so it's okay to let yourself feel some joy and not be scared of things going well for us."

I blinked, seeing Nicco in a whole new light. I'd almost forgotten we weren't alone until Pixel dramatically sighed, leaning on her hands.

"That was so beautiful. Like, I have a tear." She smiled between us, and Nicco smirked at her, looking back at the screen. I was still so flabbergasted by what he'd said I didn't even have a retort in me.

Clearing my throat, I thought about what he said and wanted to believe I could relax at some point and not fear happiness. "Thanks," I whispered, not wanting the Nosey Nelly in the van to hear me. "It means a lot to hear that."

He nodded, but I caught his smile as he scanned through some screens. When he sat up suddenly, looking closer to the monitor, I moved with him. "What is it?" I asked.

"I think they might be in trouble." I tensed at his words, scanning the small screens, trying to figure out what he was seeing. Fuck, I really was too old for this shit.

"Where? They're all too small."

Pixel leaned between us, hitting a button, and the

view enlarged with Malek and Beau. They were outside a room, picking the lock, but I saw what he meant. There was a patrol coming upon them. "Shit." I cursed. I wanted to warn them, but it might be more distracting to do that at this point. Within seconds of being discovered, they slipped through the door and shut it.

The guard stepped up to the alcove they'd been in, looking at the door, almost like he'd heard something. He walked over to it, jiggling the handle to ensure it was locked. The three of us sighed in relief when it appeared to be. From this point, we were blind as we hadn't been able to hack into the feed in the room. It was why Malek had said to try there first, believing it was a containment room. Taking a breath, I decided to trust him that he was right.

"Um, guys, we have a problem," Pixel said, typing so fast I couldn't track her fingers.

"What now?" I asked, sighing and rubbing the back of my neck. The tension had been sitting there for days.

"Incoming." She immediately jumped up, pulled her hair down, and shook it. She pushed up her boobs in her shirt and threw off the flannel she'd been wearing. I found myself staring, not because she was now half-naked, but I never would've expected her to be wearing something like *that* underneath the oversized shirt.

"Damn," Nicco whistled. "Good luck." He high-fived her before I realized she was exiting the van.

"Wait. Where are you going? What are you doing?"

She paused as she stepped out of the back, giving me an incredulous look. "I'm saving our bacon, Pops." Pixel blew a kiss, shutting the door, and I watched on the camera as she ran over to the front to intercept a car.

"She's going to get herself killed," I moaned, beginning to strap my gun on. Once Nicco had said how much Mas and I'd done to always protect everyone, it had set in, and I felt it. I was tired of this life.

"Not so fast," Nicco said, slapping my chest to stop me. "She's a Siren. I think she's capable of handling herself. Give her a chance at least."

"She's your cousin," I said, raising my eyebrow to indicate he was responsible for her.

"Even more reason to let her try." He gave me a look, and I dropped it, anxious to see how Beau was doing.

"You watch Pixel. I'll take Beau."

"I take it back. You should go after her and make sure she doesn't..." He stopped, grimacing, biting his knuckles. "Never mind. She handled it."

Briefly, I glanced over and saw Pixel kick a guy in the nuts and then flip him over her shoulder. Damn. Okay, maybe she was more than meets the eye. Going back to Beau's screen, I searched all the cameras to see if I'd missed them. Just as I was looking, I saw the door crack open. When three people emerged, I sagged in relief.

"Shit," Nicco cursed, and I looked over, not understanding. "I'll drive. You shoot."

I struggled to know what he meant, but then saw it as

Pixel sprinted back to the van, the car that had driven up moments ago now in flames. I opened the door, and she jumped into the back, out of breath, and I stared at her, unsure who she was anymore.

"Go!" she yelled, and the van lurched forward as a bullet pinged off the outside.

"Fuck." I grabbed my gun and flicked off the safety as I jumped into the front, rolling the window down. "Where're our people, Pixel?"

"Um, coming in hot. Get to the back door of the building, and I'll lead them there." She threw on some headphones, her fingers flying again. I was more comfortable with her in that setting and not the man-kicking, fire-exploding one. A car bumped the back of our van, and we swerved.

"Can you lose him?" I asked, aiming for the tire.

"I'm trying," Nicco gritted out, turning the steering wheel every which way. I focused back on the car and aimed. The shot went wide as Nicco dodged out of the way of a light post, the tires squealing as he sped up. Leaning out of the window, I braced myself against the door, praying it wouldn't fly open. Taking a breath, I let it out as I pulled the trigger, this time hitting my target. A shot rang out around us, but I let another fly, shattering the window, hitting the driver's side this time. The car rammed into the light pole we'd swerved, flipping up on its end as the momentum caught up with it.

Exhaling, I relaxed back into the seat, glad at least one

of our problems was dealt with. "How are they looking?" I asked Pixel as I reloaded.

"Um, not so good. Is that blood?" she asked, looking
up, shaking her head as she looked back at the screen.
"It's going to be close. Any chance either of you is a trick
driver and can spin it so the doors open as they exit?"

I looked over at Nicco, my eyes wide. "Trick driver?"
I mouthed, and he snorted, shaking his head.

Pixel huffed, blowing out a breath. "Figures. You
guys should really up your training program. Fine. Be
ready to speed off when I say to then. You won't have
the benefit of not stopping."

Nicco pulled around to the back and turned off the
lights. "How soon?" he asked. I moved back through the
van, opening the back doors, ready for them.

"About that. Seems they've been held up, and I don't
think my tits will get us out of this one." Pixel cringed,
and I cursed, a million different plans running through
my head.

When I knew what I had to do, I glanced at Nicco.
"Take care of Loren." Before he could respond, I jumped
out of the van and ran through the door, my gun at the
ready. Nicco had been right. I was the protector, and that
meant sacrifices. It had never meant more than it did
now. Loren needed Jude, and I could give that to her.
Even at the cost of myself.

FOUR

JUDE

My stomach was clawing at itself, and I hoped it would be food time soon. I didn't know how long I'd been here or how often they fed me. I just knew it had been long enough that they should be bringing me something soon. It wasn't a lot, but I didn't care much when I was this hungry. The rumble sounded loud in the space, and I wondered if everyone could hear it. Not that there was anyone around, but it felt nice to think there was.

All in all, being a captive of the Masked Kingpin wasn't too horrible as far as being held captive went. Since it was my first time, I'd have to wait and rate it until I had more experience to judge.

He left me alone after the first day. Seeing Elijah be murdered in front of me was pretty traumatic, though. I was mad at him for lying, but I didn't necessarily want him dead. It didn't help that they hadn't cleaned the blood off me, so I still had traces of my abductor on my skin. What I wouldn't do for a shower at this point was very limited.

The Kingpin had said I was only useful as leverage, and he apparently meant it. I guess it was a good thing since I wasn't tortured, but I was beginning to realize there were different levels of torture that weren't physical and I wasn't sure which was worse.

Especially as I sat in this stark white room, with nothing but my imagination to entertain me. Food was delivered sparingly, the men dropping it off were my only real visitors, and they weren't very chatty. I hadn't had a shower, been given clean clothes, nor access to a bathroom. Just a concrete room that I was slowly going crazy in.

Even Cameron's cell had more than this one. I was beginning to think my brother had it made as a Mascro prisoner with his soft bed, daily shower, and hot meals. Though technically, I was a Mascro prisoner, too, I supposed. Just not the right one.

Dayton Mascro was an interesting man. I couldn't believe he was Imogen, Nicco, and Atticus' father. He was the furthest thing from any of them you could be.

Leaning my head against the wall, I thought about what I should be doing right now. If I had my day right, which was hard to judge, I should be in school with Imogen. It was weird to think about school at a time like this, but I really liked where I went. And the fact Imogen, the girl I was slowly falling in love with, would be there too, just made it all the better. I wanted to share things with her and do things teenagers did. It felt dumb in the grand scheme of it all, but I guess that was why it was important.

You never knew when you wouldn't get to just be a teen in our world.

Playing my favorite game of 'what I would eat if I could,' I thought about all my favorite things that Loren had introduced me to. I was remembering the fried macaroni balls when the door opened. Peeking my eyelid open, I looked over to see which unfortunate guard got to bring me food today. Unfortunate, because at this point, I stank. When two walked in, empty-handed, I sighed, closing my eyes back.

"No food? Not cool, man."

"Jude," a voice whispered, and I opened my eyes fully this time, the sound familiar, and found a face I knew staring at me in a Delgado guard uniform.

"Am I dreaming? I really thought I would've been more creative with my rescuer. Like Dwayne "The Rock" Johnson, or I don't know, Black Widow. Yeah, that'd be hot."

"Sorry, my leather was at the cleaners. Now, do you want to stay here in this stinking pit or maybe deal with me being the one to bring you home so you can see that pretty girl you've been crushing on?" he asked.

"Wait. You're real?" I sat up, rubbing my eyes.

Jumping to stand, I wavered as I tilted to the side, the guy I didn't know grabbing me to balance.

"Um, hi." I looked to Beau, pointing. "Is he going to kill us?" I whispered.

"No. I'm not," the man I didn't know responded, and I accepted it as truth.

"Okay, cool. So, escaping?" I asked, hope filling me. The thoughts of Imogen and Loren filled my head, along with food and a shower.

I rushed forward, hugging Beau, holding onto him for a second, needing the assurance I wasn't dreaming. "Thank you."

"Of course, kid. I'm sorry we let Elijah take you." He patted my head, hugging me tight. Beau had become a real friend, and I was glad he was here, rescuing me.

I shook my head; the tears I didn't realize had fallen, wetting my face. "No, it wasn't his fault. He was being blackmailed. They had his family."

"It doesn't matter. There's a code. We don't betray our own," Beau bit out, and I decided to drop it. I didn't get the mafia code, and it would be pointless to try and argue over semantics while we were still in Delgado's place and Elijah was dead.

"Here, we're going to make it look like you're a prisoner. I need to tie your hands together. We'll keep the hood off until necessary." He tied my hands loosely together and moved me to the door. The stranger opened it, looked out, and then nodded for us to follow.

Each step I took felt like a million. Everything was buzzing around me, and I didn't know if it was from the lack of food or if this was some weird alternate reality, and I was actually asleep, only dreaming I was being rescued. I still wasn't convinced.

Something in my mind told me it was too good to be true, but I didn't want to focus on it. If I was getting out of here, I wanted to leave, no matter what. I just hoped it wasn't a setup.

"Shit," the guard I didn't know cursed, stopping Beau and my's progress. "Follow my lead."

"Sorry, kid," Beau said before he tossed a bag over my head, and everything went dark. After being left in the dark for a few days, I wasn't as scared of it as I had been. The material felt rough against my face, and it immediately became hot as oxygen was trapped inside with me. I could see a small amount of light filter through, but it didn't allow me to know what was happening. Someone tugged me, and I stumbled, my body weak from malnutrition.

"Halt! Where are you going with the prisoner?" a deep voice asked.

"If you're asking, then you're not in the know," the guard I didn't know said in a bored tone. "Can I carry on with my job, or do you want to be the one to tell the Masked Kingpin you stopped the transportation?"

I had to give it to the guy. Even *I* believed him, and I

knew it wasn't real. I heard rustling and a curse before a walkie-talkie cut in.

"Fire in the front. All available units detour to the front. In pursuit of a white van."

It was quiet for a second before I heard the telltale sound of a gun being loaded as the chamber was pulled.

"Maybe you can try that again," the deep voice said, and I could only assume he was the one pointing the gun at us.

"Nah," the other guard said before I heard what sounded like a scuffle. The bag was whipped off my head, and Beau pulled me as we ran.

Shots fired behind us, but I moved as fast as possible, which wasn't really fast in my condition.

"Sorry about this," Beau said before he picked me up and threw me over his shoulder like I weighed nothing. My body sagged into his, and I didn't argue. It was much easier to be carried at this rate, even if I did feel a little bit like a damsel. Oh well, I was getting rescued. I'd take what I could get.

The commotion in front of us had me lifting my head, and I tried to peer around Beau to see what was happening. The other guard was firing behind us, running every so often to stop and fire off some more rounds. Looking ahead, I saw a familiar face, and I felt my body relax more.

I didn't want to admit I was a little miffed to have a stranger and Beau rescue me when I had three mafia daddies who were much more suited for that role. I'd never been so happy to see Sax as right then. He was one scary mofo, and as he charged in, guns blazing, it felt like everything would be okay now. The Cavalry had arrived, and we were safe.

A second later, everything erupted into chaos around us as guards came from every direction. We were only a few feet from the door, and I watched as Sax passed us, nodding to Beau. He kept running, making it through the door as guns fired off behind us. I felt Beau falter for a second, but he didn't stop moving, tossing me into the van's open doors. I crashed into some equipment, rolling to a stop at the feet of a girl with purple hair I'd seen briefly at the manor.

She peered down at me, a broad smile on her face. "Yay, you're not dead." She scrunched up her nose. "But you reek, kid." She pulled a ball out, moving around me as she balanced on the van's edge.

"Come on," she shouted. At her words, I saw the other two men come barreling out. As Sax went to jump into the van, a guy with a big gun lifted it and shot at him. I squeezed my eyes, not wanting to watch him get hit, fear crawling up my throat.

"Fuck!" I heard him shout, the sound making me feel better. When I opened them, I found him dragging the mysterious guard into the back of the van, his hands pressing down on a bullet wound. I guess the man had jumped in front of him. I blinked, never having seen so much blood before.

"Jude!" he yelled as the purple-haired girl yelled, "Drive."

I looked up, watching as she tossed the ball she'd been holding as the van took off. Sax grabbed my hands, pressing them down on some cloth, telling me to keep them there. He started ripping things as the woman held on, so she didn't fall out the door as Nicco drove like a bat out of Hell.

We were only a few feet away when a boom erupted behind us, the heat licking us as the flames erupted around the open doorway we'd just come through.

"Pixel, you have a serious problem with blowing things up," Sax said, but I heard some admiration in his voice. "Now that you've alerted all of Delgado's men to our whereabouts, how about you help me keep this man from dying? Is first-aid part of the Siren training, or are you the one who is inept in this area?" he asked, lifting an eyebrow.

She huffed, pulling the door shut and locking it, and I felt better as we swerved out onto the open road, no one appearing to follow us.

"Of course, I know first-aid." She sat down, pulled out a kit from under the desk, and started to help Sax with the bleeding man in front of me.

I looked down, finding him watching me. "Um, thanks for saving me."

He nodded, and I didn't know if that was natural or just that he was in too much pain for words.

"You'll be fine," Pixel said, pulling out something that looked like forceps.

"You sure that you should be doing it in the back of the van? Don't you need to be somewhere sterile?" I asked.

"It's fine. I've got this, totally." She nodded, and I looked over to Sax, assessing her. I didn't think he bought it either.

"Maybe—" he started, but before he could get anything else out, she'd bent over the bleeding man and shoved the instrument into him. He cried out, jumping, and I stared in shock as she moved around, looking for something.

"If this was Operation, we'd be dead," I whispered, the lack of finesse obvious as the man finally passed out from the pain. Pixel ignored me, rolling her eyes as she stuck out her tongue in concentration.

"Almost," she whispered and then yanked, pulling a bullet out. I stared in disbelief.

"Okay, I take it back."

"Thank you." She turned to Sax, a look of triumph on her face. "Told you I was trained."

Sax blinked, nodding. "Good, because he wasn't the only one shot." Just then, I realized he was leaning against the van, his face pale as blood pooled around his leg.

"He saved my life, though, so he got to go first," he mumbled before closing his eyes.

"Fuck!" Pixel shouted, turning to me. "Sew this man up." She handed me a kit, and I looked down at it, no clue what to do.

"Um?" I looked around the van, hoping someone else would be more qualified. But there was only us, Beau and Nicco were up front as they drove and made sure no one followed.

Looking through the kit, I pulled out a staple gun, hoping it was easier to use than a needle. Squeezing the skin together, I prayed I was doing it right. My fingers began to slip on the blood as I pressed it down and I was glad the dude was out cold. It couldn't feel good. Once I had three of them in his skin, I sat back, exhaustion coating me.

Pixel looked over, assessing me. "You okay, kid?"

"Yeah. I did learn something," I said, my eyes closing.

"What's that?" she asked, doing the same thing I'd just done to Sax's leg.

"I definitely don't want to be a doctor. I'll stick with art." I slumped back against the van, no longer fighting my eyes, and I fell asleep, praying this hadn't been some hunger-induced hallucination and when I woke up, I'd be back with my family.

FIVE

ATTICUS

The thought of sleeping as we waited to hear how the rescue mission had gone was preposterous, and none of us had even tried. We were spread out in the living room, the children tucked away in their beds. The dogs had taken up residence guarding the little kids, lying in the hallway between them and us. Loren kept nodding off but then would jump, her body remembering she needed to be awake.

It was pure torture having to wait. I wasn't used to being the one on this end of things, but I knew I needed to be here for Loren and the family this time. They needed me in case anything happened. I had to be the strong one for them to lean on. I could do that for them.

So, I stood, hands in my pocket, staring at the door for what felt like a lifetime, waiting for someone to walk through it. If we didn't get Jude back, I was worried about what would become of Lore and Imogen.

We needed this win. We needed Jude.

The golden one joined me in my vigil at the door, not saying anything as he stood next to me. I was still getting to know all the traits he possessed, so I wasn't sure what his ploy was just yet.

"What?" I sighed, unable to take the quiet standoff, the solution to the puzzle not within my grasp.

"Nothing. I'm just giving you support. You're not alone, no matter how much you try to separate yourself." He held up his hand, his ring glinting in the light. "If anything, this right here proves it. You might be the head of your family, but it's not all on you in here." He circled his fingers around the room, and I rolled my eyes at him despite what he said warming me on the inside.

"Save the feel-good pep talk for someone else. The fact you think here is different from everywhere else shows how much you don't understand this life. You have a piece of jewelry, that doesn't change anything with me." I pulled my hands out of my pockets, crossing my arms. I was being more difficult than I'd intended, not wanting to admit what he said had sounded nice. I was tired of being in charge. The pressure was overwhelming.

"Keep your cool facade, but it's not going to save you from the pain if something happens."

"It will be fine," I gritted out, my eye twitching.

"I hope so. I love that kid, and I don't want to particularly think of a world without him, but," he paused, stepping in front of me so that I had to look at him, "life doesn't work out perfectly because you controlled it better than someone else or planned for every outcome." He sucked in a breath, his voice hitching a little. "Bad things happen. The unthinkable *does* occur. And when it does, who are you going to be? The man who stood apart from her, watching the door, or the man who was holding her hand, telling her how scared he was too?" He raised an eyebrow, turning to leave now that his point was made.

His words hit me like a sucker punch. I didn't want to think of the worst because I'd lived it for so long, but was I destroying the best thing in my life in the process? I looked over, seeing Loren's fear along with her strength.

"If that's what you think I should be doing, why aren't you? Why tell me?" I asked, curious.

"Last time I checked, she had two hands." He didn't pause, but kept walking back into the room, sitting next to her on the couch. I watched with some jealousy as he pulled Loren into his arms. He did it so effortlessly.

I was envious of his ability to freely show his emotions, but did I need to be? Maybe he was right. I'd been making strides for our family to be different, and perhaps that meant I had to be the most different, the one charging the way for change.

With a sigh, I took a step toward her and kept going, urging my feet to be where they wanted to be. Monroe looked up at me when I sat down. I expected a cocky smirk, but instead, he gave me a respectful nod. I stared at Loren's hand, the one with the ring I'd placed there, and I reached out, picking it up.

It still amazed me that she'd agreed to my ridiculous plan. With everything that had occurred the past few days, I hadn't really had time to digest that I was a married man. I linked our fingers, looking up at her. I didn't want to admit Goldilocks next to her was right, so I wouldn't.

"They're going to find him, Bellezza."

She looked over, showing the fear I didn't want to feel. She nodded, kissing my cheek. "Maybe we should —" Her words were interrupted as the door I'd been staring at earlier burst open, scaring everyone in the vicinity. The dogs jumped up, barking. Wells startled, cursing, and Imogen sat up, eyes wide. Nat and Cami looked around, worry on their faces.

Loren immediately jumped up, and I followed, pushing her behind me as we waited for them to come around the corner. Monroe stood by my side, making me respect him a little. I didn't want Loren rushing into danger, and he seemed to think the same. My hand moved to the gun that still felt foreign despite its constant presence.

A bright purple head poked around the corner, looking at all of us in annoyance. "A little help here. They're heavy fuckers." We all moved instantly, running to meet them. I scanned over the bodies, counting.

Nicco. Pixel. Malek.

No Jude. No Sax.

"Where's...?" I started to ask when Beau stumbled through, Jude over his shoulder. Loren rushed back into the room, clearing off the couch to lay him on. Running forward, I helped my brother and Pixel carry Malek, who was also passed out, to the ottoman.

Looking up, I tried to figure out where my best friend was. "Sax?" I asked. Pixel glanced up, panting as she caught her breath. "Passed out. You might want to call a doctor or someone. I did what I could, but yeah, not my specialty."

A snort came from the couch, and I realized it was Jude. "That's putting it mildly." He blinked, finding everyone standing around him. "Whoa. Um, hi."

Loren fell next to him, crying into his chest, Imogen joining her. Jude awkwardly patted the two crying women, and I left them to it as I tried to assess the situation, my body not knowing what to do with the adrenaline rush.

Cami was checking Malek over, asking Pixel a million questions. Nat had moved over to Beau, scanning him. When she saw his leg was bleeding, she started to yell at him, and I smiled to myself. They would be taken care of.

"Bro, Sunshine, come and help me with Sax's big ass." Nicco didn't wait for us to respond, heading back toward the garage. I took off, happy to move and leave the emotions in the room with everyone else.

"Sure, I'll just stay here," Wells said, yelling after us. I stopped, looking back for a second.

"Tell Beau to call Doc when he untangles himself from Nat." Wells looked over at the two, cringing.

"Fine," he sighed, sitting back on the couch. The surly fighter was healing, but he was nowhere near ready to carry a man. At least he accepted it for the most part. I guess we were all growing.

Stepping out into the garage, I took in the state of the van. Bullet holes had pierced the outside but wouldn't have made it inside thanks to the bullet-resistant armor. Scorch marks ran up another side, and the back door was a little dented.

"I'm guessing we didn't go undetected?" I asked, though based on the state of everyone, I'd assumed as much.

"Yeah, no." Nicco chuckled, opening the back door. "Our cousin has a bit of a blowing-up shit problem."

"Meaning?" I asked, assessing the best way to get Sax out of the van.

"She carries homemade explosives around in her purse and throws them at people who piss her off. Well, when her boobs don't work, apparently."

I stood, staring, confident he was pranking me. "Are you trying to get one over on me?" I asked as Monroe chuckled next to me, his arms shaking as he covered his mouth.

"Hey assholes, a little help," Sax groaned from inside the van.

Moving forward, I dropped the Pixel joke and put one of Sax's arms around my neck. "You just had to go and be heroic?"

"You know me," he said, groaning as Monroe went to the other side. "I can't sit on the sidelines."

"Next time, I'll just ground your ass here," I mumbled.

"Hopefully, there won't be a next time, but I just might let you if there is. Send the rookies in. I'm too old for this shit. Tell me Doc is on his way. I don't trust Pixel's first aid skills. I'm pretty sure she used nail glue and a stapler to patch me up."

"It's actually very adhesive," she said, standing at the door, holding it open for us. "Bleeders can't be choosers, Oscar."

He grunted but closed his eyes as we carried him the rest of the way. When we entered the room, I scanned for somewhere to place the giant man. Nodding toward the lounger, we laid him down as carefully as possible.

"Sax!" Loren exclaimed, immediately coming over. She started to fuss over him, and I stood back, taking in the scene. We were all here. A little battered and bruised, but we'd made it.

The part of me that had been fearful I wouldn't get to

be happy broke, and I felt the tears start to fall. Sucking in a breath, I turned and stalked toward the kitchen, needing a moment. Leaning against the counter, I calmed my breathing, relieved we were all back.

A small hand tugged at my pants, and I looked down, finding Levi. He held out a cookie and an action figure. "Here, Mr. Atticus."

I looked at him, confused about what he wanted me to do with them. Taking them, I nodded. "Um, thanks. Can I ask why, though? Not that I'm not grateful," I added quickly.

He shrugged his tiny shoulders. "Cookies make me feel better when I'm sad." I smiled, accepting his kid logic.

"Right. That's true." I took a bite, trying to remember the last time I had a cookie. When I was finished, I had to admit, I did feel a little better. "And this?" I asked, showing the action figure.

"Sometimes, the hero thinks he's only a hero in his suit. But your suit is just something you wear. Iron Man learned that." He shrugged his shoulders, his logic making sense to him. I didn't get his comic book reference, but I could appreciate the sentiment. He had no idea I was called "The Suit," but his words struck home all the same.

The Suit was a name used to make others fear me. It didn't make me the man I was. The people in my life, the choices I'd made, the experiences I had, they were what made me who I was. Seemed like Goldie and his kid had a point.

Patting him on his head, I walked him back to his room, not wanting him to see all the blood in the other one, and pulled out my phone to have Topher watch the hallway, so none of the other littles made their way down here.

Beau was waiting for me when I entered, and I nodded for him to talk to me in the corner.

"Report."

"For the most part, the plan went as we hoped. We made it in, no problem. Found Jude and were heading out with him when we were stopped by a guard. There was a commotion up front, and that was when things escalated. I threw Jude over my shoulder and booked it out of there. Sax barged in, saving us as I got Jude and me into the van. Pixel tossed something at the other guys as Sax and Stocke made it toward the van. I didn't see it, but it sounded like Stocke jumped in front of Sax, saving his life. Once they were in, Nicco took off, and whatever Pixel had thrown at them exploded. One car pursued us for a bit, but we lost them after a mile."

"I guess we owe Stocke our trust then. He saved Jude and Sax." I hadn't been sure about his loyalty. I wanted to trust my cousin, that she'd made a better decision this time when it came to men, but a part of me worried she was falling into another Darren trap. "What's Doc's ETA?" I asked, turning back to the room.

"Ten minutes. Do you need me?" he asked. It was the first time I'd ever heard him ask to leave. I saw him watching Nat and knew he wanted to be with her. I understood the need.

"If you don't need to see Doc, you're relieved. Take a few days. You've earned it. Let me know when the three of you are ready for the O'Sullivan mission. Speaking of, how is it going with the assassin?"

"That's a long story for another day. I just want to hold my girl and pretend like I wasn't shot at tonight."

I clapped him on the back, squeezing. "Thank you for bringing Jude home."

"Of course. He's important to me too." He nodded, emotion in his eyes, and I realized how much I took them all for granted.

He headed off, and I vowed to do better. Again, Monroe was right. I couldn't separate myself and still expect to have relationships with people. If I closed off from one area, it closed me off from another. If I was going to be different, it started with those around me. Shucking off my jacket, I tossed it and my tie onto the table. Rolling up my sleeves, I walked over to the people I'd come to love congregated on the couch. I wanted them to know I was here and not just supervising.

Loren saw me and reached out for my hand. Jude looked up, catching the shine of the ring.

"Wait! I get kidnapped, and you get married?"

Oops, looked like we had some explaining to do.

SIX

LOREN

Jude looked at me, and I panicked, not expecting him to ask that. "Um, well, you see." I stopped, turning to look at my friends. Cami snickered into her hand, and I caught sight of something she'd been hiding. I'd like to say I was ashamed of my behavior that followed, but, well, it worked to move the spotlight.

Pointing, I drew everyone's attention to her. "Cami got engaged and didn't tell anyone!" Okay, so it wasn't my finest moment.

Nat and Beau had been walking out of the room but stopped at my words. Nat turned, her eyes zeroing in on Cami.

"What the fuck! Seriously? You guys could've given me more notice. Now this one," she pointed over her shoulder, "will double down even harder to seal the deal. Some friends you guys are!" she huffed, stalking out of the room. Beau appeared dazed for a moment before smiling. He nodded and then chased after Nat.

Well," I said, crossing my arms to hide my ring. Are you?" I asked.

Cami held my stare, not an ounce of shame on her face. "As a matter of fact, I am. To Lark and Seb. They asked me a few days ago, but with everything." She shrugged, her eyes dropping down at Malek and then Jude. I understood her meaning.

Before we could go into more details, the doctor who'd stitched me up was ushered into the room. He looked around at the three men, unsure who to start on first. Monroe stepped in, pointing out the injuries we knew.

"Gunshot. The bullet was removed and stapled while in transport," he said, pointing to Malek. "Malnutrition, a few cuts, and bruises." Pointing to Jude and then to Sax. "Two bullet wounds, both appear to be grazes in the leg and arm. Possible stab wound on the thigh."

The doctor sighed, going to Malek, who was still passed out. I kept going back and forth between Sax and Jude, unsure who needed me the most. The doctor started working, but he looked over his shoulder when we all stayed and watched, catching Atticus' attention.

"Perhaps you could get some rooms ready for the three men? It would be easier to work without the audience."

"Of course." He nodded, looking to those of us who weren't injured. "Nicco, take Goldie and find a room for Malek. Imogen, go with Cami to ensure the spare room has everything he'll need, along with Sax's and Jude's. If you see any men up there, have them come down to help us transport them, or see if there's a gurney in storage or something."

"On it," Nicco said, jumping up to take Monroe with him, the girls following.

Atticus looked at me and Wells, indecision in his eyes. "I'll take Wells to make sure their rooms are clean." I kissed his cheek, knowing he was struggling with this but appreciating the effort he was making.

"We're still going to talk about this, Lor," Jude said, raising his eyebrow.

"Absolutely, kiddo." I kissed his cheek, brushing his hair back a little. The tears came to my eyes, and it was only Wells nudging me that had me leaving.

I took his hand as we made our way to the elevator. I knew this was a busy task, but it felt important, so I'd do it even if everything in me wanted to be back in the living room. But I knew that Doc would work better without everyone glaring at him.

Sighing, I leaned back against the elevator, the weight of the past few days finally catching up to me. Wells pulled me against his side, and I went willingly. He kissed my head, melting my heart some.

"I'm glad the kid is back," he said.

"Me too."

"Do you regret it now?" he asked, not letting me break his hold.

"Nope. I wish our family could've been there, but they will when we have the ceremony with everyone. I know it was rushed and not what any of us had planned, but I love you all. I'm happy with the results. You?"

I tried to peer up at him, but his arm around me tightened. The elevator's ding sounded, and I waited for him to move, but he stayed.

"Wells?"

"No, Kitten, I don't regret it. You're the best thing that ever happened to me, even if it started with me getting kicked in the nuts. I just didn't want you to feel like you were trapped."

"Never. This is beyond anything I could've dreamed."

"Good."

He finally let me go, and we walked forward, heading to Sax's room first. It was clean, so I pulled the covers back, getting the side of the bed ready for him. I pulled out some different clothes, laying them on the foot of the bed. Feeling satisfied, I took Wells' hand and walked back to the elevator. He'd stayed back, watching me the whole time, and I assumed he didn't feel right touching Sax's things.

The elevator dinged right away, and we stepped in to go to the floor Jude was on. It didn't escape me that it was a separate one from not only the guys but also Imogen. Atticus had another thing coming if he thought a measly floor would stop them if they wanted to have sex. I didn't think they were there yet, but watching Atticus try to prevent it was funny. Silly man.

When we stepped into Jude's room, I found Imogen sitting on the bed, holding his sweatshirt, crying softly. Wells saw her tears and motioned he'd be out in the hall. I nodded, laughing at his fear of a teenage girl crying, knowing it would be better anyway.

Sitting on the bed, I placed my arm around Imogen, pulling her to me. "Sweetie, what's wrong?"

"I'm just so happy he's back, but it hit me when I was here that he almost wasn't. It just makes me hate my father even more." She turned to me, her face hardening further. I wiped her tears, clasping her face between my hands.

"Your father will pay for what he's done, for the things he's taken from us." My words were strong, with no ounce of fear or doubt in them.

"How are you so sure?" she asked, searching my eyes.

"Because he doesn't know that everything he's done has only made us stronger, not weaker. We keep rising up. We keep moving forward. We keep trusting in love. A man like Dayton can never understand the strength it takes to do that. He thinks he's breaking us down, but really, he's just making an army of people who want to destroy him. And we will. I have no doubt. Whether by my hands, yours, or your brothers', Dayton Mascro will not get away with this."

Her back straightened, and she nodded. "You're right. I *am* strong. We all are."

"Yes, sweet girl. We are." I kissed her forehead, pulling her into a hug. It was crazy how my boundaries had kept me from doing the most natural thing in the world a few months ago. Now, it wasn't that I didn't care about ethics, because I did, but I understood that there were some things that the ethics board didn't understand. This was one of them.

"When are you going to tell him the news?" she asked, pulling back and wiping her face.

"Tell me what?" Jude asked, stepping into the room under Wells' arms. He looked between Imogen and me, trying to figure it out. Standing, I took his other side and helped him to the bed. I walked over to the dresser and pulled out some clothes for him.

"I'll let you change, and then if you want to know, I'll tell you."

"Okay." He nodded, swallowing, and I realized he looked nervous, and I wondered what he was thinking. I tried to figure out what conclusion he would've jumped to, but as I stood out in the hall with Imogen, I couldn't.

A few minutes later, the door opened, and Wells nodded for us to enter. Imogen walked in, hugging Jude one more time, and then kissed his cheek before she left.

Sitting on the bed next to him, I grabbed his hand, running my thumb across the top of it. As I tried to find the right words, he buckled under the pressure, spitting out his fears.

"I'm leaving, aren't I? I promise I didn't say anything to Immy's father. I kept my mouth shut, but I understand if I'm too much of a burden now." He hung his head, my mouth opened in shock at his words. Before I could reassure him, Wells stepped in, knocking his shoulder.

"Don't do that. Give your mom a chance to explain before you jump to conclusions. It's been a tough four days for her, and she's barely slept or eaten, so if she needs a moment, give her a moment."

"Mom?" he asked, looking between Wells and me, his eyes shiny.

I nodded, the words not needed as my tears fell. "It's official."

I pulled him into a hug as we cried into one another's arms. Wells was right that I'd been worried, and exhaustion filled my entire being as I held Jude. I think a part of me still worried it wasn't real. After a few minutes, we pulled back, and a tissue box appeared between us. Laughing, I looked up at Wells, thanking him.

He nodded, but I caught the sheen of tears around his eyes. Seemed the surly man was just as affected.

Blowing my nose and wiping my eyes, I grabbed Jude's hand. "Of course, it was the worst timing. The day after you were taken, the papers were delivered. It was a blow to my heart, but I'm glad they're here now that I have you back. You're officially my son, Jude."

"Wow, I missed so much while I was gone. I still don't even really know who the purple-haired chick is."

I laughed, nodding. "Pixel. That's a whole other story. The other thing that I think you need to know tonight is about this." I held up my hand, showing the ring. "It was Atticus' idea. Getting married helped secure everything where his father couldn't take it. I don't know how it all works, but it's been willed to all of us now, and he turned over ownership to me so that it was out of his name."

"So, does that make me a Mascro?" he asked, his face scrunching up at the thought.

"That depends on what you want, JuJu. With how you might be feeling toward a certain younger Mascro, having the same last name could be problematic. Nor do I want you to feel you have to change yours and lose your family identity. If you want to be a Carter, you can; if you want to be a Wells, Young, or Franklin, you can. It doesn't change the fact that you're my son. Okay?"

"Okay." He smiled, some of the stress leaving him. "I'm sad I missed the wedding, though."

"Oh, don't worry about that. We're going to have a huge one this summer. How about you get some rest, and we can continue more of our conversation tomorrow?"

"Sure thing... Mom." His cheeks reddened, but I loved its sound, tears forming in my eyes.

"Ah man, come on. I just got her to stop," Wells

sighed, pulling me up. He stopped after a step, holding his fist up to Jude. "I'm glad you're back, man. I missed you."

Jude lifted his own, meeting Wells, and then they did some blowing-up thing that made me shake my head. "After the Doc sets your IV up, I'll bring in Barkley if you want? She's been missing you."

"Yeah, I'd like that." His eyes started to close, and I knew he'd be out soon. We stepped out of the room, Wells pulling me into him, and I let myself think that for a moment, everything was okay. We were all safe. We were all here. And we were all *home*.

Everything else could fucking wait until tomorrow.

SEVEN

SAX

The bed creaked as I shifted, and I couldn't find a comfortable position for the life of me. It sucked being sidelined, and I was already over it. Loren was acting like the bullet and stab wounds were grave injuries. I hadn't needed surgery, so in my book, I was fine.

"Spitfire, if I don't get out of this bed, I'm liable to kill someone," I grumbled. Loren rolled her eyes as she fluffed the blankets around me. Wrapping my arm around her waist, I pulled her down to me in a swift move, making her land with an oomph.

"I'm fine. I appreciate your concern, but it's not needed. I promise." I kissed her lips and felt her relax into me. She laid her head on my chest, a sigh escaping her.

"I was just so worried. I'm glad you're not more injured. I really am tired of people getting hurt."

"You're included in that, Spitfire. And I get it." I blew

out a breath, knowing how I'd felt when she'd been hurt. "You weren't injured that long ago, and I wanted to burn the world down. So, I thank you for your love and concern, but this isn't me. Unless it's naked time with you, I'm not a lay-in-bed type of guy. I need to be up, doing things."

Her hand moved back and forth on my chest, and I imagined we were different people for a moment. Maybe I was an accountant instead of a mobster, and we lived in the middle of suburbia. We had a few kids running around and soccer practice to attend. It sounded nice for about two seconds, but then I was bored.

For one, we were better as a group, and two, well, I happened to like bashing people's skulls in every now and then. I didn't think smashing keys on a calculator would give me the same satisfaction.

"Fine, you're right," she mumbled. "It's just that you're the easiest one to hover over at the moment. Jude's already tired of my shit." Loren laughed, looking up at me. "What do you need to do?" She asked, settling her chin on her hands.

An idea popped into my head, a slow smile creeping across my face. "I know the perfect task for us. But to do it, we need to get out of bed."

"Fine. Though, I never thought I'd hear you wanting me out of bed."

"Oh, Spitfire. You know I prefer walls and other surfaces." I smacked her ass as she rolled over, climbing out, and her little yip had me grinning as I followed her. I moved slightly slower, the stitches pulling as my body adjusted to the new position.

Taking her hand, I pulled her down the hall toward the elevator. "It's time I show you a new level."

"Oh?" She looked at me, but I only smirked, not giving anything away. I hit the button for B and watched in the reflection as Loren's face opened in shock. "You have a basement? Why haven't I ever noticed?" she mumbled, looking at me. I didn't say anything, finding delight in her curiosity.

When the elevator chimed, I smiled as Loren stepped off, her head whipping around so fast I thought it might fall off.

"What? Huh? What?"

Chuckling, I steered her where I wanted her to go. Loren went along, too flabbergasted to protest. Topher nodded when we neared. He and another guard appeared to be on duty.

"Sir, Ma'am," he said, nodding in reverence to Loren.

"Hey, Topher." Loren smiled at him, looking at the other guy. "Hi, sorry, I don't think we've met." She reached her hand out, offering it to him. "I'm Loren."

I felt sorry for the guy as he fumbled over himself, wondering why the Queen would be addressing him. Loren had no clue the power she held now, which made her a great Mafia Queen.

"Matt," the man finally managed to say, shaking her

hand briefly. He didn't want to be rude, but hadn't missed my possessive grip on her either.

"We'd like to see the prisoner."

Topher nodded, used to Loren's presence, and stepped aside so we could enter. While we kept most of the prisoners at the warehouse, Atticus had opted to keep this particular one closer.

Plus, with Dayton returning, it was the one section he had no control or knowledge of, and we wanted to keep it that way.

When we walked in, the man in question didn't look up, and I felt Loren bristle a little next to me. Hardening my exterior, I looked at the man on the floor, feeling nothing but anger toward him. He was a piece of shit, and it was time we disposed of him.

"This is what you need to do?" she whispered.

"Yep. He no longer holds value, so it's time to take out the trash. If you don't want to be part of it," I said, turning to look at her, "I can do it alone. I thought you might want to, but now I wonder if that was a mistake. You fit so seamlessly in our lives that I sometimes forget you weren't brought up this way."

She looked at me, her hands clutching my forearms. "What are you going to do?" She swallowed, her body shaking a little.

Brian hadn't stirred, his spirit too broken. I knew I should feel bad about that fact, but I didn't. I was delighted about it. This man had hurt her, repeatedly made her doubt herself, and in the end, had committed the most grievous act against her by stealing her eggs. He didn't deserve to continue in this life. There was no world where I'd let him survive. He posed too much of a threat, and I wouldn't let him be able to hurt her anymore if I could help it.

"You know the answer, Loren. He doesn't get to walk away from everything he's done. Jail is too easy for him. He needs to die."

She watched me, calculating all my facial features. I didn't hold anything back. She could see all of me. When she found whatever she'd been looking for, she nodded. "Okay, but I want to be there."

"Absolutely. Mas won't agree, which is why we didn't ask." I winked, turning back to the piece of shit. "How he dies is the next part. We have a vial of the chemical Pixel made, or we could put his ankles in concrete and let him swim with the fishes."

Loren laughed like I'd hoped, and the sound filled me with happiness. I turned, quirking an eyebrow. "No swimming?"

She smiled, reaching for my hand. "No. I think the *Filibuster* is the perfect end for this piece of shit."

Her words couldn't have been more morbid, but they turned me on like nothing else. I turned, clasping her face, bringing her lips to mine. "Fuck, that's hot, Spitfire. Once this is done, I will let you take me back to bed." I kissed her lips quickly a couple of times in succession, not wanting to get too carried away with her ex-husband slumped over on the floor. He grumbled something, and I stopped, drawing back to glare down at him.

Dropping her hand, I kneeled to look at him closer. "Have something to finally say, scum?"

He looked up, his eye was swollen shut, nose broken, and lip busted, making me proud of Nicco for the damage he'd managed to do on the man. "Jac-que-line," he stuttered out, his breathing difficult.

"What about the bitch?" Loren said, crossing her arms. He tried to look up at her, but he'd lost that right, so I snapped my fingers to get his attention.

"You don't get to look at her anymore, asshole."

His one eye spat daggers at me, and I found it funny, but then he sagged, no fight in him as he tried to move against the wall. "Working with," he panted, his broken ribs not doing him any favors to speak. "The man...," he paused again, taking a breath as he grimaced, "paid m-e to sh-oot yo-u." Once he got it all out, he closed his eyes, no more energy.

I looked at Loren, and she thought it over. "Doesn't surprise me, but what would my mother have to give to him?"

"You," I said, standing. I'd come back later and give him the dose. We needed to tell Mas, so we were prepared.

We'd stolen Jude and blew up part of his property. Dayton had to be pissed, and he would retaliate. I just hoped it wouldn't be as costly. There wasn't much I was willing to let go of anymore.

Taking Loren's hand, we headed back up to the main floor. I never thought I'd have someone in my life who could handle it all, and yet, Spitfire was here with me, walking by my side and showing me how to be strong without using my fists.

We walked into the office, not even stopping to knock. If Atticus didn't want us to interrupt anything, he was in for a surprise. Not that there was anything we were hiding anymore, anyway. He was hanging up the phone as we entered, and I didn't miss the tired look on his face that we all seemed to be wearing lately.

"What is it?" I asked, already having a feeling of what he would say.

"Dayton retaliated." Loren sucked in a breath, walking around the desk to be closer. I stood back, observing him.

"Climax?" I asked.

He looked up, shaking his head. "No, Pops, along with a few other businesses on that strip still loyal to us." It was a message to both them and us. He was back and out to cause havoc.

"Pops?" Loren asked, looking between us.

I sat in the chair, the grief I hadn't expected hitting me. "Is he..." I couldn't say the words.

"Looked like no one was there. Pops called me

himself." Relief flooded me. I wasn't prepared to lose the old man.

"My mother is working with him. Brian just told us," Loren said, rubbing Atticus' shoulder. "It makes what she said at the funeral make more sense. I just don't know what her angle could be. What do you think?"

"It could be anything or she's just a means to an end for Dayton. She doesn't have anything left that could hurt you. We have the eggs and the trust. I guess it makes sense in her statement about not needing it now. Is there anyone else in your life she could target? Anything she could take?"

"No." Loren shook her head, thinking it over.

"Then we stay low and wait for them to mess up. In the meantime, we plan for our next attack."

"Which is?" I asked, rubbing my chin.

"We need to make things a little more difficult for *Dear old Dad* to operate. It's time to call in all my favors. And if a murder just happened to take place on his property, even better." Atticus smiled, and if he hadn't been on our side, I would've been nervous because it was the most sinister smile I'd ever seen him wear. I would need to make sure in his fight against his father, he didn't lose himself in the process.

We might be Mascros, but we didn't have to be Dayton.

EIGHT

LOREN

Monday rolled around, and I found it odd not to be heading to the office. Between the shooting, Jude being taken, my father's death, and the aftermath of everything that occurred, I didn't have it in me to solve other people's problems at the moment. I couldn't even solve my own.

"Yes, Doris, thank you. I'll let you know when I'm able to return. Uh-huh." Sighing, I ended the call and stared at the device in my hand. I hated to let my clients down, but this was an ethical dilemma I didn't have to wrestle with. I wasn't fit to be a therapist at the moment. I had to step away.

Hands fell to my shoulders, massaging them, and I leaned back, peering up at who they belonged to. Nicco stared down at me from above, a cheeky grin on his face.

"I've come to distract you."

"Oh? I could use some distraction." I licked my lips,

thinking something of the naughty nature might be just the thing.

"Hmm, now I'm reconsidering what I'd planned." He leaned down, taking my lips with his, delivering a passionate kiss. Far too soon, he pulled back.

I found myself pouting, having enjoyed the kiss. "More," I demanded.

Nicco chuckled, pecking me briefly. "I promised I wouldn't get up to any hijinks but to grab you out of your wallowing, and deliver you to the distraction intact."

"Fine. This better be good." I sighed again, turning in the chair and stood. I left my phone on the table, not needing it anymore. Everyone I cared about was in this house. If they needed me, they could find me. One less thing to worry about. I never did like the damn thing.

Nicco linked our hands together, pulling me along. He had a mischievous smile, and I knew he was hiding something. I just couldn't figure out if it was good or bad for me.

"First, we have to make a brief pit stop in the war room. Mas wants everyone to start giving a daily update, so we all know what's going on. Come on, Mrs. Mascro. The King needs his Queen."

My face blushed, and I didn't miss how nice it felt to hear those words. I never thought I'd like being the Queen of anything, but when Nicco said it, goosebumps spread over my body at the sound. I kind of liked being all of *their* Queen.

We stepped into the room, and I found the rest of the guys there, along with Pixel and Cami. She smiled at me as I entered, and I returned it. Though, most surprising was discovering Jude and Imogen at the table.

"Bellezza," Atticus said, nodding toward a seat at the front. I let go of Nicco's hand and took it, realizing everyone was looking at me. I nodded to all the faces I loved and even saw some of the guards along the wall who looked on in reverence. It was weird.

"This is our first official house meeting, but I'd like to do this every morning where we can all briefly give an update on the assignments we're all working on. If you're at this table, you're part of the family and included in the decisions that will be made. Those in this room are privy to our private matters, and anyone found sharing information outside the people here will be punished. We do not take to gossip. Our trust and privacy are worth a lot, and if you've been allowed into our circle, we value yours. Don't lose that."

He cleared his throat, and I shifted, liking how he commanded a room. Thoughts of how we could recreate that voice later drifted to my head when I realized Atticus was staring at me. It seemed non-working me was a horny bitch.

"I'm not sure what my job is now," I said. "I've taken

an official sabbatical from the practice and transferred all my clients except for one. I've made arrangements to see her off-site." I looked around, feeling put on the spot. "I, um, that's all." I glanced down, feeling anything but the Queen I was meant to be now. This was why I wasn't ever in charge. I faltered at the scrutiny.

"I might have something for you if you're free later?" Atticus asked, and I realized the importance of his question. *He was asking.* Everyone else might get an order, but I had a choice. He was subtly reminding me of my position in his very Atticus way.

"Of course, Husband." I smiled, liking how that made his ears tinge just the slightest. He cleared his throat, loosening his tie, and it seemed I wasn't the only one who liked our new roles. He nodded to the next person, and I listened as everyone gave an update.

"Checking in with Pops and the other businesses affected by Dayton's rampage to get them relocated and taken care of, and then checking in with the prisoners at the Warehouse. I also need to stop by city hall," Sax said, and I realized how much he did for Atticus and the family.

I was about to step in and say I could help when Atticus did it for me. Despite Sax stating he was fine, I could tell how fatigued he was from his injuries. It would be helpful if he could lessen one thing, but something he'd never ask for.

"Monroe, maybe you could help with the city hall task?"

"Oh, yes, I could do that," Monroe said, nodding.

"Perfect. Sax get with Monroe after this. Nicco?"

"Meeting with the Cappos—Lucca and Jasper—to get a headcount of foot soldiers. Then coordinating with Pixel on our new security measures for the house and businesses."

Atticus nodded at Nicco, pleased with his report, moving on to Wells. He looked shocked for a moment and then cleared his throat. "Training." He didn't say anything else, and Atticus approved.

"How are your injuries?" he asked, steepling his fingers.

"I'm fine," Wells retorted, his jaw tightening.

"That wasn't what I asked. You might be okay fighting injured, but that is not something I am comfortable with. Not only are you important to this family and your *wife*," he said, stressing the last word, "but to our club. If you're not ready, then we wait. Doc needs to clear you before I sign off on you returning to training, or do you want to try that again?"

I watched as Wells debated, his teeth grinding back and forth, his face set. Finally, he glanced at me, and something on my face must've soothed him because he let out a breath. "I'm still sore but improving. I plan to work on low-impact exercises to build my endurance and regain some of the momentum I lost. I promise not to overdo it. I know my body and my capabilities."

"Very well. You can return to training, but this will be a different conversation if I find you're minimizing your injuries."

I knew where Atticus was coming from, and I respected him for saying something, but I knew Wells would struggle with someone telling him what he could and couldn't do. I would need to talk with them both, so this wouldn't become an issue.

Monroe had a few cases he was working on, but was going to take a leave of absence once they were closed so he could be more available to the family. Cami was watching over Malek as he healed and was returning to Climax tonight. She seemed okay, but I was worried she might be jumping back into normality a little too soon, but I'd trust her judgment.

Pixel was working on the security with Nicco and had given Sax the dosage for Brian. It was now up to us to determine when and where to unleash him. I knew Atticus had a plan, and I trusted him. I didn't care at this point as long as he was dealt with. I was tired of thinking about Brian.

The teens were petitioning to return to school. I hadn't realized Atticus had pulled them out and wanted them tutored here for the rest of the semester.

"Attie, you said it yourself the school was secure. Give us a guard, and we'll be fine. I think it's safer to go to school, honestly," Immy pleaded, her hands begging him.

Atticus started to protest, and I could see a fight on the horizon. Imogen didn't want to budge on this.

"What are your concerns?" I asked, asking my husband and not the mafia boss. He turned his eyes on me, and I could tell most of it was fear. He was worried they'd be retaken, and I knew he didn't want to deal with that.

I clasped his hand under the table, squeezing. "Imogen, let's give it a week. Let things settle down with your father, and then we can revisit it," I said. She started to protest, but I watched as Jude nudged her, stopping her. She sighed, agreeing to wait one more week. I felt Atticus squeeze my hand, thanking me for not making him the bad guy.

It was then I realized I did have a purpose as part of this family. I just needed to figure out how to use it. I was a bridge between the two worlds.

Nat called in with Beau and gave an update on how their undercover mission was going. Once everyone had given their plans, the meeting was dismissed, and they all hurried off to do their tasks.

Nicco grabbed my hand, pulling me down a corridor. I let him lead me, trusting he knew where he was going. When we came upon Wells a few feet later, I realized he must've been following him.

"Crash, feel like trying out a new room that might

help your training?" Nicco raised his eyebrows, leaving it up to the surly man to decide.

He turned, the denial on the tip of his tongue when he spotted me and stopped. "Kitten, are you part of this deal?"

I shrugged, looking between them. Something had changed, and I didn't know if it was more concentrated sexual tension or angst. But the air between them almost crackled with it.

"I guess you'll have to take a chance," I said, smiling. I could see the indecision on Wells' face, and the moment he decided to give in.

"Fine," he gritted out, and I felt Nicco's body almost vibrate at the response.

"Follow me then, if you dare." Nicco was practically bouncing on his toes at the excitement.

He took us to the floor with the gym on it, but instead of turning toward it, he headed in the opposite direction. I hadn't ever been this way and was even more curious now. Perhaps I should get a tour of the place and everything held in it if I was going to be living here? Yeah, that might be helpful.

He stopped in front of a door and took my hand, holding it in front of a touchpad. "Mas had this room programmed with all the adults' fingerprints as part of the new measures with Pixel. It's not that this room is secretive, but," he paused, smirking, and pressed my thumb down on the scanner. The door beeped and swung open. Inside wasn't what I was expecting, as humid air and chemicals assaulted our noses.

"Holy shit, you guys have a pool!" I looked at Nicco, my mouth hanging open as I took in the gleaming waters. He smiled wider, liking that he was getting to surprise us. Even Wells had changed the surly frown into an expression of awe.

"That's not all," Nicco said, pulling me and reaching back to grab Wells with his other hand.

I smiled when Wells was too stunned to notice, not dropping Nicco's hand. I caught the tilt of Nicco's lips and wondered what his plan was. The more I got to know Nicco, the more I realized how much he enjoyed teasing others and pulling them into things that scared them. He'd done it for me, and I could see him doing it for Wells. It only made me realize how beautiful it would be when Wells let go of whatever he held onto so firmly.

"There's also a hot tub and this European bath that's basically like a giant Epsom salt bath with healing abilities. I thought you could both benefit from it."

It really was a sweet gesture, and despite whatever naughtiness he had in store, it had come from a place of caring.

"So, why is this room locked so heavily?" I asked, scanning it as I looked for anything that might seem top secret.

"Mas didn't want any of the young kids to stumble in

here and not be supervised in case they fell into the water."

I stopped, turning to stare at him. "Wow. I didn't even think about that. Even if he doesn't know it, Mas really is a great father." I sat down on one of the benches, processing everything. "So, do we just get in naked?"

Nicco laughed, moving closer, and I saw Wells look at me, heat in his eyes. "That's always an option, Beautiful, but there are suits in the locker room. You two get changed, and I'll be back in a few minutes. I need to check on something first."

He pecked my lips briefly, then spun to walk out of the pool area. When he passed Wells, I laughed when he slapped him on the ass. Wells jumped, so shocked by the move he didn't even have a comeback.

When the door closed, I stood, collected my stunned husband, pulling him toward the changing room.

"You going to be okay?" I asked, chuckling.

"I honestly do not know how to take him." He looked at me wide-eyed.

"I think he likes you, and if I know Nicco, he'll help you find the part of you that you didn't even know was hiding. He did that for me. Try not to be so scared." As we walked, I laid my head on his shoulder, enjoying the softness he now showed me.

"It doesn't bother you?"

"No, why would it?"

"I guess I just assumed you wouldn't want us to mingle."

"Surly." I smiled, the name no longer being a barb but a loving endearment between us. "I love you all, and being with you five is the best thing I've ever done. I don't want you guys to go out and have sex with other women or men outside our family, but if there's something within it between you guys, I'm not going to stop it. Besides, I fell in love with all of you. I hope you guys love one another as well, even if that's not romantic with everyone. Now that we're married, it's kind of for life."

I leaned up, kissing his face, and felt his body relax. He rested his forehead on mine, staring intently into my eyes. "Thanks, Kitten. I guess I needed to hear you say I wasn't a freak, or I don't know, that it wasn't a bad thing."

"It's a wonderful thing." I kissed him again but stopped, not wanting to get too carried away. We found lockers with our names on them containing new swimsuits in our sizes.

"I'm starting to wonder if that man sleeps," Wells mumbled.

"Not very much," I admitted. "He thinks of everything. One day, I hope he realizes how amazing he is."

Wells pulled me into his arms, his bare skin hitting mine. "With you by his side, I have no doubt he will."

Clasping our hands, we grabbed some towels and headed out to the bath. As we stepped into the water, the door opened, and two people entered. Looked like Nicco wasn't done scheming for the day, and the bathwater wasn't the only thing that was about to be hot and wet. At that thought, I realized I'd been hanging around Nicco too much. Oh well, there were worse things than bad, dirty jokes.

NINE

MONROE

When Nicco had shown up in my temporary office, stating he was my next appointment, I'd been skeptical. Standing in an area I hadn't known existed until now, I knew I'd been right to be.

"This is my next appointment?" I asked, raising my eyes to him.

"Yup. I couldn't exactly put dick appointment, or you might've ignored it. Plus, you having to announce to the whole family you were going to get your socks rocked didn't seem like the kind of thing you wanted others to know."

He winked, moving toward me, leaning close. "Come on. I have a feeling Crash isn't going to let himself break free until you do. So, the question is, Sunshine, are you ready?"

He stood facing me, blocking Loren and Wells, for the time being, making it just the two of us. We were similar in height, so this close, I could see into his gray-blue eyes clearly. Nicco was daring me, pushing me to see how I'd respond. I didn't know which response he wanted, but I wasn't afraid of him. Not the way he thought, at least.

Taking a step, I brought the toe of our shoes together, engulfing his smell of leather and ink. I watched as he swallowed, his Adam's apple bobbing with the movement, and I realized I'd disarmed *him* for once. I grabbed his hips, surprising him yet again, his eyes going wide at the move.

"I think the real question, Casanova, is whether you are." I kissed his lips briefly before pulling back, walking over to the other two. They'd been watching, and I found them both sitting stunned. Winking, I hoped I hadn't overstepped. When they both licked their lips, I knew I'd been right. While I didn't feel for Nicco the way I did for Loren and Wells, I wouldn't shy away from playing if he was inclined, especially if it made the other two more aroused.

Though, if I had to guess, he wanted to use me to show Wells it wasn't the huge ordeal he was making it out to be and to face his own feelings again. But what Nicco needed to realize was, I wouldn't be used as a prop. I might be the "golden retriever" one, as they all liked to call me, but it didn't make me weak. Nicco would either realize that or miss out on getting to know me and, ultimately Wells, more intimately.

Because I had a feeling that Wells was holding out due to some obligation to Loren and me, and once that obstacle was removed, he'd have to face his own feelings.

I started to remove my clothes when I realized they were in actual swimwear. "It seems my appointment before lunch is a date with you guys." I smiled at them, loving their attention.

Loren leaned against the side, smiling at me. "I can't say I'm mad about that. Do you have time, though? I don't want you to miss anything."

I looked over at her and Wells, my heart racing at the sight. "I always have time for you two. Now, should I pretend and go put on a swimsuit or just strip down naked now?" I asked, lifting my brow.

"Oh, kinky. Let's just strip down, Sunshine." Nicco came up behind me, apparently unfrozen from his stupor. Smirking, I ignored him, walked over to the soft chairs, and started to place my clothes there as I undressed. I laid everything as carefully as possible so it wouldn't get wrinkled, but I'd probably have to put on a new suit anyway. Worth it.

Dropping my boxers, I tossed them onto the chair, walking proudly to my husband and wife. Nicco walked next to me, and I kept my eyes forward, not wanting to give him the benefit of checking out his dick. I already knew from Wells he was pierced, and while I wanted to see it, it felt important right now not to look.

I was momentarily stunned at how good the water

felt when I stepped in. "Okay, is this like some miracle spa water or something? This feels incredible."

"It's spring water, and it's a European bath with Epsom salt. It does have healing properties," Loren explained, pulling me closer to her. "Hi," she said, smiling at me.

"Hey, Lo." I kissed her nose, reaching over to grab Wells' hand. "How did Nicco rope you into this?"

"Did I see you kiss him?" he asked instead of answering.

"He was trying to push my buttons, so I pushed back. Why? Did it make you jealous?"

"No." He shook his head, and I watched him as he contemplated something. "I think I finally got it, that's all." He looked up at me, staring into my eyes. "You're amazing, Monroe. I don't tell you that enough."

"You do, and thank you." I leaned over Loren, kissing Wells deeply, wanting to display to him I understood what he was trying to say.

When I released him, I smiled, laying back so I could float in the water. "This is nice." I closed my eyes, letting my body feel the water for a moment. It was quiet as we all floated, relaxing. I didn't know how long we stayed serene, enjoying the peace when Nicco had enough and decided to spice things up.

"Seriously? We're all alone, two of us are naked, and still, no one is doing anything other than floating? Wow. I guess you do lose your sex drive when you turn thirty. I'm doomed next month."

"You turn thirty next month?" Loren asked, sitting up.

"That's the part you focus on." He swam over, cupping her face between his hands. "Yes, Beautiful. I turn thirty in May. But right now, I just want to fuck you. Can we do that?"

She smiled, nodding. "Yes."

He sealed his lips over hers, and I watched them for a few minutes, noticing the different ways she kissed each of us. It was nice to know we all had our unique approach. I moved over to Wells, watching him observing them, desire evident on his face. I pulled him into my arms, sitting back on the bench seat.

"You don't have to be afraid of liking someone else. Even if you just want to screw around with him, it's cool."

"I keep hearing you and Loren say that, but something in my brain keeps stopping me. Can we just keep it us? I think I'm too worried I'll mess it up when everything is perfect."

"Of course, babe. I love you." I kissed him, relishing the way his lips felt against mine. I reached around, finding his cock already hard through his swim trunks. Slowly, I pulled him free and stroked it up and down, his head falling back onto my shoulder. "This is nice, you letting me be the more dominant one for a change."

He chuckled. "I'm glad you're enjoying yourself. I have to agree, though; this is nice."

His eyes were focused on Nicco and Loren, who were kissing, his hands playing with her nipples. He'd removed her top, and I decided to do the same with Wells' trunks. Once his ass was bare, my cock nudged between his cheeks, finding a home.

We both watched the show as Nicco began to bring Loren to orgasm, his fingers doing things under the water we couldn't see. I was slowly stroking Wells. Enough to feel good, but not enough friction to make him combust.

"Want to join the fun?" I asked, nipping his ear. I watched as he swallowed, but then gave in and nodded.

Nicco had placed Loren up on the edge, and she was laid out like a buffet course for us to enjoy. We both raised ourselves out of the water and walked over to where they were. Nicco looked up from where he was feasting, but didn't stop. Loren beckoned us to join her on the ground, so we both took a side, kneeling. But as I lowered, my knees began to ache, and I knew I'd regret that position in the morning.

"How about we move to the bed instead of trying to get comfortable on this cold, wet, and hard floor? It sounds like an accident waiting to happen."

"Sure thing, Pops." Nicco smirked, licking up Loren in a long stroke before he pulled back and raised himself out of the water. I couldn't help but be enthralled for a second as the water rolled down his delicious body, touching his tattoos and muscles. He was cocky, but for good reason. When his dick rose up, the metal glinting in the light, I found myself entranced by it.

"Call me what you want," I said, licking my lips, "but nothing stops the fun like a broken bone. Besides, with more room, we can have more fun."

Wells grunted, helping Loren up. Once his hands were on her, he couldn't stop and began to kiss her. Loren didn't mind, and they managed to walk and kiss their way to the couch. This time, I stood, a dare in my eyes as Nicco sized me up. When he got to my dick, he licked his lips, then drew his eyes to me.

"*Fun*, you say?"

Walking forward, I grabbed his cock before he had time to move and stroked his piercings. He groaned, his eyes closing as they rolled back in his head. "Yes. Can you keep up, *Casanova*?"

I kissed him again, this time for longer, pulling away before he could take control. I knew I was playing a delicate battle of power with him, but it was one I wanted to win. Nicco didn't get to push our buttons without having a few of his own pushed. Dick for cock, and all that.

Spinning on my heels, I walked off, smirking the whole way. Loren and Wells had stopped to watch us, both of them with hungry eyes.

"Fuck, that was hot, Roe," Wells admitted. I winked

at him as I lowered to the bed, took Loren's face between my hands, and kissed her passionately. The three of us fell into a rhythm, comfortable with our roles as we began to pleasure one another. When I felt a mouth on my cock a few minutes later, I didn't think anything of it at first.

Pulling back to kiss over Loren's body, I was surprised when it was Nicco's head below as he tweaked his fingers on Lo's clit with one hand and fondled my balls with the other. I turned my head to seek out Wells and found his eyes fixed on what was happening as he thrusted into Loren from behind.

I was worried he wouldn't be okay with it after what he'd said moments ago, but when he swallowed, looking up, I knew he was more than fine with what was occurring, even if he didn't know it himself. His pupils were blown, and nothing but pure lust stared back.

"Fuck, that's hot," he whispered. "What do you think, Kitten?"

Loren's eyes flicked open, and she took in what was happening. My hands were massaging her breasts, but I lost focus as Nicco continued to suck me. Loren got a mischievous smirk on her lips, and I watched as she took her hand and threaded it through his hair. With her hold on him, Loren sped him up, making me unable to do anything but throw my head back in ecstasy. Before I was ready, I was spewing my cum down Nicco's throat from one of the best blow jobs I'd ever had.

"Shit. That was incredible," I admitted, sitting up when the blood returned to my head. Nicco smirked, fisting his own. Wells had his arms wrapped around Loren as they moved together, and I found myself wanting to be hard again as I watched them. I'd never had a short refractory period before, but it wasn't surprising that I wished I did with all these sexy people around. I could almost feel my dick wanting to rally.

"Is there any lube around?" I asked, figuring I should know what we were working with. Nicco shook his head, turning to look at me. "No. We should definitely stock these rooms, though."

Wells grunted, pulling Loren back to him, and I knew he'd found his release. When he drew back, he rolled over toward me, his shoulders touching mine, and we watched as Nicco swooped in, pulling Loren onto his lap.

It was the best type of porn because it was our wife and Nicco, and they put on an excellent show. Their bodies moved together in a way I was almost envious of, but I couldn't compare as it wasn't fair to Loren. We all had our moments with her, and that's what mattered.

"I have to admit, I didn't feel how I expected when I saw his mouth on you. I was a little jealous, but the overall eroticism of the moment outweighed it. I came so hard in Loren, I don't think my balls will recover."

Chuckling, I entwined our hands as we watched. Before this, I would've thought it was weird to lay naked on a pool bed, my cock out after being spent, my husband next to me as we watched our wife get railed by one of her other husbands.

Yeah, it was an odd world I lived in now. But I couldn't say I didn't love it because I did.

I'd once told Wells that it was the foster kids' dream ending, and I realized how right I'd been. We had a family here, not just for us but the kids too, and I loved what we were creating. It worked because it was special, and no one would take that from us.

We would all make sure at whatever cost.

TEN

WELLS

W iping the sweat from my brow, I panted as I tried to catch my breath. After the sex bath, I'd been working in the gym for the past few hours, training. At first, it was nice. It helped me focus on what I was doing. But as I fell into the routines I knew, my mind began to wander.

Flashes of Nicco and Monroe together replayed in my mind. And if I was honest, mostly of Nicco. The sight of his body brazenly displayed before me had given me the opportunity to gawk, and I'd taken advantage of it. Nicco's body was a work of art. From the dips and lines of his muscles to the ink he displayed, I didn't know where to look the most.

When I watched him and my Monroe together, I was jealous. But not in the way I'd imagined. I wasn't jealous Nicco was with Monroe, but that Monroe got to taste Nicco. Watching Monroe be more dominant with the cocky man had my blood surging. It was hot to see that side of him be ignited, even if it wasn't from me. We had our roles with each other, and it was good he could branch out of himself with Nicco.

So, where did that leave me? Could I let go of this block I seemed to have with him? I didn't know why I was holding on to denying myself so much, but it felt like I might break apart if I let go.

"You look like you're thinking something serious," a voice said, pulling me from my thoughts.

I turned and blinked, wondering if my thoughts had somehow conjured him. Returning to the bag in front of me, I pulled my arm back and hit it, trying to calm my heart. "What do you want, Nicco? I'm busy."

"I'm here to help." I could hear the smile in his voice, making me grind my teeth. Always so playful, that one.

"Don't you have important meetings to attend or something?"

"Already done. Spoke with Lucca and have it all settled. Now, it's time for me to check in on my fighter. Six weeks until the big fight. I can't have you sullying the Mascro name."

I rolled my eyes, not answering his lame attempt to bait me. I focused back on the bag in front of me, my breaths coming out in short bursts now as I jabbed and punched. Concentrating on the object in front of me, I didn't expect it when he pulled it, my fist missing it as the momentum brought me forward. Stumbling, I glared at the man who beamed at me from the other side. Stupid, cocky man.

"Come on. Let's spar."

"No." I gave him my back, going to the water cooler.

"Ah, come on, Crash. Don't tell me you're scared of sparring with me?"

"You wish," I snorted. Draining a cup before filling another one.

"Then what's stopping you? Come on. Just one round and see if it's worth it."

Sighing, I looked back at the man. "You're not going to stop until I give in, are you?"

"Nope." He smiled, his eyes twinkling.

Shaking my head, I couldn't deny the fun he tried to bring and how nothing seemed too dark for him. Tossing the paper cup into the trash, I really looked at him.

"Fine." Walking into the center of the room, I stood with my hands on my hips as I waited for him to tape his hands up.

"What rules?" I asked, stretching my arms over my head.

"Rules? What are those?" He smirked.

Rolling my eyes, I decided to be the responsible adult. "No junk shots or headshots. Everything else is fair game. Five minutes."

"Five minutes. I'll try not to knock you out in two."

Laughing, I shook my head. "Is there any part of you that's never cocky?"

"Nope." He winked, strutting over. He looked way too good in those loose workout pants and tank. "You ready?" he asked.

I set the clock on the bench and met him in the middle. Tapping knuckles, we waited for the buzzer to sound to tell us to begin. Once it did, my focus zeroed in on his form, looking for any weaknesses.

He kicked out, but I dodged it, dancing back on the balls of my feet. I wanted to assess him before I took him down. Nicco was lithe and had good range. He wasn't as green as I thought he'd be. I struck out to see how he'd respond and was surprised when he didn't fall for the easy kick, blocking me instead.

"I've surprised you," he said, his smirk growing wider.

"I'll admit you have. I wasn't expecting you to know what you were doing." I did a quick jab, catching him off guard that time, and I smiled, liking I'd gotten one over the cocky man.

"Fuck, that stings." He laughed, stepping back. We went back and forth a few times, dancing around each other. Our bodies fell into a dance of steps neither of us knew, but somehow we seemed to understand. Nicco got a few kicks in, and I got a few hits in. Overall, we were both playing it too safe to make any real headway.

"Come on, Crash. Show me the big guns."

I shook my head. "You heard your brother. If I do too much, I'll be sidelined."

"And you don't trust me not to rat you out?" he asked, his face falling a little.

"I don't know. You're his brother. I'm just your fighter."

Nicco watched me for a few seconds before he rushed me, taking me by surprise, and jumped on me, knocking me to the ground. He pinned me beneath him, our chests heaving from the exertion.

"I hate that you don't think you can trust me," he admitted, his blue-grey orbs staring intensely down into me.

"I don't trust anyone other than Monroe and Loren. It's just facts. And they had to battle their way through my armor to get there." My voice was soft, the realization I didn't let people in hitting me.

"What do you think I've been doing? I've been trying to find the secret password. I want to be let in, Wells. Why won't you let me?"

The cocky guy was gone, and he stared at me, full of intensity, waiting for my answer like it meant everything. I opened my mouth, shutting it a few times.

"Why?" I asked, the one word the only thing that would leave me. It came out in a breathy whisper, but he easily heard it since he was still on top of me.

"Do I need a reason?"

I shook my head. "I don't trust people who give things away for free. Nothing in my life has ever worked that way. It took a lot for me to let Loren and Monroe in.

To think that more than two people are interested in knowing me is absurd. I don't get it. I'm a failed stockbroker who was too stupid to see the pitfalls before him. The only thing I have going for me is the love of two people who are too good for this world. Outside of training dogs, I have no redeemable qualities. People don't like me. I was always the angry one with too much baggage, and Monroe was the golden boy. Even you all call him that. I'm just the one who's happy with the scraps."

It flowed out of me, unbidden. I hadn't meant to be so vulnerable with him, but something about Nicco made me want to share. If only to prove I wasn't worth the wasted breath to him. I didn't expect to have anything more than what I already had. It was more than I ever dreamed of, to begin with.

Nicco pushed on my chest, drawing my attention. "Wake up, Wells. None of us are good enough for those two if you put it down on paper. Thankfully, that isn't the measuring stick we use here. You're in the mafia, for fuck's sake. Open your eyes and see the life waiting for you to wake up and take it. Stop waiting for someone to hand it to you." He moved closer, our lips a breath away. "Take. It. Don't apologize for being you. *Don't*."

His eyes bored into mine, waiting for me to do as he said. For some reason, having this tattooed mafia prince on top of me, spouting for me to take the things I wanted and not apologize for who I was, clicked something in me. I'd gotten so used to living by the world's definition of who I should be that I forgot I wasn't in that world anymore.

"Fine. I will," I growled, grabbing his head and pulling his face toward mine, slamming our lips together. I knew he was waiting for me to cross that line, to show him I was willing to take what I wanted.

The kiss was brutal as we battled one another. It was so different from Monroe. Nicco was similar to me in so many ways; we just chose to cover up our scars differently.

Rolling, I pinned him to the ground, liking my advantage above him. I ground myself into him, loving the sound he made. Nicco's moan was liquid heat, spurring me on, the whole sound coursing through my body. My hands were in his hair, and I grasped it by the ends, pulling his head back.

"Happy?" I sneered, still a little pissed he pushed me to this even if I'd wanted it.

"I will be when you quit fighting me and get naked already. I have an ass to claim."

I scoffed. "Like hell are you claiming my ass with your studded dick!" I narrowed my eyes at him, daring him to try. I'd knock him out so fast that he wouldn't remember his first name.

"Ooo, I kind of like when you get all domineering, Crash. You going to punish me, Daddy?" he teased.

"I'll punish you, but don't call me that."

I shoved my hand down his pants, not being gentle. This wasn't the time for that kind of moment. I found him easily, the studded member eagerly waiting to meet me. Nicco's eyes rolled back, his moans increasing as he thrusted up, trying to gain more friction. Sitting up, I let go of his hair and pinned his hips between my thighs. I watched him as I stroked him, licking my lips.

"You're too fucking sexy."

"Why do you make that sound like a bad thing?" he teased.

"Because your stupid tattoos and abs make me want to do stupid things."

"I thought we already agreed you were only doing things you wanted." He lifted his eyebrow, challenging me. Huffing, I squeezed him, watching as he groaned.

"Roll over," I commanded, waiting to see if he'd follow. I leaned up, giving him only the barest amount of space to move. He reached in his pocket, pulled out a bottle of lube, and handed it to me. Smirking, he sat up without question, and I wondered if I'd been played. Had he wanted this all along?

Nicco freed my cock while I debated, and all thoughts fled me, and I groaned as he wrapped his lips around my dick. "Shit," I cursed, losing all pretense of controlling this.

Nicco sucked me down, and I found myself struggling to hold back. I'd wanted to show him who was the boss in this dynamic, proving I was the alpha asshole, but when he wrapped his lips around me, I lost all thoughts and just wanted him to keep doing what he was doing.

When I came down his throat, I blinked as he trailed kisses up my body, reverently kissing the tattoo he'd given me, before landing on my lips. Nicco kissed me long, taking his time before he pulled back.

"You can get me back later if you want." He kissed me again, much more gently, the earlier aggression gone. "I have an idea. Come on."

We stood together, and I was a bit dazed, if I was honest. Two orgasms in a day had my body feeling spent. I grabbed my bag, tossing a shirt on, wondering what the enigmatic man had up his sleeve this time. I couldn't deny that he hadn't steered me wrong so far.

Nicco grabbed my hand, pulling me along, and I found myself excited. He was right. This wasn't the same as the real world, and I could be more than just the man I was with Loren and Monroe. They gave me the foundation, but I could break out some, expand my wings and soar to a height I never thought possible. And it started with trusting these other men explicitly.

ELEVEN

LOREN

After spending some time with the kids and dogs, I found myself alone for the first time in a week. Sitting down on the edge of the bed, I glanced around the room, observing the details. My life had changed so much, and I hadn't had time to process any of it. I feared I was one wrong look away from falling apart.

Brian had shot me. Jude had been kidnapped. My father had died. I wasn't a practicing therapist anymore. I got married. I was a mom.

In a weird sense of things, my life was all the things I'd expected it to be all those years ago. Granted, I'd never imagined being married to five men, with three of them being in the mafia, but I found myself liking the turn of events. In fact, everything I'd wanted had come true in a way. It just looked slightly different.

I was married—to five men.

I lived in a big house—with a mafia family.

I was a mom—to an abandoned foster kid. Plus, a

stepmom to Levi. We gave blended family a whole new meaning, and I loved it.

Those things in of themselves were amazing and were probably what was keeping me from swirling to the bottom of the barrel.

Because the rest, it was a lot to take in.

Death and mayhem were a regular part of my day now. I didn't know if the fact I was okay with it said more about me than I wanted it to.

The two hardest things I hadn't completely dealt with were my father's death and the loss of my job.

While I hadn't been close to my dad, it felt worse because I'd been robbed of the chance to get to know the real him. Another victim of Dayton's skewed view of reality.

When I really thought about it, it made me furious he'd taken that from me. I had such a deep ache in my soul, and I wondered if it would ever be repaired. Some things weren't capable of being healed. We just had to hope they scabbed over, and we could move on.

And now, I didn't even know who I was. My sense of identity had been taken from me too. Before, when everything else had fallen apart, I had it to cling to, and now it was gone.

How did I crawl out from this rubble? How did I rebuild when I wasn't sure which direction to go?

Was this even something I could fix? I honestly didn't know. Despair sat heavily on my chest, the familiar feeling wanting to wrap its arms around me, promising me a return to the dark abyss I'd grown so accustomed to.

I was tired. So tired of dealing with everything that it felt comforting for a minute to let myself fall back into the inky darkness, letting everything around me fade away.

As I laid back on the bed, whispered promises of avoidance swirled around me, the fog falling into place. I could just stay here for a while and let everyone else figure it out. I was owed that much.

Closing my eyes, I drifted off, letting everything on the outside fade into the background.

A HAND FELL over my face, pushing my hair back, the soft caresses feeling at odds with the torment I felt inside. I blinked open my eyes, trying to make sense of the dark shape next to me.

"Bellezza," Atticus said, alerting me to his presence. "The knee-jerk question I want to ask you doesn't seem right for this moment. I know you're not okay, but I want you to know that you don't have to be."

He stared at me with his dark umber eyes, and I saw his love shining back for me. It was something I'd never found with Brian—the perfect reminder this wasn't the same. In fact, *I* wasn't even the same. The emotions might feel similar, but that was it. They were fleeting, ever-changing with circumstances.

Whereas the strength of my character and the love of these men weren't. *That* was what I needed to grasp a hold of with every fiber of my being. We'd all come this far, our hurts and pains, battle scars that shone brightly of the true warriors we were. We didn't have to be broken here. Together, we could stand strong, supporting one another.

I wrapped my arms around Atticus, pulling myself into his lap. He sat back against the headboard, holding me. I hadn't realized it was what I needed, but once he hugged me, the dam broke, and I shed all the tears I had been holding in.

It was the first time I'd cried with an audience, but I'd never felt more cared for and supported. Atticus didn't rebuke me. He didn't shush or tell me it would all be okay. He just held me, letting me get it out and providing me with his strength when I was low.

When they finally began to slow, he handed me a tissue, and a weird sob laugh combo emerged. Blowing my nose, I dabbed my face with another, wiping away the remains of my heartache.

Placing them on the bedside table, I immediately went back into his arms, wanting the comfort and warmth he emitted. His voice surprised me when he started to talk, and I leaned into his chest, enjoying feeling the deep rumble through my entire body.

"I never got to mourn my mother, something I regret knowing what I do now. At the time, I hadn't been sad because I thought she'd abandoned me, and I filled the loss with other things to occupy myself. With everything we've uncovered, I find myself thinking about her more. I can hear her laugh at times in Imogen's. I can see her smile in Nicco's, and I can see her love for her children in you."

"But I thought they both had different mothers?" I asked, not getting his meaning.

"They did. Dayton has taken them from all of us, I suppose. Another thing to add to his extensive list of sins. What I'm failing to express, Bellezza, is that remembering them doesn't always have to be about the life they lived. Imogen never even met my mother, but I can hear the same joy in her laugh. With Nicco, the mischief she had in the games we made together, and with you, the love. You missed out on knowing your father as the person he was, but it doesn't change the past. Even when we wear masks, we often still show others who we are underneath in small moments. It's hard to hide everything."

I let his words roll over in my mind, his meaning sinking in. He was right. And perhaps, something I always knew deep down. I hid the things I didn't want others to see, but they were still there. And when I wore the physical mask at Illusion, it didn't make me suddenly braver. That had to have come from me, to begin with. My father might have been pretending to play a part, but it wasn't all a lie.

"I guess that's true. Thank you for sharing that with me. I'm struggling with expressing how I feel, and I'd contemplated letting the darkness take me over. We've been dealing with so much, and I haven't had a moment to process any of it." I paused, and I appreciated that at this moment, Atticus was giving me what I needed instead of demanding answers like the mafia boss he was.

That was when it hit me. We could be more than one thing. It felt so simple, yet it felt like a colossal epiphany had just occurred within me.

"I just realized that while it might feel similar, it's not, and in fact, I have so much more this time in my life. I've lost my father and my job, but I have a family, a home, and a love so powerful that it has changed my world. Everything else will come in time, and I just need to take it step by step. More importantly, I need to make sure I take time for myself because it's so easy to manage everyone else when there are this many people in my life that I could lose sight of myself, hiding in the shadows of everyone around me."

"Bellezza, I don't think you could ever hide in the shadows. Your beauty and love shine brightly, drawing us all to you. But I get what you mean about making sure that you're a priority, and I'm fully on board with that. Just tell me if you need something, and I'll make it happen."

"I know you will, my love." I cupped his cheek, bringing it down to kiss. "And there might be times I need you to step in and tell me, but I think it's important for me to recognize it in myself too."

Atticus kissed my nose, tightening his arms around me. "The good part is that we're in this together." He lifted my hand, kissing the ring, and I knew without a doubt he was right. Our love would change our world because it already had.

A FEW DAYS LATER, I found myself needing some girl time, so I called Cami, Nat, and Stacy for lunch. Nat couldn't get away from her undercover assignment, but Cami and Stacy eagerly replied. Cami was even bringing Lark, which made me excited to spend time with the blond beauty when I had more clothes on.

Topher followed me into a restaurant, and I noticed he was more alert than before. When he'd asked me who I was meeting, I noticed his ears had gone a little red. He looked nicer today, too, taking time to comb his hair, shave, and I daresay, he even wore cologne. It made me curious about whom he was dressing up for.

The hostess appeared immediately when we stepped into the lobby, a big smile on her face. "Mrs. Mascro, right this way. We took the opportunity to provide you with a private room. Please let us know if there's anything we can do to improve your time here today."

It took me a moment to realize she was talking to me. I was still getting used to being "Mrs. Mascro." At least she'd been friendly and hospitable. I liked that she wasn't trying to kiss my butt or be fake, but genuinely wanted to do her job well.

"Here you are." She motioned for us to step into the room. I stopped, remembering my position.

"Thank you..." I paused, waiting for her to give me her name.

"Megan." She smiled, almost holding her breath to see if she was in trouble or not.

"Thank you, Megan. You've been most hospitable." I smiled kindly at her, remembering my epiphany. I could be both strong and nice. I didn't have to lose sight of that.

She smiled, her shoulders relaxing as she waited for us to step into the room. Cami and Lark were already sitting, and as we entered, they stood, waiting for us to get closer so they could hug me.

"Lor! You look so good!" Lark exclaimed, and I beamed as she pulled me into her arms. She always smelled amazing, and I loved how much she put into her hug. The girl gave good hugs.

"Quit hogging her, Lark," Cami teased, pulling me from her fiancée to give me a hug. I'd seen her around the manor a lot, but it was different when there weren't a lot of mafia men around.

Though, as I said that, I watched as Topher went to stand by Malek on the back wall and wondered if he was here because of Cami or if he'd been assigned to her through Atticus. It was curious. I was more surprised he was healed, but he was probably like Sax and refused to be bedridden, if at all possible.

Cami went to ask a question, her mouth open, when Stacy walked in, and everything halted.

"Topher!" she screeched, running across the room toward him. She flew so fast in her heels that I didn't know how she didn't topple over. She launched herself into his arms, kissing the reddening guard, and his earlier behavior now made sense.

The three of us gawked at our friend as she smothered him in kisses. I turned to Cami, a look of shock on my face. "Did you know?"

She shook her head, unable to tear her eyes away.

"I think it's cute," Lark said, picking up a breadstick and biting it. "They totally hit it off at the club a few weeks back."

Cami turned to Lark, her eyes wide. "You had gossip and didn't share? That's fiancée 101, babe! I'm appalled."

Lark just stuck her tongue out, and I laughed. When Stacy finally disentangled herself from my blushing guard, she walked over to the table, acting like nothing had happened.

"Nope," Cami said, shaking her head. "I don't care if he's there listening in; you're going to share all the details now, girl. Leave nothing out." Cami braced her head on her hands as she peered at Stacy, blinking, her eyes huge.

Stacy didn't seem to care that we had an audience and regaled us with her exploits. I had to stop her at one point, as I didn't need that much information about one of the men who routinely guarded me.

All in all, it was a fun lunch with women who had come to mean the world to me. My relationships with them were another success for me, bringing a smile to my face.

Laughter, shenanigans, and girl talk had been precisely what I needed.

As Topher and I left a few hours later, I didn't miss the way Stacy kissed him bye and told him that he better call her this time or she'd hunt his ass down.

He kept looking over at me as we walked to the car, his cheeks still red. Eventually, I took pity on the man. "Don't worry. I won't say anything. I'm happy for my friend. Just don't break her heart."

Topher relaxed, nodding. "I think I'm more likely the one to be hurt. Stacy is a force to be reckoned with. I've never met anyone like her."

"She's a good one. I'm happy for you both then."

I bumped his shoulder as we rounded the corner, smiling at him. When I turned back, we both stopped at the sight in front of us. Fury boiled over in me, and I let it rise to the top. Topher already had his phone out, probably calling it in or for backup, but I was done waiting on the sidelines.

TWELVE

LOREN

The earlier fog of grief fell away as I walked toward the man who thought he could play with our lives like we were chess pieces.

"Well, if it isn't my former client. How are you, Dayton?"

He smirked, rubbing his chin as he took me in. Since it was lunch, I'd dressed in some black skinny jeans, black boots, and a red sweater that had a deep V that showed off the top of my black lace bra. Dayton's eyes trailed up my body, and I held back the shiver of disgust that wanted to take over me. When his eyes landed on my hand, his face shot up, looking at me differently, a question in his gaze.

"Mrs. Carter, how nice to bump into you here. It looks like congratulations are in order. Might I ask who the lucky man is?"

I felt Topher at my back, letting me know the cavalry

would arrive soon. It bolstered my confidence, and I knew my time was limited before Atticus swooped in, attempting to rescue me. This was one time I didn't need to be.

I smiled darkly, shielding myself from allowing my anxiety to take root. Crossing my arms, my hip jutted out, my heeled boots giving me a great silhouette as I stood across from him, power pose on display. He watched me, looking for any sign of weakness to strike out against.

"I think the better question, *Dayton*, is how your son is such a better man than you? He seems to have managed what you never were able to. I think it's time you leave and admit defeat. You're not winning here."

He smiled, enjoying my strength like it was his favorite candy. He pulled his hands out of his pockets, and I felt Topher tense. Dayton clapped, looking me over again. "It seems you've found your power, Mrs. Carter. I'd like to think I had some part in that."

Scoffing, I rolled my eyes. "Sure, because a narcissistic asshole such as yourself would believe it was because of you."

"I'm glad you're finally giving me my due credit, Mrs. Carter. Now, tell my son that he owes me a club. I'll be fair and fight him for it instead of just taking it. I'm a good father like that."

A squeal of tires could be heard coming around the

corner, and I knew it was Atticus. Dayton nodded to a man who moved to open the door of their vehicle, the one that was purposefully parked behind ours, so we couldn't have left if we'd wanted to. As his door began to close, I stepped back, making my way to the vehicle that pulled to a stop. Before his shut, I called out, knowing what I needed to say.

"Oh, and Dayton?"

The door stalled, staying open a smidge. I almost wished I was on the other side so I could see his face when I delivered the news, but I knew it would be better if I was out of view to get away.

"It's Mrs. Mascro. I'm a true mafia Queen. Show some respect."

Topher opened the door behind me, and I hopped in, my breathing coming quick as the door closed and we sped away before I could think any more of it.

I turned, taking in Atticus. He was breathing heavily as well, his hands tight on the steering wheel. Once we were a few blocks over, he quickly pulled over into a parking lot, turning off the engine as he lowered his head to the wheel.

"Attie?" He held up a hand, and I knew he needed a minute. I took it as well, using the quiet to calm my own heart. I'd stood up to Dayton Mascro, the Masked King-pin. And I daresay I held my own reasonably well.

A laugh bubbled out of me, the hysteria overtaking

me. "I just told your father to admit defeat and that he was a narcissist." I laughed more, the tears starting to fall. "And then I told him I was Mrs. Mascro. I wish I could've seen his face." I turned, finding Atticus looking at me like I was crazy. To be fair, I felt a bit crazy.

He blinked, collecting himself. "You what?"

"I told him to show some respect. He tried to intimidate me, cornering me when you weren't around. It was a stupid power move, and I didn't let him have it. Your timing couldn't have been better if we'd planned it."

Atticus' mouth hung open as he listened. I pulled his face to mine, kissing him deeply. His eyes were dilated when we pulled back, and I was half tempted to push his seat back and have my way with him, but the two-seater sports car wasn't ideal for recreational activities.

Apparently, I didn't care that it was mid-afternoon in a parking lot. If my mother could see me now, she would indeed have a stroke. Something about that brought a smile to my face.

"Every day, I wonder how I could love you more than the day before, but you go and do something, proving me wrong. You truly are our Queen."

"Sorry if I scared you or made it more difficult. I just couldn't let him try to intimidate me anymore. Something in me snapped when I saw him leaning against his car, blocking ours."

"Part of me wants to reprimand you, but that's

because I was scared, not that you did anything wrong, Bellezza. I'm trying to learn the difference."

"Oh, Attie." I braced my forehead to his. "I'm only brave because you've shown me how."

"Um, guys," a voice said from the speakers, startling us both.

"Fuck, sorry, Pixel," Atticus cursed, turning to look at the screen in the middle of the car.

My cheeks heated as her face appeared. Guess I'd been too occupied earlier to notice. I was suddenly thrilled I hadn't decided to get some dick mid-afternoon if she'd been there the whole time.

"I just wanted to let you know that I've successfully been able to track his car. I know where he's staying," she said, smiling wide.

"You're brilliant, Pixel. We're headed back now. Have everyone gather in the meeting room. It's time to strike."

"You got it!" she said before the screen blinked off.

We turned toward one another, and the earlier hysteria returned, Atticus joining in this time, tipping me over more. The car filled with the sound of our laughter, and I relished the moment. We needed more of this. Where we could remember there was more to life than corrupt fathers, jealous mothers, and greedy men wanting more than their share.

Once we'd wiped our eyes, Atticus drove us the rest of the way at the speed limit. It explained how he'd gotten there so quickly if he had Pixel changing lights or something. I decided not to ask. Some things were better left to the imagination regarding the mafia.

TWENTY MINUTES LATER, I found myself seated around the table that had become a necessary part of my day. Every morning and sometimes afternoons, we gathered and gave an update. It felt nice to have these meetings and keep everyone abreast of the situation.

Sax, Nicco, and Wells were present this afternoon when we walked in. Topher was already along the wall, nodding to me when we entered, having driven the car back without any parking lot stops. A few other guards and men I was still learning the names of filled the rest of the table.

Pixel sat in her regular seat, a computer screen in front of her. She'd become such a constant presence here that I was beginning to feel like I should make more of an effort to get to know her better. Everyone seemed to only use her for her tech genius, and I could see how she could fade into the background at times, despite her loud colors and personality. People tended to only talk to her when they needed something.

She poked her head up, catching me staring at her. Pixel blinked, smiling. "You need something, hot stuff?"

Laughing, I shook my head, focusing back on what

Atticus was saying. I decided I'd catch her later and make her do something with the girls.

"We've been able to track Dayton's car to where he's staying in the city. This gives us two options. Do we try to overtake the compound with him in the city, or do we strike his place here and send him back to the suburbs?"

"Which would give us the best strategic advantage?" someone asked, and I thought it over.

"I think the better question is, what does your father expect you to do? He's always thinking a few steps ahead, and who's to say this wasn't a setup to get us to fall into a trap. So, which option is he expecting, and which one would actually give us the leverage or advantage?"

The room was quiet as everyone considered what I said. "You make a good point, Loren. Perhaps, the better option is to strike out against an area he'd never think we'd go for."

My phone buzzed on the table, pulling my focus from the room. Seeing the caller, I motioned to take it out in the hall.

Once I was clear, I hit answer and pulled it to my ear. "Hello?"

"Hello, is this Mrs. Carter?"

"No, this is Mrs. Mascro."

"Oh, apologies. I, um, well," the voice said, stumbling. I knew what they meant, though, so I took mercy on them. It wasn't their fault they had to make this call.

"I was Mrs. Carter before I remarried. Is there something I can do for you?"

"Oh, yes, um, well." The person cleared their throat, clearly nervous. "We need you to come down to the police station. It seems your ex-husband was murdered, and they need you to identify the body."

"Murdered? Are you sure? What happened?" I asked, attempting to sound like I was shocked.

"He was found at a club called Evolve, the details of his death are still being investigated, but they need someone to identify who he is to start their investigation."

"Why me? There isn't anyone else? We divorced over three years ago."

"You were listed as the emergency contact on his medical information. Do you know of someone else I should call?"

Sighing, I rubbed my forehead. "No. It's fine. I'll do it. Which station?"

I knew I needed to do this, but the thought of having to go through it had all the energy draining from me. Thinking of Brian dying and actually seeing his body were two different things. I hung up once she told me the address, and I leaned against the wall, closing my eyes.

"Everything okay, Spitfire?"

I opened my eyes to find Sax standing in front of me. "They want me to claim Brian's body," I said with no emotion.

Sax's face tilted up in surprise. "That doesn't sound right. What station?"

I told him, not understanding his concern. "What's the issue? We knew they'd probably call me to do this."

"Yes, but he shouldn't have been discovered yet. So either we have a mole, or someone tipped them off. Did they say where he was found?"

I nodded, stating the location. "Isn't that where we'd planned?"

Sax rubbed his jaw before something lit up in his eyes, and he walked back into the room, stopping Atticus from whatever he was saying. I followed at a slower pace, trying to piece together what Sax had figured out.

"Stop. I know what we need to do," he said, grinning wide. "It's time to throw a party."

Blinking, I didn't understand what that had to do with anything, but Atticus and even Nicco had smiles covering their faces as I looked between them.

"Anyone care to explain?" I asked, leaning against the door. "I have to go and identify Brian's body, so the quick version would be appreciated."

"What do I do best, Bellezza?" Atticus asked, turning his attention to me. My face reddened as I stuttered, not knowing how to respond to that. He rolled his eyes, smiling as he walked toward me, taking my hands.

"Secrets, Bellezza, secrets."

I still didn't get what that meant, but I could tell they were excited about it. "Okay, sure."

Atticus chuckled, the sound doing things to me. "It's time to cash in a few. We'll hit Dayton on multiple fronts, so he can't possibly manage them all. Then, we go for what we're really after when he's occupied."

Thirteen

Nicco

I watched Loren closely as she listened to the officer tell her where they'd found Brian. She held herself strong, her face impassive as she nodded. Wells stood next to me, his arm brushing mine the barest amount, and I smiled, happy he wasn't avoiding me any longer. After our tryst in the fitness room, I'd taken him to my art studio. It felt right to show him something vulnerable of mine after he'd shared his heart with me.

Loren shifted, and I zeroed in, squeezing her hand when the examiner said he would lift the cloth so she could confirm his identity. She nodded, steeling herself. If Pixel's drug did what she claimed, it wouldn't be a pretty sight. When the sheet was pulled back, I grimaced. His face was still bruised from the beating I'd given him, but it was unmistakably Brian. His skin was bloated, and he looked more like a beached whale than the man we'd seen a week ago.

"It's him," she said, nodding. Loren turned into me;

whether to hide her view or needing some comfort, I didn't know. I rubbed my arm up and down her back, soothing her nonetheless.

"Do you need anything else from my wife?" Wells asked. The guy eyed him since I was the one comforting her. I smirked, lifting my eyebrow, daring him to say anything. He quickly turned away, looking back to Wells.

"No. If she can just sign the paperwork on the way out, we'll send his personal effects once they've been cleared through evidence."

Turning Loren, I led her out of the foul-smelling room, keeping her close. Wells stayed even with me, and I smiled. He might deny it, but he liked being near us both. Once we were clear of the police station, we all let out a collective sigh.

"He was clearly found too soon. It's suspicious," Wells said, tapping his fingers on his pant legs.

"I agree. Do you think Dayton knew and tipped them off?" Loren asked, biting her lip. She looked between the two of us, looking for an answer I didn't have for her.

"No clue, but we have a few errands to run before returning to the manor. Come on." I herded them toward the waiting SUV, hoping to distract them. We slid in the open door, settling ourselves. I, for one, was glad to have that over with.

"So, one ex down. Have we heard anything about Brittni?"

"Nothing yet," Wells confirmed, checking his phone.

I watched as he put it in his pocket, his hand grazing my leg as he did. A tiny groan slipped past my lips, and I moved, my leg rubbing against his. I caught Loren hiding a smile as I tried to shift the growing appendage in my jeans inconspicuously. The simplest touch from him set me off.

"So," she said, leaning forward a little, "you two get it on yet?" Her eyes were mischievous as she looked at us. Picking up her hand, I brought her wrist to my mouth, kissing the soft skin of her tattoo.

"As a matter of fact, we did. Well, sort of. Wellsy finally succumbed to his love for me." I grinned wide, winking at Loren.

The scoff next to me could've been heard two towns over, making me smile wider. "No, Wellsy?" I asked, turning to him and pinning him with my eyes. He faltered, swallowing.

"I think it was you," he said, giving me a grin that could melt icebergs. It was so powerful that I stopped, wondering if I was dreaming. Clearing my throat, I was overcome by feelings I hadn't expected, turning to look at Loren to escape his gaze for a moment.

"There you have it," I said, shrugging. "So, you ready for another tattoo?" I asked, changing the subject.

"Hmm, I don't know. Maybe once everything is over."

"I'll hold you to it, Beautiful." I kissed her knuckles, threading my fingers through hers. The rest of the ride was quiet and I ran through my thoughts, wondering what my father was up to. When we pulled up to an office building, we got out and headed inside. I wasn't used to others coming with me on jobs, but it was nice not having to do this alone, if I was honest.

I walked up to the receptionist, smiling at her. "Hello, Gloria, can you let Mr. Charles know that I'm here."

"Sure thing, sweetie." The older woman winked, picking up the phone. I walked over to the sitting area, and Wells and Loren followed.

"So, what are we doing here?" Loren asked, taking a seat. "Cracking some skulls? Doing a shakedown?"

A laugh erupted out of me, not expecting her question. "No, Beautiful." I shook my head, my eyes watering from how hard I laughed. "Not everything we do is violent, you know."

She looked at me sheepishly, her face tinting a little red. "Sorry, my knowledge is limited."

"I know. Wells, I could actually use your help on this. This is one of the accountants we use, and there's been a few discrepancies lately. Feel up to going through some books with me?" I eyed him, waiting to see what he'd say. His eyes widened, and his mouth opened, gaping a little.

"Um, sure. Though, don't forget I bankrupted half of Chicago."

"I disagree," I said, shaking my head. I stood when I saw Mr. Charles walking toward us, but kept my gaze on him. "You took the fall. You were set up to fail in that situation. Believe in yourself, Wellsy. You just might surprise yourself."

He nodded, and they both stood, following me. It felt nice to be the one to push him to believe in something outside of the ring.

As I neared, I shook the older gentleman's hand, not missing when he swallowed, some nerves showing. Okay, there might be some violence involved, after all.

"Nicolai, I wasn't expecting you today."

"That's kind of the point, Glenn." I didn't make any apology for being here. We paid him a decent salary to manage our legitimate businesses; he could take our visit whenever we goddamn pleased. Atticus had been having difficulty reaching him as of late, so he felt a personal touch was needed. With the way the man was acting, it seemed his hunch was correct.

Mr. Charles led us into an office, eyeing my companions. "So, what do I owe this visit to, Nicolai?"

"Mr. Mascro has been having a difficult time reaching you, Glenn. So, I wanted to stop by and see if there was anything we could help you with. I brought our financial advisor with me. If you could please bring out the books for us to go through, I'd appreciate it."

Sweat began to bead on his forehead as he nervously shuffled on his feet. "Um, yes, of course." He looked over at Loren and Wells, almost like he was debating something.

"I wouldn't think about running if I were you. The whole building is surrounded by guards. You won't get more than two feet from the door." It was complete bullshit, but he didn't know that. Wells cracked his knuckles, acting as the muscle, and I smiled into my hand. That man was going to be my undoing. When Loren stepped into her role as Mafia Queen, I couldn't have been more proud and turned on.

"Mr. Charles, is it? We haven't met. I'm Loren Mascro. I can't help but notice that you seem a little stressed. Is there something you wish to tell us?"

He swallowed again, his brow sweating more at the mention of her name. "Um," he stuttered, pushing up his glasses.

Loren walked closer, gently patting his hand. "We can help you if you tell us everything, but keep it from us now, and my husbands won't be as lenient."

It was then I realized how much Loren fit with us. I'd always known it, but she gave us a softness we'd been craving. Atticus wanted our family to be different, but we often fell into old patterns, not able to see how to go about getting things in new ways. But here, Loren showed this man some fierce compassion in her own way.

She was strong and beautiful, avenging the misfortunate left and right.

Mr. Charles crumpled under her kindness, sinking into a chair next to his desk, spilling all of his misdeeds.

Dayton had been thorough, but it seemed we might have caught it before it ruined us.

And all because Loren showed a little compassion. She was the Beauty to all our Beasts, showing us how to love.

Wells leaned close, his body pressing into mine. "She has no idea how amazing she is."

"Nope, but we get to show her every day from here to eternity." I smiled over, forgetting he'd moved closer. I got stuck in his eyes for a minute as we stared at one another.

"Yeah, we do," he finally said, licking his lips.

The door shutting brought us back to the present, finding our smiling wife in front of us. She leaned back against the desk, crossing her ankles. "I really wish we had long enough to explore the looks on your guys' faces."

"Raincheck, Beautiful." I winked, stepping closer to her. "You were amazing, by the way. You were meant to be our wife, even if you don't see it." I leaned in, kissing her nose.

"I'm still figuring out my place in this world, but I like to think I'm grasping it. Thank you for reminding me." She kissed my cheek, reaching a hand out to Wells, pulling him closer. "You're my heart; I hope you know that."

"Fuck," I cursed, "now I wish we had more time. You

can't go spouting grandiose declarations and not expect me to show you how it makes me feel."

I watched as her eyes dilated, and I knew she was two seconds away from giving in to my wants when the door opened, Mr. Charles returning. He cleared his throat, sitting a box down on the table.

"Um, here's everything. The real ones."

"Excellent," I said, not dropping Loren's eyes. "We'll be taking them with us."

I stepped away and motioned for Wells to grab the other box, and the three of us headed toward the door.

"I'll be in touch about the future of our business." I looked the man up and down, showing him that while Loren might have a softer approach, we weren't opposed to cracking some skulls if needed.

I couldn't be certain, but a small wet spot appeared on his pants as we turned to leave. A weird grin filled my face at finally being able to scare someone enough to pee themselves.

My life was weird, but I loved it. The future I'd dreamed of months ago no longer felt like me, and I knew I'd only been kidding myself.

These people, this life, this was who I was always meant to be.

When we got back to the car, the sexual tension was high, but it started to dwindle as we made a few more stops. Grinning to myself, I couldn't wait to see how they reacted to the last visit. Thankfully, I had something up my sleeve to push the limits and stoke that fire.

"Can I stay in the car for this one?" Loren yawned, leaning back against the seat.

"Yeah, me too," Wells said, snuggling closer to her. I knew his intention was to have some alone time. I saw as she blushed, also picking up on his reason.

"Nope. You're gonna want to come," I said, pausing, "in this store." I looked over at them, winking. They looked between themselves and then glanced out the window as we rolled to a stop at our destination.

The Right Spot sign glowed brightly against the darkening sky. Opening the door, I held it for them both. Loren and Wells looked up at the sign and the blacked-out windows, trying to piece it together.

"This seems suspicious," Loren whispered. I grabbed her hand, smiling the whole time as I walked toward the door. Hitting the buzzer, I waited for them to ask for our name and password.

"Mascro party. Backdoor."

"Good evening, Mr. Mascro. We look forward to serving your party this evening."

The door buzzed open, and we stepped in. The swanky storefront was decked out in dark purple velvet with gold accents. When Madame Emma walked out, Loren slapped my arm, turning to me.

"Why do I feel like I'm being set up for something?" she asked.

Before I could answer, Madame Emma greeted us.

"Mr. Nicolai, how nice to see you again. I'd kiss you in greeting, but I hear congratulations are in order?" She smiled, looking between Loren and me.

"All three of us," I said, winking.

"Apologies, congrats to all of you. Thank you for visiting our establishment. We look forward to serving you today. Is there anything, in particular, you're looking for?"

"Yes, actually." I turned, looking at the two next to me. Their faces were both filled with apprehension and curiosity. "I believe we're in the market for two backdoor diamonds."

FOURTEEN

LOREN

W hen Nicco said backdoor diamonds, I was momentarily confused. Was that a type of diamond I hadn't heard of? Like the tiger lily one? When Wells stalled, looking over at him in shock, I had a feeling it was exactly what it sounded like.

Glancing over at Madame Emma, I tried to gauge her reaction. She smiled wide at me, motioning for us to head back behind some doors. When we stepped through, I stopped in my tracks at the sparkling cases around us.

This was a sex shop. A legitimate sex shop.

For some reason, I hadn't been expecting it despite his use of backdoor and Madame Emma being here. Okay, that was a lie. I'd assumed something sexual when she'd glided out, decked out in her leather and thigh-high boots, but a sex shop hadn't been on my list for some reason.

"You brought us to a sex shop?" I asked, looking at

Nicco. I knew the answer, but I needed him to say it out loud.

"Not just any sex shop, Beautiful, the *premier* sex shop."

"He's not wrong," Madame Emma stated with a smug smile on her face. "For backdoor, I'd suggest these." She gestured to a case a few rows in, and I walked toward it in a daze. I wanted to look at so many things around me but also felt slightly embarrassed.

Sure enough, when I made it to the cabinet, rows of butt plugs were displayed on little velvet pillows. You'd almost believe they were real jewels with how they were shown off. Some of them sparkled, some of them lit up, and a few others appeared to move with you. I'd never seen so many varieties of butt plugs. Not that I was a connoisseur of them to begin with, but that was beside the point.

"Wow, that's, um," I mumbled, my words dying on my lips.

"I can see that this is your first time, so I'll give you some space. Let me know when you make a decision or have a question. Nicco, you know where the key is."

He nodded, rubbing his hands together in glee as he moved around to the back of the cabinet, bending down to open the back. Apparently, he was well acquainted with Butt Plugs 'R Us. So much so that he was allowed behind the counter.

"I feel like this needs some context," I finally stated, realizing my nerves made me a little bitchy.

"It's not what you're thinking, Beautiful," he said, looking up to catch my eyes. I huffed, crossing my arms. Wells moved closer, pulling me into his body.

"What? That you either visit this place a lot, or... nope, that's all I got," Wells said, a dry chuckle leaving him.

"Yeah, that." I kept my eyes focused on Nicco, watching every move he made.

"If I didn't know better, I'd say you're both jealous." He straightened, two cushions in his hand that he placed on the glass surface, sliding them closer to us.

"Here, look at these while I tell you guys a story."

I looked up at Wells, my head on his chest. He peered down at me, his eyes softening slightly at the move. "I guess we should hear him out, Kitten."

He tapped my hip, and I moved with him closer to the ominous things on the glass. Nicco watched us, some apprehension in his gaze now. I didn't mean to make him doubt himself, and I realized I was being a chicken. Not once had Nicco led me into anything I hadn't enjoyed. I trusted him with my body, and I needed to trust him with this.

Smiling, I dropped my arms and moved closer to look at the items he'd laid out. "Okay, tell me about them and why you're familiar with this place. I'm curious."

He relaxed, leaning down to peer at me, meeting my

eyes. "You know that we hire Madame Emma for the club, right?" I nodded, moving closer to him. I couldn't help but be drawn into Nicco. I grabbed his hand, needing to touch him.

"Well," he said, caressing my thumb, "as part of the agreement to train our staff, we financed this place with her. We needed a legitimate business, and this way, she gets to expand, and we get access to all the things we need to run a sex club."

My cheeks heated. He was right. I'd jumped to the wrong conclusion. "So, that explains how you're so familiar, but I'm guessing these are for Wells and me?"

Nicco nodded, licking his lips. He looked up, his eyes drawing to the man behind me. "Yes. We've talked about exploring more things, and I thought this would be the best option to get you both prepared."

"I'm not letting you take my ass," Wells hissed. Nicco rolled his eyes, not backing down.

"Maybe try it before you dismiss it completely. If you don't like it, I'll wear it, or I'm sure Monroe will be game. It's honestly better than you're both making it out to be. I promise. Nothing but pleasure."

"Have you worn one?" I asked.

"Of course." I looked back at Wells, who seemed to deflate at that response.

"So, why these? Educate us."

"Well," he started, going into his explanation. I realized after silicone, angled, and vibration, I quit listening.

I trusted Nicco, and he was clearly more experienced in this area. Why wouldn't I let him lead me in this as well?

"I'm game," I said before he was finished. "I trust you. I'm sorry I doubted you." Nicco smiled down at me, making my insides flutter. I loved how he could give me a look even now, and it felt like the first time.

"What about you, Wellsy?" he teased.

Wells' hands on my hips tightened as he debated. Eventually, he sighed, placing his head between my neck and shoulder as he breathed. "Fine," he mumbled into it, sending tiny vibrations through me.

"Perfect." Nicco beamed, moving to place them back in the display. He opened a drawer, pulling out two boxes and what looked like two packets of something. Nicco walked back around the counter, grabbing my hand to pull me in a different direction. Wells stumbled since he wasn't watching, but quickly caught up as Nicco pulled us into what looked like a private dressing room. He shut the door, and I looked around at the space.

"Is this a sex room?"

"Sort of. If people want to try things out, they can."

I wrinkled my nose. "Isn't that unsanitary?"

He chuckled, the sound more throaty than usual as he occupied himself with taking the two plugs out of the boxes. "Strip," he said in lieu of an answer.

"But," I started when he walked forward, placing a finger against my lips.

"There's a process, but most people who come here

buy and try, no need to return. Sometimes, you just need a place, or the need strikes you, so they have it here. Don't overthink it. Now, strip. Both of you."

I glanced over at Wells, who shrugged, pulling his shirt over his head. Joining in, I pulled off my shirt and jeans, folding them up. When I was left in only my underwear, I looked up at Nicco.

"All of it." He leaned back against a wall, clearly enjoying the show if the hard outline of his dick in his jeans was any indication. Clasping my bra, I unhooked it, dropping it to the floor. Now that I was pretty sure this would lead to something sexual, I was finding my footing. Slowly, I slid the panties down, kicking them into the pile of clothes I'd made.

Standing with my hands on my hips, I lifted an eyebrow and waited for my next order. Wells wrapped his arm around my waist, pulling me closer to him. I peeked over, seeing that his dick was starting to grow as we stood there naked.

"Put on a show for me," Nicco said, sitting back on the lounger.

I didn't have to be told twice to kiss my surly lover. Turning in his arms, I went up on my tiptoes, bringing our lips together. Our kisses weren't as aggressive as the first few times, but there was still a bite to kissing Wells that I didn't get from the others. Each one felt like a war between the person he was and the person he wanted to be. I didn't know how to tell him I loved him for who he was—brokenness and all. He didn't have to be at war with himself anymore.

Cupping his face, I pulled back a second, forgetting Nicco. "I love you, Wells. You. Don't hate who you were, because I love *every* part of you."

He blinked, moving his hands to my hips and pulling me closer. His cock made itself known, bumping into my lower half, eliciting a soft moan from me. "How do you do that? See into my doubts?"

I smiled, love shining out of my eyes. "I'd like to say it's my superpower, but I just know you." I kissed his nose, deciding to share some vulnerability. If you couldn't be open while naked in a sex shop, when could you?

"And perhaps because I've thought them, too. If I've learned anything this past year, it's that I had to embrace all aspects of myself—dark and light. I can't rise to my full potential if I'm denying a crucial component of my identity. It doesn't always mean it's pretty, but it's mine, and no one else can claim that. There's power in that understanding. We're all here for you. You don't have to be worried about any of us leaving."

Another body pressed into us, their warm hands wrapping around us. Wells tensed for a second before relaxing. We turned our heads together, finding Nicco peering at us. "As much as I want to be dominating and tell you both off for forgetting the assignment, Loren's not wrong, Wells. When you let yourself be free in moments, it's beautiful. You're so much more than you realize."

Nicco leaned forward slowly, giving Wells time to move if he wanted to. I saw the moment for what it was. Before, if they kissed, it might have been a moment of passion or something fun, but this was full of intensity and with purpose. If they kissed here, it would mean something, and Nicco was giving Wells an out. When he didn't move, Nicco closed the gap, bringing his lips to Wells. I sucked in a breath at the kiss, biting my lip with need.

It was so different from Wells and Monroe. Theirs was a love woven from years of friendship and first loves; this was one of passion and unexpectedness, of discovering new parts of yourself and not being scared to crack that door open more.

Nicco bit Wells' lip, pulling back. He held his stare for a moment, emotion heavy in his eyes as I watched. His lips tilted up, and I heard as he smacked Wells' ass. "Now, show our woman how much you love her." He kissed me quickly before returning back to his perch.

Wells took Nicco's words to heart, lifting me up, and I wrapped my legs around his waist. His lips immediately found mine, and a new passion was unleashed in him. He walked toward the wall, stopping when my back pressed against it. Our kissing turned sloppy as we tried to devour one another's mouths. When I felt his fingers near my core, a whimper left me.

"Need you," I gasped, moving my neck for him to kiss. He greedily obliged, kissing down my nape, his finger plunging into me in quick succession. I quivered with need as he pulled his finger in and out. It wasn't enough, and I wiggled, trying to find more friction.

"Fuck her," Nicco said, sounding closer. "Plunge your thick cock into her tight pussy and make her see stars, Crash. Do it, or I'll take over, and you won't get your reward."

With a growl, Wells' hands lowered to my hips, tilting me slightly before he positioned me over his cock, thrusting up in one movement. Moaning, my head fell back against the velvet wall, its smoothness feeling nice against my naked flesh. My hands braced on Wells' shoulders as he moved me up and down, and I soon climbed toward an orgasm.

"Yes, Wells. Fuck our wife." I looked over to Nicco, wanting him closer. He stood, his cock in his hands as he watched our show. I beckoned with my finger, drawing him near. I pulled his head close, kissing him. Using him as leverage, I wrapped one arm around his neck, moving my other to his dick. In tandem with him, I wrapped my hand around his, helping him to fist his cock. Nicco groaned into my kiss, and I felt my walls begin to tighten.

My head fell back as curses left me, and I moaned. "Yes, fuck, yes."

"Come for me, Kitten," Wells said, and I fell over at

his command. He picked up his pace, thrusting in me as my hand moved with Nicco's. When warm liquid hit my belly, I knew Nicco had found his release, and I toppled over the edge, stars lighting up my eyes. Wells gripped me tighter and pulled me down firmly, holding me to him as he spilled in me.

Their heads leaned against me as we all tried to catch our breaths.

"Shit, that was hotter than I expected," Nicco said, a laugh leaving him.

It set Wells and me off, and he groaned when my walls tightened from the sound. "Naughty, Kitten," he wheezed.

Nicco stepped back, walked over to a cabinet, and pulled out some wipes. He walked over to us as Wells lowered me to the floor. We all managed to wipe ourselves clean, tossing the wipes into the trash. I moved to my clothes, figuring we were done, when Nicco stopped us.

"Nope. Not yet. Both of you, hands on the lounger, asses in the air." I looked at him, swallowing as I nodded. Wells didn't move, his jaw tightening.

"Trust me," Nicco said, pleading with his eyes. Wells sighed, moving forward, and placed his hands next to mine. Nicco's warm hands rubbed over my ass before I felt a cold drizzle. His finger then pushed in and out, and I wondered if I'd orgasm again. I was beginning to get turned on as he plunged his digit in and out. When I felt something thicker begin to bridge the opening, I tensed.

"Relax, Beautiful. Wells, distract her." Wells did as he said, pulling my face to his. His hands moved over me, and I soon forgot Nicco was behind me as I fell into his kisses.

I felt Wells tense a moment later, and it was the only reason I realized that Nicco had left me and moved over to him. I hadn't felt the plug when I'd been kissing Wells. Even now, it wasn't entirely uncomfortable. Just a little pressure. I kept kissing Wells, moving my hand down to his dick to help persuade him. He grunted as I grabbed him, panting with the effort. When I had him hard and throbbing, I felt Nicco move away from us.

Pushing Wells down on the bench, I perched over him, lowering myself onto him. I was so turned on again. I just needed a little to push me over. It didn't take long as we found our orgasm together. The plug was snug with his dick in me, and I wondered how long I'd have to leave this in for.

This time when we cleaned up, Nicco allowed us to put our clothes on. Madame Emma winked as we walked out of the shop, and I prayed it wasn't because she either heard us or I was walking funny.

Yeah, I'd pretend it was neither.

FIFTEEN

ATTICUS

The only part I hated about having legitimate businesses was the amount of networking I had to do. However, in this sense, I hoped it would lend to my plan to shove my father out. He could try all he wanted to open his club, but without the proper connections, there was no way he'd get all of his ducks in a row. It was simple, but it worked, and for once, I gladly sipped a cocktail with men I thought were boring.

"So, Atticus, I hear you recently got married? And here I thought you were the one to envy, the rich bachelor." The man chuckled, thinking his joke was funny.

"You obviously haven't met my wife. She makes me better every day. I wouldn't trade her or our family for anything." My little speech effectively shut up the buffoon as he swallowed his drink in a nervous gesture.

"Well, yes, of course. Congratulations."

The conversation changed after that, and I had three of the city council members in my good graces by the end of the cocktails. They were also eager to attend the secret gala we were hosting in a few weeks. It seemed like everything was aligning as we'd planned.

When I returned to the manor a few hours later, everything felt different. For the first time in a long while, I felt optimistic that I was ahead of my father. Having a family to fight for had given me a new purpose, a drive to succeed.

At first, I'd been dead set against the possibility of him being alive. Mostly because I'd wrestled with the knowledge that I'd killed him for so long, that it felt like a slap in the face to be told otherwise, when I'd finally come to terms with it. The other half, though, was denial. If my father was still alive, it meant it wasn't over. That I hadn't been enough, and he would take out his vengeance on Imogen and me. And well, no one liked to think of themselves as a failure.

It was trusting Loren and seeing the results from the bones that had me grappling with my new reality. When Jude had been taken, and half of the family had walked away, I knew what he was really after.

Dayton Mascro wanted to be the best. He wanted to win some arbitrary award he'd created to show who was top dog. At what, I wasn't sure, but I didn't think it mattered. Because, however, you sliced it, it was point-less. Whatever Dayton was after didn't exist, or at least not where he was looking for it.

If I had to guess, my father wanted the feeling of

complete power and adoration from those around him. He was a true narcissist, and only being perceived as the best would tickle his fancy. My father failed to understand that the path he was taking would never lead him to what he was after.

Unconditional love, acceptance, and respect were things you couldn't make people give you through fear. So while he was plotting our deaths and overtaking the city, searching for enough power to fill the void in his heart, I was finalizing a plan to take him out of our lives once and for all.

I didn't need to win against Dayton. I just needed him gone. I'd already won the lottery of life and had everything he so desperately wanted.

Leaning against the doorframe, I watched the people I cherished, the ones who gave me their love unconditionally. This was home. This was everything. And it was something Dayton would never have or understand.

Immy colored on the floor with Lily and Olivia. Levi played a game with Jude and Monroe on the coffee table. Wells and Loren were sitting on the couch, laughing with Nicco and Cami. Topher and Malek played cards with Sax and Pixel, and it looked like she was winning. Food and drink were spread across the room, and I watched as my family was happy to be together, just spending time in each other's presence.

Loren looked up, catching my eyes, and motioned for me to join them. Smiling, something I found myself doing more and more, I walked into the room. Shouts of hello rang out from the others, warming my heart, confirming everything I'd concluded earlier.

Loren stood up, motioning for me to take her seat. "Where will you sit, Bellezza?" I asked, a smile in my voice. Wells stood, letting her sit in his spot, and moved to the floor. They moved gingerly, sitting down slowly. I wondered what it was about, but the smirk on my brother's face had me believing he either knew or was the reason.

I linked our fingers, taking her hand in mine, instantly calming at her touch. I brought her hand up to my lips, kissing it. "How did today go, Bellezza? Are you doing okay?" I asked softly. It wasn't a secret, but it wasn't something she wanted to discuss in front of the kids.

"It was okay. Not as hard as I thought. Does it make me a bad person that I'm glad he's gone? Brian can't hurt me any longer."

I pulled her close, noticing she tensed for a second before settling into my arms. I kissed the top of her head, loving the smell of her shampoo as I did. Laying my head on top of hers, I kept her in my arms, locking my hands around her.

"Not at all. In fact, I realized that about my father tonight. I don't need to beat him because I already have. I just need him gone so I can live the life we've created."

She peered up at me, a smile on her face. "That's beautiful, Attie. How did your meetings go?"

"Good. Everything appears to be in full swing for our secret party. All the city officials I met with are on board, willing to help us stop Dayton. He'll never expect us to use legitimate sources. It's where he lacks imagination. Will you come with me tomorrow to meet someone?"

"Absolutely. Just tell me when."

"I love you, Bellezza," I whispered, kissing her softly.

Gagging sounds erupted next to me, and I turned, glaring at my cousin. "Camila, do you have something to offer?"

"Oh, sorry, had something in my throat." I rolled my eyes. Looking at the kids, I caught a couple of yawns, and suddenly the idea of having Loren to myself seemed like the best reward.

"Ah, look at the time. Isn't it bedtime?" I asked.

"Ah, man," the kids said, but no one argued. Cami took Olivia and Lily, Malek following her out. Levi ran over to give Loren a hug goodnight, and she kissed his cheek. I caught the happiness on her face at his gesture, and it made my own grow. Monroe bent down, kissing her deeply before walking out with Wells. He was still walking gingerly, making me even more curious.

Nicco leaned back on the couch, giving me a look like he knew what I was up to and wasn't going to let me get away with it.

"That includes us?" Jude asked, looking at me. I glanced over at him and Imogen.

"Um," I stuttered, pausing. Looking down at Loren, I decided to let her take this one.

She laughed softly, shaking her head. "Don't stay up too late. Your tutor will be here in the morning. If you want to return to school, you can't fall behind."

"Movie or video game?" Jude asked Imogen as they stood, heading off toward the media room. I was glad to see Jude bouncing back after the whole ordeal. He was a strong kid. But it didn't mean I trusted him alone with Immy. I nodded to Topher, who grinned, standing to follow. I didn't care what Loren said. They wouldn't be having sex if I could prevent it.

Once everyone had cleared out, it left only Loren, Sax, and Nicco. I glared over at Nicco, wanting him to leave. He groaned, standing. "Fine, but you owe me, big brother. Besides, I left you with a gift." Nicco smirked, making me interested for different reasons now. When I glanced down at Loren, I found her cheeks blushing.

"Okay, now, I've gotta know."

Loren giggled, making my heart take flight. Sax moved over closer to us, watching us with heated eyes.

"I have a good guess, considering how she's been acting," he murmured, licking his lips. "Did you happen to visit *The Right Spot*, Spitfire?"

She nodded, biting her lip. Arousal blared to life in me at the realization as the pieces connected. Leaning in,

I brought our lips together in a searing kiss. I moved her onto my lap, feeling Sax take her spot on the couch. My hands started to roam when a throat cleared, bringing me back to the present.

Turning, I glared at the guard who stood there, interrupting my time. "What? And it better be life or death."

"Sorry, Mr. Mascro, but you have a guest. They wouldn't leave."

Dropping my head, I counted to twenty to pull myself together. Standing once I was collected, I buttoned my suit jacket and stormed out of the room. Loren and Sax followed as we made our way down the stairs. Standing at the bottom were two police officers. I stalled, not having expected them.

"Atticus Mascro?"

"Yes," I said. "What can I do for you, officers?"

"You're under arrest for the attempted murder of Dayton Mascro and arson. You have the right to an attorney." I tuned out everything as contingency plans rushed through my head. I turned to Sax, nodding for him to take the lead.

"Call Max and get Monroe."

I didn't resist when they moved to cuff me. It didn't escape my notice how loose they left them, my reputation lending for something good. I couldn't bring myself to look at Loren as thoughts rushed through my head, but as they tapped me to begin moving, I looked up, needing to see her.

She stood firm, her head high, giving me the confidence I needed. She nodded, sealing the declarations I'd made earlier in my heart.

I had to remember what this was—a desperate move by a desperate man.

We had him scared, and that meant something.

SIXTEEN

LOREN

Watching the officers escort Atticus away was difficult. I knew this wouldn't stick, but I hated seeing one of the men I loved being taken from me, even if it was just temporary.

"Come on, Spitfire. We need to rally everyone, and I need to make some calls. Can you gather the others in the war room?"

"Yes, of course." I kissed his cheek, letting him know I had this. If I focused on planning, I wouldn't spiral into a million thoughts of how Dayton might use this to his advantage and either take Atticus out or attack when he thought we were vulnerable. Fuck that. We were strong. We wouldn't be overtaken by bogus charges.

Well, okay, so maybe the attempted murder was accurate, and he had caused the fire in the warehouse, but there were valid reasons. Like the fact, his father was a psychopath and a murderer. Just to name a few.

Walking down the hall, I first stopped at one of the

kid's rooms, finding Monroe and Wells. I motioned for them to come out into the hall. Monroe kissed Levi's head, and I chuckled as Wells ambled over. He grimaced as the butt plug moved. I didn't know what Nicco had planned or how long he'd intended for us to wear them, but now was not the best time.

Of course, I couldn't exactly say, "Sorry, officers, but I've been wearing a butt plug for a few hours now, and I really need my husband to plunder my ass. So, could you come back tomorrow?" Yeah, doubt that would work.

"What's going on?" Monroe asked.

Blowing out a breath, I grabbed both of their hands. "It seems Dayton is trying to get Atticus arrested. He was just taken to the police station."

"What the fuck?" Wells cursed, shaking his head. "Does that mean I don't get this fucking thing out anytime soon?"

I wanted to laugh, but I was in the same position, so I shrugged, not knowing what to tell him. "Looks that way," I sighed.

"Who's the lawyer?" Monroe asked.

"Sax is calling them. Attie asked for you as well."

Monroe's chest puffed up at the comment. "Really?"

I nodded, smiling at him. "I need to get the rest of the crew. Go ahead and meet everyone else in the war room." They both kissed my cheek, walking toward the room I was beginning to think got more action than my bedroom, and *I* had five husbands.

I quickly made my rounds to the rest of the people I needed to gather and had everyone back in the war room within a few minutes. Jude and Imogen stayed in the media room, and I promised I'd keep them updated. While Atticus was letting them be part of the business more, I knew there were things they didn't need to be involved in, and this was one of them. The fact they didn't protest told me they agreed.

When I stepped into the room, everyone turned to look at me, and I realized they were waiting on me.

Me.

I stopped, taking that in for a second. Pulling my shoulders back, I strode the rest of the way into the room, leaving Atticus' chair unattended. It didn't feel right sitting in it. So, instead, I took my seat and looked at Sax.

"What's the status of the lawyer?"

He smiled, giving me the encouragement I needed. I wasn't fucking this up. "He's going to meet Atticus at the station. He'll send over the file once he's there so we can see what evidence they have."

"So, what should we do in the meantime?" I asked.

"We need to call a judge to get him released and show Dayton that we aren't scared. We need to double our men at all locations, so he can't breach any of our properties while we're busy with Atticus."

"He's trying to attack us like we want to do to him?" I mused, seeing the logic. Dayton had to know Atticus would be out in a few hours. So, what was the real reason for the arrest? "He's not after Atticus." I looked around the table at everyone, my fear spiking in me. Seemed my earlier paranoia wasn't such an absurd thing now. "What could he really be after?"

Pixel shrugged, leaning closer. "It could be anything. The club, the manor, a person." She tapped something on her phone, ignoring us.

Glancing at the others, I hoped they had a better answer. "He's burned down the youth center and vandalized people aligned with us. He's tied Evolve and Upswing into a legal battle. It only leaves here or the club," Nicco said.

"Don't forget your shop," I pointed out.

"Nothing there he wants. It's not connected to the family."

"At this point, it feels more revenge-oriented. He could go for it," I mumbled, my thoughts racing. There had to be some kind of clue.

"The only places he ever talked about were the Masked Kingpin and someplace over on Shelby Street," Malek offered. "He never took us there, but I heard it in passing once, and it sounded important to him."

I looked to Sax and Nicco, figuring they'd know if that meant anything. Sax shook his head, but Nicco looked like he was trying to pull a memory, so I waited to see if he was able to. He tilted his head, blinking back at us.

"It sounds familiar, but nothing is coming to mind. I think I either visited there, or maybe I lived there for a while. I'm not really sure, though. It's vague."

I reached over and squeezed his hand. "Okay, well, I guess we sit tight until we hear back from the lawyer." My shoulders fell a little. I'd wanted to have some brilliant idea that saved the day, to show Attie we hadn't been sitting on our asses while he was gone.

"Or," Pixel chimed in, drawing our attention. "We could set off our own attack and take out two birds at once."

"What do you mean?" I asked, leaning closer.

"Dayton is currently at dinner with your mother, Jacqueline."

I stared, stunned, assuming I'd heard her wrong. I'd known they were working together, but this solidified it, making it real. I hadn't expected them to be so open with it. Out in public sent a whole other message.

"Wow, okay." I swallowed, rubbing my hands on my legs. "Which attack are you referring to?" I asked, looking up at her.

"The one where we make them both look like fools." She grinned wide, and not for the first time, I was glad she was on our side. I looked at the guys, wanting their confirmation. I didn't want Atticus to leave us alone, and we screwed up our first thing without him.

"It's brilliant, Cous," Nicco said, beaming at her.

Sax grinned wide, grunting his approval. Monroe had a calculated look on his face as he thought through all the details. When he nodded, along with Wells, I felt good about this. We'd strike back, letting Dayton, and my mother, know that we weren't scared.

We were Mascros, and we'd stand tall, fighting back every step of the way.

"Do it," I said, giving her the go-ahead. Pixel's smile widened, and she made a big show of lifting her finger in the air as she dramatically brought it down to hit a button on her phone.

"And done! That always feels so good to do. Time to unleash the birds." She giggled, and I rolled my eyes, but I couldn't deny it was brilliant.

"Well, then I guess we just wait until Atticus returns. Thanks for joining us. Um, Nicco, I think Wells and I could use your assistance."

I gave him a look, and he laughed but nodded. "Fine. But man, what a way to ruin a good time."

We hobbled out of the room and followed Nicco down the hall. He chuckled as he opened a door for us to enter. I realized then that Monroe and Sax had followed.

"Nope, no way. I'm not doing this in front of a crowd," Wells huffed, folding his arms over his torso.

"What? Afraid I might catch feelings for you like this one?" Sax asked, pointing at Nicco. "Have no fear, Grumpy. I'm solely a Spitfire man."

"Grumpy, I'm not grumpy; you're grumpy," Wells muttered, almost pouting. Nicco laughed, eyeing us.

"If you want it out, you gotta pay the toll." Chuckling, I walked over and kissed him before bending over. He brightened at my kiss, his eyes dancing. "It's such a crime to waste this," he mused, rubbing my ass almost lovingly.

"Sorry, I didn't think it was appropriate to ask the police officers to come back later because I'd been wearing a butt plug for hours," I deadpanned.

The guys snorted, and I could feel Nicco shaking with laughter. "Oh, Beautiful, how I wish you would've. Fine. But I get to play another time then. I'm owed."

"Sure." I pushed my pants down, not caring everyone was watching. Nicco eased the plug out, and I felt relief at the intrusion being gone. Though, it hadn't been as horrible as I'd imagined, and now that it was out, I almost missed the pressure. Sitting down would be easier, at least. I stood up, fixing my clothes as I looked between Wells and Nicco. He stood with his arms crossed still, a look of annoyance on his face.

"Alright, Wellsy. You going to pay—"

Wells walked over, grabbed Nicco around the neck, and yanked him, kissing him aggressively. After a few seconds, he let go and dropped his pants. Monroe leaned into me, fanning himself.

"Shit, that was hot." I giggled, agreeing.

"Even I was a little turned on," Sax murmured,

making me giggle more. These men were meant for me, and I couldn't imagine life without them.

Once Wells was butt plug free, he fixed his pants, a look of relief on his face. Sax walked over and looked at the two backdoor diamonds. "You're an asshole, Nicco," he said, chuckling.

I didn't understand what he meant until I looked closer and noticed the one Wells had been wearing was bigger than mine, and not the one he'd shown us at the store. Wells seemed to realize it as well and turned, slapping Nicco.

"You're so wearing it next time," Wells declared, trying to hit Nicco again, who dodged his arm, taking off out the door.

Monroe shook his head, smiling. He wrapped his arm around me, and we walked out together with Sax in tow. As we neared our set of rooms, Pixel appeared, skidding to a halt.

"It's happening. Come on, I have it on the screen." She put her hands together, perfectly impersonating an evil dictator, chuckling as she threw her head back in a maniacal laugh. I looked at the guys, and we all grinned, following her. It was time to watch the great downfall of Dayton Mascro begin. You couldn't mess with us without consequences. It was time he learned that lesson.

SEVENTEEN

PIXEL

Bouncing on my heels, I was practically vibrating with glee as I waited for the group to follow me. When Aunt Phea had ordered me to come here, I wasn't sure what to expect. However, it was an opportunity to get out of the house and away from all of my sisters and cousins, so I'd eagerly jumped at it. I never expected it to actually be enjoyable. I liked Loren and the Mascros. They were good people, and they didn't treat me like I was lesser-than because I was more of a 'behind-the-scenes' Siren.

It was nice to be appreciated for my genius for once.

The fact they let me run wild with my ideas also suited me. It was a level of trust I wasn't often given. Back home, I was Pixel, the screwup. Or, Pixel, the one who always went too overboard. Perhaps my least favorite moniker was Pixel, the Siren with no game. Being surrounded by your gorgeous family day in and day out only reminded you how much you failed at being an actual Siren.

The real reason I was behind the scenes was that I sucked at being a true Siren.

It had been a total gamble for me to distract the guards on the rescue mission, and truth be told, I hadn't done well with it either, considering I'd blown it up. Oops.

Yeah, I had a penchant for explosives. They were too fun not to play with.

"So, what do we have?" Loren asked as she took a seat.

I clicked a button on the remote, and a screen lowered from the wall. Once it was in position, I hit play from my laptop. The live feed came into view, and everyone turned to watch it.

"It's showtime," I said, smiling as I zoomed it in onto our target. Jacqueline Hanover and Dayton Mascro sat at a table with a few others. I didn't know who they were, but the others did based on the looks around the room.

"Son of a bitch," Oscar the Grouch sneered, looking at the table in disgust. I didn't inquire who it was yet; it didn't matter. The main event was about to occur.

"Wait for it," I said, watching a separate screen on my laptop. The moment the numbers cleared, I looked over at the projector screen. "Now." I turned up the sound so we could all hear.

The waiter looked nervous as he walked over to the

table, bending down to whisper into Dayton's ear. The Kingpin's face turned red, and he slammed his fist onto the table, making everyone around him jump.

"Rerun it," he demanded.

The waiter looked nervous but held his ground. "Sorry, sir, but it's been run three times, and the company is saying we should report it stolen at this point. Do you have another card?"

Dayton's face began to glow red with irritation as he stared at the waiter. "Here," Jaqueline said, producing a card and handing it to the waiter. He hurried off, wanting out of Dayton's murderous gaze. Jacqueline patted Dayton's arm like he was a misbehaving schoolboy, his deadly gaze turning to her. He jerked his arm free, turning back to his guests.

"This is my son's doing," he stated, daring them to argue. It didn't take long for the waiter to return, this time with the manager in tow.

"Sorry, ma'am, but it appears your card was declined as well."

At this point, the whole restaurant was watching. I could only assume that Dayton had wanted to be seen, giving himself a solid alibi. The downfall of that was it also gave us a larger stage to set them up and watch them fall.

Jacqueline didn't seem to care that everyone was watching, or perhaps it was a more significant faux pas for her to be accused of being poor. "No, that's not correct. Try it again!" she exclaimed, her voice rising in volume.

A few people I'd sent in started to pull out their phones, recording the incident. Once I saw them being streamed with the hashtag we'd made, I set my bots free, lighting up social media. This would be trending before they even left the restaurant.

As Loren's mother started to escalate, I realized Dayton was being too quiet. I looked up and found everyone watching. Turning my head, I found him staring right at the camera feed we had playing. He mimed slitting our throats before he stood, dropping his napkin on the table. He pulled Jacqueline with him, not listening to the manager yell for them to stop and pay their bill.

The rest of the men around the table looked around worriedly, trying to figure out what was happening. Dayton and Jacqueline made it to the door but then were accosted by paparazzi outside, hurling questions at them left and right.

"Is it true you're bankrupt?"

"Did you sell your daughter to become richer?"

"Why did you fake your own death?"

"Are you the real reason behind the D&D Trade corp stock crashing?"

"What are your plans now that you're back?"

"Do you believe you're above the law?"

As they attempted to fight off the cameras and

reporters, we watched as Dayton looked around for his men. The men the Mascro guards had already bound and gagged twenty minutes ago. The next part was my little secret that I'd set up, wanting to put them both in their place.

Water dumped over the building edge, dousing them when they moved into the spot, followed quickly by birdseed. Then a crate of pigeons and doves were released and they descended onto the pair. Jacqueline screamed as she ducked behind Dayton, who didn't seem to care. He looked around, searching for something.

He wrenched his arm free from Jacqueline, apparently having enough of her screeches, and marched himself, ignoring the birds as they pecked and pooped on him, to the SUV parked at the end of the block. The paparazzi continued to take pictures of the madness, knowing a front-page story when they saw it. Jacqueline was curled up into a ball now, swatting away the birds as best as possible. Strangers tried to help her, but she only hit them away, apparently not knowing the difference.

Everyone in the conference room laughed at her plight, and a sense of pride filled me that they weren't mad at my digression from the plan. I beamed, watching as Dayton finally made it to the SUV. The car pulled away as he went to open the door, and not even I had anticipated what would happen next.

Leaning against a flashy sports car in a suit was none

other than Atticus himself. I guess he was released from police custody already.

Dayton stopped, and I wished I could see his face. The cameras I had access to were only on his back at the moment. The Siren I had there followed at a reasonable distance, but I wanted to see it all. Quickly, I entered some codes and found a camera on the corner of a building that might give a better angle. When it loaded, it showed a side view of Dayton. He smiled at his son, stopping in his tracks.

"I didn't think you had it in you, Son."

Atticus grinned, not breaking his laid-back stance. "Oh, this? This wasn't me. I've been in police custody until five minutes ago, remember? When we left the station, I saw the debacle you were making on social media, and I had to come to see it for myself. You're everywhere. You won't be able to escape this for a while. You know, in case you were planning on doing anything shady soon."

I wished the film was clearer; the grainy angle was not enough to make out the facial expression of the Masked Kingpin. The Siren present continued to sneak around some cars, finding an excellent spot to keep the recording going. Thankfully, she wasn't filming live any longer in case there were things shared we wouldn't want everyone to hear. From her spot, I could make out more of his expression and see how red he was getting at the embarrassment of the whole ordeal.

Atticus nodded, and I looked to see what he was referencing when a few men made their way to Dayton. "Looks like you have some messes to clean up, Kingpin. If I were you, I'd remember just who you were dealing with. I'm not some snot-nosed little kid. I'm better than you in every way that counts, and we'll be the ones standing at the end. So, if you keep coming at me, know this, Father. You. Will. Lose."

Dayton let out a raucous laugh, throwing his head back. It was all for show as he tried not to show his emotions. Atticus rolled his eyes, climbing into his car just as the men reached Dayton.

We all watched as his car pulled away, and the Siren flipped the camera, coming into view. "Need anything else, Pixel?"

"Nope. Great job, Songbird." She nodded, hanging up. The video feed on the screen cut off, but was quickly followed by an incoming call. Answering it, I sent it to the screen so everyone could see it.

"I'm guessing you guys were behind that?" Atticus asked as he drove.

"Yep. How did we do?" I asked, typing in some more commands as I shifted the money I'd stolen into a charity.

"It was risky, but I can admit it felt good to see my father sweating. What happened?"

As the rest of the group filled Atticus in, I shut down the bots before setting off another attack on Jacqueline.

She'd be finished after this. In a lot of ways, she was the easier of the two. She cared too much about her image and didn't have the same protections a mafia crime lord did. There would be nowhere for her to go, no money in her accounts, and no standing within her circle. And when she was served with criminal charges tomorrow, there'd be no future for her either. Jacqueline Hanover was toast.

Sitting back, I glanced around the room, the pride of a job well done simmering in my belly. I always dreamed of an environment like this but never fully achieved it back with my family. Perhaps a permanent change of location was in store for me. It might be nice to stay here and feel like a valuable member of the group instead of the annoying Siren who couldn't even pass seduction training.

I just needed to keep proving myself useful. Turning to Nicco, I kicked his chair with my foot.

"So, Cous, what's a girl gotta do to get a tattoo?" I wiggled my eyebrows, waiting for him to respond.

"A tattoo, huh?" he asked, rubbing his jaw. "That could be arranged. I'll call the shop tomorrow and see what my schedule is."

I nodded, feeling like a plan was coming together. These were my people, and I was glad to have finally found them. Now, I just had to convince Aunt Phea.

EIGHTEEN

LOREN

When Atticus returned home, I held him for a good five minutes, needing to reassure myself he was back with us.

"So, what happened?" Sax asked.

Atticus looked up, sighing. "I'm beat. Can we recap in the morning?"

"Yeah, sure thing."

Atticus linked his fingers in mine and pulled me to his bedroom. The rest of the guys nodded, slapping him on the shoulder or back as he passed, happy he'd returned to us. A few minutes later, we crawled into bed; Atticus wrapped his arms around me, pulling me close. I was content to lie in his arms, feeling his presence behind me.

"He's getting scared, Bellezza. We just have to hang on for a while longer. I have faith in us to succeed," he whispered. His thumb brushed against my palm, and I snuggled back into his embrace.

"Me too," I agreed, pulling his hand up to kiss.

We didn't say anything else; nothing else needed to be said. We would defeat Dayton, or we would all perish. There wasn't really any other option. None of us could survive in a place he was. It was as simple as that.

It was Dayton or us, and we all prayed it would be us.

THE MORNING CAME TOO SOON, but I found myself waking with a sense of urgency. Today was the day that my mother was gone from my life for good. I could feel it in my bones. She would pay for what she'd done, and I would never have to deal with her again. What happened from this point forward would be her choice, but I didn't have much faith in her redemption. Jacqueline Hanover was too self-centered for that.

Getting dressed alongside Atticus, I felt the power couple we were becoming. Him in his dark slate suit, me in a flowy silk top and black dress pants, we looked like a million bucks. And since I no longer saw how much my clothes cost since Atticus had stuff ordered and delivered, we very well could be wearing close to that. But it was more of the people we were becoming beneath our expensive trappings.

Atticus was focused, determined, and compassionate.

Those were three characteristics I knew would take him far in this fight. He'd embraced the things that he felt were minor and showcased the genuine growth he'd made.

"What are you smiling about?" he asked, adjusting his tie.

I finished applying my lipstick, my smile even more prominent once I was done. "Just how much we've grown, and how our clothes reflect the people we're becoming."

He moved over to me, a small smile lifting the corner of his mouth as he wrapped his arms around my middle from behind. His head dropped to my shoulder, and he stared at us in the mirror, taking us in.

"And what do you see, Bellezza?"

I turned, wrapping my arms around his neck. "A powerful man who doesn't have to step on others to achieve his success."

"Hmm, and what about yourself?"

I tilted my head thinking, my eyes calculating as I thought about it. "A woman who is both soft and strong, who goes after what she wants, and doesn't let others determine her worth anymore."

Atticus' eyes lit up, sparkling with something. "I couldn't have said it better myself. The moment I met you, I was enraptured by your presence. I didn't understand what it was at the time, but now that I know you, it was your goodness, your light. You see people for who they can be, never judging their past mistakes. I needed someone to believe in me, and you gave me that. You are all you said and so much more. I'm glad you're able to see that for yourself."

"Better be careful; you might give me a big head," I said, dropping my eyes. It still felt weird hearing compliments and accepting them as truth. While I knew my worth, there was still that voice of doubt that wanted to deny what others said.

"I don't think you could ever think too highly of yourself, Bellezza." He kissed my nose, bringing my eyes up to his. "Let's go have some breakfast with our family and finalize our plans. We're taking out our foes today."

Walking into the kitchen together, the sound of chatter and laughter filled the space. Almost everyone was already present, sitting around a large table with pancakes, eggs, and sausage in the center. The cook, Mrs. Gilbert, nodded as we entered, motioning for us to take a seat. Atticus kissed my head as I sat, walking over to grab us both some coffee. I sat and took in the presence of the others, enjoying just sitting and listening. The dogs laid on the floor at the feet of the kids, in heaven as they ate up the scraps dropped to them.

"I want to go swimming. Can we, Dad?" Levi asked, looking up to Monroe.

"Me too!" Lily added, bouncing in her seat. And like I'd come to notice, Olivia jumped in. She adored Lily and wanted to do everything the older girl did.

"Me too, Lily," Olivia said.

Monroe looked over at us, and I nodded, not seeing the problem. "I think that can be arranged. Do you all know how to swim?" I asked, figuring it would be important to know that.

"I do!" Levi said, raising his hand high.

"I'm still learning," Lily said, slightly dropping her head.

"I can show you," Levi offered, making Lily blush, but she nodded, smiling at him. I noticed how Levi puffed out his chest a little at the action.

Olivia started to cry, and we all froze for a second before Cami swooped in, gathering her into her arms. She was becoming a natural mother to the little girl, and I wondered how things were going between her and Malek. I knew she was engaged to Lark and Seb, but I couldn't miss the sparks that flew between them and wondered what that meant now.

"I can help you too," Levi offered, biting his lip. He didn't like it when she cried.

"You hear that, Liv?" Cami cooed, "Levi will help you, too. I bet we can get you some floaties, and you'll be golden. I'll even swim with you if you want."

"I'll come too," Imogen offered. I'd noticed she had a soft spot for the little kids, and I remembered how excited she'd been when she watched Levi, making me wonder how many kids she'd gotten to be around.

"I just need some swim shorts," Jude mumbled.

"There are some in the locker rooms," Atticus offered, sitting down next to me with our cups of coffee. "If there's a size we need, we can have someone get some."

The kids started to chat more excitedly about their plan to swim, making me happy to see them so excited about something amid our war. These little moments let me know we were doing the right thing. We all deserved a life where we didn't have to look over our shoulders or worry about someone taking out a person we loved.

"You should call Lark and Seb to come over," I suggested to Cami. She looked up, her face brightening.

"Okay, yeah. Thanks."

Atticus squeezed my leg under the table, offering me some comfort. It was the reassurance I needed that I was, in fact, the lady of the manor as he suggested. I just needed to get used to making decrees and being comfortable with them. Baby steps.

Once the kids were set on swimming, they quickly finished their food and pulled Cami and the teenagers out of the room. Monroe stood to follow when Jude spoke up.

"I can help Levi if you're okay with that," he said. Levi nodded enthusiastically, taking Jude's hand. The maternal part of me wept at the sight, and I held back the tear that wanted to fall. My two sons. I'd meant what I told Monroe; Levi was my son now too.

"Oh, yes, thanks, Jude. That would be great." He smiled at him before dropping his eyes to Levi. "Listen to everything Jude has to say. If he has to come back and report you weren't being careful or put anyone in danger, then no more swimming. If you're going to help teach the others, you need to ensure you follow all the swim safety rules, so they know them. Understand?"

"Yes, Dad." Levi nodded, a serious look on his face. Monroe had done well to make it about teaching the girls. Levi pulled his little shoulders back, a look of responsibility on his little face. When they left, I turned to Monroe, impressed. Before I could say anything, Atticus beat me to it.

"I can tell you're a good lawyer just from that."

Monroe beamed, shrugging his shoulders. Wells laughed, slapping him on the back.

"You should've seen him in the group home. He could always get us out of trouble."

The guys laughed, the atmosphere feeling nice. Nicco cleared his throat once the laughter died down, leaning forward onto the table as he assessed his brother.

"So, what happened last night?"

Atticus sighed, placing his fork down. "Max was able to get everything thrown out. They didn't have any evidence that wasn't circumstantial, and with my iron-clad alibi, they had to let me go. I don't think it was an actual attempt to get me arrested. I believe Dayton used it as a diversion, but that also failed. I'm not sure what was planned, but based on his pissed-off expression when he saw me, he didn't get what he wanted, so it's a win in our column."

"Score one for Pixel's crazy scheme," Nicco said, chuckling.

"Where is she?" I asked, realizing she hadn't been around the table earlier.

"She got a message from Aunt Phea this morning, and had to return home for something. She said she'd be back though and would be bringing a surprise when she did," Monroe answered.

"I'm kind of going to miss her," Sax grunted, taking a sip of his coffee, making me smile.

"So, what do we do now? Where are we on the plan?" I asked, looking around the table.

"We stay the course. Taking out Jacqueline is our priority today. It's time to remove one more player from the board. Natalia will also have an update for us later. I have a few more meetings to finalize the plans for the secret party, but most of it is all set."

I looked at the clock on the wall, realizing it was almost time for Jacqueline's demise. "Can we get the TV turned to channel 8?" I asked.

Within a second, the TV came on, the news reporter standing in front of the house I'd once called home. Wells turned the volume up, and we all watched in antic-ipation.

"If you're just tuning in, we're at the home of Jacque-line Hanover, former Miss North Shore, and socialite.

After the disturbing footage from last night where she was mauled by birds, we were sent information linking Jacqueline to the potential death of her late husband, Kenneth Hanover, along with colluding to steal and harbor the eggs of her daughter, Loren Carter. Criminal charges have yet to be filed, and we're left wondering why. Are the elite so far above the law that they have different rules?"

The screen split, showing a news reporter back at the station. "It's troubling, Samantha. We've reached out to the police, asking them why charges aren't being filed. They have yet to comment on the case. We have someone who'd like to remain anonymous but says they have some information to share on the phone. Go ahead, caller. What do you have?"

"Am I on?" a woman's voice asked.

"Yes, ma'am. Go ahead, tell our viewers what you told us."

"I've known Jacqueline for years, and I believe everything they say about her. She was awful to her daughter. It doesn't surprise me she was doing something shady. In fact, there was once some money stolen from the club. She was in charge but blamed it on an employee who was fired. I don't doubt it was her if what I've heard is true."

"Why do you think there haven't been any charges?" the reporter asked.

"The elite operate on a different level. It's not right,

but it's how it is. Maybe now, with the press getting wind of this, they won't be able to hide behind expensive lawyers."

"Not that she could afford one," one of the news reporters mumbled.

I smiled at the way the people were turning from my mother. She'd always been so immaculate, so untouchable, and now she would have to pay for all the sins she'd committed.

"Frank, we have movement coming up the road. It looks like a police cruiser." The reporter and the cameraman took off, following the car as they pulled up to the door. The policemen looked over but didn't tell the cameras to go away.

"It looks like they're taking some action," the reporter whispered. We all watched as they knocked, waiting for the door to open.

"Police, open up."

It took a while, but eventually, Jacqueline Hanover answered the door. The woman who came into view was a sight to behold. Her hair was patchy, her skin marked with red spots haphazardly covered with bandages. "Yes?" she asked, holding her head high. I had to give it to my mother. She never stopped believing she was better than everyone.

"Jaqueline Hanover, you're under arrest for accessory to murder of Kenneth Hannover, robbery of Loren Carter, forgery of documents, and fraud."

The reporter turned back to the camera, a broad smile on her face. "Well, it looks like this North Shore socialite will finally be held accountable for her actions. Stay tuned for your local weather."

The reporter had a huge smile that mirrored my own as we watched my mother be cuffed and placed in the back of the car. In some ways, it was satisfying to see her finally be held responsible for the atrocities she'd caused, but in another, it didn't feel like it was enough.

But no matter what, Jacqueline Hanover was out of our lives and no longer a threat to me or my family. From this point forward, what happened to her was up to her and the courts.

And if we happened to have a judge in our pocket, so be it. Justice would be served.

Jacqueline Hanover was done.

NINETEEN

LOREN

The morning had left me on a high, knowing my mother would finally have to answer for her crimes. So, when Atticus told me he had another surprise for me, I blinked, not knowing what he could mean.

"Cover your eyes, Bellezza."

Doing as he said, I let him lead me to where he wanted. We were on the side of the building that was used for his office and some of the guards' rooms. I didn't know what he could have for me here. I hoped he didn't think someone tied up was the perfect present for me. Outside of Brian, Darren, or Dayton, I didn't really wish vengeance on anyone else enough to see them tied up to something.

"I'm not going to puke, am I?" I asked, my anxiety beginning to climb my throat at the thought of a beaten prisoner.

"No, Bellezza." Atticus chuckled, helping to ease some of my worries. I heard a door open, and then he led

178

me into a space. It smelled nice, at least. Surely, if I was about to be presented with a hostage, it wouldn't smell peaceful and soothing. Though, wouldn't that be a mind-fuck to get prisoners to lower their guards? Maybe there was something to that.

"Okay, open your eyes." I blinked them open, adjusting to the light, and found myself standing in an office. It was painted a soft gray and had light blue and navy accents. There was a comfortable couch, two chairs, a bookcase, desk, and a lamp. A bright mosaic rug sat in the middle, tying in all the room's colors.

"It's lovely." I glanced over, trying to gauge what response he wanted from me before I caught myself. "I don't understand, though, and I was about to pretend, but I don't have to do that anymore. So, sorry, but you lost me. What does it mean?" I muttered, fidgeting with my hands.

Atticus laughed, his whole face lighting up at the sound. I heard Sax and Nicco chuckling behind me, and I turned to look at them. Sax leaned against the door, and when he saw me looking, he moved, showcasing a sign on it.

Loren Carter, MA, LMHC

Gasping, I covered my mouth with my hand as it sunk in. They'd made me an office. Twirling back around, I hugged Atticus, jumping a little as I did.

"It's really for me?" I asked, stepping back.

"Yes, it's all yours. I wanted to put Mascro, but Cami

told me that you had to change it with the licensing board or something first, and you might want to keep it as Carter to keep a lower profile in this field since Mascro isn't exactly inconspicuous. There's a separate entrance on this side that the guards use, so when you have sessions, it will be closed off to anyone else to give you privacy. I know how important confidentiality is for you and your clients."

I could hear the teasing in his voice, an earlier battle between us coming to mind. "We didn't want you to lose this part of you, but now it's in a controlled space where we can make sure no one can ever hurt you."

"Wow, I don't know what to say."

Sax walked over, pulling me to his chest, kissing me deeply. "Say that you love it and that my fantasy of fucking you over your desk can come true now."

"I, um, what?" I blushed, my face heating. "I'm not sure that's the best idea. I'd be thinking of that every time I was in session, and it wouldn't make me a very good therapist."

"I beg to differ, but fine. We'll just have to use Atticus'."

Atticus laughed, a smug look crossing his face. "Already did," he boasted, making me giggle.

"Mine too," Nicco beamed, winking.

"So, I have a thing for desks." I shrugged, causing Sax to laugh.

"Fine, I'll find something that's mine. In fact..." He

trailed off, his eyes lighting up. My body shivered at the ideas running through his head. Whatever it was, I knew I'd love it.

"Besides showing you this office, you also have an appointment today," Nicco said, bringing me back to reality.

"Um, what? How?"

"Seems Doris had a soft spot for me. When I told her what we'd done, she insisted on helping out by calling the one client you were still going to try and see while you figured things out. She's agreed to help get you set up on her off hours if you'd want it."

"Oh wow, you guys. This is..." Tears developed in the corner of my eye, and I knew I would cry. "This means the world to me. I didn't know how much I needed this until you gave it to me. Thank you."

"You're our wife, Loren. We want nothing but the world for you. If you need something, you can ask, and in those times you don't know, trust us that we will. We're in this together, remember?" Atticus pulled my hand to his mouth, kissing my ring.

I nodded, smiling wide, the tears managing to stay back at his reassuring words. "So, what time is she arriving?" I asked, straightening my clothes and looking around the room with a new perspective. It absolutely was perfect for counseling and for me. It was calming and warm.

"In about five minutes," Nicco said, looking at his watch.

"Shoo then. I need to get myself oriented and not feel so out of place." I pushed them out of the office as they laughed at me, but I wasn't joking. I needed to feel at peace here too, so I could then focus on what I was doing. I already felt a little anxious. It had been almost a month since I'd been shot and last done a therapy session. So much had happened since then.

Sitting down at the desk, I smoothed my hands over the surface, enjoying the feel of the wood. Taking a moment to open all the drawers, I found pads of paper, pens, post-its, and an assortment of office supplies. There was also a brand new laptop in the next drawer and some files on the bottom. When I turned to the other side and opened the drawer, I was momentarily stunned by what I found.

Reaching in, my hand wrapped around a silver frame, and I pulled it out. Inside were photos from the art benefit. One was our table as we chatted, another of me dancing with Nicco, and the last of Jude on stage speaking. I hadn't known they'd been taken, the professional photographer blending into the background seamlessly.

A knock on the door had me wiping my eyes as I looked up, finding Atticus smiling at me. "It's to make do until we can get a real family photo made of all of us."

"I love it." I pulled it to my chest, wrapping it in a hug. "It's just missing a few people."

"I didn't know if you could have our photos, so we put them on the side so you could decide, or at least have them near you when you needed to remember the people who loved you."

"Don't ever say you're not romantic, Attie."

"You make it easy, Lore."

I beamed at him, wishing I had more time to show him how much I loved him. Atticus must've read the desire in my face as he stepped toward me. A buzzer on the phone went off, startling us both.

"Press it," he said, smiling softly.

"Hello?"

"Loren? It's me, Jill. I'm here for my appointment."

"Oh yes, one-second dear."

"Come on, I'll show you to the door."

I stood, walking toward him, and he grabbed my hand, leading me toward a small entrance a few feet away. He demonstrated how to use the safety features, which included a video camera of the area and a panic button that would send an alert to the rest of the house and guards. Atticus kissed me quickly on the cheek before walking in the opposite direction. Schooling my features, I put myself back into therapist mode and opened the door.

"Jill."

She turned at the sound, smiled at me, and practically

rushed me as she quickly walked over. "Loren! I'm so glad you were able to start sessions again. How are you? I heard what happened on the news about the break-in. That must've been scary! And the fire! I'd been there that same day." She spoke a mile a minute, firing questions at me, showing her concern.

Taking her hand, I squeezed, trying to calm her down. "Jill, I'm okay. Thank you. I'm glad you're safe too." I avoided any other topic about the fire, not wanting to think about my father dying in the middle of a session. "How about we go to my office, and you can catch me up on how your progress has been?"

She nodded, her face blushing when she realized how she'd bombarded me with her questions. Pulling her along, I directed her to the space that was now my own.

"Take a seat wherever."

"Wow, this is beautiful. I love it," she said, sitting on the couch.

"Thank you, my husband surprised me with it." It hurt my heart to say only one, but I didn't want to get into it with a client on the why choose motto I'd taken in my personal life. I still had some boundaries left in me.

After some catching up, Jill began talking about what she'd been working on in her journal while we'd been on a hiatus. I'd given it to her to do as homework until we could meet again.

"The other day, I was writing, and I didn't even know what I was writing, but when I looked back on it, I realized how much had poured out. I'm starting to let go of what was done to me. It feels weird to say that, but it's not as triggering anymore."

"That's great, Jill. There's something I want to caution you about. There's this concept in therapy where sometimes, when you start to feel better because the therapy is helping, you jump in too quickly, too soon, and end up setting yourself back more than when you started. It's hard not to when you're feeling the powerful effects of healing, but I just want you to make sure you're pacing yourself. Therapy is hard work at times. It takes learning the skills and mastering them on small intervals to be ready for the big things."

She nodded, thinking about what I said. "That makes a lot of sense, actually. In skating, if I get too cocky and try to throw a jump I'm not ready for, I'll injure myself more than if I'd just waited until I'd built up the muscle memory and stamina for it. So, you're saying I shouldn't be trying to throw triples when I'm still learning doubles?"

I smiled, liking that she figured out an analogy that worked for herself. "Exactly. I do hear and see the growth you're making, and I commend you on the hard work you've put in. I just don't want you to fall backward. It's hard getting to where you are, and to have to find this place again after losing it would be detrimental to your progress. So, how about today we pick something you've been working on and deal with it, using the skills we've gone over so you can see how to use them in small situations first."

"Okay, I think I know something that would be good. In many ways, I see Donald as the worst part of the whole thing, but really, it was Alek and the other men on the Council. They..." She shook her head, realizing she was heading down a dark path. "Yeah, you're right. I'm not ready to face that yet. Let's deal with the director."

Over the next thirty minutes, I worked with Jill to recount her traumatic experience and helped her find new ways of thinking about it, identifying that she wasn't to blame and that while there were different choices she could've made, it was pointless to dwell on them.

"The thing to remember, Jill, is that yes, you could've told someone sooner, but there's no way of knowing if that would've changed any outcomes. It could've even been a worse one. The brain likes to try to find the solution, to avoid making the same mistake. What it fails to realize is that life isn't black or white. Nothing is ever the same circumstances or situation. You change one thing, and the whole outcome can shift. So, spending time trying to figure out where you messed up only makes you go crazy. It's already happened. So instead, work on changing the narrative, letting go of the shame, and not letting it control you. Your past is just that, your past. It doesn't have to be your future."

Jill nodded, wiping her eyes. "Thank you. I never

thought about it that way. It's not something I ever plan to put myself through again, so there's no reason to replay all my mistakes repeatedly."

"It's easy to do. We all find ourselves lost in that loop at times. Acknowledge the things you can learn from, accept the things you can't change, and work to do better next time. That's all we can promise ourselves. To do better. Be better. You're already working on that by coming to therapy. You're not letting your past hold you back, and that's a courageous thing to do."

"I'm glad you're back. I missed this."

"Me too, Jill." I smiled at her, her words meaning everything. I hadn't realized how lost I was until I stepped back into this role, finding my own sense of purpose. Now, I could do it on my terms and help the family.

"Well, I think the best way to end a heavy session like this is to dance it out. What song do you want today?"

She laughed, jumping up. "I know the perfect one." As she played the song on her phone, I stood up with her, dancing it out. It might not seem professional to let myself dance without abandon in my office with my client, but I'd found there was nothing more powerful at times than just letting go with the movement and a song.

When the music ended, we collapsed on the couch, laughing. "You're gonna be okay, Jill."

She looked over at me, smiling. "Yeah?"

"Yeah." I squeezed her shoulder, being mindful not to

cross too many boundaries in one day. "Okay, let's get you scheduled for your next appointment."

Once she was gone, I sat back in my chair, falling into the familiar habit of notating my session. As I finished, a smile spread across my face. This was the life I'd always wanted, and now I had it.

As I finished up, my cellphone rang, and I picked it up, forgetting it was there.

"Hello?" I answered, not knowing the number.

"Loren," Nat sighed into the phone. "I'm so glad I caught you."

"Nat! How are you? How's your mission?"

"It's fine. The O'Sullivans aren't working with Dayton. But I have news. Can you gather everyone and meet us here?"

"Oh, sure. Who's everyone?" I asked, some trepidation building.

"Whoever is available, but especially the women."

"Okay, send me the address, and we'll be there as quickly as possible."

"Thanks, Lor. It's good to hear your voice. See you soon." She hung up, and I stared at my phone, wondering what else had just been dumped into our lap.

Standing, I closed my office and headed back into the main house. Time to be the Mafia Queen.

TWENTY

SAX

I pulled into the long driveway of the address Nat had sent, wrapping along the long bend until a house came into view. It had taken an hour to get here, and I was hoping we weren't walking into a trap.

"It's not a trap," Loren said, smiling over at me as she patted my hand.

Grunting, I put the car into park and looked around the place. It was weird to drive a car, but we hadn't wanted to draw attention by taking one of the SUVs in case Dayton had someone watching us. Cami leaned forward, reminding me she was here.

"Swanky. What do you think Nat's gotten herself into?" she asked.

"Let's go find out." Loren opened her door, stepping out. I watched as she stretched, her shirt rising some. A smack on my shoulder had me jumping, and I glared over at the nuisance.

"What?"

"You got it bad, is all."

I rolled my eyes, heaving myself out of the car. We hadn't exactly taken a large vehicle, and my long legs were screaming at me after being in the nondescript sedan. The cracking sound felt good as I turned from side to side, rolling my neck. Checking my sidearm, I shut the door and walked over to my girl.

Atticus had a meeting he couldn't get out of, so he left this up to Spitfire to handle. I kept trying to remind myself that since Atticus had only sent me, he had faith in our ability to handle it sufficiently. It was a big step for Mas, letting go of some of his control, especially when it came to Loren. Hopefully, it wouldn't bite us in the asses.

"You ready?" she asked, biting her lip. Loren held out her hand to me, and I took it as I pulled her close. As she collided with my chest, her tiny gasp sent chills down my spine. Tilting her chin, I grasped it with my other hand and kissed her.

"You got this, Spitfire." I might have my own concerns, but I didn't want her to think they were about her capability. If anything, I trusted her to keep us out of any trouble. Loren had a way about her that made others want to listen to what she had to say.

She nodded, taking a deep breath. I watched as she strengthened something inside herself, some fire coming to her eyes. "Thank you." Quickly, she pecked my lips and stepped back, holding my hand. Cami smirked at us from the steps, but I ignored her. With her staying in the manor most nights now, she'd become more and more like an annoying little sister, a constant pest.

"You ready?" Loren asked her.

"It's just Nat. How bad do you think it is?"

"It sounded serious on the phone." Loren reached out, ringing the doorbell, and the three of us waited to be let in.

When Beau answered the door, I felt instantly better. He smiled when he noticed us, stepping back to let us through. "Hey, guys. You made it!" He clapped me on the shoulder as we entered, and I wondered what weird situation we'd encountered.

"Hey, Beau," Loren greeted, squeezing his arm as we passed. A low growl rumbled out of me before realizing I'd done it. Loren didn't say anything, but I caught her smirking at the sound.

Nat came around the corner, taking a few steps into the foyer, and I instantly wished I was anywhere else as girly screams and chatter erupted. Loren dropped my hand as she pulled Nat into a hug with Cami, and the three of them began to animatedly talk a mile a minute as they caught up on things. You'd think they'd been separated for years the way they were carrying on.

Beau stepped up next to me, and we both watched the scene unfold. "It's good to see you, man."

I looked over, trying to gauge how things were going. He appeared relaxed, a soft smile on his face as he watched them.

"I can't say the same until 1 know what we've been dragged into."

He snorted, peeking up at me. "Fair. But it's not what you're thinking. Come on, Byron is out by the grill. How do you like your steaks?"

Checking on Loren one more time, I turned and followed him through the house. When we stepped out through the back door onto the deck, I stopped speechless.

"I know, right?" Beau chuckled. "It takes a minute to get used to after being in the city."

The deck wrapped around a sparkling pool. A massive outdoor kitchen with a large flat-screen TV mounted on the wall was to the left. On the other side was a pool table, dartboard, and a foosball table. It was the perfect outdoor man cave. I followed him over to the grill where Byron stood, flipping steaks. He nodded as Beau reached down into a fridge, handing me a beer. I looked at the beverage, almost like it was a foreign thing.

"What the fuck?" I finally asked, looking up at the two men. "I thought you guys hated each other but were on this undercover mission with Nat to infiltrate the O'Sullivans. But instead, you're out here living a life of luxury, all happy family while Nat's daughter is with us?

If you wanted a vacation, okay, but this? I'll say it again. What the fuck?"

The two men, one of whom I considered a friend, turned to one another before doubling over in laughter. Having heard enough of their mockery, I tossed the beer at their heads and stalked off, not caring if I hit one of them. I hoped I did.

There was shit going on in our life. It was on them if they didn't want to take it seriously. I wouldn't participate in it or make Loren have to either. She'd lost her father and had been dealing with so much, she didn't need someone she considered a friend throwing how good they had it in her face. We'd come under the impression they needed our help, but this was just cruel.

I stormed into the back door, stalking through the house, looking to where they'd gone. Hearing voices, I followed them, stopping outside a room when I heard them talking.

"That's why I need your help, Cami. These are good people, and they're being taken advantage of. If we can take out the woman holding this over their heads, then we'd have a powerful ally on our side."

I leaned against the open door, listening, trying to figure out what level of danger we were in.

"I don't know, Nat. This is a big ask. I left that lifestyle behind."

"What about Pixel, then?"

"She went back home for something. What do you

see happening?" Loren asked, and I smiled with pride that she was keeping the conversation on track.

Before I could hear a response, the two goofs I'd left outside found me. "Sax, I'm sorry, okay. I wasn't trying to make light of anything. Please, just come back and hear what we have to say."

I glanced over, taking in Beau and Byron's stances. They seemed sincere, but it was hard to wrap my head around what was happening here. Peeking back in the room, I found Loren watching me. As always, she seemed to know what I needed from her and nodded at me. Sighing, I turned and followed the guys out.

Byron went back to the grill, and I noticed some other people were out there now mingling around. I followed Beau to the pool table, and he handed me a stick, nodding to the other people in greeting.

"What is this place?" I asked, not moving until he told me something.

"It's the O'Sullivans' main residence."

"So, your mission?" I asked, keeping my voice low.

"Success. They're clean, or at least when it comes to Dayton."

Something in me relaxed at the news. It couldn't be as bad if it was something other than Dayton. "So, why the secrecy? Are you guys staying? You seem pretty homey."

I took the chalk this time, moving it across the tip as he racked the balls. "No, man. We're Mascros for life. But I can't deny it hasn't been nice to be away from the city and everything that entails. I'm sorry, though, if it seemed insensitive. Things are so much more laid-back out here. There isn't the same rush to get things done or fear that someone will beat you to something."

"If it's not Dayton, then what is it?"

"Nat will explain. She wanted to be the one to tell the girls since she needed their help."

"And what are *we* then?"

"Arm candy." He beamed, bending over to strike the white ball. The solid and striped balls scattered at his hit, going in every direction. A solid purple ball banked into a corner pocket, and he smirked over at me, thinking he had it. He hit two more in before missing, then it was my turn. Slowly, I bent over the table, lining up my balls, and systematically sank all of them, leaving only the black 8-ball.

"Fuck," Beau cursed, causing me to smile wider. Glancing up, I pointed to the corner pocket.

"8-ball, corner pocket." Keeping my eyes on him, I hit the white ball and heard the satisfying sound of the balls making contact as it sailed across the felt before dunking into the pocket. Standing, I walked over and placed my stick on the wall, leaning against it.

Beau hung his head, laughing. "Shit, man. I forgot how good you were at this. Come on, steaks should be ready. You can hear it all from them."

Grunting, I walked with him over to the table by the pool, already laden with food. The girls had come outside and were talking together with another woman. Seeing Loren, I walked over, wrapping my arms around her from behind. She leaned back, not breaking her stride but letting me hold her.

"Ah, this must be one of your men," the older woman said, eyeing me.

I raised an eyebrow, not caring to respond. If Spitfire wanted to, she could, but we didn't owe this person anything as far as I was concerned.

"Brianna, this is Saxon, one of my husbands." She peered back at me, smiling. I loved hearing her say those words. We stared at one another for a moment, lost in each other's eyes.

"Ah, yes. I remember those days. Come, let's eat."

Loren moved her head back, acknowledging the woman, and we followed them over to the table that was full of others now. Nat and Cami sat with Byron and Beau, but the two seats left were near the head of the table where Brianna was seated. She motioned to them, and I took the hint, pulling out the chair for Loren.

"Thank you for agreeing to listen to us, Mrs. Mascro. I know that you don't owe us anything. Nat was kind enough to offer, but I told her we couldn't ask that of you."

"It sounds like you need help, though," Loren said, taking a sip of her drink.

"You're not wrong, but with the war coming, you have enough on your plate," the woman said, taking her

fill of food before passing it over. The rest of the occu-
pants were quiet as they handed food from one person to
the next. Several of them eyed us, but none appeared
hostile. It was more of a weariness, like they'd grown
tired of whatever fight they were in.

"Nat was telling me that you're being blackmailed?"

The matriarch sighed, realizing Loren wasn't one to
let it go. I admired her attempts to keep us out of it,
showing me she wasn't accustomed to asking for help.
She didn't know Loren, though. If someone needed
something, she'd do whatever she could to help them. It
was just who she was.

"Yes, by my daughter, actually."

Muttering went around the table at that, and I
wondered what all she'd done to these people.

"I believe that Pixel, Cami, and I could do this, Lor.
Selena doesn't know us, and we could be in and out with
our skill sets combined. With the blackmail lifted from
them, the O'Sullivans would be freer to help us."

Loren looked back to Brianna, gauging her. "What's
she holding over you?" she asked, taking a bite.

I placed a bit of food in my mouth but was too busy
to taste it. I was more focused on the conversation and
understanding the risk.

"My late husband, the former boss of the O'Sullivans,
was not a nice man. For many years, I turned my head at
his philandering ways, keeping myself safe. When he
was occupied with his mistresses, he left me alone. I

know that isn't right, but years of abuse left me too weak to stop him or care. He spoiled Selena, giving her everything she wanted. I thought it was okay. As long as she was happy and not being used, then at least one of us would make it. When I learned my husband had moved on to the younger females of the family, I couldn't stand by any longer. So, one night I poisoned his food and then fed him to the pigs on the farm."

She said it so matter-of-factly that I had to stop and make sure I heard her correctly. In fact, I practically choked on the bite of food I'd just taken when it processed. I looked down at my meal, wondering if we were about to suffer the same fate.

Her cackle rang out, along with the rest of the family around the table. "Oh, dear, you have nothing to worry about. I don't kill to just kill. He was a rotten man and needed to go."

Loren squeezed my leg under the table, and I cautiously picked up my fork. "How is she blackmailing you then?"

"The mistake I made was allowing Harvey to spoil her. She became her daddy's daughter and saw no wrong with what he did. Our family was divided then, the ones who didn't see anything wrong with what Harvey was doing, and those who did. She took the half of the family that sided with Harvey, making us pay a monthly fee in order to keep our secret. Everything we do, everything we get, it mostly goes to her. This house is all we have left, and I fear she'll soon try to take it. She's a tyrant and needs to be stopped. The only thing she has against us is a recording. If we got the recording, we'd be free, and Selena wouldn't be able to survive without our monthly dues. Right now, we're weak, but if we had her off our backs, we'd be a force to be reckoned with. The O'Sullivans are strong and resourceful. We can help you in your fight."

Loren looked to Cami and Nat. "It's your decision, ladies." Cami looked back and forth between Nat and Loren. Nat had a pleading look on her face, and I could tell Cami would give in, before she did. Sighing, she nodded.

"Okay, I'll come out of retirement. We'll just need to get a hold of Pixel and see if she'll be back soon."

The table seemed to let out a collective sigh at the news, the chatter starting up again as everyone returned to their eating. We didn't stay much longer, saying our goodbyes once we'd eaten. As we walked out to the car, I stopped Loren for a minute, needing to say something before we had an audience.

Leaning forward, I heard her breath hitch as my lips touched her neck. "You were sexy as Hell back there, Spitfire. When we get home, I think it's time I pay my respects to our Queen."

Stepping back, I adjusted my cock as I slid into the car. I watched as she took a few seconds to gather herself before walking over. Her steps were full of swagger as she opened the door and got in.

Buckling her seatbelt, she glanced over, licking her lips. "How quick can you get us home?"

I made it back in a record thirty minutes.

TWENTY ONE

LOREN

The car ride was quiet as we thought over the things Brianna had shared with us. Or, at least I was thinking them over so I didn't cause Sax to wreck the car so I could have my way with him. Need was pulsing through me so fiercely, that when we finally pulled into the underground parking garage, I was out of the car and headed into the house quicker than he could turn off the engine.

"I'm going to go check on the kids," Cami teased, excusing herself from the heated looks Sax and I shared. She turned down the other hallway leaving us standing in front of the elevator. I looked up, tapping my foot as we watched it descend.

"Fuck it." Before I could turn and ask Sax what he meant, he lifted me over his shoulder in a move that reminded me of one he'd performed on one of my first visits to the house. Laughing this time, I let him carry me wherever he wanted to go.

"I like the way you think," I said when he sat me down on a flat surface a few seconds later. I didn't even look around to see where we were. It didn't matter when I had the sexy man in front of me. Slowly, Sax kneeled down, taking my feet and removing my shoes one by one. The whole time his eyes stayed on mine, his motions communicating his steps before he could get to his prize.

Unbuttoning my pants, I stepped out of his hold and slid them down, standing only in my underwear and top. Sax continued to peer up at me, nothing but awe and adoration on his face. The heated frenzy was still there, but I could see the pure love for me shining through his eyes. I tilted his face up, cupping his jaw, smoothing my hand over his beard.

"I love you, Saxon."

His eyes fluttered closed as he placed his hand over mine. We stood like this for a second, taking a moment to recognize the love we had for one another. As he opened his eyes, I could see the hunger there now and knew I was about to be devoured by the man in front of me. A wicked grin spilled over his face as he pushed me back down and lifted my leg up to his shoulder. Caressing my ankle with his hand, he took his nose and breathed in my skin as he trailed his lips lightly over my flesh the whole way up to my center.

He licked the wet spot through my silk panties,

making it wetter as he began to tongue fuck me through the material. Bracing myself back on the surface, I pushed my cunt further onto his face, needing more. His growl of approval sent shivers up my body and a round of goosebumps across my skin.

"More, Sax. I need more." I heard him open something, but I was too focused on his tongue, which was now licking me under my panties. I was really regretting keeping them on at this point. Leaning up, I looked down to tell him to remove them when I found him grinning up at me. In the next second, my panties were ripped off, and my wish was granted as the cool air greeted my wet pussy.

Sax wasted no time covering me with his mouth as he pulled my thighs closer to him, both my legs wrapping around his head now as he plunged his tongue into me. Gripping his hair, I held on as he tongue fucked me to kingdom come.

"Fuck, yes, yes," I moaned, thrashing my head back and forth. When he pulled back, I expected to feel his fingers entering me, filling me fuller. Instead of his warm hands, something cold and round plunged into me, hitting me deeply.

"Shit!" I screamed, falling back onto where I was. I still hadn't figured out where we were, the pleasure I was receiving taking all of my focus.

"Watching you come undone is the sexiest thing in

existence," Sax purred, nipping my clit as he continued to plunge whatever it was into me.

Words and my surroundings escaped me as I climbed higher and higher, the climax building to a crescendo.

"Come, Loren. Shower me with your cum."

As he pinched my clit and thrusted the object into me, I couldn't do anything other than what he demanded. I came so hard, my entire body tensed up as white lights exploded behind my eyes, sound leaving me. My body continued to quake with aftershocks as I laid there, pleasure coursing through me, and before long, my eyes closed, my body completely spent.

WHEN I WOKE a few hours later, it took me a few minutes to remember how I ended up in bed. Lifting my head, I found two bodies pressed into me from the front and back. The arms around me pulled me closer, bringing a hard dick into contact with my bare backside. Gasping, I peered back, staring into Atticus' eyes. They heated at my sound, and his hand lowered, lifting my leg up higher on his hip.

He kept watching me as he teased his cock in little thrusts until he pushed all the way in. Moaning, my eyes fluttered closed at feeling him inside me. Atticus bent down, taking my lips in his as he moved us together. Small pumps of his hips managed to have me climbing as we lazily kissed one another. When hands traveled up my front, I pulled away and found Sax grinning at me.

"Looks like you're ready for round two, Spitfire."

His big hands covered my breasts as he tweaked my nipples, one hand moving up to wrap around my neck, bringing my face closer to his. Atticus took the waking of Sax as permission to draw back more, and he began to thrust into me deeper, pulling my hips to him as he pistoned into me.

"You're a fucking wet dream. I love watching you respond to him." Sax lowered his hand to my clit, rubbing it as he began to suck on my nipple. Reaching down with my own hand, I found his hard cock ready and dripping for me. Squeezing, I started to stroke it up and down in tandem with Atticus' thrusts. My orgasm was climbing again, and I wondered briefly if I'd be able to walk after. Atticus leaned up, pulling my head back as he hooked my knee into his arm, giving him a new position to thrust even deeper.

My hand froze on Sax as Atticus plundered me and all I could do was squeeze as waves of pleasure washed over me. Atticus stilled a moment later, a long, languid moan leaving him as he released his orgasm into me. He moved to withdraw, and before I could adjust to being empty, my hand was forced off Sax's cock, and he thrust up into my waiting pussy. He rolled over onto his back, bringing me with him as I adjusted to being on top.

I looked over at Atticus, who watched me with hungry eyes as he lay there in his post-orgasmic bliss. "You're beautiful on top, Bellezza. Give me a show."

The words spurred me on, and I found a rhythm on top of Sax's massive dick. Slowly, I moved my hips, bracing my hands on his abs and pecs, massaging his muscles with my hands as I rode him. Sax's hands landed on my ass, and he fondled my cheeks, letting me control the speed for now. As I began to bounce more, I found my sweet spot, my clit rubbing up against his pelvic bone just right, and leaned forward so my breasts swayed with my movement.

Placing my hands on the sides of his head, I used my hips to move up and down, my own breath hitching at the feel of him in me. "Shit, Sax. You fill me up so good," I purred, my words coming out a little drunk sounding from all the orgasms I'd had.

Sax reached up, threading his hands through my hair, and tugged a little, bringing my face to his, kissing me deeply. When I couldn't take it any longer, I sat up, riding him faster as I found my release again. Sax reared up, pumping up into me simultaneously, holding me to him as he came inside me.

With heavy breaths, I leaned against his chest for a moment, letting my heart rate fall back to normal.

Atticus moved me off Sax, and I realized he was cleaning me, caring for me in his way. He didn't care that I had Sax's cum in me; he just wanted to care for me. While it seemed he was always comfortable with Sax from the beginning, I knew he was a long way from squinting.

Once he was done, he deposited the washcloth in the hamper and snuggled back into bed with us. We laid there silently for a while, the only sound our breathing. Moving my hair aside, Atticus kissed my neck tenderly.

"How did the meeting go?"

I loved that he'd had confidence in me to handle this and hadn't demanded we tell him the minute we'd returned. Atticus never failed to surprise me with how much he believed in others.

"It went well. What Nat said is true. They're not involved with Dayton, just a family skirmish that keeps them from being great. Nat wants Cami and Pixel to help her with a job, and then it will allow the O'Sullivans to provide us with more assistance once the encumbrance is removed."

"Do you think it's wise?" he asked, stroking my belly with his thumb. Sax rolled over, watching me as I spoke. His hand came up to my face, tracing the outlines of my features. He was so gentle that I stopped for a minute to let him caress me. My eyes fluttered shut at the soft touch, but I didn't forget what Atticus had asked.

"I told them it was their decision. I believe Brianna is

a good woman, and the alliance of their family would be a good thing, but I didn't want to risk them if they weren't committed. It seems fairly simple, and Nat's confident that the three of them, along with Beau and Byron, will be able to succeed."

"If you ever doubted your role here, I hope you hear how much of the Queen you sound. You make us better, Bellezza. All of us. I've seen Cami and Nat grow in confidence since meeting you. Your touch isn't limited to just us, but all of the Mascros. I can't wait to see everything you're able to accomplish."

He kissed my neck again on the pulse point, and I sucked in a breath. Sax stared at me intently in front of me, and this moment felt powerful as we lay in bed, talking about the dynamics of our family. I liked how it felt, and I knew I was embracing this life more and more each day, becoming the version of myself I was always meant to be.

"It felt nice to go there and be listened to, feel needed. I liked it," I admitted.

"We will never not need you, Spitfire," Sax whispered.

"And I will never not need you. The five of you showed me who I could be, and the family we've built is everything I've ever wanted. This is the life I dreamed of." They both kissed me, happiness radiating through them. Outside of having my other three husbands here, the moment couldn't have been more perfect.

"How did your meeting go, Attie?"

"Good, Bellezza. I'll tell you all about it in the morning. Sleep for now."

"Fine," I grumbled, closing my eyes for a second before they popped back open.

"Sax?"

"Yes, Spitfire?" he asked, his voice becoming heavy with sleep.

"Where did you ravage me earlier, and what was it that you used? I came so hard I blacked out before I could find out."

A bellow erupted out of Sax, startling Atticus behind me. "Shit, Sax!" he hissed.

"Sorry," he soothed, laughing.

"Well?"

"Oh, just Atticus' desk and the new fountain pen he'd bought recently."

"Christ!" was muttered behind me as shock settled on me at his declaration. After a second, a giggle erupted, and then the other two bodies in bed joined me.

"A... pen?" I asked around my laughter.

"Without the ink, of course. I'm a gentleman like that." Sax chortled, causing us to lose it again.

"I'll never be able to look at that pen now without getting an erection," Atticus groaned.

"That was kind of the point."

"Why do I feel this just created a competition

between the two of you to see how far you can push this?"

"I have no idea what you're referring to, Bellezza," Atticus said, barely able to keep a laugh from his voice.

"Well, as long as I get orgasms, I don't really mind. Game on, boys."

TWENTY TWO

JUDE

A sound at my door had me jolting, and I sat up, straightening my clothes. I'd fallen asleep at my desk working on an assignment. The first night I returned, I'd passed out, just happy to be back with my family. I didn't really think about what I'd gone through. But ever since, each night became increasingly harder for me to sleep. As it was, I bet I only got about two hours last night, and finding myself in random places passed out was becoming too common.

"Come in," I said through a yawn as I turned in my chair. Loren's head peeked through the door, bringing a smile to my face. "Hey, how's it going?" I asked.

"I came to ask you the same thing." She smiled, sitting on the corner of my bed. I shrugged, not really knowing how to answer that.

"It's kind of hard to say. I'm glad to be back, to be here, but I won't lie and say it hasn't affected me. I've had some dreams," I admitted.

Loren moved closer, taking my hand in hers. Tears welled in her eyes as she listened. "Do you want me to find someone for you to talk to? I know you might not want to talk with me about it."

"Actually, I think I'd rather talk with you. It's not the easiest for me to open up to strangers."

"I'm glad I'm not considered a stranger anymore."

"Of course not. You're my mom."

It was the first time I'd said the word, and the tears that had been developing trickled over, falling down her cheeks. "Wow, I never knew how great it would be to hear someone call me that. I'm glad it was you, Son."

Loren pulled me into her arms, and I soon found I was crying too. It felt nice to be cherished by her, to be loved so much she'd been willing to risk anything to save me. No one had ever wanted me that much before. I'd always been the burden.

But here in this family, I was welcomed and seen as a valuable member.

Loren patted my head, her hands running through my hair, soothing me in a way I'd never been comforted before. It shouldn't have felt so significant, but it did. It felt like the culmination of things I'd experienced had led me to be here in this moment where I would know what it meant to be truly loved. That knowledge healed something broken in me.

When we pulled back, wiping our cheeks, I couldn't

deny I felt lighter. It felt good to cry and be hugged by my mom. She cupped my cheek, patting it softly.

"How are you feeling about returning to school?"

"Honestly? I think I'd rather wait until after summer. There's only a month left at this point, and having to explain my absence feels like a bigger thing than I want to make it. I know Imogen wants to go, but I'm not sure if we should while this war is going on with her father. I think Atticus made the right call."

"I can't deny that I love having you closer and protected. I don't want to lose you again, but I know it's not feasible to keep you here under lock and key forever. I can honor your wish to wait until next school year, and if you need someone to be the bad guy, I can do that for you. Just promise to talk to me if it's something else you're worried about."

"I promise. I don't think it's anything else other than people asking questions. I don't feel like being in the spotlight. At first, I was excited about going, just wanting to get back to my normal routine, but I like the tutor and having the time to actually deal with something for once instead of rushing to survive is nice."

"Okay, honey. Is there anything I can do right now?"

"I'm just having trouble sleeping. I keep... having nightmares about that place."

"That's perfectly understandable. I've had a few too where I have to wake up and remind myself you're here. What usually helps me is to put something next to my bed as a reminder of what's real. It could be anything from a picture to a coin or even a piece of string. It's just a reminder that you're here and not there."

"I like that. What do you use?"

Loren smiled, a blush coming to her cheeks. "I have the picture you made saved on my phone. I look at it a lot and remind myself you're safe. I've also used a tube of lipstick. Something tangible to remind me to be in the present and not in my head."

I nodded, thinking. "I could use a watch face that I kept from my dad. It doesn't work anymore, but I've always had it with me. Would that work?"

"It could, but sometimes if they have sentimental value, it's harder to tell if it's real or fake because your brain knows about it. It's why something random works, because it's not like your imagination will try to trick you with something that means nothing. But give it a try. Everyone is different."

"Thanks, I will. It feels nice to talk about these things and not be in it alone," I admitted, my cheeks reddening.

"I'm glad. You never have to be alone ever again. You have me and everyone in this house. We all love and care for you, kiddo."

"It feels nice. I like being part of this family." I stopped, a smile coming to my face. "Who should I call Dad?"

Loren let out a sharp laugh, slapping my knee. "How's your little game with them going? Have you rearranged the order lately?" she asked, raising her eyebrows.

I shook my head, laughing.

"What you refer to them as is between you and them. I won't tell you that you have to call any of them anything other than what you feel comfortable with. They all care for you and will be there for whatever you need. I told them we were a package deal." She paused, taking a deep breath. "Speaking of, have you thought about your last name yet?"

"I'm still considering. My parents weren't the best, but I don't know if I'm ready to let go of that just yet."

"I understand. You're part of us, no matter what your last name is. I hope you know that."

"I do." I smiled, feeling lighter just from talking.

"Can I ask a personal question?" She grinned, and I had a feeling I knew what it would be about.

"Go ahead," I groaned, dramatically falling back into my chair.

Loren laughed, sitting up straighter. "Is there something brewing besides friendship between you and Immy?"

My cheeks heated, giving away my answer, and I nodded. "I don't know how she feels, but I like her. I've never really had a girlfriend before, though, so I don't know what to do."

"Well, I think the best place to start is to talk and see if you're on the same page. Then, make it whatever you want it to be. Don't let others make decisions for you or tell you who you must be. That's one thing I wish I'd learned sooner."

"So if I had two girlfriends, or Immy had three boyfriends, that wouldn't be an issue?"

"Not for me! Atticus might see it differently, but he'll get over it. If you want a boyfriend and a girlfriend, or just one, I'm cool with it. I just want you to be happy, Juju."

"I am, Loren. I promise."

"Good." She reached over, squeezing my knee. "Okay, I'll let you be. If you need advice, though, on dating, Nicco is actually really good at listening and helping you figure out things. He helped me when I didn't know how to feel about all the new things I was experiencing."

"Thanks; I'll keep that in mind if I ever get the courage to do something."

Loren leaned up, hugging me one more time, and then quickly kissed my cheek before she walked out of the room. I turned around and stared at my math home-work, but couldn't focus on it. Closing the book, I stood to see what everyone else was up to when there was another knock at my door. Walking over, I opened it, surprised to find Immy standing there.

Instantly, my insides warmed, and I felt happier just seeing her. "Hey."

"You busy?" she asked, smiling at me.

"Avoiding the Math homework. You?"

"Same. Want to go out to Wells' place and feed the dogs with me?" She bounced on her toes, a bigger smile spreading across her face.

"You know the answer to that," I teased. I turned around and toed on my shoes, tucking my phone into my pocket. "Who's taking us?"

"Topher and the new one, Stocke, I think," she said, her nose scrunching up a little in thought.

"Oh yeah, he's cool." We walked down the hall together, and I didn't miss how our hands brushed against each other. She didn't move away, so I took that as a good sign and reached down, linking our fingers together.

I watched her out of the corner of my eye, trying to gauge if she hated it or not. When she didn't drop it, I smiled and relaxed, hoping it meant she liked it. Together, we walked out to the garage, finding the car waiting for us.

When we climbed into the backseat, I was surprised to find it empty. We didn't usually get this type of alone space. There was always a guard nearby or another adult. Scooting in, we both buckled our seatbelts as the SUV took off after a few seconds.

"Wow, I'm shocked we're back here alone. It always feels like we have a babysitter."

Imogen laughed, nodding. "I know. My brother is so

paranoid that if two teenagers are alone together unsupervised, they will immediately have sex."

My face warmed at the word, and I laughed nervously. "Yeah, that's insane. We can control ourselves a little more than that. Besides, I haven't even kissed anyone. I'm pretty sure that usually comes before sex." I blushed at the word, my face feeling like it was molten lava at this point.

Immy looked over, a small smile on her face. "You know, I've never been kissed either. We should be each other's first."

I turned, my eyes wide. "Um, what?"

She moved closer, our legs touching. "Do you want to kiss me, Jude?"

I nodded, no longer able to find words. She leaned closer at my movement, her eyes closing, and I followed suit. When our lips met, it felt like the earth aligned, and everything finally made sense. Or at least while our lips were pressed together.

Imogen pulled back after a few seconds, fluttering open her eyes, and we stared at one another for a while, just watching.

"That was nice," I finally found the words to say.

"Yeah." She smiled, taking my hand.

"Immy, I uh, I like you a lot. As more than a friend, and I wondered…would you be my girlfriend?"

She rolled her eyes, kissing my lips again quickly. "Duh. I don't kiss everyone."

She sat back, leaning into me, and I relaxed as we held hands. We didn't talk the rest of the way out to Wells' house, but we didn't need to. Imogen and I understood each other in a way I hadn't ever with anyone else. We were both victims of our circumstances, making us survivors. We didn't need to talk because sometimes there were moments where words weren't needed.

Twenty Three

ATTICUS

I tossed the card down onto the table, tired of looking at my father's face. I'd made flashcards of everyone's picture with the secrets I'd gathered written on the back and was making a chart on a corkboard. My plan was to place the ones together that would enact the most damage to my father's empire. He was spiraling based on the few phone calls I'd already received.

The phone rang again, and I sighed, glancing over at the desk. The image of Loren sprawled out on it as I took a phone call replayed in my head, and I had to shift my cock as I made my way over to it. Leaning against the wood, I picked up the receiver, bringing it to my ear.

"Yes?"

"That's how you answer the phone?" my father asked. I'd been expecting him to call any day now, so I wasn't surprised he'd finally caved. He was playing right into my hands. I kept silent, not giving him anything.

"I know what you're planning," he spat out after a minute of silence.

"Oh?" I asked, feigning interest.

"You won't find anything on me, Son. You'll lose, and then I'll use your bitch of a wife and your sister to further my plans."

I gritted my teeth, knowing he was baiting me. I wouldn't let him get a reaction out of me. "Is that all you called about? To make idle threats? If I didn't know any better, Father, I'd say you were the scared one."

He scoffed, only confirming my assessment. I wanted to gloat on this small win, but it was too soon to declare victory, especially up against a foe like Dayton. He wouldn't go down easy.

"The only thing I'm scared of is whether or not I can get your bloodstains out of my white shirt. I'll see you tomorrow night."

"Oh? Do we have a meeting I don't remember making?"

"Don't think you can throw an exclusive party, and I won't come."

"I don't remember inviting you. Only members with the password will be let in. It would be a shame for you to be turned away at the door."

"I have my ways, Son. I'll bring you a gift."

He hung up before I could say anything else, but it didn't matter. The trap had been set, and it was ready to be sprung. My father would get what was coming to him tomorrow night.

Walking back to the table, I picked up his card, smiling. Placing it in the center of the board, I stuck a push pin into his forehead, feeling some small pleasure from the act.

Tomorrow night, Dayton Mascro would crumble.

A FEW HOURS LATER, I was going blind from staring at the computer screen. Rubbing my eyes, I was surprised when a knock sounded at the door. Looking up, I was even more surprised when it was Jude. He walked in at my nod, one of the dogs trailing behind him. I should probably learn their names since they would be a permanent fixture in my life now.

"What can I do for you, Jude?" I asked, sitting up.

"I was wondering," he started, fidgeting with his hands. He swallowed, straightening his back as he seemed to gather his bearings. "I was wondering if I could cash in my favor. I know I technically haven't earned it yet since we didn't start school, but... a favor is a favor, right?"

I smiled, liking his tenacity. "Sure, Jude. I think you've earned it. Sit and tell me about this request."

He smiled, some of the tension leaving him. "Well,

it's kind of two parts, you see. You remember how you asked me last time about my feelings for Imogen?"

My body stiffened as I nodded, focused on his face. "Yes."

"And I told you it was a conversation I needed to have with her first?"

I nodded again, no words this time. I watched as he swallowed, holding my eyes the whole time.

"Well, we had the talk, sir, and we've decided to be together."

"Be... together?" I asked, my teeth grinding as I tensed my jaw. "So, you're what? Coming to tell me you're going to have sex with my little sister? Is the favor not to kill you?"

Jude spluttered, his face turning red. "Um, no, I mean, be together as in boyfriend/girlfriend. No sex!"

His words had my pulse slowing some, but not entirely. I stared at him, waiting for him to explain more. When he just kept staring, I let out my breath, knowing I couldn't use my usual intimidation tactics on Jude. He was family.

"Is that all? You're dating?"

"Um, yes, I mean no. Yes, we're dating, but the favor I wanted to ask was if we could go on a date. I know that Topher will have to accompany us, and I'm okay with that, but I figured we wouldn't be allowed to do something on our own without your permission first. So, that's what I'm asking. Can we?"

I observed him for a moment, mostly so I didn't respond out of anger. The brother in me wanted to lock Imogen away and never let her meet another boy. But that wasn't practical. I knew if I did that, she'd rebel and end up doing more dangerous things than dating a nice young man like Jude.

In all honesty, he was the best option, even if I didn't like it. Jude had the courage to come to me and ask, while also understanding our family. He appeared to prioritize safety by knowing they'd need a guard. When I broke it down like that, he was the best-case scenario. The family thing could be a little complicated, but that never stopped us before.

Sitting forward, I clasped my hands together as I peered at him. "You'd stay with the guard the whole time?"

"Yes, sir." He nodded, his face serious.

"You wouldn't try to leave or lose them?"

"No, I swear."

"And you won't try any funny business? My sister has been through a lot already, and I don't want to see her progress falter because of a hormonal teenager."

"To be fair, Mr. Mascro, I'm not ready for that either. I know teenage boys tend to make stupid decisions, but I hope you see that I'm not like my peers. Until I met Loren, I had to fight just to survive each day. It was more about making sure I had food and clothes to wear than getting naked with someone. Plus, I've seen what that can lead to, and I know we both have plans for our future. It doesn't mean that we won't want to cross that line someday, but I can assure you it's not now."

I tapped my fingers on the desk, studying him. I didn't like the thought of my baby sister having sex at any point in her life, but I knew it was unavoidable. Everything he said was honest, and I appreciated that Jude was mature and able to understand things I hadn't even been able to at his age.

"Just one thing," I said, giving him a critical eye. He sat up straighter, nodding. "I think you can call me Atticus now. You've earned it."

His body sagged with relief and it felt like his whole being brightened with that one comment, and it brought a feeling of warmth I hadn't let myself feel for anyone outside my circle in a while.

"Okay, Atticus." He grinned wider, moving to stand, and I knew I needed to say something else to him.

"Jude, wait." He stopped, looking at me in that way where he gave you all of his attention. "I hate that the marriage thing was done without you. That hadn't been my intention. I wanted to talk with you about it, actually."

"Me?" He touched his chest, his mouth open in surprise.

"You're Loren's son and I wanted to make sure you were okay with the arrangement. We're going to have a huge reception once everything with Dayton is dealt with, and I'd like your help with something."

"Anything," he said, his face lighting up.

"Perfect." I told him my idea, and he nodded, his face filling with curiosity and interest the more I spoke. When he left a few minutes later, I sat back, hopeful about the future for once.

TWENTY FOUR

LOREN

Clasping the necklace around my neck, I stepped back and took a look at myself in the mirror. The emerald green dress glimmered in the light, and I couldn't help but fall in love with the ensemble. Stacy had done well picking it out for me. The necklace sparkled as the diamonds and emerald caught the light, and I wondered if I'd ever worn anything as expensive as this before.

The answer was an easy no.

Stepping into my stilettos, I picked up the clutch and black lace mask off the dresser and headed out the door. It was time to don a mask for an entirely different reason tonight. When I came to the staircase, I grasped the railing, taking extra care in my shoes. The slit in the dress moved with each step I took, showcasing my long legs as I descended.

It was like out of a movie as I approached the five

men below, all decked out in suits. Each one looked different, but they were all scrumptious and all mine. Atticus was the first to step up, taking my hand and helping me off the last step.

"You look magnificent, Bellezza."

Smiling, I wrapped my arm in his as we made our way out the door. I eyed the others as we passed, and I prayed we got to have a private celebration after, where I could peel each layer of the sexy tuxedos off of them. Sax growled as I passed, making my whole body quiver.

My eyes trailed over Nicco, loving that his tattoos stood out on his hands and neck. I still needed to spend some time licking them up and down. Monroe and Wells stood at the end, looking just as delicious in their black and white. Monroe winked at me, causing me to lick my lips at the flirty behavior. Wells gave me one of his classic surly expressions, his eyebrow raised as I passed, and I could hear the reprimand he wanted to give in my head.

Yes, I definitely needed to have time with all of my husbands tonight. It would be mandatory, I decided.

When we stepped out the front door, I was momentarily confused until I saw the limo at the curb. Ideas of what mischief we could get up to in it before making it back home started to swirl now. I rubbed my legs together, needing some friction to stave off the desire pulsating below.

"You look so fuckable, Bellezza. I have half a mind to say screw the party and just have my way with you in the back; this dress pooled around you as I slide my cock in you," Atticus purred into my ear, his breath cascading down my neck.

My breath hitched, and I paused on the step, my hand gripping him harder as a wave of desire rushed through me. "Shit, if you don't stop, I'll come right now."

"Well, that sounds like a challenge," he teased, nipping my earlobe.

I didn't know what had gotten into Atticus, but it seemed like taking down his foes was a huge turn-on for him.

The car door opened as one of the guards tried to hide his smile, and I slid in, taking a moment to gather my dress to keep it from wrinkling too much. Because I wasn't blushing after being caught by the guard. Nope.

The other guys filtered into the car, and as the door shut, I felt like the sexual tension raised a notch. Fanning myself with my mask, I tried to cool off my insides. I could not ruin my dress before taking Dayton down a few pegs.

"I don't think that's going to help, Beautiful," Nicco teased, licking his lips as he adjusted the massive erection he was sporting. I could even make out the line of piercings and wondered just how tight those pants were.

"Perhaps we should discuss the plan again?" I asked, needing a distraction.

Atticus chuckled but obliged. "You each have your

area and the person you'll be watching. Nicco, you'll be on Mr. Thompson, the building inspector. Monroe, you have Judge Ryan. Wells, you have Mr. Shultz, the fighting commissioner, and Sax, you'll be on Jones, the police commissioner. Which leaves me with the mayor and Loren his date. You have the secrets you're to use and see if you can find any other information on what Dayton is up to. He will be there, and he'll have his spies as well. The advantage we have is knowing the club, the players, and what moves he'll try to make. We just have to lead him into position and let him set the trap himself."

"What if he doesn't fall for it?" I asked, hoping there was a backup plan.

"He will," Atticus said with some steel. He turned, his eyes softening when he looked at me, noticing my fear. "But if he doesn't, we're prepared for Plan B with the media and virus that Pixel made before she left. It's not ideal as we won't gain as much leverage, but either way, my father won't be walking out of there the winner tonight. We're going to knock him down and make it harder for him to get back up."

Everyone nodded as I looked around the car, and I prayed that everything would go as planned. We couldn't afford for it to fail. At this point, everything came down to this party and the secrets we held.

The limo pulled up to the club a few minutes later, all

of us in our own heads as we thought through our information. It had successfully killed all the lust in the car as no one had even looked up from their lap.

Atticus held out a hand to me as I stepped from the limo. Our masks were on now, our roles fully in place as my husbands walked ahead. Sax stayed back, his role as guard in place. Nicco strode forward, waving and smiling for the cameras. Monroe and Wells walked hand-in-hand together. The red carpet entrance was packed with people milling about, hoping to get a shot of us or someone famous.

Camera flashes went off every second, and I placed a megawatt smile on my face. It was the moment all of my upper crust training was made for. Too bad my mother wasn't here to see it firsthand. Doubt they had this coverage in jail. I snorted at that thought and Atticus tilted his head slightly, his own mask of indifference in place.

"Nothing," I whispered, linking my arm to his. The paparazzi had done such an excellent job for us last time that we'd opted to use them again. Though it meant we had to be careful not to be caught doing anything, since we were only toeing the line tonight, it wasn't that much of a risk. It would mostly be for all those who wanted to be seen, including Dayton.

Once we stepped into the club, I took a moment to admire all the details that Atticus had put in place. The club was transformed with lights and hefty velvet drapes of fabric hanging from the ceiling. There were even some acrobats on big rings, performing in certain spots, twirling around. Waiters dressed in tuxedos and masks mingled with trays of drinks as they effortlessly moved in and out of the crowd. A five-piece wind ensemble sat on the stage, playing a melodious tune.

The whole scene rivaled any masquerade ball I'd ever envisioned. It was seductive elegance at its finest, and we were about to strike down an evil man while wearing couture. It didn't get much more upscale than that.

"Go time," Atticus mumbled, kissing my cheek and walking to intercept his target. He was to occupy himself with the Mayor until his father arrived. We knew that Dayton would make a scene, and we had to be ready to strike when he did. We couldn't allow him to have any foothold here. Not on our territory.

The woman I was to cozy up to was headed toward the bar, so I followed, hoping my recent success at making friends would pay off. Sitting my clutch down, I turned and gasped, catching her attention. "Oh, wow, your dress is stunning."

She smiled, looking down at it. "Thank you. It was a gift."

"Oh, well, whoever he is has excellent taste."

She eyed me, taking in my dress. When she spotted the necklace, she turned more toward me. It seemed Stacy was right. If I looked like I was someone to be envious of, she'd be more willing to talk to me. Something about always wanting what we couldn't have and if you acted like you were someone, others believed it. I never realized how much reverse psychology went into dressing people.

"I could say the same about your man." She lifted an eyebrow, motioning toward my necklace. I leaned in conspiratorially.

"He has great taste. I couldn't believe he got it for me. I'm kind of scared to wear it. I'm not used to these types of events. Plus, it's from my boyfriend, and my husband doesn't know."

Her eyes went wide at that, and just like I'd hoped, her smile became bigger. "It seems we have something in common."

"Oh?" I asked, taking the drink from the bartender.

She leaned closer, whispering. "I'm here with my *boyfriend*, too." She raised her eyes at the word, making sure I understood.

"Well, to boyfriends with good taste," I cheered, raising my glass to hers. "I'm Loren."

"Gabriella." We both took a sip, turning to look out at the crowd. I caught her looking over, eyeing me occasionally. Her blue eyes stood out from her mask, and I felt terrible for lying to her, but I had to remember the bigger picture.

"Have you ever been to something like this?" I asked when she grew quiet.

"Occasionally, though this is more luxurious than most of the things I get toted to."

The therapist part of me picked up on her sadness, and I fought to not pull that string. "Oh?" I asked, losing the battle with myself. "That sounds suspiciously like unhappiness." She tensed, and I berated myself for stepping over the line. "Shit, sorry. I have a knack for picking up on people's emotions, but I'm crap about staying in my lane, so to speak. Ignore what I said," I rambled, losing the calm tone I'd been imploring. I cringed, looking over at her.

Something in either my words or expression eased her, and she let out a low chuckle. "I don't know why, but I like you, Loren. You're not like most women at these places, even though you're by far prettier than any of them."

I smiled at her compliment, but it did nothing to quell the pit in my stomach at using her secrets against her. "Thank you. That's kind of you. I'm sorry I pried. It really is one of my worst traits."

"I might regret this, but you seem like you genuinely care, not one of those women who are only nice to me so they can get close to my date. But I guess you don't need to when you have a man like yours." She lifted her eyes over my shoulder, and I turned, finding Sax watching me. I waved, turning back, a look of love on my face.

"Yep, you're not using me," she assessed, deciding something. I bit my lip, hating myself a little. Atticus said the family he was creating was different, so maybe that meant I could be a different type of Queen too.

"Actually, I was. But I can't. Please, if you follow me somewhere private, I'll explain everything. I think we could help one another, Gabriella." She tensed at my words but nodded, following me. I could feel my shadow watching, so I knew he'd know where I was going and tell the others if they needed me.

I couldn't use this woman. She was innocent for the most part. While I disagreed with her choice to sleep with a married man, it didn't mean I wanted to embarrass or shame her. Perhaps there was a way for us all to help one another.

Stepping under the rope that sealed off the upstairs, I picked up my dress and climbed the steps, which was exceedingly harder to do in these heels. By the time I made it to the top, I was cursing my decision, but I couldn't deny how much quieter it was.

"Okay, talk," she said, her kindness gone as she placed her hands on her hips, staring daggers at me.

I took off my mask, hoping it would let me show my sincerity. "My name is Loren Mascro, and I'm married to Atticus Mascro." At the name, she tensed a little but held her own, making me like her even more. "Actually, I have five husbands, but we won't get into that. I was supposed to get you to talk and then blackmail you with a secret I know," I admitted, swallowing. She crossed her arms, her eyes conveying all the ways she would hurt me. "But that's not who I am. I'm a therapist by trade, and, I hope, a good person. I don't know what difficult things you've dealt with in your life, but I can hear a broken soul. You're hurting, and I can't add on to that. I won't."

"So, because you think you know my story, you're what? Offering me therapy advice? You're crazier than I thought." She turned to leave, and worry climbed my throat, desperate to spill out.

"Wait, no, that's not it. A man is coming here tonight, and he's evil. He's hurt my family in so many ways. We threw this event to put the right people in place at the right time to stop him."

"And how do I play into that?" she asked, turning around.

"This man has acquired significant wealth and prestige, and if he gains political connections, he will be unstoppable. I know your secret, but I won't use it against you. If you need help, though, I can do that. But it's your choice."

"What did you hope to gain from me?" she asked, stepping closer. "I'm a nobody. I'm just here to look pretty."

"Oh, Gabriella, you're so much more than that." I took her hand, squeezing. "I know you want to go to school, and you started being an escort to pay for that. Then things happened, setting you behind. I'm not one to judge your choices, but I'd like to help you have different ones if you want them. I'll help you regardless of what you decide. It's not an either/or decision."

She observed me, looking me over from head to toe. I pleaded with my eyes for her to trust me. "I still need to know what you wanted from me," she said, standing her ground.

"Fair." I nodded. "My husband is brokering a deal with your date, the mayor. If he needed some persuasion, then that was where you came in."

"Threaten to out me to his wife?"

"Or the press. But I know in situations like this, you would pay more than he would, and I knew I couldn't use someone like that. I'm sorry."

"You would really help me?" she asked, some hope in her voice.

"Of course. No woman should feel trapped. If you need help, I'll do whatever I can. I promise."

She watched me for a few more seconds before she decided something, a sense of strength stealing over her as she thought through something.

"Okay. I'll help you too."

I sighed, walking forward to squeeze her hand. "Thank you, Gabriella. You're saving people's lives."

"That kind of feels nice, actually."

I put my mask back on, and together we walked down the stairs, helping each other not trip over our dresses. Once again, it felt nice to be part of the mafia and do something my way. I was learning I could be who I needed to be without losing who I was.

Nodding at Gabriella, she set off to schmooze her date and get us the information we needed. So far, everything was falling into place.

So, of course, that was when Dayton had to make his entrance. Showtime.

TWENTY FIVE

NICCO

My face was beginning to hurt as I talked with the building inspector, my mega-smile in place as I complimented and talked him up. I realized that Atticus had earned his resting asshole face honestly. After so many conversations while being pleasant, the last thing I wanted to do was chat up more people.

"You know, I've been thinking of getting a tattoo, living on the wild side a little," Mr. Thompson boomed, sloshing his drink as he leaned closer to whisper. "I hear it's great with the ladies." He nudged me, making a lewd gesture with his hands, and I realized I couldn't do it any longer.

"Actually, getting a tattoo is a serious decision and shouldn't be done on alcohol. Tattoo artists work hard for their craft and should be treated as such. You'll be wearing this for the course of your life, so it needs to be thought about with precision. I encourage people to think about it for a few days before committing just so it's not an impromptu drunken choice."

The man sputtered, stunned at my response. He started to open his mouth, gaping like a fish, when he was saved from responding by Dayton's entrance. The music stopped as he paraded into the middle of the floor, acting like some big shot. Everyone stopped what they were doing and looked, giving him the attention he sought.

His eyes were obscured with a black plastic mask that covered the top portion of his head, but there was no denying it was Dayton. He oozed power and arrogance, spreading his arms wide as he turned in a circle, grinning wide at everyone. It was a bit manic, and for the first time, I saw some cracks in his composure. Dayton was unraveling, and it made me feel lighter on the inside. It wasn't that I doubted our ability to take him down, but I'd learned to never underestimate his ability to survive.

"Who is that?" Mr. Thompson asked.

"No one," I said before remembering my role. "Just someone who thinks he can bend the rules to get around inspections. Did you know that he has a new venue, and I heard he paid off the city so they wouldn't do a full inspection? Makes you wonder what he's hiding."

"He what?" the man gasped, his former boisterous personality fading to encompass the hard-nosed, rule follower he was.

"Oh, that's right. You said you work in that department, didn't you? Did you know?" I gave him a disgusted look, like he was responsible.

He shook his head quickly, his jowls flapping with him as he did. "No! This cannot stand. What building did you say?" His face turned red as he pulled out his phone in haste.

"Oh? Hmm." I tapped my chin in thought, making it seem like I hadn't planned for him to respond precisely as he was. Snapping my fingers, I pointed at him when I had it. "The Masked Kingpin. It's a fighting arena on the east side."

He typed it in and then turned the phone to show me. I nodded when it came up, trying to keep my glee from pouring over at how well this was going for me.

"David was on that one. I never liked him. He was always too shifty. I'm going to have to report this and do an inspection myself." He turned like he was looking for something as he patted his pockets. When he was satisfied he had everything, he turned back to me. "It was nice meeting you, Nicco. I'll take what you said into consideration about the tattoo, and maybe I'll pay you a visit. Do you have a card?"

I opened my wallet, pulled out an Ignite Ink card, and handed it to him. "I look forward to hearing from you then. Bring that in, and you'll get 20% off." He smiled wide at that, eagerly taking the business card and placing it in his wallet. "I'd be honored to have such a respectable businessman like yourself come. We need more people like you." I patted his shoulder as he walked by, nodding and hoping I hadn't laid it on too thick there at the end.

Sax walked over once the building inspector was gone, a smirk on his lips. "You got a little something," he said, pointing to the tip of my nose. I went to wipe it when he broke out in a laugh, and I realized he was making fun of me. Rolling my eyes, I looked back over to see what scene Dayton was trying to pull now.

"Ha, ha," I said, leaving his ill-mannered joke alone. "How did yours go since you have such an opinion on mine?"

"Easy-peasy."

I looked over, taking in the big man. "Why does that not fill me with confidence? I've never known you to say that phrase before."

He shrugged his shoulders, taking a sip of something he held in his hand.

"What did you do?" I asked, giving him my full attention now.

"Nothing. I had a conversation with him, and he's already agreed to look into Dayton. I also dropped a hint about the dead body, so there should be a team discovering bloated ex #2 as we speak. I'm just efficient."

I snorted, shaking my head. "I feel like that's only half of what happened."

"Not my problem." He shrugged, taking another sip of his drink as he looked out onto the floor.

Sighing, I decided to leave it for now. I followed his gaze to Loren, who was arm in arm with Atticus as they spoke with the mayor and his date. They were all smiles, so I hoped it meant things were going well.

"What about Goldie and Crash?" I asked, looking for them. I found myself needing to know they were okay more and more as my feelings for the two men grew. I realized it wasn't only sexual desire I felt for them, especially Wells.

Sax snorted this time, my attempt to hide my eagerness apparently not as hidden as I'd hoped. He grabbed my head, turning it in the direction of the two men. Both were still with their marks, but Wells didn't seem to be faring as well as Monroe. He took a gulp of his drink as the fighting commissioner looked around, almost bored.

"You good with watching Dayton if I go rescue him?" I asked, already moving in that direction before he answered.

"Yeah," I heard him snort as I walked away.

Making my way through the crowd, I nodded and smiled at people, forgetting most wouldn't know who I was with the mask on. When Wells came into view, I knew I'd made the right choice coming over.

"Mr. Schultz, it's nice to see you here this evening. How are you finding the establishment?" I asked, pasting that smile back on. I clapped Wells on the shoulder, leaving my arm around him. I felt him relax into me, something changing inside.

"Oh, Nicco, how are you?" he asked, smiling at me. "I was just talking with Mr. Young here about the big fight you're having in the summer. I'm looking forward to it."

"That's excellent. I know there were some issues with some fighters scraping in at the last minute at our opening. It made us wonder if the integrity of the fighting program had fallen and whether we were better off switching to a different fighting style. You don't know anything about that, do you?" I asked, raising my eyebrow. "Wells was stabbed during that altercation."

The man gulped, looking at Wells a little differently now. "I didn't realize that was your fight, Mr. Young."

Wells grunted, taking a drink. I squeezed him, hoping to help calm him. I knew he was more worried about Loren during that fight, but it didn't mean he hadn't been affected by the incident. Something like that left a mark long after the injury healed.

"Yeah, well, not something I like to remember," he finally said, setting his glass down.

I was suddenly grateful my brother had made us all learn the secrets of all the guests here tonight since Wells seemed to have fallen into a sullen state with the mention of the fight.

"Yes, well, as you can see, it was pretty traumatic for us. Which reminds me, do I remember correctly that you have a daughter who attends River Valley? My sister is thinking of going there. They've been so accommodating and excited about her attending that they even offered us a seat on their board of directors. I guess there's been some suspicion that some students' parents are getting kickbacks from the board for jobs. Sounds like a mess, but it could be worth looking into." I shrugged my shoulder, playing dumb. "Have you heard anything about that?"

"Um, no. I haven't. I'm glad they're not letting it go." He swallowed, his brow starting to sweat. "Do you know if they had any suspects?"

"Oh, yes, there was a list. Wasn't there Wells?" I asked, looking at him in mock concern. "Wells is very involved with our children's schooling. In fact, he might be the one to sit on the board." I smiled, loving the teasing I could do to Wells.

"Yep, that's me. All about education." His words were gritted, but he smiled. I didn't miss the slight elbow to my ribs he gave me.

"Wow, that's so considerate of you. You know, now that you mentioned it. I definitely am free the week of your opening. I'll make sure to have our best referees there and that no other fights are happening simultaneously, so there's no mixup on people switching at the last second. I'll even be there for the weigh-ins and checks myself. How does that sound?"

"That sounds amazing. What do you think, Wells?" I

asked, turning to beam at him.

"I think it sounds like a much better situation than last time, one where I'll definitely have no time to be on a board since I'll be spending it training."

"I'm sure the school will understand," I said, mustering up some fake concern. Looking back at the man in front of us, I could tell he seemed relieved. We'd let him continue for now as long as it was in our favor and no one was getting hurt. But he was stupid if he thought that we wouldn't keep an eye on him once we learned of his shady dealings.

"Well, it's been great catching up with you, but I think I will call it an early night. Excuse me, fellas." He nodded his goodbye and made his exit as we watched him go.

"Two down." I kept my arm around Wells, testing how long he'd let me. Looking over, I waited for him to turn.

"What?" he asked, eyeing me.

Smiling, I shook my head. "Nothing. How's Sunshine doing?" I asked, looking for him. Wells pointed in the other direction, and I found our golden boy schmoozing like the best of them with the judge.

"He was always better at getting people to like him than I was," Wells mumbled, taking a swig of his drink.

"Nah. I think it's more that you don't waste your time on people you don't deem worthy. Not the other way around."

"What's that say about you then?" he asked, looking into my eyes again. I bit my lip as I peered down at him. He was only an inch or so shorter than me, so our faces were very close at this angle.

"Obviously that you find me adorable and lovable."

"Hmm, is that so? I think you're more annoying than adorable." His breath skated over me, and I held back the shiver that wanted to course down my spine.

"But you're not denying the lovable?"

He paused, looking back and forth between my eyes. "No, I'm not." His hand reached up, pulling my neck down to him, our lips meeting in a soft kiss. It was brief and over before I could do anything, but it had happened, and it meant something to me.

Smiling, I grabbed his hand, pulling him toward Monroe. "Let's go see if we can wrap this up so we can stop Daddy Dearest and then have hot sex in the limo ride home."

His steps faltered a little at my words, but he picked up the pace, pulling me toward Monroe quicker.

I spotted Dayton out of the corner of my eye, his sneer only making me smile more. It didn't hurt that no one was talking to him, ignoring his big show of an entrance and going on about their business. It seemed like two things would be solidified when we left here tonight.

Dayton's downfall only being the second best to Wells submitting to me.

TWENTY SIX

LOREN

When I first walked over with Gabriella, Atticus examined me quizzically, a look of uncertainty on his face. It didn't help that the moment I reached him, his father walked in, acting like he was some bigshot everyone should focus on.

The crowd stopped to stare, giving Dayton a moment of the limelight he craved, but they turned away when he didn't say anything, drawing back to their conversations. Atticus pulled me closer, keeping one eye on his father as he began talking with the mayor again.

I supposed that Dayton expected us to make a big deal of his arrival, or perhaps he wanted us to make a play publicly. I realized that was his weakness. He was too arrogant to think anyone would make moves against him without taking credit. While he was busy trying to draw attention and favor, we were making deals and sabotaging him right under his nose.

At the end of the day, Atticus didn't need the fanfare;

he just needed his father out of the picture so we could live the life we were creating. That was the reward in the end—the chance to live.

"How did it go?" Atticus whispered, his fingers tapping against my side as he gripped me.

"I improvised, but she's on board."

Atticus peered into my eyes intently for a moment before a smile spread across his face. "You always surprise me in the best ways, Bellezza." Leaning forward, our lips met, tuning out the rest of the room. I could relish in his kiss and everything it promised for a second.

Drawing back, he pulled me tighter to him, turning back to our guests. "Excuse us, newlyweds."

The mayor smiled, looking me over. It wasn't predatory but more assessing, as if he was measuring our worth in votes. "Congratulations to you both. Your husband was telling me about the fire at the youth center. It's devastating. I'd be interested in hearing more about how you're working to help our city's youth. Perhaps we can set up a meeting?"

I glanced at Atticus, a smile on his face as he peered down at me. It seemed we had both deviated from the original plan. "That would be lovely, thank you," I said, turning back to the man. "I'm very passionate about helping others." Smiling, I peeked at Gabriella, hoping she understood. I wouldn't go back on my word.

She whispered in his ear, and I watched as the man

became putty in her hands. I almost envied the skill, but I didn't really need it when I already had five husbands myself.

"It was lovely meeting you both. I look forward to hearing from you this week, Mr. and Mrs. Mascro. Please, excuse us." Gabriella winked as they walked away, his hands possessively over her. I hoped she would call and we could help her. She had spunk, and I liked that about her.

"Well, that's settled. How about we see if we can take out some trash?" Atticus asked, pulling my body to his.

"Hmm," I hummed, wrapping my arms around his neck. "I quite like the idea of dancing."

"Oh? If the lady wants to dance first, then we shall." Atticus took my hand from around his neck, spinning me out. The dress fluttered around me as I did, the cool silk rubbing against my body in the most delicious way. I eagerly returned to his arms, and we fell into an easy step, following along to the music. Every few beats, he'd spin me under his arm and then bring me back, making me feel like an actual princess at a ball.

"You never cease to amaze me, Lore."

I smiled; because one, I was out of breath, and two, what did you say to something that sweet? Some applause broke out when the song ended, and I blushed, realizing we'd had a crowd.

"It's all for you, Lore."

Atticus spun me out, and we did a bit of bow, and I

truly felt like my face was going to fall off from the amount of smiling I was doing. I felt so light and happy; I'd forgotten for a millisecond that we were actually here to remind Dayton he wasn't as powerful as he thought.

In order to take down Dayton, Atticus knew we had to do it on multiple fronts he wouldn't see coming. He'd expect us to come at him full force, plotting behind his back like he'd done to us. And while that was part of it, we were smarter.

Atticus wanted to change the Mascros for good, and this was the first step, by separating them from Dayton. We weren't just after Dayton; we wanted him to never be able to gain any following ever again. We couldn't just kill him; we had to destroy him for his legacy to die.

So, first, we'd embarrassed him and tarnished his name with the incident at the restaurant. His powerful allies would be questioning his power after that night.

Second, we'd donated all of his and Jacqueline's money to charities across the city, including a new youth center the mayor was interested in helping sponsor.

Third, we would take his business and stop him from gaining any footing in the criminal world. He might be able to work underground for some things, but for the empire he was building, there would be a lot of hands he'd need to grease to get his club opened now. Without any capital and the blockades we'd placed on the people he needed, we'd effectively stopped him from gaining any momentum, and ultimately, power.

He was stalled in the water. Which only left one more thing—the family.

Since we hadn't acknowledged his entrance the way he wanted, he made his way onto the dance floor, knocking people over as he charged toward us. I pushed my shoulders back and tilted my head high, knowing he wanted to see fear. He'd tried to intimidate me once and had been successful, but he wouldn't be this time. This time I was next to my men and knew what game he was playing.

At the thought of my husbands, I felt them trickle down next to us, standing at our back in solidarity. It didn't matter what Dayton thought, we were a united front, and nothing could break us.

"Did you need something, Dayton?" I asked, steeling myself to keep my voice steady. I couldn't falter now. I'd made it this far.

He sneered at me, not liking that I was the one talking. Which was precisely why I was. Atticus stared at his father indifferently, showing no emotion, and I could almost picture the others' faces. Dayton grew angrier the longer they continued to ignore him, making me even more confident in my assessment of him.

He would hate being spoken to by me, the inferior one of the group. The fact they weren't even showing emotion in his presence would also trigger him. Each little thing we did to chip away at his sanity brought us a step closer to his downfall, and he *would* fall. That was a guarantee.

"What? You think now that you're prime pussy, you're better than me?"

Tittering, I shook my head. "No, Dayton. I'm better than you because I'm a good person, unlike you. Now, you've made a scene by stopping the party, so please, tell us what you want. Otherwise, remove yourself from my vicinity."

My dismissal had him grinding his jaw, his fists unclenching as he attempted to rein in his emotion.

And this was where I shined. Dayton might think I was weak because of my profession and understanding of emotions, but he forgot one little thing. I was an expert. I knew the telltale signs better than anyone, and while he might've fooled me at first with his game in my office, I'd come to know his mannerisms very well, and right now, he was very close to exploding in rage.

This knowledge bolstered me, and I took a step forward. Atticus held onto my hand, attempting to pull me back, but I didn't falter. I felt the power of their love and faith in me coursing through my veins, giving me strength. This would be the last man to make me feel small.

"I'm sorry, I can't hear you. Did you say something?"

He gritted his teeth, muttering through them. I looked around the room, realizing it was now or never. The entire place watched, waiting with bated breath to see how it would unfold. Everyone liked a good show, it was time to give them one.

"Well, then. I guess you can leave, since you have nothing to say. Such a shame, since we had everyone here to listen."

He looked around, noticing the crowd, but it seemed to incense him enough to continue with whatever agenda he had.

"You know, it's been entertaining playing with you and my son, but I've grown tired, so I just wanted to come by and let you know that everything will be mine as of tomorrow." He grinned wide, a smug look on his face as he waited for us to implode.

"Oh? How do you expect that to happen?" I asked, crossing my arms. The men stepped up, apparently over me being closer to Dayton without them. It was enough to make him smirk like he had something figured out.

"You'll see," he said, keeping himself tight-lipped.

"Well, as fun as it would be to watch us prove you wrong, again, I'm growing bored of this conversation, so how about I just go ahead and tell you that won't be happening."

"And why is that?"

"The simple fact that the properties you're trying to overtake no longer belong to Atticus. Admit it, Dayton, you were outplayed. You have no money and you'll be the one with no assets or businesses as of tomorrow. The only thing you have left is your name, and let's face it, that's starting to be equated with a lunatic."

Dayton began to seethe, his face turning purple as the rage built in him. His eyes zeroed in on my ring, snapping him.

"There's no way you've done what you're claiming. Even if you had, I still have the family. They wanted me as their true leader!" he practically shouted.

"You sure about that, Dad?" Atticus asked, raising his eyebrow. "When I gave all the family members their rightful dues, they quickly returned to the fold. A few stubborn ones remained with you, but you'll see that you no longer have the men you thought. You're done."

"No, that's not possible." He shook his head, some of his earlier demeanor unraveling as the words sank in and the fear of what we were saying being true grew.

"You've been so busy focusing on us, you weren't even paying attention to your own family. What was it you always taught me? Hit them where it hurts. I think I've hit you now in all the sore spots. Did I miss anything?" Atticus turned to us, mimicking counting the things we'd taken from Dayton on his fingers. "Business, money, men, pride... Nope, I think that's it. What do you say, little brother?"

"Oh, I'd love to have the honor of escorting Daddy Dipshit off the premises." Nicco smiled wide, walking forward, and I stood with my head high as Dayton tried to figure out what was going on.

The two guards who'd entered with Dayton gripped his arms, and it was the final thing to seal our words in his mind, confirming everything, as his own men escorted him from the floor. He started to fling himself from side to side, and he managed to get an arm free, reaching for the gun in the guard's holster.

He turned, pointing it at me, and I stood, firm, unwavering. The last thing I noticed was the smile that spread across his face.

When the gun went off, I stared, not letting him know how scared I was we'd miscalculated, praying that everything wouldn't fall apart right at the end. The impact hit, hurting more than I'd imagined, but I fell with all the grace I could muster in my gorgeous gown.

More guards swarmed him, tackling him to the ground as the gun scattered across the floor that I'd just waltzed across. I laid there thinking of that one perfect moment as I closed my eyes for a second, taking a breath. When a hand smoothed the hair back from my face, I looked up into Nicco's gray-blue eyes, a smile on his face.

"You did great, Beautiful." He reached down, giving me a hand, and I clasped it, standing to my feet. I glanced down at the gunshot, the fabric torn from the bullet, and I thanked the heavens that the seamstress had been able to sew kevlar into the gown. Atticus hadn't wanted to take any chances this time, stating too many of us had already been shot, and no one had argued.

The others circled me, the gunshot being a little too real for them as we watched Dayton spiral out of control. He lost it when he saw me standing, going wilder, trying to find another gun. I tensed for a moment, worried he'd try to take a shot at one of the guys, our bet he'd try to take me out first, not playing out a second time. When the woman in red taffeta walked up, pressing a taser to his neck, I'd never felt prouder or more relieved.

We'd done it. Dayton Mascro had fallen.

TWENTY SEVEN

LOREN

E verything seemed to happen in a flurry of
movement as men took Dayton away, and the
party guests began to disperse after the chaos. Atticus,
Sax, and Nicco had to deal with the business side of
things, leaving Wells and Monroe with me. Cops
swarmed the area, but with the police chief present, it all
went smoothly, like we'd hoped.

Gabriella had walked over, squeezing my hand to
make sure I was really okay. "I see what you mean about
dangerous men," she said. "I thought you were dead,
and I realized how sad I was that I hadn't taken you up
on your offer. So, this is me asking for your help."

I gave her a hug, thanking her for stepping in and
tasering Dayton. She left quickly after with the Mayor,
stating she'd be in touch, and this time, I knew she
would be. Wells hadn't left my side since we'd been
released from questioning, holding me close to him as

we sat on a couch. Monroe was on my other side, softly caressing my hand.

"Do you really think it's over?" Monroe whispered like he was too afraid to ask it out loud.

"I think so. I'm not sure how he could recover from this. We took everything he held dear. To a man like Dayton, that's equivalent to death."

"Regardless, we're done," Wells stated firmly. "No one else will be put into harm's way for that man. I don't care that you were protected. It felt too real, Kitten."

"It was the best option, Wells. You know that. And in front of all these witnesses, including the police chief, there's no way for him to weasel his way out." Even though I was the one saying it, I couldn't help but wonder if it was true. Part of me had to believe it, or I'd go insane with worry. Dayton had to be dealt with. We all needed the reprieve.

"We're done," Atticus said, stopping in front of our huddle. "Let's head home." He reached his hand out, and I realized how much had been lifted off his shoulders tonight. Taking his hand, I let him pull me up, the other two following. Together, the three of us walked out, meeting Nicco and Sax at the door.

Walking out into the cool night, I stopped and took a deep breath, filling my lungs. Opening my eyes, I looked at all my guys, feeling like things had cemented between us. We'd been to war together, most of us having battle scars to show for it, but we'd come out the other side stronger, together.

Atticus opened the door, and I smiled, scooting into the dark limo. The men followed, and we all sat in silence as the car took off.

Sax leaned close, whispering in my ear. "I happen to recall you telling me about a certain list you had and limo sex being on it. Now's your chance to see if you can make that wish come true." His breath cascaded over the curve of my neck, sending tingles all over me. Sucking in a breath as the words penetrated my mind, I rubbed my legs together in anticipation. It felt wrong, but also like the culmination of life to celebrate with a group orgy.

I glanced over at Atticus, finding him watching me. Sax started to unzip the back of my dress, deciding for me. I knew if I said stop, he would, but I also appreciated him taking the lead before I talked myself out of it.

My eyes lifted, meeting Nicco, Wells, and Monroe on the bench seat. The three of them eagerly watched as Sax kissed down my throat, waiting for a signal from me. Licking my lips, I pulled my dress down, the top falling easily.

"Fuck, Bellezza," Atticus groaned, causing me to turn to him. His eyes were heated and focused on my breasts. I watched as he rubbed himself on the outside of his pants, the growing hardness becoming visible the longer he stroked himself.

A gasp had me looking up and over to the guys.

Before I could investigate, Sax's lips sealed over my breast, making my eyes roll back as he sucked my nipple hard, biting it a little. The remainder of my dress was removed, and I found myself in only my panties as two bodies next to me began to kiss and fondle me. Remembering the three across from me, I opened my eyes to find Monroe on his knees, sucking Wells' cock into his mouth as Nicco and Wells kissed one another passionately.

When Sax's finger found my clit, it was a battle to give in to the pleasure I felt while watching the show in front of me. Atticus gave in to his desire, stripping his clothes off as he moved me into his lap. With Sax's help, they brought me to a quick orgasm as everything crashed around me, and I found them lifting me onto a cock, the sudden fullness taking me by surprise.

Opening my eyes, I began to bounce as I rode Atticus facing outward, and found the men across from me had also removed their clothes. They moved closer to me, bringing all the men I loved within reach. Sax was licking up my core as Atticus made small thrusts. It was apparently too close for comfort for Atticus as he grunted, shifting me.

"I have a better idea." His voice had Sax peering up, a satisfied look on his face, and I wondered how much of this he'd orchestrated. My sexual escapades were constantly being expanded between him and Nicco—not that I was complaining. Nope, not one bit.

Atticus lifted me off him, and everyone moved, letting the mafia boss have his control. He scooted into the center of the seat we'd been on, reaching into a compartment I hadn't known was there and pulling out a bottle. When I looked closer, I realized it was lube, and I swallowed. My eyes heated a little, and I glanced up, locking them with Atticus'.

"We got you, Bellezza." At his words, Sax took the bottle and began to prep my asshole. My body tensed until Nicco moved next to Atticus, much to his dismay.

"Keep your metal dick to yourself, Brother. I don't need you touching me with that thing."

"Ah, Big Bro, are you scared mine might be better?" Nicco teased, winking at me.

"Hell, no," he growled, moving closer to me. "You can do whatever you want to yourself, but it doesn't mean I want to be close to it." Nicco laughed before finally giving in to Atticus' wishes.

"Fair enough, Bro." He leaned in, acting like he would kiss Atticus' cheek, before detouring and kissing mine. Atticus swatted at him, making a high-pitched sound I wouldn't believe could come from him if I hadn't watched him make it. Everyone laughed, and it seemed to ease the tension that we were all about to have sex together as a sixsome.

Shit. I was about to have sex with five people at once. Okay, now that was a lot of dick to control.

"Stop thinking, Spitfire. Just relax." Sax said, soothing

me with his big hands. Leaning more into Atticus, he used his hands to distract me. Once he was occupied with my nipples, Nicco pulled my face to his, giving me a long and deep kiss. My hand snaked out, finding his pierced cock, and I gently rubbed it, my fingers skating over the piercings.

Rubbing my thumb over the tip, I teased him gently with touches as I lost myself in our kiss. Another body settled on the other side of Atticus, much to his displeasure. He grunted, and I could almost imagine him squinting as he moved his leg to not touch another man.

Breaking my kiss, I turned my head, finding Wells sitting next to me, using some of the lube to prep Monroe. That was when I realized that Sax had pressed his thumb into me, lowering me onto Atticus' waiting dick. I gasped with both sensations at once, my eyes closed tight as I tried to adjust to the feeling. Monroe's groan had me opening my eyes, and I watched as he lowered himself on Wells. The act had me swallowing at how hot it was to watch two men I loved enjoying each other.

He leaned back when he was seated, letting Wells take control, and I watched as the pleasure racked his body. Atticus began to thrust deeper as Sax worked more fingers into me, getting me comfortable with the girth I was about to experience. I tried not to focus on that and only on the enjoyment I saw in my two husbands.

Nicco pulled my face back to his, wanting to be in on

the fun. We all found a rhythm, and I reached a hand out to grab Monroe's dick as it twitched. Being connected to all of them at once felt powerful, like I could feel the love from all of us seeping into us from our connection.

When Sax pushed his cock in a few minutes later, I was ready and welcomed him. The tight feeling of them both was too much, and I erupted when Nicco reached down, despite Atticus' growl, to flick my clit. My body spasmed, causing Atticus to lose himself, sputtering his cum up in me with one last powerful thrust.

"My turn," Nicco demanded when Atticus stilled.

He rolled his eyes but didn't deny his brother. Except when he opened his eyes, he narrowed them at Nicco. "Move your dick first. I don't want any part of you to touch me if it's not necessary."

I couldn't help but smile at how much it unnerved him. I wasn't sure if it was because they were brothers or if it was just anyone who wasn't Sax, but it brought me great enjoyment all the same.

"Fine," Nicco huffed, moving over to the other seat, so Atticus scooted out and over without any accidental cock touching.

I glanced over at Monroe and Wells and realized they'd even stopped to watch Atticus. Monroe winked at me, and the giggle I'd been trying to hold back fell from my lips, setting off the others.

"It's not funny," he huffed, making us laugh more. Nicco swooped in once the coast was clear, wasting no time to slide up in me with his studded dick. One moment I was laughing, and the next, a strangled moan was leaving my lips as I adjusted to him.

When he grabbed Wells' face and smashed their lips together while he thrust up into me, it was all I could do to hold on and not combust on the spot. Sax grabbed my hips, pushing himself in me further as he fucked my ass. The two of them found a rhythm, and I was cresting my next orgasm within minutes. Monroe was close as well, his labored breathing cluing me in, so I reached over, tugging on his balls as we both fell over the edge.

Sax came as well, erupting with a loud groan as he held me to him, pumping his cum into me. Nicco took the opportunity to twist us when he pulled out, so I was now sitting facing the others instead of lying on him. Atticus had his clothes half on, but I noticed he hadn't done up his pants, and I wondered if he was finding himself hardening again from the show.

"Wells, show our girl how good your tongue is," Nicco demanded. I expected Wells to say no, but instead, he smirked, dropping to his knees to lick up my pussy while Nicco fucked me from behind with abandon. The two of them worked well together, and I somehow reached that cliff again, my body spent from the activities.

Stars erupted, my body tensed, and I almost blacked out as I came again.

"Shit, okay, I'm done. I think I'll die if I cum again."

"Sounds like a challenge," Nicco said, nipping my neck. "But I'm spent too, so you're safe tonight."

Laughing, I weakly looked around the limo, the smell of sex and sweat in the air. Everyone was leaning back, relaxed as we all caught our breath. Shirts were left unbuttoned, and some hadn't even bothered to put their clothes back on yet.

"How much longer until we're home?" I asked around a yawn.

Atticus laughed, drawing my attention. "We've been back for about twenty minutes."

"Really?" I asked, then laughed. "Well, I don't even care that they all know we defiled this limo. It was on my list, dammit!"

The guys broke out in laughter, the feeling of right-ness settling around us. We eventually got dressed and headed inside. I stopped by and checked on the kids. It was too much of a habit now, to make sure everyone was where they were supposed to be, to not stop.

Their sweet faces were why I was willing to take a bullet tonight. No one messed with my loved ones. I'd fight until I couldn't fight to save them. I was a mom now, and that meant something to me. I think Dayton finally understood just why a woman's love was the most powerful emotion in the world.

TWENTY EIGHT

LOREN

Life fell into a normal balance after the secrets party. It was now the end of May, and school was ending. I debated how much time I wanted to take off for the summer. I wanted to be able to do things with the kids and maybe even go on a vacation. We all seemed to adjust easily as we began to pick up the pieces of our lives that Dayton had tried to demolish.

"What are you thinking?" a voice asked, bringing me out of my musings.

I looked up from the computer; the last note I'd been writing was waiting for me to hit submit on the screen. Holding up a finger, I finalized everything and turned it off, gathering my stuff. It was much easier now when all I had to grab was my phone, and half the time I forgot that.

Smiling, I walked over to Sax, who'd come to escort me to dinner. They'd learned quickly that if someone didn't come to get me, I had a tendency to keep working or lose time staring off into space like I'd just been doing. Apparently, when your mind was always focused on thinking for others, it found any second it could to think.

When I didn't answer him, honestly having forgotten what he'd asked, he stopped us, pushing me back against the wall. Towering over me, he peered down at me in concern. His thumb trailed across my cheek, and he searched my eyes.

Despite it being a month later, they were all still concerned I wasn't handling the takedown well. Granted, I'd been shot, but it hadn't been real. Not really.

"I'm okay. Sorry, what did you ask me? I was lost in my thoughts of frolicking somewhere on a warm beach that isn't Chicago."

Sax relaxed at my words, a smile gracing his lips. "That sounds nice. Tell me more, Spitfire."

"Well, I was wondering how much time I wanted to take off for the summer and if we could go on a trip, along with all the other things I'd like to do with the kids. Levi is at that fun age where he wants to explore things, and Jude and Immy have their own interests that I'd like to know more about. It's just nice having people to plan things with," I admitted, my cheeks tinting a little.

"The sight of you in a swimsuit sounds good to me. Even better, not in one." Laughing, I slapped his chest playfully before giving him a kiss. Stepping back, I grabbed his hand, pulling him along with me. Now that I knew it was dinnertime, my stomach had gotten the memo and was hungry, wanting food.

"You can see me naked after you feed me," I said, tugging him along. Sax grunted a little but let me pull him.

We walked into the new family room that Atticus had designed. It wasn't as formal and stuffy as the other one, thankfully. The table was a large circle with another circle in the middle that we could put food on and spin. It made it easy with nine people to serve on a regular basis. The kids, along with Wells and Monroe, were already gathered around the table, scooping food onto their plates.

I never thought I'd be one of those people who'd have a personal chef, but now that we did, I didn't know if I could ever live without Mrs. Carlson. She definitely made life easier, cooking for all of us. In fact, I was pretty sure I'd gained a few pounds from her delicious meals as well.

Sitting down, I kissed Levi on the head as I pulled him into a hug. "Hey, kiddo, how was the last day of school?"

He beamed up at me as he excitedly began to tell me all about their field day and the prizes he'd won. I was surprised how well he'd taken his mother's death. I think it helped that he had the older kids to lean on as well. They'd lost parents, too, so they were a good source of comfort for the boy.

"Wow, that sounds like a lot of fun," I said, smiling at him.

"It was the best." His face turned sad, and I wondered if this was the moment it hit him that his mother was gone.

"What's wrong, bud?" I asked, playing with this hair.

He shrugged his tiny shoulders, looking up. "I just wish you were my mommy."

I stopped, stunned for a moment, scrunching up my face. "I'm confused. Why do you think I can't be? I know I'll never replace your mom, but I could be a bonus mom for you if that's alright?"

"Really?" he asked, his eyes lighting up for a second before his face dropped. "That's okay. I know that Jude needs you to be his mommy. I just wanted you to know I wish you could be mine, too."

Pulling him close, I snuggled down to understand where the confusion was coming from. "Levi, is there a reason you think I can't be yours too, bud?"

"Landon at school said you'd have to choose. He also said that I couldn't have five daddies, even though Jude told me I did now. Since I still have a daddy, I didn't want to be selfish and keep you. Jude needs you," he whispered, keeping his eyes low.

"Ah, buddy, whoever this Landon kid is, well, he's wrong. Did you know that our hearts are capable of loving lots of people? It's not a limited thing. I can love you and Jude the same amount. It doesn't ever run out.

So, I can be your bonus mommy and Jude's, and you can have five daddies if you want. Our family is about acceptance and love. Okay, kiddo?"

"Really?" he asked, his little shoulders dropping in relief.

"Really. Which means you and Jude are brothers."

His eyes lit up, and I realized how poorly we'd handled this talk with everything going on. Levi threw his arms around me, hugging me tightly. He kissed my cheek. "Love you, Lommy."

"Lommy?" I asked, wondering if he had developed a sudden speech impediment.

"Yep. It's Lo and mommy—Lommy." My heart was about to burst, so I snuggled him close. When I let go, he jumped off my lap and ran around the table to Jude.

"Jude, we're brothers. For real!" Levi shouted, causing everyone to stop what they were doing. Jude looked up, a question in his eyes, but I nodded, hoping he'd understand.

"That's awesome, little man. Secret shake time." They fell into their secret handshake, slapping their palms together in varying motions, before shouting, "Misfit Penguins."

Laughing, I fell into the arm that wrapped around me from the other side as I wiped my tears. Wells kissed my head, and I let him give me some of his comfort for a moment. At times, my heart was so full that I wondered if it would spill over and burst.

Once everyone settled, Levi returned to his seat, and we continued eating. Nicco and Atticus came in a few minutes later, kissing me before taking the open spots. The nice thing about this table was that there wasn't any hierarchy here. We were just a family, eating together. The guys had fallen into an easy acceptance that Atticus was the boss in most other areas of their lives, but when we were in our family spaces, it wasn't that way, making it equal for all of them to have a say.

However, there were still some actions we adopted when Atticus was around. For instance, roll call had become one of my favorite things we did. With a family our size now, it was important for each member to get a chance to speak, and this allowed us to do so.

"How was everyone's day?" Attie asked, looking around. We all nodded as he buttered a piece of bread. "Who's turn is it to start roll call tonight?" he asked. Levi eagerly raised his hand, earning a soft smile from the mafia boss.

"Okay, Levi, hit us with your day." And just like that, we fell into our dinner conversation as we ate.

"I beat Lily in the 50-meter dash," he said, earning a lot of congratulations.

"Well done," Atticus replied, patting him on the head from his seat. From there, it was my turn.

"I had some really good sessions today, and I thought that we should all go on a vacation this summer if everyone agrees." I looked up to meet Atticus' eyes and found him smiling at me. He nodded once, letting me know it would be safe for us to do so. "So, start thinking about some places you kids would like to visit. Give us your best suggestions, and then we'll all decide. Sound good?" The kids all nodded, their faces full of excitement.

"My day wasn't as exciting," Nicco started, giving me a wink, "but the new youth center is almost completed. It looks like we'll make it in time for the grand opening next week after all."

Applause went around for that news, everyone having been involved in the development and decisions of the new place. Jude and Immy had helped out a lot since they were still homeschooled and had free time after tutoring.

"Yes, I'm so excited for everyone to see the things we've done," Jude added, raising his fist to bump Nicco's over the table. "I'll add that Immy and I completed our Junior year today and are officially Seniors."

More cheers and slaps went around at the news, congratulating the two. "Did you decide where you wanted to go to school next year?" I asked after swallowing some food. They'd been debating if they wanted to return to the school Jude had attended before the kidnapping or start somewhere new together.

Immy nodded, a smile on her face. "Yeah, we want to give Timber Valley a shot." She took a drink, trying to hide her blush, and I wondered what that was about. "My day was good. I spent it finishing some plans at the youth center and taking my last final. I also played a new piece of music today."

"Oh! Will you play it for us later?" I asked, wanting to hear how she got on with her music. It was no longer a trigger for her, and she'd started to play more and more, her love of the instrument returning.

"Sure." She smiled, her blush returning.

Wells cleared his throat, helping to switch the attention to him. "I have that practice match this weekend. I'm feeling confident about my prospects and winning. Nicco and I have solidified a solid training regime to help me win."

"I want to go!" Levi said, bouncing in his seat.

"Sorry, little dude. It's past your bedtime. I'll record it, though, and let you watch it after."

"Ah, man. I want to be older, so I can do the cool stuff." He fell back into his chair, sulking a little.

"You'll be older soon enough, Levi," Monroe said, ruffling his hair as he reached around Atticus. "I had a good day meeting with the teams and getting our business in order. I also had the preliminary meeting with Jacqueline's lawyer." I tightened my grip on the fork at her name, taking a deep breath. The hearing was soon, and I was ready for it to be over with. Maybe after that was when we would go on a trip. That sounded like a great idea, actually.

"That leaves you, Sax," Levi said, looking over at the big man. I think he was both fascinated and a little scared of Sax, but he had a solid case of hero worship going on for the big man.

"Humph," he grunted, setting his fork down. He cracked his knuckles a little, looking over at Levi as he answered. "I dealt with some bad people and reminded them who was in charge. I also got my new guitar in, so I played a little on it."

"Oh? I can't wait to hear that," I said, fluttering my eyelashes at him. Something about Sax playing guitar was always a surefire way to get me hot and bothered.

"So it seems we have the youth center opening in a week, the fight, and then our wedding celebration at the end of summer. Perhaps after the court hearing would be a perfect time to go on that vacation, Bellezza?" Atticus asked, looking over at me.

"You read my mind." I smiled, appreciating his thoughtfulness. "So, where do we think we should go?"

The rest of the meal was spent with everyone lobbying ideas of perfect getaways from Disney World to the Grand Canyon. I realized I didn't really care where we ended up, just as long as we all went together.

TWENTY NINE

LOREN

The gavel banging down sent a shiver through me, and I felt as if the last weight pressing down on me had lifted as the words left the Judge's lips. "The court finds Jacqueline Hanover guilty of all charges."

I didn't need to hear the rest. It didn't matter when her sentencing hearing was or what they sought fit to punish her with. The words I needed to hear had just been spoken, validating everything I'd gone through and felt for years.

And now I was officially free of her manipulations. Jacqueline Hanover would no longer have any say in my life. In fact, she would no longer have any space in my head or heart. She was guilty, and that was all I needed to know.

"Loren, you ready?" Monroe asked, nudging me. Silently, I nodded, standing with him as we left the courtroom. News reporters stood outside the closed doors, waiting for a response from us. I ignored them, not having the energy to deal with being polite. Sax met us and helped block the crowd with his frame, effectively moving us quickly through the hallways and out the back door down the stairs. An SUV was waiting when we exited the courthouse, and I eagerly slid in.

A sigh of relief left me as I sat back, a huge smile spreading across my face as the other two climbed in. "It's done. Jacqueline will be held responsible for her crimes, and I will never have to see, speak, or think of her again. I'm finally free."

Monroe picked up my hand, kissing it. "You are, Lo. I'm so proud of you. You were so strong today."

"That was some pretty impressive lawyer mumbo jumbo you said up there," Sax added, teasing his new buddy. I loved how the guys were making their own relationships with each other and finding some commonality between themselves. Sax and Monroe were two of the most opposite men on paper but had found a connection, and I loved the bromance they had going on.

Atticus still held himself back from the others somewhat, only letting Sax in, but I saw him softening and knew that he'd learn to trust the others just as much, as the years passed. Years. I liked the sound of that.

"Why, thank you, muscles. You held up that wall well, scaring anyone who dared look at us funny."

Sax puffed up his chest, nodding in agreement. "You hear that, Spitfire? Goldie thinks I'm muscular. I can't wait to tell Grumpy."

Chuckling, I leaned against Monroe, letting him support me for the ride. He'd said I'd been strong, but it was only because I knew I had them supporting me. It was much easier carrying the weight of your burdens and others when they were spread out. When we pulled up to a building, I didn't know a few minutes later, I looked at them, confused.

"Why are we here?"

Neither responded and before I could grill them more, the door opened, answering my question.

"Girl! Get out of the car. It's pampering time. No dicks allowed. Come on!" Nat demanded, tugging on my hand.

"Go, Lo. The whole place is rented out. It's the bachelorette party you never got to have. We figured you could use some relaxation after today, and then later, you're going to Climax, where we'll meet you," Monroe explained, kissing the tip of my nose.

I hadn't thought I had any energy in me, but the thought of hanging with my friends and dancing later with my guys had me kissing them both before I bounded out of the car. As soon as I was free of the vehicle, Nat tugged me and pulled me into the spa.

Stacy, Pixel, Cami, and Lark stood inside, waiting for us. They cheered and placed a pink sash over me and a crown when I entered. Pulling it away from my chest, I read the words inscribed on it. 'Lucky Bitch.'

Laughing, I noticed the others had them as well.

Cami's said 'Loud and Crazy,' Lark's 'More than my looks,' Pixel's 'Smarter than you,' Stacy's 'Small and Feisty,' and Nat's 'The one you should worry about.'

"Oh my goodness, these are great. I didn't realize how much I needed this until I was right here. Thank you, guys. You're all the absolute best friends I could ever ask for."

"But I'm your favorite, right?" Nat asked, winking.

"God, I've missed you," I said, pulling her into a hug. They'd completed their mission with the O'Sullivans, but I hadn't seen them much since. I knew they were working on something new, but they'd all been hush-hush about it. She tugged me toward a room where attendants waited next to tables for all of us.

"Massages first, then facials, and then mani/pedis. It's a full spa treatment! Now, strip!" Nat said, slapping my butt.

The girls chuckled, but we all did as she said, going behind our screens to discard our clothes. "Too bad we can't get massaged with our sashes on," Stacy hollered, and we all laughed, realizing the same thing.

"Yes, but they'll be there later," Nat reassured.

Once we were all settled, the conversation fell away as our bodies began to be massaged and oiled until we felt like limp noodles. The forty-five minutes went by fast, and we were soon led to the next room in fluffy robes, where we sat in laid-back chairs.

"So, Stacy, are things going well with you and

Topher?" I asked, realizing I hadn't heard the latest gossip.

"It honestly depends on the day of the week," she sighed, and I wished I could've looked over to see her facial expression.

"Oh? That doesn't sound good," Lark piped in.

"It's just, he'll go days without responding to me, and sometimes I won't even see him for weeks at a time. When we're together, it's good, like so good, but I wonder if he has a secret family or something."

The crazy thing was he did in a way, but not the type she was worried about.

"He does work a lot. I bet it's just that. He doesn't seem like the type to string you along," I offered. The others were quiet, knowing it was a hard line to walk with how much we told Stacy. She was the only one still on the outside. I knew she suspected something, but probably like me initially, it was easier not to guess the truth.

Deniability and all that.

"Yeah? I guess that's good to hear then. Maybe I'll just ask him. It can't hurt anything."

We all fell quiet, and I wanted to kick myself for ruining the good mood. Searching for a safe topic, I decided to pull Lark and Cami under my bus of desperation. "So, Lark and Cami, how is your wedding planning going?"

"Funny you should ask that," Lark said, her voice

strained. "It's temporarily on hold. There's been a few adjustments we're all trying to figure out."

"Does that adjustment happen to go by the name of Malek and have the cutest little girl?" I asked.

"Ugh," Cami groaned. Apparently, I'd hit another sore subject among my friends.

"Okay, okay. Forget I asked."

"No, it's not that. You're right; it's just... it's complicated," Cami said, offering no more.

"Well, I'm here if you need to talk about it."

"Thanks, Loren," they both said, and I heard the love between them.

"Okay, Nat, Pixel, anything interesting in your life where I won't stick my foot in my mouth?" I asked, chuckling.

The assistant moved over, peeling the mask off, wiping my face down as she did, and we all quieted for a moment as we gained control of our facial muscles again. Once our pores had been opened and purged, we were sat up, and the little baths at the bottom began to be filled. It made it easier to talk, and I could see my friends' faces this way.

Glancing over, I raised my eyebrows, waiting for them to answer. Nat sighed, shaking her head. "I'm good. Lily keeps bugging me to come to see Levi, so maybe we can set something up for the summer?"

Nodding, I smiled, liking that I got to plan playdates. "Of course. I'm thinking of only working a few days during the week over the summer so I can have more time to do things with the kids, and we're even planning a vacation."

"Ah, that sounds like fun," the girls said, some of the fun coming back into the party. I guess I just needed to talk about myself more. But I couldn't let her get away with not answering what I really wanted to know.

"Byron and Beau? How's the double B life treating you?"

"Not going to let it go, are you?" she asked, smiling.

"Absolutely not. You once told me to 'spill the deets for my peeps' if I remember correctly. Well, we're all your peeps, so dish!"

The girls chuckled, all eagerly looking at her to share. Her cheeks blushed a little, and I realized it wasn't that things were going bad for my friend but good, and that scared her.

"They're both good. We're still figuring out how to be a threesome, but I think they respect one another despite their bickering. The job we had to do," she said, clearing her throat, "was good for them. Lily adores them both, and my mom keeps telling me to stop being an idiot and move in together. I'm just not sure I'm ready to lose that independence yet."

And there it was.

"Oh, Nat. It's okay to be scared, but I don't think you have to be. I've seen both men around you, and they worship the ground you walk on. They've both waited years for you to be ready, taking whatever morsel of yourself you would give them. They're not going to run away, and they've shown they're not Mason. Trust your heart. It's a good one."

Her eyes were watering a little as she nodded at me, accepting what I had to say. "Despite you going all therapist on me, I appreciate what you said. Thanks, Lor. I'll definitely think about it more."

Smiling, I reached over, clasping her hand. "Love you, girl."

"Ah, you're going to make me cry," Stacy said, shooing away the tears around her eyes.

"Well, good. Because I love you all." They all beamed at me, and I held onto this feeling of true friendship, knowing that it was a rare commodity I didn't want to ever take for granted.

"Pixel, anyone you got your eyes on?" I asked, bringing the conversation back around. She shrugged, a coy look on her face.

"Too early to tell." She didn't elaborate, and I realized I still needed to hang out with her more. Pixel had been quiet since she'd returned, and I wondered what that was all about.

"Oh, Lor," Nat started, but was interrupted when the women all stood, declaring us done. I blinked, not realizing they'd been working that long on our hands and feet for me to space out.

"Ladies, if you'll follow us, we have the last area for you."

I raised my eyebrow at Nat, who shrugged. "I thought it was over."

Some apprehension began to build, and I worried we were being led into a trap. I reached for my bracelet but realized I'd taken it off when we'd gotten undressed. Reaching into my pocket, I searched for my phone, but it was also missing. Shit. Were we about to be ambushed?

Shrieks filled the space as the girls entered before me, and I tensed, wondering what danger lay behind the door. Walking through, I took a deep breath, remembering I wasn't a coward, nor would I let my friends deal with the shit alone. Pushing my shoulders back, I stepped into the room, preparing to take down whatever threat lay ahead.

Which turned out not to be the threat I'd imagined, but a scary sight all the same.

THIRTY

LOREN

"**W**hy does it have to be so pink?" I asked, looking down at the dress I'd been given to wear with disdain. "This is so not my signature color."

Nat snorted but ignored my complaints as the limo pulled up to Climax. We had our sashes back on, and we were all decked out in hot pink bodycon dresses. It wasn't a horrible dress outside of the color. A team of makeup artists and hairstylists had perfected our looks, and I was amazed at how fast they'd worked. Dinner had been catered in while we were getting pampered, so we were able to nibble on things between hair and makeup turns.

Overall, it had been a fun day, and now we were headed to the evening entertainment. I always enjoyed my time at Climax, especially when it ended with sexy times with one, or more, of my men. I didn't want to admit I was anxious to see them all, having gotten used to seeing them all the time now. These past few hours had felt weird without one of them nearby.

"Cheer up, Lor. It's not that bad," Cami said, nudging me.

Rolling my eyes, I pasted a smile on my face. "I'll remember this, you know. What's your least favorite color? I will dress you in it and see how you like it."

Lark laughed, shaking her head. "I'm sure Cami can rock anything, but she'd probably be more down with no clothing."

The girls laughed, and Cami shrugged, not denying it, but I caught the faint sign of discomfort and wondered how she was doing with everything post-Darren. It sobered me a little, and I realized that wearing hot pink with my friends to celebrate my marriage wasn't horrible. I was grateful we made it to this point, actually.

"Fine, you're right. I do look good, don't I?"

Everyone nodded, and we managed to climb out with no flashing accidents. Once we were clear of the limo, I realized how odd it looked outside. "There's no line," I stated, blinking.

"Duh," Cami said, grabbing my arm and pulling me. "You really think your husbands would let random men stare at you when they can control it?" She gave me a look like I was dumb for even considering it.

"I mean..." I started, but then realized how right she was. "Okay, you're right." Laughing, I smiled, knowing how loved I was.

We stepped through the door, a guard I'd seen around before nodding in deference to me as we passed. It was still weird to think I was their Queen, or whatever.

Now that we weren't under attack, things had settled down in the mafia world, and I hardly even knew what was happening. It was more for my own sanity than anything. Atticus had tried to include me, but it was better for me to step back, since my family was safe.

The hallway was dark as usual as we made our way deeper into the club, and I wondered which side we'd be entering tonight—Illusion or Verity. Images of what happened the last time I'd been in Verity began to play through my mind, and my body responded in accordance—my nipples tightened, and my core began to throb. Shit, hopefully, my husbands would be near soon, or I might orgasm from memory alone.

Cami and Lark directed us to the Verity side, and when we entered, I had to stop to make sure we were in the right place. In the middle of the club, a stage had been built with a pole on one end. It looked similar to the one from the Obsession room now that I thought about it.

"What is this?" I asked, looking around at the others. A few people were working at the bar, but for the most part, it was empty.

"Sit down and find out. The show's about to start," Nat said, beaming at me. She was practically jumping in her heels, she was so excited. The six of us sat down in an extended couch area that was set up at the front of the stage. The moment we were planted, drinks were delivered to the table in front of us, and the lights dimmed. I knew someone was watching us from somewhere, and I wondered again if it was any of my husbands.

The music started, and neon lights flashed on the stage as the girls whooped and hollered for the show to begin. I was still too stunned to relax, so I grabbed the drink and took a big swallow. The cold liquid rushed down my throat, the bite of alcohol almost drowned out by the sweetness of the fruit.

"Mmm, what is this?" I asked, turning to Cami.

She'd been watching me, so I wondered if she had a hand making the drink. "It's the Lady of the Manor. I made it just for you, per Atticus' request. Do you like it?"

My face heated, and I nodded, taking another sip. "It's really good. I'm going to be in trouble if I don't slow down."

"That's kind of the point," Nat whispered, leaning close to my side. "Let go, girl! It's your bachelorette night in reverse."

"I don't know what that means, but okay. You're right. I haven't had a true day off in forever, and it would feel nice to not worry about everything for one night." Lifting my glass, I tapped it to hers. "Cheers."

"That's my girl!" She kissed my cheek, and we laughed at the silliness. It felt nice to let loose. I should probably do this more often.

"Welcome, ladies. Tonight, you'll be entertained by some of our best performers. Enjoy!" a voice said over the speakers. It sounded familiar, and by the way Nat did a full-body shiver; I'd guess it was Byron's.

"Looks like someone is here," I teased, and she took a sip, blushing.

Before I could tease her more, smoke began to fill the area as a man walked out. When the song started playing, the girls cheered. I felt a little out of the loop at their easy recognition, but I sat up, eager to see what they were excited about. The body began to dance to the rhythm, and I had to appreciate how well they could move. The light fell on them when the song started, and I realized it was Nicco. His lips began moving to the words, and I finally understood what was happening. He was doing one of those lip sync battles we'd watched on TV the other week.

As the song played, he danced his heart out, making us laugh and giggle as he got into the words, portraying the iconic "Single Ladies" dance.

When it finished, we all stood, applauding his efforts. He strutted over, jumped off the stage, and pulled me into his arms.

"That was not the dance I was expecting, but I loved it nonetheless. In fact, I think it was better. I don't really want anyone else seeing your body but me," I whispered.

"Why do you think we opted to embarrass ourselves? We don't want you looking at other men, Beautiful."

"Well, I'm glad we're on the same page." I kissed him when what he said sunk in. "Oh, please tell me that you're all going to do this?" My eyes rounded as I waited for him to answer me.

Nicco smiled, his eyes even getting in on the action. "Not just us, but Beau, Byron, Topher, and even Seb. If we were going to embarrass ourselves, they also had to."

Laughing, I kissed him again, pulling him toward the couch to sit with us. Nicco obliged, dragging me into his lap as the next performer came out. When the fog cleared, we found Seb lip-singing a classic Dolly Parton song. "He pulls off the boobs," I whispered to Cami, laughing. She and Lark were in tears as they watched him prance around the stage with his balloons.

Over the next hour, we were entertained by Monroe, Wells, Topher, Beau, and Byron. The only two left were Sax and Atticus, and I had to say, I was the most eager to see the both of them. This was so out of character, I had no idea what to expect. It seemed Sax was up first. The music started, showing us his back as he tapped his foot to the music, and I lost it.

He had on a long wig, and when he turned around to sing, it was everything. He belted out, "Natural Woman," making anyone who would dare give him grief about it think twice because his performance was so good. I never thought the giant of a man, who often wore a scowl, could perform and move so well. We all stood when he hit his final pose, clapping and bowing in his honor. He tossed his wig over his shoulder and strutted off stage with all the grace of a diva.

"I don't know how anyone could top that," I said around a wheeze. We'd learned after the second one that we had to score them as well and pick a winner. It was apparently the only thing that made them all take it seriously. They wanted the bragging rights.

I'd had a few drinks by this point, so I was feeling good and enjoying the evening. To be honest, it was the best bachelorette party I could've ever hoped for.

We all started to cheer when the next song started, already loving it. When Atticus came out on stage, my jaw fell open, and I wondered if my heart had stopped. Nicco pushed it up, mimicking that he was wiping some drool.

"I don't even care. That's hot."

The men laughed at me, having replaced the girls around me as their guys finished and joined us. Atticus was in tight jeans and a white tank-top, rocking the iconic Freddy Mercury look as he lip-synced along to "Bohemian Rhapsody." We were all shouting it out by the end of the song, singing along with the music as we danced in our section. Clapping loudly, we roared our applause as he took his bow and joined us at the foot of the stage.

"So, Bellezza, who's the winner?"

"Like I could choose." I laughed, shaking my head. "I loved every single one of them because it was you all. Thank you, this was the best night ever."

Atticus smiled, walking over and pulling me to him, kissing my lips as music started to play over the speakers. The six of us were in our own little bubble for a few moments as we danced and laughed, reminiscing our favorite parts from their performances.

"You happy, Lore?" Atticus asked me a few minutes later as I snuggled down into his embrace.

"The most happiest," I said, kissing his chest.

"I'm glad."

The girls all began to break off, leaving with their significant others, and I felt bad for Pixel when I realized everyone else had paired up. When I looked around the space, I found her talking to one of the bartenders, easing my guilt slightly.

"Come on, let's go home, Wife."

Saying my goodbyes, I hugged my friends, thanking them for the perfect night. As we stepped out through the back door, reality crashed into us again. There was no such thing as a night off in the mafia.

THIRTY ONE

SAX

I mmediately, I pushed Loren back as I surveyed the area. It was doubtful anyone was still here, but I wouldn't take the chance. The past month had been too quiet, and I'd been waiting for something to happen. Atticus had told me to calm down, but it wasn't in my nature.

"Take Loren back into the club," I said, knowing Monroe and Wells would listen. Once the door closed, I pulled out my phone and called the police chief. We couldn't let this go unreported. Even if it didn't point any fingers, I wouldn't let Dayton think he got one over on us.

"It's late. This better be important," he sighed into the phone.

"It is. Send one police car down to Climax. No lights. Tell them to come around to the back. This needs to be done the right way, but without any media attention. Got it?"

"Yeah, yeah." I could hear him moving, and it was enough for me to know he'd do what I asked. Hanging up the phone, I jogged back into the club and headed to the break room. Opening a cabinet, I pulled out a box of latex gloves, a flashlight, and a trash bag. Once I had the items, I returned outside, putting on the gloves.

Slapping the box at Nicco, he nodded, following suit. Atticus was on his phone, I assumed it was to call in other guards or check on the kids, probably both. He'd become just as paranoid as Loren, and between the two of them, I didn't know how long it would be until they convinced each other to place GPS units on all of them. It was bad enough as it was now with their constant shadows for the kids, making them roll their eyes anytime they shifted and had an audience.

Though, I wouldn't have done anything different. Plus, it was nice that I wasn't the one making a fuss, so no one complained about me being too protective. The joke was on them—I always knew where they were. I'd keep my secret for now, as it was fun to watch the others scramble.

Shining the light, I surveyed the damage as I felt Nicco reach my side.

"Is it me, or does this seem a little petty for Dayton?" he asked, crossing his arms as he thought.

"He's in jail. Maybe it's all he has the reach for anymore?" I shrugged my shoulders. "If it's not Dayton, then we have another enemy, which isn't something I want to consider. It's the obvious choice. He wants us to know he can get to us even behind bars."

Nicco grunted but seemed to agree as he started to take pictures with his phone. Whoever had done this had taken their time, and it made me question whether or not we had another leak among us. Atticus had set aside time a few weeks ago to go through and vet everyone, letting those who seemed to be loyal to his father go. The Rawles were under new leadership now, since Ethan had sold us out, and it was the only way Atticus would let them stay in the underground. However, they were no longer on the committee, being replaced with another family, the Vazquezs.

It was a different landscape for Chicago, with two of the founding families no longer reigning. The Mascro name was also changing. We were rooting out the corrupt and putting people who wanted to prosper the right way into place. It had been a busy month over-hauling the family, but too quiet.

And now we had to show Dayton he didn't scare us.

Atticus walked over, a sigh leaving him as he watched Nicco and me. I couldn't help but snort at him, dressed as he was. It was almost funnier to be caught in this weird getup than the actual destruction of our vehicle.

"Thomas is bringing us a new ride. They'll be here in a few minutes and will take over the cleanup. When will the police be here?" he asked, knowing I'd call the chief.

"Should be soon." Just as I finished, a car pulled around the back, and we froze, making sure we weren't about to be ambushed. When we spotted the police cruiser, my shoulders dropped, and I walked over to it.

"Evening, officers. We haven't touched anything, just assessing the damage."

They both nodded, pulling out their own flashlights and evidence bags. Between the five of us, we quickly took pictures, collected the evidence, and bagged it for them to take back in under five minutes.

"We'll have someone out to tow it to impound," one of the officers said, nodding. He finished writing a report on his pad, handing it to Atticus. "We'll be in touch." They headed back to their cruiser just as the other SUV pulled up. The guys stepped out, and we all waited until the police had left before walking to the car.

"Strip the inside. Don't leave anything behind," Atticus ordered, tossing Nicco the keys. "I'll grab Lore. Let's head home."

The part of me that wanted to check on Loren and make sure she was okay tugged at my heart, but I calmed it, reminding myself she'd been with the other two idiots. She wasn't a damsel in distress, so I needed to curb my cavemen tendencies to wrap her up in bubble wrap and never let her leave the house.

So instead, I slid into the passenger seat next to Nicco, exhaling. It was quiet for a minute as we listened to the team of guys begin to dismantle the inside of the

SUV. They removed weapons and listening devices, so they didn't fall into the wrong hands. Only then could it go into police custody when it was a shell of itself.

"Do you think he was looking for something?"

"What would we possibly hide in a car?" I asked, turning my head.

"I don't know. It just seems so strange. To vandalize a car and leave it for us to find."

"I think you're focusing too much on why instead of the what. He did it, Nicco. It doesn't need to make sense."

"Yeah, okay." He leaned his head back against the headrest just as the door to the back opened. I glanced around, checking them all over. They might've been out of my sight for only half an hour, but I still wanted to make sure they were good. Loren's hot pink dress hugged her body in all the best ways, and I really wish the night wasn't ending this way. Figured, just something else Dayton was stealing from us.

When she sat back, I could see the tiredness in her body as she buckled in, leaning against Monroe. "It's so weird to be in a normal car," she said, a yawn breaking free.

I looked around at the guys, the love for our woman shining in their eyes. It didn't take long for her eyes to close as we headed home. It might seem like I was being overprotective, the measures I'd go to keep our family safe, but it was nights like this that showed me how much they were worth, and I'd do anything to keep Loren as happy and carefree as she'd been before we stepped through that door.

Anything.

Especially because I'd rocked that wig.

"HAVE you heard anything from the police?" Atticus asked, stretching. We'd gotten a little sleep when we'd returned, but we'd been up for a while, combing through the evidence and cameras we'd collected. We needed to know if we had a mole or if Dayton had found someone to do his dirty work.

"Not yet. I can give the police chief a call." Putting the photos down, I picked up my phone and dialed his number. I didn't wait to hear what Atticus said. Even if he said no, I'd still call, knowing he'd want to know.

"I'm starting to regret giving you my number, Mr. Wessex."

"And here I thought we had something special." He chuckled, and I waited for him to get somewhere quiet, the children in the background not ideal for what I wanted to talk to him about. Once I heard a door shut, I started, not wanting to waste time. "Anything?"

"Nothing concrete yet. There was a partial fingerprint

on the door that they were running through the system. If it pings, I'll let you know."

"It's Dayton," I sighed. "He got someone to do it. It has to be."

"I'm looking into it. He's not supposed to be able to integrate with the other inmates, so I'll call the warden myself. I know how important it is he stays where he is."

"Good. I'd hate for our special bond to be ruined so soon, Chief."

"There's no need to pull that trigger yet, Sax. I'll be in touch." He hung up before I could, and I smiled, knowing I'd rattled the man. I didn't plan to reveal his secret, but he might work a little harder if he was more worried. Sometimes you just had to properly motivate people.

When I looked at the time, I knew I had to bring up the elephant in the room. "You can't cancel again."

Atticus glanced up a scowl on his face. He was regretting allowing Jude and Immy to go on their date. He'd already postponed it three times for various reasons and told them he would make sure it wouldn't be this time. I feared Imogen would go full rebellion on him if he did.

"Topher's going with them. They'll be fine. It's now or never, Mas. You can't keep them in glass cases their whole lives. They've been training with Grumpy. They'll have a guard. Let them go. I'm sure it will gain you some bonus points too."

His scowl deepened, but he sighed, rubbing his hand across his face. "You're right. I just don't like it."

"It could be worse. Imogen could decide she wants five boyfriends too," I teased, wanting to wind up Atticus.

His head snapped up, his finger pointing at me. "Don't even give her the idea. One is enough."

"At least you agree that Jude is a good match for her. He's a good kid. You know this."

"Yeah, yeah." He sighed again, and I worried he'd need blood pressure medication before this was all over. "Fine. They can go, but I get to tell them." He jumped up, but I slid the chair in his way, stopping him as I called Imogen on my phone. Her face lit up the screen, and I smiled at her as I held her brother back.

"Immy, your date is a go. Be ready."

She squealed, thanking me. "You're the best, Sax! Love you the most!"

I beamed over at Atticus, who'd finally stopped trying to get by me, a deep frown on his face. "You hear that, Mas? I'm the best!" Looking back to the phone, I said my goodbyes and placed it back on the desk.

"You're an asshole," he grumbled, sitting back in his chair.

"Yep." Grinning, I flipped back through the photos we'd printed when something caught my eye.

"Mas, look!" I pointed to the image, looking up at

him. His face transformed once he realized what it meant as well. It was the logo for the Masked Kingpin.

"Busted, Dad."

Taking a picture, I sent it to the chief so they could use it for whatever they needed. However Dayton had managed to make friends, he was about to find himself in isolation. I couldn't deny that it made me feel like I'd sleep a little better at night. Until Dayton was formally charged and sentenced, I wouldn't discount his ability to con people into believing whatever he wanted.

At least for now, we had him contained, which was better than the alternative.

THIRTY TWO

IMOGEN

Rushing from the music room, I couldn't wait to tell Jude that we could finally go on a date. When he'd told me about Attie owing him a favor and that he was cashing it in to take me out, I practically passed out from happiness. We'd called each other boyfriend/girlfriend, but so far, that hadn't been anything different outside of kissing. Though, I didn't mind the kissing. I liked it a lot actually, but I was really looking forward to this date. I had no idea what it entailed, but thankfully, it hadn't been something that couldn't be rescheduled a million times since Attie had continued to push it off.

But now it was happening.

Walking past a few other volunteers at the center, I smiled, my face feeling like it would break from happiness. The youth center was reopening in two days, so we were all putting on the last-minute touches. It had been a lot of fun and a good distraction from everything else. The best part was getting to be part of something outside of the Mascro name. I understood why Nicco had done it in the first place—it felt good to give back.

Jude was helping with the mural as I walked over, and I stood back as he and Nicco finished a section. As I watched him, I got a little lost and didn't notice the person stepping up beside me.

"Wow, that looks really cool," a girl said, and I looked over, realizing it was Jill.

"Yeah." I smiled, nodding. "I can't wait to see it when it's finished."

"I wish I could draw. But the best I can do is stick figures." She laughed, and I agreed with her.

"Same. I think my brother took all the art genes."

"Oh, so Jude's your brother?" Jill asked, a blush appearing on her cheeks.

"No, Nicco. Jude's my... my boyfriend." I shrugged, my cheeks beginning to redden as well.

"Noted. Stay back." She lifted her hands, smiling, and I was glad I wouldn't have to stop being friends with her. Jill was cool, but Jude was my person, and I would always pick him.

"Hey," Jude said, spotting us. He walked over, and butterflies erupted in my stomach as he neared. We'd kissed a few more times since the first one, and each one felt like my heart would burst into a million pieces. His finger grazed my pinky when he neared, and I clasped it, wanting to touch him.

"Guess what?" I smiled, barely able to keep it together.

"Seriously?" he asked, his smile matching mine.

Nodding, I threw my arms around his neck and squeezed. When I pulled back, Jill was looking at us oddly.

"What's the big secret?"

"Oh, nothing like that. We just get to have our first date tonight. My brother's finally letting us go."

"Wow, he sounds kind of controlling," Jill muttered, and my defensiveness reared to life.

"It's not like that. There have been some family concerns, and we had to wait until it settled, and now, it is." I clasped Jude's hand fully this time, feeling brave. "So, what's the plan?"

He blushed adorably, making the butterflies fly around a million times faster. "It's kind of a surprise."

"Well, I can't wait to hear about it. I need to head out. I have practice soon. I'll see you guys tomorrow," Jill said, waving.

"See you tomorrow," I responded, but barely even glanced over. The only one I was focused on now was the cute boy in front of me. "So, what time do we head out for this date? How much time do I have to change, and what should I wear?"

"You don't have to change."

Shaking my head quickly, I pressed a finger to his lips to stop him. "Sorry, but this is a big deal to me. I've never gotten to do anything a normal teenager has, so I'm going to make this one the epitome of every classic teen movie I've ever seen. So, yes, I need to change and make one of those staircase entrances while you stand at the bottom and look at me with goo-goo eyes. It must happen."

Jude laughed, stepping a little closer. "Okay, Immy. Whatever you want. But you don't need a staircase for me to look at you that way." His eyes bore into me right there, and I knew if we weren't in the middle of the youth center, he would've kissed me. Despite my earlier comment about feeling good helping others, I kind of wished we weren't.

Screw that. I wanted to be kissed!

Okay, bratty teenager moment over. I could wait for my kiss. I planned to receive a million from this boy.

"You guys ready to head to the house?" Nicco asked, breaking the moment.

"Yup, let's go!" I pulled Jude along as we headed out toward the back parking lot. Nicco chuckled but obliged, granting him my favor.

"Wait!" Jude exclaimed, stopping me. "I need to grab something from the office and tell Cameron something."

I barely reined in a groan, but nodded, letting go of his hand. Nicco chuckled next to me, bumping my arm as we continued on our way.

"You okay there, Momo?"

"Yeah, just excited and ready to be back."

It wasn't that I didn't like Jude's brother, but he'd been constantly around since he'd been let out of the holding area and allowed to redeem himself. It had been a few weeks now, and I was beginning to see more of him than anyone else. I knew I shouldn't be so disgruntled, Jude had his brother back, but a selfish part of me worried he'd choose him in a situation over us, if it came down to it. It was stupid and selfish, but it was how I felt.

"Jude will never betray you, little Sis. He's one of the most honorable people I know. Even when his brother came back into the picture, he reached out for help immediately. He has a good head on his shoulders. He's not going to ruin that just to keep his brother in his life."

I stopped, hanging my head at being called out so easily. "Do you think Jude knows I doubt him?"

"Nah. He thinks you hung the moon. He's too busy making sure not to say something dumb or fart to pick up on your weird jealousy of his brother."

Scrunching up my nose, I slapped him on the shoulder. "Ew. Why?"

Nicco laughed, pulling me along, and we made it to the SUV. Topher opened the door for me, and Nicco kissed my head before jumping on his bike. Jude joined me a few minutes later, and we were headed back to the house, a million and one butterflies swarming in my stomach.

I was about to go on my first date.

"KNOCK, KNOCK," Loren said, stepping into my room. The door had been cracked, so she stepped further in, spotting me in front of the mirror.

I pushed the fabric down for the hundredth time, debating if I was too overdressed or not. "How do I look?" I asked, biting my lip. I'd picked a magenta pink top with a floral skirt that swished when I walked. The gladiator sandals, though, were my favorite part.

Loren came and stood behind me in the mirror, her hands resting on my shoulder. "Oh, honey, you look beautiful."

She smiled at me, and it eased my nerves. I never had this moment, not just going on a date, but a mother who would come and check on me, helping me with my hair and makeup before a date. I loved my mom, but we'd never had this, and I was happy to have Loren in my life.

"Thanks. I'm nervous but excited. Do you know what he has planned?"

She shook her head, my shoulders dropping in disappointment. "He hasn't told me anything. I think he's been planning with Nicco. Which means you'll have a blast. He's one of the most creative of my husbands with ideas."

Gagging, I laughed. "Ew, don't." Loren rolled her eyes at my reaction. It didn't bother me; I was happy my brothers had found happiness; it was just weird to think about. I didn't judge their unconventional relationship and loved the family we'd created, but it didn't mean I wanted to think about what that all entailed. I was still trying to figure out what to do with one guy.

"Come on, he's waiting." Those words made goosebumps appear on my arm, and I nodded, grabbing my purse. I didn't have much in it besides my phone and some lip gloss, but it felt like something I should carry.

When we got to the staircase, Loren kissed my cheek and walked down ahead of me. I peeked around the corner and saw the top of Jude's hair. He seemed as nervous as me, shuffling on his feet, blowing out a breath. When Loren reached him, she kissed his cheek, whispering something in his ear, and I watched as his face reddened, but he also relaxed as his shoulders dropped. He looked up, meeting my eyes, and it felt like everything else around me stopped.

It was the moment I'd always dreamed of, and it was better than in any movie. My nerves disappeared, and I stepped forward, taking hold of the banister. The whole way down, I didn't focus on anyone else, just Jude. I couldn't even tell you who all was there because the only thing that mattered was the boy smiling up at me.

When I reached the bottom, he held out a hand, and I took it. A throat clearing broke our bubble, and I looked over, spotting my brother. Attie raised an eyebrow, but I just clasped Jude's hand firmer, daring him to say anything. Loren nudged him, and he sighed, letting it go.

"You have to promise that you will stay with Topher the entire time. You won't try to run away or do anything stupid. While things are safer, it's never safe for us. So, please, take precautions. You're too precious for anything to happen to the both of you." I could hear the worry in his tone and knew how much this was costing him.

"We promise," I said, dropping Jude's hand and walking over to hug my brother. His arms wrapped around me, pulling me tight to him. He kissed my head before letting me go. Patting his cheek, I stepped back and met Jude. Together we walked out with the whole world at our feet.

"Did it meet your expectations?" he whispered later as we rode to wherever we were headed.

"Yes." I smiled, squeezing his hand. "Do I get to know what we're doing yet?" I asked, peeking at him from under my eyelashes. I watched him smile, his head shaking no.

"Not just yet. But we're almost there."

A few minutes later, we pulled to a stop, and I tried to peer outside to see where we were. It was pretty nondescript, giving nothing away since we were in the back. Topher opened the car door, smiling wide at us both.

"Come on, lovebirds." My cheeks wanted to redden at the name, but I ignored it, taking it in my stride.

When we stepped through the back, I was still confused until we walked out of the backroom, and sound began to seep through.

"Bowling?" I asked, a smile lighting up my face as I bounced on the spot.

"I've never known a girl who wanted to bowl before so much," Topher commented, but again, I ignored him.

Tugging Jude's hand, I pulled him through the last door as we stepped out into a mega-fun zone. On one side were bowling lanes, the other an arcade full of games, and the back had a rock climbing wall and bumper cars. The place was massive, and I knew we could spend a couple of days here trying to do it all.

"What do you want to do first?" he asked.

"Bowling, definitely."

Together we headed over to a lane. There were already balls set out for us and socks and shoes in our sizes. "Well, that's thoughtful," I commented dryly.

"One of the stipulations to decrease access." Jude's face blushed more as he shrugged, taking his shoe off.

"Hey, I'm not mad. I understand. It's actually nice. It saves us time to do other things. That line is long." I nodded toward the line, all the people glaring at us, and I realized how nice it was to have special privileges. I could be my own version of normal.

We started to play, and I realized how much easier the video game made it after my third gutter ball. "Okay,

I thought I'd be better at this," I pouted, sulking as I dropped down into the chair.

"Here, come on." Jude pulled me back up and grabbed my ball, showing me how to hold it. When he moved behind me, I melted. Okay, I could get used to this. A cute guy showing me how to do something. Definitely on board with this plan. Peeking over my shoulder, I found him close, and he stopped, realizing it too. He leaned down when a throat cleared, ruining the moment.

Gee, thanks, Topher.

Swallowing, Jude went back through the steps and gave me some tips. His hand stayed on mine, helping me pull the ball back and pushed when it was time to release. It stayed a little straighter this time, and I hit two pins.

Jumping up, I spun around, throwing my arms around his neck. "Yes! Thank you." I found myself wanting to lean in again when Topher nudged us out of the way so he could go.

Rolling my eyes, I started to make plans in my head to get him back.

I managed to get a little better as the game went on, scoring 50 points by the end. Jude won with 130. We decided not to count Topher's since he was well in the 200s. Jerk.

"So, what next?" he asked, putting his shoes back on.

"You pick this time. Just maybe not the rock climbing."

He smiled, and I couldn't wait to see what he would choose. Walking over to the air hockey table, we played a few games, and I found myself much better at this one. In fact, I beat him in all three games.

"Okay, that's a bust. How about some food and then arcades?"

"Sounds perfect."

The next few hours flew by as we gorged ourselves on nachos, pretzels, and hot dogs in between games of Skee-ball, pinball, and car races. My feet were starting to kill me, so I wasn't even upset when we had to leave.

"I had an amazing night," I whispered, carrying the stuffed animal Jude and I had won with our tickets. I bumped his shoulder, and he smiled.

"I'll give you guys a moment. Don't make me regret it." Topher stepped forward between us, giving us the eye. "I need to make sure it's clear. Don't come out until you see me, understand?"

We nodded, just happy to have a second to ourselves. Jude turned to me, and I suddenly felt shy. "I'm glad you enjoyed our first date. I couldn't have asked for a better person to go on this with."

"Not even Jill?" I asked for some stupid reason.

"Jill? From the youth center?" he asked, looking at me strangely. He stepped closer, his hands landing on my hip.

"Yeah, she was asking about you. Sorry, stupid girl moment where I felt insecure for a second."

"Well, let me assure you that you're the only woman for me." I liked how he said woman, and when he stepped closer, I sucked in a breath. His lips met mine, and I leaned into him, pulling him closer. This was the kiss. The one I would remember from our date. It was passionate and sweet and full of everything I wasn't ready to say yet. When he pulled back, we stared at one another for a second, our breathing heavy.

"Wow," he said, brushing my hair aside.

"I never want to stop kissing you, Jude."

He smiled so brightly that I needed sunglasses. Giggling, we both turned toward the door when we realized Topher had been gone longer than he'd said. A pit formed in my stomach.

"Should we go and look?" I asked, pulling out my phone.

"He said not to."

I dialed Atticus as I nodded. "What's wrong?" he asked the second he answered.

"I'm a little offended you immediately go there," I groaned, biting my lip.

"Imogen, how are you? How's your date?"

"Topher went to check it's clear, but he's been gone a long time. I didn't want to walk out there."

"Good thinking. I'll call you back in a second. Don't go anywhere."

"We won't," I snapped, not liking that he assumed the worst when we'd done what we were supposed to all night.

"He's going to call someone," I said to Jude when I hung up.

"I think I see him," Jude said, peering through the small window. "Come on."

"We should wait," I started, but the door was already opening. When I saw Topher standing by the car, I relaxed, realizing it was safe.

He spun when he heard us, panic on his face. "Stop, don't come any further."

I noticed something at the foot of the car. No, not something, *someone.*

"Wait, is that..." Jude said, the coloring draining from his face. Turning to him in shock, I panicked about what to do. Not once in the teen movies had a date ended with a dead body.

THIRTY THREE

LOREN

When Atticus had gotten Immy's second call saying there was a dead body, I was immediately transported back to the night my father died, and I realized that while I'd been playing happy family, I'd ignored my grief. And now that we were faced with another death, I couldn't put it off any longer.

Especially when Jude needed me.

Quickly, those of us at the house jumped into a car to head to the scene. Atticus was on the phone the entire ride, talking to Topher. Nicco called the police chief since Sax wasn't with us. I realized that we should probably let him know as well. What did I even say? Words felt difficult, freezing on my tongue.

Monroe squeezed my hand, breaking me out of my circle of thoughts. It was only the four of us since Sax had been over at Pop's and Wells was training. He'd wanted to leave with us, but I told him to stay. There wasn't much for him to do, and it was better for him to train with the fight only a week away.

I think the only reason Monroe came was for me. He always seemed to know when I needed to lean on him. Cuddling into his arms, I looked at my phone and pulled up Sax's number. Staring at it, I tried to practice how I could word what was going on to him.

Hey, Sax, we...

Sax, there's been...

Babe, I need you. Jude...

It seemed I couldn't get the words out, even in my head. Logically, I knew my brain was protecting me, not letting me think about it, but it was a really inconvenient time for it to have an aversion to things. Monroe grabbed the phone out of my hand, saving me once again from having to figure it out right then. I sighed into him, not even fighting him on it as he called Sax and told him the news. Listening to their conversation, I began to process it a little.

"Hey man, there's been—. Oh, you're already there? Okay, good. We're en route." He paused, and I felt him shift a little, and I wondered what he was doing but was also too tired to care. "She's okay, I think. Yeah, okay." Monroe stopped again, pulling back more, forcing me to look at him.

"He wants to talk to you." He held out the phone to me. Slowly, I reached out for the device, watching as my fingers wrapped around it and brought it to my ear.

Everything felt like it was moving slower; that feeling of quicksand returning, and a spike of fear rushed through me, jolting me out of the funk.

No. I wouldn't fall back into that person. I wasn't her anymore. I was strong. Grieving didn't make me weak. It was a natural part of life. I could do this. I would do this. Jude needed me. I was a mother now.

Feeling more present, I lifted the phone to my ear, clearing my throat. "Sax?"

"Spitfire, you okay?"

"I'm, yeah. It's just making me think of my dad." There I said it.

"You don't need to put yourself in this situation. We can handle it."

"Jude needs me. I can do this."

"You can, Spitfire. I love you."

His words were said with such reverence that they brought a smile to my face, lifting some of the sadness away. He was right. I could do this. I was so used to being alone that having others help shoulder the burden was still odd to me. But if I'd take a moment to open my eyes, I'd realize I didn't have to do everything on my own anymore. I could grieve my father and be present for my son. I didn't have to manage everything. In fact, it wasn't good for me to try.

That was a trap I no longer would fall prey to.

We rolled to a stop a few minutes later, and I took a deep breath, centering myself. Monroe squeezed my hand, and I stole his strength. Stepping out of the car, my anxiety and grief fled me the second I spotted Jude and Immy huddled together. Jude looked so shocked and sad that my maternal instinct kicked in, and I rushed over to them.

Wrapping them into a hug, I squeezed their heads to me, letting them cling to me. "I'm so sorry this happened, kiddo." There weren't any other words to say, so I just held them both, and Jude finally broke down into tears, letting out his shock and grief.

"Can I see him?" he asked after we'd stood there for a few minutes. I pulled back and wiped the tears from his face, searching his eyes.

"Are you sure you want to? It will be the last image you have of him." As much as I wanted to protect him from this, I knew I couldn't make the decision for him. He had to choose if he wanted to or not. He glanced over at Imogen and then back to me, biting his lip.

"I... I think I want to. I just need to know. He deserves that much from me."

Nodding, Imogen and I grasped his hands as we walked over to the body lying near the SUV. Topher stood there talking with Atticus. They noticed us as we approached, and Atticus stepped away, coming to me.

"Hey, I wouldn't go any further. The police are on their way and will take care of it. How about you guys head home in the car we came in, and I'll head back with Topher?"

Jude shook his head, a determined look on his face. "I want to say goodbye. Please, Atticus."

My husband regarded him, calculating every little sign to determine if this was something he could withstand. He looked over at me at the end, almost like he was asking my permission. A tiny sense of warmth filled me at that.

Smiling, I nodded. "If Jude wants to, I support his decision. We'll take the car after. We don't need to be here for anything else."

Feeling appeased, Atticus stepped back but stopped his sister. "It's not something you should see, Immy."

She gritted her teeth, holding her head high. "I want to support my boyfriend." I noticed Jude's cheeks tinting red at the mention of the word, and I had to give it to Immy for standing up to her brother in solidarity for Jude. He looked over at me again, and I shrugged my shoulder. They were both almost eighteen and more mature than most adults; they could decide this for themselves even if it was different from what I wanted.

Atticus sighed when I didn't deny Immy, stepping back to allow us to pass finally. Gritting my teeth, I pushed my shoulders back, preparing to see a dead body. Maybe I should've been more worried for myself?

Topher bent down as we approached, lifting a jacket he'd placed over him, making me like Topher even more for that small act of kindness. He'd tried to give Cameron some decency in his last moments.

Jude sucked in a breath, turning his head into me, and I nodded to Topher that he could put it back. Directing the kids over to the waiting car, Monroe opened the door for us as we neared. Quickly the four of us slid in, and the vehicle took off. Jude and Immy were quiet on the drive, off in their own worlds thinking. It was a lot to take in, and the idea to start a group for the teens at the youth center became even more necessary. They needed this. They'd all been through so much, and sadly, they weren't the only kids who had.

Settling back into Monroe's arms, I let him comfort me as we rode, but at least this time, I didn't feel so consumed by my own grief. I'd need to deal with it, but channeling it into something good felt like an excellent place to start.

THE NEXT FEW days passed in a blur as we dealt with the authorities, and we all went back to being closely monitored. Between the wrecked car and now a dead body, we couldn't discount Dayton's attempts. Especially with the youth center opening today, causing a battle to ensue over breakfast.

"No," Atticus said, not even looking up from his coffee. "You're not going."

"That's not fair! We've put in more work than

anyone. We deserve to be there, to celebrate the opening," Imogen argued.

"I think it would be nice to get out of the house, too," Jude offered. He'd been so withdrawn, I'd started to worry about him falling into his grief and not returning to us. The fact he wanted to do this spoke volumes to me.

"Attie," I started, and his umber eyes swung up to me, fire in them. That might've deterred me in the past, but now it just made me want to strip him down on his desk again and have my way with him. "You have extra security in place, and we'll all be there. It's probably the safest place. Besides, who's to say it wouldn't be worse for them to be here alone? Maybe that's the plan to lure us away thinking the threat is elsewhere?"

His jaw clenched as he stared at me, and I wondered if the fork he was strangling would ever go back to the right shape. His eyes never left mine, and I stared back, not backing down.

"You know I'm right," I whispered. I didn't want to fight him for dominance over scrambled eggs and toast, but this was important, and he needed to let go of control at times.

I watched as he took a deep breath, his eyes closing as his chest raised up and down with the action. After a few of them, he opened his eyes and nodded. The kids exhaled in relief and began to squirm in their chairs.

He turned back to them, stopping their celebration. "You will be accompanied by multiple guards and will not leave the public area. If anyone needs something, send someone else. No going off to places where you can be taken. If you can't agree to that, you're not going."

"Fine!" Immy huffed as Jude said, "We agree."

They jumped up from the table, heading up the stairs to finish getting ready for the day. Atticus looked over at me, a growl on his lips. "You going to deliver on that promise in your eyes, Bellezza?"

Looking around, I realized that we were alone for the first time in days. Quietly, I slipped out of my chair and slid to my knees in front of Atticus. Unzipping his pants, I surprised him when I pulled out his cock and began to lick it up and down. It was hard as a rock, and I'd have to remember he liked it when I didn't back down.

"Fuck, I didn't think you'd actually do it," he wheezed, his breathing becoming more rapid. Knowing I probably wouldn't have much time, I deepened my hold on him, sucking him further into my throat. Taking his balls, I rolled them between my fingers as I pumped his length with my other hand. My own arousal began to increase, and I rubbed my legs together to gather some friction.

Twirling my tongue around his dick, my lips wrapped around him as I took him further into my mouth, trying not to gag as I swallowed to open my throat more. With a curse, Atticus began to twitch, spilling his cum down my throat. Licking my lips, I pulled back, a smile on my face at a job well done.

Before I could sit in my satisfaction too long, I was hauled up into his arms, and as he carried me over to the island and laid me back on it. He didn't waste time, pulling up my nightgown and sealing his lips over my core. I was so wet and turned on by our morning escapades that the moment his finger entered my pussy, I was detonating around them.

"Ah, fuck," Wells hissed, walking into the kitchen just as I came. I looked at him upside down, a coy smile on my face as my body trembled. Atticus stood, fixing my clothes and pulling me off the counter. He glanced at Wells, who now stood frozen in the doorway, a tent in his pants. Atticus pulled me over to the table and sat back down like we hadn't just defiled one another.

"Maybe next time you'll be on time for breakfast," he said, picking up his coffee to take a sip.

Sputtering, Wells broke his stance and managed to join us at the table. Laughing, I grabbed my mug of coffee, taking a sip, a massive smile on my face. Who needed creamer when you had *that* to wake up to?

THIRTY FOUR

ATTICUS

nxiety filled me as I scanned the crowd, waiting for Dayton's next strike. I thought I was past this, but it seemed just as we started to relax and be happy in our lives, he struck, reminding us he was still there, waiting.

Even in prison, my father still managed to get at us.

I couldn't live like this. I had to do something—even if it meant tarnishing myself a little more in the process. And perhaps that was my father's end goal. I'd worked so hard to change our family and make it something other than underhanded and feared.

But the truth was, I'd sacrifice my soul to keep them all safe, and the world wouldn't be safe with Dayton still in it. He'd shown us that.

Dead or alive, he was a virus, and we needed to eradicate him before he spread too far, infecting all the areas of our lives. I had too much to care about now to let him try to take it away.

So, after tonight, I'd make a choice I'd thought I'd made already, and rid the world of Dayton Mascro. It was time.

"Boss, there's someone at the entrance asking to speak with you," one of the guards said into the comms.

Sighing, I stepped out from the shadows and made my way toward the front. The fact that I was missing out on this joyous occasion with my loved ones was one more thing my father had stolen.

No more. Life was too short to live it stressed and watching over our shoulders for him to figure out a way to attack us. Decision made, my steps felt a little lighter as I made my way to the front.

Mitzi smiled at me as I passed, but I nodded, not wanting to stop and talk with her at the moment. Several guards stood at the front, and when I neared, they parted, allowing me to see our visitor. I wasn't expecting it to be an older woman. Stopping, I took her in.

There was something vaguely familiar about her. She stood tall, her head high in a regal fashion as I observed all the details I could. She was dressed to impress in an elegant gown with jewels glittering on her ears. It was subtle, and yet I knew they were worth a lot.

"Can I help you?"

She smiled coyly, the corner of her lip hitching up a smidge. "You sure have grown to be a handsome man."

Her voice hit my ears, and I immediately knew who it was. "Aunt Phea." I smiled, but the anxiety didn't lessen. What did her visit mean? When Pixel had returned, she hadn't told me anything, stating she was on a leave of absence from the Sirens. She'd been sullen and withdrawn, keeping to the lab I'd made her instead of interacting with everyone else. The night out at Climax had been the first time I'd seen her interact with the others since she'd returned. "I'm sorry, but I didn't realize you were visiting."

At my acknowledgment of the woman, the guards stepped back, giving us some space. She observed me, a curious look on her face, and I couldn't decide if it was respect or glee.

"I thought it was time I pay my nephew a visit, and this seemed like the best opportunity as any. We have some things to discuss."

Watching her, I gauged her answer, weighing her words. "Of course, but as you can see, we're a little busy tonight. Perhaps, you could come and join the festivities, and we could chat tomorrow?"

"Thank you for that welcoming invitation." She stepped forward, patting my cheek. "But I'm afraid the chat cannot wait until tomorrow. First, let's have dinner, shall we? I'm dying to meet the youngins responsible for this."

She walked off, headed toward the center, and I stood there watching her back. My face gave nothing away, while inside, the pit of anxiety felt like it was opening to cavernous levels. Swallowing, I took a step, following the elusive woman, praying she wasn't about to drop a bomb on us. I was about over information being delivered at a function.

When we stepped into the atrium, I spotted Loren and held her eyes for a second. It was enough for her to stop her conversation and walk toward us.

"Attie?" she asked, looking from me to the woman who'd stopped when she'd noticed Loren.

"Bellezza, this is my Aunt Phea. She has some news to share with us after dinner."

Loren peered into my eyes, searching for everything I wasn't saying. Like the amazing woman she was, she seemed to pick up on what I couldn't say and nodded, squeezing my hand. I looked at her dressed in her red gown and knew how lucky of a man I was to have her as my wife. She smiled, turning toward my aunt.

"It's so lovely to meet you, Phoebe. We're honored to have you here tonight to celebrate the opening of the new youth center. Thank you so much for letting us borrow Pixel. She's been an integral part of our team."

I couldn't help but smile fondly at my wife as she welcomed our uninvited guest like she was royalty. Loren might think at times she didn't belong with us or have what it took for this life, but she proved to me that she was perfect for us each day. Wrapping my arm around her waist, I pulled her closer, the anxiety ebbing as she neared.

Looking back at my aunt, I noticed she watched us

with an all too observing eye. Whatever she was up to, I hoped it wouldn't destroy us. I was at my limit.

Leading her to our table, I decided to stay with my family this time instead of retreating to the shadows to lurk. I had every inch of this place covered digitally and humanly. Everyone here was vetted, and I trusted them. In short, there was no way that Dayton was ruining this party tonight.

"Aunt Phea," Pixel said, standing and walking over to her. "I wasn't expecting you." She clasped the older woman's arm, helping her to a chair. I didn't know if that was expected of the younger generation or if Aunt Phea played more feeble around others to catch them off guard. It seemed like the latter to me. There was nothing weak about Phoebe Costa.

Loren introduced the rest of the table, falling into her hostess role perfectly. Everyone looked at her when she was done, curious about her presence.

"It's so lovely to meet all of you. I've heard so much about each and every one of you. It's nice to put a face to the tales."

I narrowed my eyes, looking over at Pixel. Had she been a spy the whole time, right under our noses? My glance must not have been as subtle as I hoped, if the chuckle Phoebe gave was anything to go by.

"Now, now, Atticus, it isn't like that. Please, I'll explain once we've had our meal and the presentation. I'm eager to hear all about this new center."

It oddly felt like I'd lost all control over the table with that comment as everyone turned to her, following her orders. Clenching my jaw, I breathed in deeply, reassuring myself it didn't matter. I didn't need to control the table. There were other, bigger, things at play here, and I needed to focus on that, not entering into a pissing contest with my elderly aunt.

Taking in a deep breath, I let it out slowly, feeling my whole body relax. As the next hour passed, we ate our meal and listened to various donors speak about their vision for the youth center and why they'd given. It was boring as fuck, and I found myself gazing around at my men, looking for any sign of a threat.

When Jude, Immy, and Loren got up and talked about the groups they were starting here, including a photography, music, and therapy group, I did stop to listen. But once they were done, I went back to my scanning, not caring how much someone else had given and how awesome they thought they were for doing it. My narcissistic, murdering asshole of a father was trying to destroy my family. I didn't really care to pander to their self-inflated egos.

And people said I didn't have my priorities right.

Seemed like something else Loren had helped shift in me. I no longer cared about profits other than what it could provide for my family. I was more interested in the legacy we would leave and getting to live it.

"Attie," Loren leaned in to whisper, "whatever it is,

we'll handle it. That's what we do, remember? We're Mascros. We get shit done."

Smiling at her, I touched her hair, the silky strands falling through my fingers. "I don't think that's exactly how it goes, but I like your version."

Grinning, she kissed my cheek, patting my leg. When the last speaker was done, it felt like I'd run a marathon of emotions. Whatever she was going to share with us, I was just ready to get it out in the open. This secret bull-shit was killing me.

Or perhaps it was just the anticipation. Either way, I was done waiting despite my earlier attempt to avoid it.

Applause sounded around us as everyone stood, acknowledging the official opening of the Second Chance Youth Center. The name had been a last-minute change to honor the people who'd been taken from us too soon, and the part they played in giving us hope for change. I was proud of Jude and Immy for recognizing both Cameron and Kenneth as part of that.

Mitzi stepped off the stage, and music began to play, indicating the dance and auction part of the evening had commenced. Nodding to Sax, he led us to a private room, our party trailing after. Looking around, I took in the faces of all the people I'd come to care about, even if some of them didn't know it.

Monroe and Wells sat next to Jude, engaged in a conversation about hockey. Imogen was talking with Nicco and Pixel, and Loren sat next to Sax, a spot open on her other side for me. My Aunt walked up to me, and I could tell she expected me to take a seat. The command made me bristle, but I reminded myself it was about more than control. This was about our family, and I needed to know all the facts, even if I didn't like them.

"Thank you all for gathering. As I mentioned, it's been marvelous to put together the faces to the stories that Cleo shared with me." We turned to her, watching as she swallowed, her face becoming pale. "I wasn't sure about you, Atticus, when you called. But you are a Costa, and we take that seriously. When I sent Cleo, I thought she'd return, tell me how awful you were, and then we'd be done with you. I could wash my hands as having done good by Shayna and move on."

She paused, looking around at all of us, stopping to peer into each and everyone's eyes like she could see into their souls. "Imagine my surprise when Cleo returned and, instead of confirming what I believed, she told me of a family with values, kindness, and strength but who needed some direction. She told me of a vision she had where we could merge our two families together, creating a new era for both the Costas and Mascros. I was taken aback by this idea. Costa women have made a name for themselves without the help of men. We stand against injustice, taking what we want and deserve, providing a better life for those in our midst. I laughed at her, told her she was foolish and that perhaps she wasn't as strong as I thought she was if she could go on a mission and be influenced so greatly by the people around her."

Thoughts swirled in my head at everything she said, along with some anger that she would think of us that way. Admiration for Pixel grew, and I turned to her, nodding my respect. She'd been truthful to herself and us, and I was proud to call her cousin.

"So, what changed your mind? Why are you here if you think we're a lost cause?" I asked when she didn't continue.

She smiled, and I tried not to let the slight patronizing tilt get to me. This wasn't about my pride, I reminded myself.

"Because I'm woman enough to admit when I was wrong. I've been watching you over the past month as you work to rebuild your family and make a new path. I thought you might've been all talk before, but you backed it up with actions, and that spoke to something in me. I know that you didn't get to know your mother well, but I can see some of her best qualities in you, Nephew. So, I thought to myself, maybe my darling Cleo has a point."

"So, you're here to join forces? Why now? Why tonight?"

"Because I think we can help one another. Cleo wants to start a Siren program within your midst, bringing young girls and women into our folds, helping to increase our numbers and provide your women with skills that will increase your family's dominance."

Imogen gasped at the news, a smile spreading over her face, and I had a feeling I was about to enter another battle soon with her, one I already knew I would lose.

"That still doesn't explain why here."

"Ah, clever but impatient, you are, Nephew. As for the why, well, I like to get dressed up and do not have as many opportunities as I once had. But I also come bearing some news that I think will greatly impact your answer." She stopped, looking around, ensuring she had all of our attention. "I have it on good authority that one of your enemies has escaped custody. So, I took it upon myself to send out a few operatives to ensure his capture. She should be calling you any minute now."

We all stopped our movement, the room going quiet as we all waited to hear a phone ring.

"How—" my words were cut off as a shrill ring rang through the room. Loren picked up her phone, a sheepish look on her face.

"Hey, Cami, it's not a good time. Wait, what? Okay, we're on our way." She hung up, looking at my aunt with new eyes. She blinked once before turning to me. "Darren, Cami has Darren."

THIRTY FIVE

LOREN

I wasn't sure how he'd done it or how Phoebe had known, but sure enough, sitting tied to a chair was Darren Delgado, my one time stalker. Cami was practically vibrating, and I worried she was going to lose control as she paced back and forth. The slap mark on Darren's face alone told me she'd gotten in at least one good strike already.

"Camila, focus," Atticus boomed, gaining her attention.

When we'd gotten the phone call, the kids had been taken back to the manor with Wells and Monroe, while the rest of us met Cami at the location she'd given us. Apparently, it was the warehouse the Mascros used to house people they were questioning, the very place that Wells had been shot. I learned something new every day.

Phoebe had said she'd meet us the following day to discuss more details, but had other people she needed to touch base with first. The woman was a mystery to me that I yearned to figure out, but I was pretty sure that was the point. She kept you guessing, so you never knew which version of her was true.

"Where did you find him?" Atticus asked again, getting Cami to calm some. Darren glared at all of us but kept quiet.

"I got a phone call from one of the Sirens I know, Canary, telling me to be at a location at 8 o'clock. That I needed to stop someone from hurting anyone else. Malek was with me, so we went there together and that's when we found him, breaking into a house."

She lifted a finger, pointing at the man who'd held her captive. I could see the battle waging within her, from wanting to fall back into the woman she told me she was around him, and the woman she'd been fighting to return to. Walking over, I took her hand, trying to give her some support.

"You did good, Cam."

Squeezing her hand, I felt her relax at my words. Atticus nodded to Sax once Cami had given him all the information she had, and he walked over, pulling Darren's head back so he was forced to look at him.

"How did you escape? Whose house were you breaking into?"

"Like I'd tell you," he sneered, fighting to hold back the wince from the hair grab.

"Honestly, it makes no difference to me. But it could

buy you a less painful death. Your choice, asshole. You only get the offer for the next five minutes."

Sax patted Darren's cheek, dropping his head back down and walked away, setting a timer on his phone. He showed it to Darren before turning his back, effectively ignoring him.

It was pretty good psychological warfare on their part, alienating the prisoner. I'd be scared if they weren't my men. It should make me a little put off, but watching Sax manipulate Darren had my blood pumping a little and my pussy throbbing.

"You have a choice, Cami," Atticus said, looking at her. "Do you want any part in his death? Do you need your revenge?"

She didn't answer right away, thinking over the words. I watched as she glanced over to Malek and I could tell she wanted to know his opinion, valuing the bond they shared.

"Go, talk it over. He has a say as well." She nodded, giving me a hug and walked over to Malek, and they began to whisper together. Atticus turned to me, observing my stance.

"You doing okay, Bellezza?" he asked, taking my hand.

"Yeah, I'm good. Cami needs me, so I want to be here."

He dipped his head in understanding, accepting my answer before walking over to converse with Sax. Nicco took the opportunity to come over and wrap his arms around me from behind, pulling me to his chest.

"You never cease to amaze me, Beautiful."

"How's that?" I asked, leaning my head back.

"You're so good at all this and you don't even realize it. You just step in, helping everyone, making them feel at ease. It's such a gift and I'm truly in awe of you most days."

"That's sweet of you, Nicco, but I don't think I'm doing anything. I'm just being there."

"And that's what makes you amazing. Most people don't show up the way you do. Just take the compliment." He kissed my nose, making me smile.

"Okay, thank you." I yawned, looking back at the space. It felt odd to be standing in an interrogation room. "You know, I didn't know a place like this existed. It makes me wonder what else I'm clueless on."

"I thought you wanted to be?"

"I guess you're right, but then when I learned about it, it just felt like I was hit upside the head with new information. I know I can't have it both ways. It's still all new, I suppose."

"Honestly, I like that you're not in too much of it. It helps keep it separate. Not that there's a lot of crime amongst us anymore, but there are still some unsavory things we do that I'm glad don't touch you. I don't want you to ever look at us differently or for it to sully you in a way that it changes you. I'm probably asking for the impossible. To have it and not let it affect us."

I thought about what he said, tossing the words around in my head. "I get what you're saying. And I guess that's why I choose to stay out of it. Not that I'm worried I'd look at you differently, because I wouldn't. I see all the parts of you and I love them, no matter how dark. But I think I'm worried if I embrace too much of my own darkness, not only would I not recognize the person I'd become, but you guys wouldn't accept her either. I guess, in a way, we have the same fear."

"I want to be contrary and say the same thing you said to me. No matter how much you change, I won't feel differently. I accept you as you are. And I hope that we grow and change together."

"Who knew you could have such deep conversations while waiting for a madman to decide how he wants to die?" I joked, pulling his hand up to kiss.

We fell into silence as we waited for the timer to go off. Darren was stewing by this point, and I had no idea what he would choose in the end. He was stubborn, and a loose cannon, making his actions impulsive and impossible to predict. Cami walked over with Malek, a firm look in place, as she waited next to us. When the timer beeped, Sax spun on his heels, holding up the phone.

"Time's up. Decision time. Will you take it, or will you choose to die a horribly painful death?"

Darren kept quiet and Sax sighed, shaking his head. "Okay, your choice man."

"Camila?" Atticus asked, looking over at him.

"It's enough for me to watch him die. I don't need to be the one to do it. I've realized that having that on my conscience would be worse, and I don't want to give him anything else." Her voice was steady, and I noticed her shoulders were pushed back, her decision solidifying something in her.

As I watched her, I didn't miss how Malek reached down and grabbed her hand, squeezing it quickly before letting it go. I was so curious about that dynamic, but it seemed to be complicated at the moment. I needed to get her alone so I could talk to her more freely instead of in a spa with a lot of other people in range, including her fiancé.

"I'm proud of you, Cami," I said, beaming at my friend. "You're so strong."

She smiled over at me, nodding her thanks, and I watched as something else in her seemed to repair itself right in front of me. The warm glow I often felt in sessions spread through me, and I knew I was where I was meant to be. This confirmed it.

Atticus nodded at Pixel, who walked over with a syringe. "This will hurt," she said, smiling. "I call this one 'Dumbass.'"

She took the big needle, lifting his tongue as Sax held his head firm. I watched in a weird curiosity as she emptied the contents under it. Darren tried to move his head, but Sax held him down, allowing Pixel to release it all without a problem.

"How long?" Atticus asked.

"First signs will begin soon, but it will take over ten hours before it kills him. It's going to be excruciating."

At the mention of death, I knew I didn't need to be there for it anymore. Walking over, I pulled Cami into a hug, holding her to me closely. "We need to sit down and chat soon. Promise me that you'll call."

She nodded, clinging to me for a second. "I promise. Thank you, Lor."

Kissing her cheek, I stepped away before I walked over and kissed Atticus and Sax goodbye. Nicco waited for me by the door, holding out a hand. Together, we walked out, and I leaned my head against him, everything catching up to me.

From the threat of Dayton ruining the opening, to Jude's brother's death, there had been a lot going on. Tomorrow there was a memorial service for Cameron, and I was worried about it triggering my grief again.

I needed to face it before it ate me alive. It was time.

Maybe it would be a good opportunity to reach out to Marcus and finally have that chat about my father.

TEARS slid down my face as Jude spoke of the love he had for his brother, and how he was glad he got to know the version he was in the end. Topher had told us how Cameron had been working so hard at the center, and it had to be the fact he was working late that night that made him vulnerable to attack with everyone else gone. Dayton was grasping at straws, or perhaps repaying a debt he felt Cameron owed him. It was hard to know with Dayton.

We knew it was Dayton because the same insignia we'd found on the SUV for the Masked Kingpin had been carved into his chest. He wasn't trying to hide that he was responsible. Dayton wanted us to know.

The fact he hadn't tried anything the night of the opening either meant we'd done enough to halt him or he'd been stopped on the inside. I knew Atticus wanted to go and talk to him. I wasn't sure how I felt about it, but it was his father, so it was ultimately his decision. I'd be there after it to help him put the pieces together if Dayton tried to destroy our foundation.

Because he could try, but he wouldn't succeed. We would stand. United.

Jude walked over, and I pulled him into a hug, letting him cry for the loss of his brother. I knew it would hurt, but we'd be there for him. He had a family now and wouldn't be alone ever again.

"You sure you want to come to this lunch with me?" I asked when he drew back, wiping his face.

"Yeah, I think it will be good for you and I'm curious. Plus, I think it will help me not think of today too much. In a lot of ways, I lost my brother a long time ago. I just hate that the moment I started to get him back was when he was taken again."

"If you're sure, then I'd love the company."

"Let me say goodbye to Immy, she's been taking Cam's death harder than I thought."

Nodding, I let him go, walking over to Monroe and Wells. They both instantly surrounded me, giving me their focus.

"Hey, Kitten, how are you feeling?"

"Okay. There's been a lot going on, but I think this will be good. You guys headed back?"

"Yeah, I have a sparring session with Nicco." Wells blushed and I couldn't help but take the opportunity to tease him.

"Oh, is that what you call it? You wouldn't happen to need a backdoor diamond, would you?" I teased.

Wells' eyes smoldered as he stepped closer, grabbing my hips. "Next time, I get to be the one to have you wear it. Understand?"

Licking my lips, I nodded, caught up in the sexual tension to care about anything else. "Yes."

"Okay, before this goes to far and I say fuck it, I was wondering if you wanted to take the kids to that movie in the park tonight?" Monroe asked.

Blinking the lust away, I turned my gaze toward him,

his words beginning to penetrate my thoughts. "Yes, that would be lovely. I think the kids would enjoy that. Maybe we should see if Lily wants to join us? I think it might be too late for Olivia."

He smiled his golden smile, effectively making me fall for him all over again. "I can call Maren and see if that would work. Maybe we could do a sleepover since it will be late afterward and it would give her a night off. I heard things are going well with her and Ryan." He wiggled his eyebrows, making Wells and I laugh.

"You're such a gossip," Wells teased, looking at him fondly. He turned to me, making me look at him. "We'll take care of it. You go and have lunch with your father's secret lover." Wells winked, blowing me a kiss in such a manner that was like Nicco, I was stunned to the spot for a second. When I glanced over at Monroe, he laughed, nodding.

"Yeah, I see it too. They're hanging out a lot. It's kind of cute though." Monroe pinched Wells' cheek as he tried to get away.

Feeling better, I walked over to grab Jude and headed to the car. It felt weird to be driving somewhere, but I'd wanted to for this. I didn't want to explain why someone chauffeured me around or why there were multiple men watching me. I knew they'd be there, but acting normal felt like a safe bet for this occasion. Jude was quiet on the drive over and I kept glancing at him, checking to make sure he was okay.

"I'm good, Mom." He smiled over at me, the term making me melt into a puddle of goo.

"It's okay if you're not."

"You take your own advice?"

Sighing, I smiled. "You're right. It's just easier to take care of others. I'm… dealing as best I can. I guess you understand how it feels. I didn't get to know the real version of who my father was until it was too late. I bounce between anger and sadness, not knowing which one I feel the strongest most of the time. I'm hoping that Marcus can give me a better glimpse of the man I never got the chance to know."

"I hope so too. I want that for you." He paused and I could tell he was thinking something over. "Can I ask a random question?"

"Always, kiddo. Ask away."

"Do you think I could learn how to drive? I know I don't really need to with all the people who drive us and the L-train, but…" he shrugged and I glanced over, catching his cheeks pinking. "I think I'd like to know."

"Absolutely. Though, I'll admit, I might not be the best teacher. I'm sure Wells or Monroe would be great at it. Wells is more patient than people give him credit for, and Monroe has that sense of being about him that just makes you calmer. Either alone or together I think they'd be great teachers and I know they'd love to teach you."

"Awesome, I'll do that." He smiled brightly, and I was glad to give him something to look forward to.

"So, my turn to ask a random question." He nodded as I pulled into the parking lot, placing the car in park. Turning to him, I looked at him seriously. "Who's your favorite Daddy?"

Jude's face was frozen for a second before he burst out laughing so hard he had tears running down his face. "Oh, wow, I wasn't expecting that. And I can't tell you."

"Why not?" I huffed, getting out of the car.

"Because. It's my game, my rules. It takes all the fun out of it if they think they can find out from you."

"I wouldn't tell!"

Jude gave me a side-eye, clearly not believing me. Grabbing his arm, I walked into the restaurant with him, smiling over nonsense and feeling like maybe today wouldn't be as bad, that the grief would lessen some, and I'd be able to breathe a little easier.

THIRTY SIX

ATTICUS

The guard following Loren and Jude checked in that they'd made it to the restaurant and were sitting down with her father's lover. Knowing they were safe for a while, I climbed out of the car and headed into the prison side door with Sax on my heels. The guard standing there nodded before opening it for us and allowing us entry.

I'd leveraged a lot of secrets to make this happen, but it was worth it. Darren had already managed an escape, which meant it was only a matter of time before Dayton found a way.

Our shoes echoed off the walls as we walked down the dark corridor, following the painted lines on the floor that directed us to the interrogation room. When we made it there, another guard was standing outside.

"He's inside. You have ten minutes before I have to take him back."

Nodding, I glanced at Sax, who understood my message. *"Keep everyone out."*

Taking a deep breath, I stepped into the room and came face to face with my father. The sneer he wore on his face wasn't surprising, but what was, was how small he looked in his prison jumpsuit. I'd always seen my father in suits, his broad shoulders spanning the width of the whole room, it seemed.

But here, in this muted room devoid of color, he looked like an ordinary man. His hair was longer around the edges, his face scruffy with an unshaven beard, and his skin color was similar to the walls around him—gray. There was nothing distinguishable about him here.

"I'm surprised it took you this long, Son."

"Oh?" I asked, leaning against the wall. I didn't want to be any closer to the vile man than necessary. I was here to assess and say my piece. Plus, I had no doubt he would try to take advantage of the situation if I overstepped. I wouldn't give him any access that wasn't necessary.

He sneered again, clearly not amused I wasn't giving in to his baiting. "So, what do you want? You're clearly here to learn something."

Smirking, I dropped my arms and relaxed back on them. "I'm not sure I have anything else to learn from you, Father. I was more curious if you'd come to your senses and was willing to apologize."

"Me?" he rolled his eyes, the idea never crossing his mind.

Why would it? He was Dayton Mascro, the king of everything. He didn't apologize to anyone.

"Your dream isn't going to come to fruition. I'll be out of here soon, and then I'll be free to take back my reign from you and that worthless cunt you married. I know what buttons to push with her. You should've seen how much she squirmed in sessions when I talked about certain things. I know what makes her tick and how to destroy her, and I will. I will take you down, along with that worthless daughter of mine and the bastard. None of you will be able to stand against me. Better enjoy your time because it's all about to be mine."

Sighing, I dropped my head to gather my composure. While I knew he wouldn't do those things because I planned to end him before he had the opportunity, I didn't relish having to listen to him talking about the people I loved. It was a tactic he was using. I just had to keep remembering that.

With one last breath, I raised my head and stared him in the eyes. "Out of curiosity, what was your end game? Takeover all the families? Turn Chicago into your own little kingdom?"

"You think so small, Son. Chicago was only the start."

The arrogance and greed this man possessed were astounding. "Ethan told me that when you were younger, the four founding families were all friends and that you had all fallen in love with Shayna. The plan was to share her and unite the city once and for all. But in the end, your selfishness wouldn't allow it, and you stole her away from them, breaking the peace among the families. Was it worth it?"

He snorted, laughing at me. "Oh, Son. It wasn't about having some pussy; it was about taking what others wanted. By stealing Shayna, I made myself the best, the envy of all. I was able to accomplish what they couldn't. I was top dog."

"That must've really stung then when you found out about Benny," I chided, unable to keep the smirk from gracing my face.

Dayton's eyes narrowed as his face began to turn red. "Benny was a waste of space, and he got what he deserved in the end. He was always jealous of what I had. Raping his girlfriend and telling him that he was a father was the best payback. He died thinking he had a son. Ah, the look on his face." He leaned back, bracing his chin in his hand. "That's top three in deaths for me."

It was odd, but that statement helped separate my father from me. I didn't enjoy killing and only did it out of necessity to protect the people I loved. But Dayton *liked* it. It was obvious by the look on his face. Plus, anyone who had a top five murder list was clearly unhinged. Sadly, if I hadn't met Sax or Loren, I probably would've ended up the same way. They both saved me from my worst self.

A knock on the door reminded me I only had a few minutes to spare, and I needed to use them wisely. If this was the last time I spoke with him, I needed to learn everything I could.

"Before I go, Father, there's one thing I wanted to ask you." I paused, waiting it out. He rolled his eyes, huffing as he sat up.

"Go on. You'd be surprised how busy my social calendar is in this place."

Smiling, I stepped forward a little, bracing my hands on the table. I needed to see his eyes when I asked. "Do you have any regrets, Dayton? Any, at all? The things you did to Imogen? To Loren? To me?"

He took a long moment, looking between my eyes as he gathered himself. "The only thing I regret is not killing you that day in the warehouse."

It was all I needed to hear. For some reason, the small boy who'd idolized his father had held onto hope that it had been real, that there was a part of him that would reconcile the things he'd done. It was foolish, but I couldn't carry on with my plan without knowing. Perhaps, I just wanted to feel the pain of his rejection, justifying my behaviors from this point forward.

Because I could be merciful if I wanted. But I no longer wanted to.

There was no doubt, no shred of hesitancy now as I walked toward the door that the world would be better without him.

Turning the handle, I stopped, glancing over my shoulder, finding him smirking at my retreating figure. "Oh, one thing, Phoebe Costa asked me to give you her regards."

If I hadn't been watching and didn't know my father as well as I did, I might've missed it. But at the mention of my aunt's name, his pupils dilated, his breath hitching for just a second.

Seemed like Dayton Mascro had some common sense, after all, and I was suddenly glad Aunt Phea was on my side. She was one scary lady; his reaction proved it.

Walking out, I left all the baggage of a boy who wanted to please his father behind, all the fear of never measuring up to the expectations he had for me, and the self-loathing that I was weak for caring about others.

I left it all, striding forward as a freer man with plans to eradicate the virus once and for all.

THIRTY SEVEN

LOREN

The lunch with Marcus had gone well, and I was discovering my father in a whole new light. It felt nice to have these memories of him, even if they weren't firsthand. Marcus was even thinking of volunteering at the center so he could hang out with Jude more.

It had been a few days since the memorial, and I'd been watching Jude, making sure he wasn't falling into a depressive hole like I had. But as I was learning with Jude, he always surprised me, proving he was far more prepared for this life than any of us gave him credit for.

Today was the first meeting of my group for teens, and I was nervous and excited about what it could become. I was setting up the last bean bag when Immy walked in, a tray of cookies in her hand.

"Hey, Lor, where do you want these?"

"Um, wherever there's an empty spot on that table works." I pointed in the direction, fluffing the chair one last time.

Jude followed a moment later, with pitchers of lemonade and water in his hands, and sat them down next to Imogen's tray. Walking over, I hugged them both, always feeling better when I could.

"You sure you guys want to join? It won't be weird with me being the leader?"

Since it was an informal group, offering a safe place for them to talk, I wasn't as concerned with the boundaries. I was merely going to be the leader, directing them to help one another. If what I hoped occurred, it would be a good chance for them to find their own strength and recognize it amongst their peers.

"Yeah, we're excited," Jude said, peeking over at Immy. She'd been a little withdrawn, and I hoped Cameron's death and return of her father hadn't set her back any.

"I think it's great you're doing this and would love to be a part of it," she finally said, offering me a smile.

"Okay, well, I won't tell anyone about our relationship, so that's up to you guys to disclose if you want to. Which also means I'll talk to you both as I would everyone else, no special treatment."

"Ah, bummer, and here I thought having a therapist as a pseudo mom would finally be my in," Immy teased.

Laughing, I pulled her close and kissed her head; her words meant more to me than she probably knew.

"Love you too, Immy." Drawing back, I straightened

my clothes before I got too emotional and lost it before the group even started.

"I'm going to put some music on. You have a few minutes before others should hopefully arrive, so now's your chance to pick your seats." I smiled, some butterflies entering my stomach at the reality of starting a new venture. I prayed it would be what I wanted it to be for these kids.

Selecting some soft music, I fiddled with straightening things when I heard voices, too nervous to turn to see if people were actually arriving. Hands settled on my waist, making me jump when I realized I hadn't heard anyone walk up. The warmth and weight were familiar, so I looked up, peering behind me at their chuckle.

"Beautiful, you okay? You seem a little jumpy."

"I'm good, just nervous that no one will show up or that I'll suck at it if they do."

"You'll be great, Beautiful, just as you are at everything you put your heart into." Nicco spun me around, kissing me briefly. "I kind of want to be bad and have my way with you, but I know it's not the time or the place. But have no fear. I'll be scouting out the perfect hot-for-teacher location."

Giggling, I slapped his chest, knowing that while he was 100% serious, he was also helping to ease my nerves in his Nicco way.

Pecking his lips, I hugged him close, stealing his warmth and love. Taking a deep breath, I exhaled it slowly, letting it flow through my body and purging all the negative energy. Pulling away, I pushed my shoulders back and nodded. Squeezing his hand, I left him and walked into the room. I was excited to see five teens sitting around the circle, snacking on cookies and drinks. Okay, so at least some kids had shown up. This would work.

"Hey guys, I'm Loren, and I'll be your mentor for the teen group. Just a few rules to go over. This is a safe place to talk about the things going on in your lives and find comfort from one another, building bonds. This is not a therapy group but a place you can share your own troubles and find support from someone else who's been there. That being said, I am a mandated reporter for the state of Illinois, so if you do say something in this group that deems reporting, I will have to share it with the proper authorities. I won't do this behind your back. I would let you know and sit there with you if you wanted when they came to talk with you. Any questions so far?"

They shook their heads no, so I smiled, taking another breath. "Okay, the next rule is that since this is a safe place, it means that what you share here, unless reportable, stays here. You can talk about anything you feel comfortable sharing and have the confidence that it won't be spread around. If I find someone sharing things they were privy to in this group, not only would you be kicked out of the group, but you'd be placed on a suspended membership to the youth center. There are consequences for using someone else's pain to your advantage, and I won't allow that. It's hard enough to speak about these things without the fear that someone you don't trust will find out. Does everyone understand?"

They nodded yes, but I needed their verbal acknowledgment on this one. "I'm going to need to hear you say it, guys." I smiled, hoping to soften my tone a little.

"Yes, Loren," they said, Jude and Immy the loudest. I smiled at them in thanks.

"Other than that, I want you guys to have fun and respect one another in here. Any questions?"

No one said anything, so I smiled wide and realized I was overcompensating for them, so I dimmed it, reminding myself to breathe again. "Right, well, does anyone want to start? Anything anyone wants to share?"

Silence met me, and I regretted my decision to do this for a brief second. Why did I think I could? I was insane and apparently liked torturing myself.

Slapping the negative thought out of my head, I remembered that teenagers hated being first in these types of situations and a little nudge went a long way. I needed to make it more focused, so it wasn't so scary.

"How about we all go around and introduce ourselves first and say what we hope to gain from the group?"

Nods and a few smiles met me, and I relaxed, gaining

my footing. I looked to Jude when no one started, hoping he'd help me out. He rolled his eyes but sat up.

"Hi, I'm Jude, and well, I hope to get everything Loren said. A place to connect with people who understand that life doesn't always deal you the hand you expect. The youth center has always been an important part of my life, so I'm happy to be here and take part in what it offers."

"Thank you, Jude." I smiled, nodding to Imogen to go next.

"I'm Imogen; most people call me Immy. Um, well, I'm looking forward to making friends my age. I've been homeschooled most of my life, and this one here," she nudged Jude, "is my only friend who isn't over thirty. No offense, Lor." She giggled, her face blushing.

Raising my hands, I laughed with her. "None taken."

The next kid swallowed when he realized it was his turn. "Hi, I'm Chuck, and I'm here because the flyer said cookies." He shrugged his shoulders, his cheeks blushing, but I liked his honesty.

"Welcome, Chuck. It's nice to have you. Let me know if you have a cookie preference." His shoulders relaxed at that, and he nodded, taking a bite.

"I guess I'm next," Jill said, fidgeting slightly. "I'm Jill, and um, I guess I'm here because I've been trying to do things that are different from my normal routine, and my therapist," she paused, briefly raising her eyes, "mentioned this place, so I thought I'd give it a try." She shrugged, fiddling with a napkin, and I hoped I didn't make it too uncomfortable for her.

"Welcome, Jill. It's nice to have you with us."

The last kid looked like he wanted to be anywhere but with us, and I hoped he wasn't being forced. He sighed when we all stared, sitting up from his spread-out position. "I'm Elliott." He didn't share anymore, staring at me like he dared me to ask him to do so.

"Welcome, Elliott. I hope you find this place to be whatever you need it to be." He nodded once, and I hoped it was an acceptance that I wouldn't force him to do anything. This wasn't that type of group.

"Okay, well, now that we all know one another's names, maybe we could do one of those dreaded things called an ice-breaker?" I fake gasped as they all laughed.

Over the next twenty minutes, they seemed to warm up to one another, chatting and finding things they had in common. When it was almost time to end, I realized how quickly it had gone.

"Before we end, maybe we can say something we're looking forward to this week? Having goals and positive things, big or small, are good ways to motivate us to keep moving forward. I'll even start."

They all seemed to sigh in relief as I thought about what I could share. It was odd being able to be this open with teens. "Well, I'm looking forward to spending time with my family this weekend and going to my husband's fight match."

Elliott seemed to perk up a little at that, and I wondered if maybe seeing if Wells could spare an hour a week to do a class would be possible. Perhaps he could move Jude and Immy's training here so others could join as well? It was something to think about.

I was surprised when Jill volunteered to go next. "I'm excited about seeing two of my former skating coaches, Sawyer and Rey, this weekend. They're coming in from Utah to compete in a competition. They're so close to making the Olympic team. I'm excited to watch them and get back to skating in a way that I used to love." Her smile dimmed a little, and I tried to give her a look of praise that I was proud of her for sharing.

"That sounds awesome. I've never been to an ice skating competition. I can't wait to hear about it next week and how your visit went." She nodded, some of her nerves leaving her as she settled back into her seat.

"I'm looking forward to seeing my third favorite dad... Well, I'm looking forward to going to a fighting match. And just so everyone knows, Loren is my mom. It feels weird not saying it," Jude provided, slumping back into his chair, and I laughed, smiling at him.

"It's true, but no favoritisms. If anything, I'll be sterner with him," I said, looking at the others. No one seemed to care, so I relaxed. Jude gave an enthusiastic nod, making the other kids laugh.

"Um, I guess it's my turn," Imogen started, "I'm looking forward to spending time with my family and boyfriend. My pseudo-little-brother wants to make pancakes this weekend, so I'm looking forward to that." She smiled, her face a little red, and I nodded at her, smiling at what she said.

Chuck cleared his throat, shuffling his feet a little. "Hm, well, I guess I'm looking forward to not being in school." He shrugged his shoulders, but it was a start.

"That leaves you, Elliott. Anything you're looking forward to?"

"Nope," he said, laying his head back and closing his eyes. I could tell he'd be difficult, but I had hope that this group was exactly what he needed.

"That's okay, maybe next week you will. Well, that's my cue to head out and let you guys hang. This room will be open to socializing for another hour. I hope to see you all next week."

They all hollered their goodbyes, and I walked out, feeling happy with the progress. This could be the start of something amazing and a new venture for our family, giving back to others who felt alone and in search of somewhere to belong. We could be that for them, or at least let them not feel so alone until they found their own family.

When I turned the corner into the open rec area, I wasn't surprised to find someone waiting. What was surprising was that all of my husbands were there.

"Um, hi. Don't you all have things to do? We have the fight coming up tomorrow?"

They all smiled at me, melting my insides, and I was surprised when it was Monroe who spoke up and not Atticus.

"We're here supporting you, Lo. That's where we needed to be. Come on, we're having a date night. Jude and Immy will be taken back to the house by Topher and they've agreed to watch Levi. I'm not sure who's more excited, him or the teens. We haven't had much time for all of us in a while, and before everything goes down, we thought it would be nice to spend time together. You can tell us all about your group over dinner."

Tears welled in my eyes, and I nodded, realizing how desperately I needed this. "You guys are the best." I didn't know how I got so fortunate to meet them when I needed them the most, but I was glad I had.

That night as we ate dinner, I shared with them how the group went, and they all gave me updates on their days. I'd felt our bond before, knowing we could make this work, but that night, it felt transcendent and like anything was possible if we were together.

As we stepped into Upswing the following night, I prayed that it was enough.

Thirty Eight

DAYTON

The damn guards had done nothing but talk about the fight all week, and I was to the point I would kill the next one who mentioned that miscreant's place. Atticus was a misguided fool, taken in by pussy, and I would remind him why I was the King.

At the end of the row, the guard did his pass, giving me the signal, and I slipped out, dressed in a guard uniform. The outfit had been delivered an hour ago, and I'd been waiting in my cell ever since. Time was funny here. A single minute could feel like an eternity.

When he turned right, I went left, keeping my head down as I approached the other guard. I quickly wrapped my arm around his neck from behind, cutting off his air supply, waiting for him to go slack. Once his oxygen was depleted, I dropped him to the floor, taking his badge, taser, and keys before stuffing him into a closet.

That should buy me enough time to escape and kill my son, taking back my empire. He'd thought he had me by having me arrested, using his secrets as currency to keep me behind bars. It only proved how much of a weak-willed man he was by choosing the lesser path.

All he'd done was give me time to prepare for my next attack. He assumed he had this place locked down, but he wasn't the only one with dirt on people. Coming here had been a vacation, and Atticus would soon learn there weren't any walls that could contain me. I was a force of nature, barreling through whatever lay in my path to get to my prize.

And tonight, that was Upswing.

My feet didn't make a sound as I padded through the halls, scanning my way through each door without issue. Seriously, they made it too easy to escape for anyone with two brain cells and deep pockets. Of course, the pockets were much shallower than I wanted, thanks again to my spawn. Just one more thing I'd be correcting when I was free of here.

"Good evening," I said, nodding at the front.

"Hmph," the man grunted, his eyes on his phone, but he opened the door. As I stepped through the last one, I felt a sense of relief and freedom that was unparalleled. It might've been easy on the inside, but I didn't relish anyone watching me take my daily shits. Out here was where I belonged.

Walking down the street a ways, I found the car waiting at the curb for me like my lawyer said it would be. Climbing in, I changed into a suit, wadding the guard uniform into a ball and tossing it far away from me. Peering through the bag next to me, I selected the gun I wanted, loading it and sliding it into my holster.

They'd caught me off guard last time, but I'd be the one in control tonight, taking them by surprise.

As we pulled up, I took in the arena that was lit up like they were hosting the Super Bowl. The parking lot was packed, and it made what I was about to do even better. There would be so many people to witness me overtaking my son. A delicious sense of satisfaction filled me, making me smile.

I'd kill Atticus first, then the big one. My bastard next before I defiled that slut of a wife of theirs. The others could watch, and then I'd kill them altogether. My daughter would be sold, helping me regain my fortune, and I was sure I could also fetch a good price for the boy. Plan outlined in my head, I smiled as I thought about my return.

The car rolled to a stop at the back entrance, and I stepped out, buttoning my suit. Striding in like I belonged, I made my way through the labyrinth of back halls. I could hear the announcer and crowd over the PA, and it seemed like their fighter was losing. It made me smile even more knowing it would be a double blow to them tonight.

Coming to the tunnel that would lead me to the floor, I grinned as excitement coursed through me. It was time to take what was owed and remind these pups why I was called the Grim Reaper.

Except when I stepped through, nothing made sense.

THIRTY NINE

ATTICUS

"Hello, Father."

I didn't say anything else, wanting to watch his face. My insides danced in glee as he began to turn purple. It fell from smug to confused before landing on rage.

"What is this?" he turned, taking in the empty stadium aside from me and the ones I'd come to depend on—my family.

Loren, Sax, Nicco, Wells, and Monroe stood behind me in an empty ring, safe from my father's ministrations.

"I believe this is the mouse taking the cheese and falling into the trap. Snap!" I clapped my hands together, the sound echoing around the deserted arena now that the fake sound we'd pumped in had stopped. He sneered at me, his eyes moving over my head. I could imagine how they looked behind me, all majestic in their poses as they stared Dayton down.

"It doesn't matter. I can still take you out!" he roared,

spit flying everywhere as he reached for his gun and pulled it free. This time, he was more clever and didn't waste a second before he pulled the trigger, aimed for my chest.

The sound went off, and he blinked as he looked down at the gun, wondering why it hadn't shot like he wanted.

"I don't understand," he whispered before tossing the prop gun onto the ground and leaping for me. I heard Loren gasp behind me, but I'd been prepared. I knew my father wouldn't go down without a fight.

Dayton lurched forward, and I dodged, stepping to the side. Slowly, I rolled up my sleeves as we circled one another, taking in my father for the last time. He looked even worse than he did a week ago. He was sweating, his brow dripping, and I smiled that the formula we slipped into his water seemed to be working. He wheezed, his eyes drooping as he reached into his pocket to pull out a crude shiv.

While this hadn't been part of the plan, I wasn't worried. One, the effects of the drug "Old man," as Pixel had named it, would be hitting him about now. And two, I learned to never underestimate my father the day he sold his own daughter to gain power. He always had an escape plan, even faking his own death. So, I would never make that mistake again. I was ready for anything he had to throw at me. If he managed to attack me, it would be my fault for not paying attention.

His steps faltered slightly as he blinked again, his hand re-gripping the shiv. "What... what is going on?"

"Now, who isn't listening, Dayton? I told you. You lost. You fell into my trap with such ease, I almost feel bad for killing you this time. *Almost.* You *will* die tonight and never be a threat to my family again." My words had never been said with such conviction before, and I meant every last one of them.

He sneered, drool dripping down his chin as he hunched over and lunged for me. He must've been saving up all of his energy because he managed to slice my shirt, but nothing else. He tumbled to the ground where he stayed, panting from the exertion.

"Really? I liked this shirt." Sighing, I unbuttoned and removed it. He peered up at me, his eyes wide when he saw my new ink.

"What have you done...?" he wheezed, his voice trailing off at the end like he no longer had words.

"Oh, this?" I asked, pointing at the symbol of a lion and rose. "Do you like it? You gave us the idea, actually. You kept leaving your moniker all over our things, so we took it upon ourselves to mark what was ours. You can never touch our hearts. Loren saved us from that fate." He sneered at the mention of my wife and I smiled even bigger. "My brother designed it, you know, the one you thought you'd use against us? Well, he's got real talent, that one."

"Ah, thanks, big Bro," Nicco cheered from the ring. I

peered over, finding him sitting on the side, leaning against the ropes as he swung his legs out.

"It's an abomination," Dayton spat, attempting to reach out for me one more time. I stepped on his hand, taking a small ounce of pleasure as he cried out. I wriggled the shiv out of his palm and threw it far away.

"No, that's where you're wrong. What you made our family was an abomination. Now, I'm resetting history, correcting the course of our lineage, and making it the family it always should've been. I'm just sad you won't live to see it. I know how much that would kill you." I smiled, liking the irony. "The Costa Sirens and the Mascros are now joined, bringing a new chapter to our family. Your murder is the last one I'll ever commit. It's a new era, Dayton, and you're shit out of time." I patted his cheek, unable to help myself from patronizing him one last time.

"How?" he asked, and I smiled, liking that he finally accepted his fate.

"Easy. I did what you taught me. I used your own hubris against you. I knew you'd escape eventually, so I made it happen. I had the guards talk about the fight so you'd come here, intent on settling the score. We had everyone we know and a few rentals parked outside and created a sound feed to give the appearance we were here. Each step you took was orchestrated by me. You were so bent on destroying us; you never stopped to question that I could've fooled you. Ergo, your demise."

I bent down, getting closer to the dying man on the floor. "The gun was fake, and your current condition is thanks to a brilliant cousin of mine who created a time-release formula to make you feel like an old man. I don't really understand the science behind it, but basically, it made your pain receptors think you were ninety, so everything hurts. And because she's Pixel, you'll even…"

I scrunched up my nose, waving a hand in front of my face.

"Yup, there it is. You even have the pleasure of shitting yourself. If they were to do an autopsy, it would show you died of a heart attack. But you won't be getting one of those. I haven't quite figured out if we should return you to your cell and let them find you or just feed you to the rats here? I'm leaning more toward the rats, but I'll let the daughter you tried to sell make the final call. She deserves that much. To know, once and for all, that you're gone from this earth. Enjoy your last few seconds, Dayton, because you're done."

He tried to groan, but it was already too late for him. I waited a few minutes, my experience with him last time flashing back, and I knew I wouldn't leave until I was confident he was dead. Hesitantly, I reached out, placing my fingers on his neck, and waited to feel a pulse. I relaxed when nothing could be found, my head dropping to my chest. When a tear fell down my cheek, I realized the weight that had been lifted.

A hand touched my shoulder, and I looked up into the eyes of the woman who'd saved me from myself. Who showed me I could be a better man than my father.

Standing, I wrapped my arms around her, holding her close, needing to remind myself I wasn't the hard mafia boss I pretended to be sometimes, but a man. A man who was broken and had been put back together by love. A man who was finally free of the restraints an evil dictator had placed on him. A man who had hope and a reason beyond duty to get out of bed in the morning. A man who had been forged through flames and had come out better. A man who loved others beyond measure and was loved in return. A man who was no longer alone. A man who'd learned that the actual definition of family wasn't about fear or obedience, but that a real family was made from respect and love.

"It's done," she whispered, rubbing my back. Nodding, I drew away, and she wiped my face, staring at me adoringly. "I love you so much, Atticus. Never forget that." Leaning up, she pecked my lips, sealing her words to my heart. When she stepped back, I saw the rest of them waiting to comfort me.

I would've laughed a year ago at the idea that I could consider five other men to be my best friends, people I trusted explicitly and sought out, but I did. I still didn't want to touch dicks with any of them, but joining forces to bring our wife pleasure was the ultimate experience of love and trust.

Walking forward, Sax pulled me into a brief hug, slapping me on the back. "You did it, Mas."

Nodding, I stepped forward to Nicco, who pulled me into another hug, holding me tight. "I'm so glad to have discovered the truth. I'm honored to be your brother." He squeezed tight, and I pulled back, catching the mistiness in his eyes that matched my own.

Monroe and Wells each clapped me on the back, giving me nods of respect. They fell into line behind Loren and me as we walked toward the tunnel on the other side. A team of Sirens were waiting to take Dayton away for now.

"He's ready," I said, and they bowed their heads in respect as they walked past. Stepping out into the warm summer night, I felt the last of the tension leave me. The villain of our story was dead, and now we could live our lives free of his torment.

And I, for one, couldn't wait.

Forty

LOREN

The difference tonight as we stepped into Upswing was tremendous. Last night, we'd been poised to take down a madman, and tonight, we were celebrating the start of our new beginning.

"You're gonna be amazing. Don't forget your reward for winning," I teased, kissing Wells on the lips. He snorted, pulling me closer.

"I'm not sure the consequence is as significant this time," he purred, kissing my neck.

"Oh, did I not tell you?" I smiled, waiting for him to pull back and look into my eyes.

"No, what?"

"Nicco said the new reward was letting you take my ass, but the consequence was him taking yours. Your diamond is in your locker in case you lose." I kissed him quickly, walking away, leaving him stunned. At the door, I paused, turning my head over my shoulder. "I'm already wearing mine."

Winking, I blew him a kiss for luck and made my way to the VIP area. It was still early so none of the fights had started, but Wells wanted to have some time to center himself. I imagine after that parting gift he'd need a minute to wrangle the beast between his legs.

I was greeted by Monroe smirking at me when I stepped into the VIP lounge. Nicco was chatting with a few people, and the teens were gathered around a table with Sax. The only one missing was Atticus.

Monroe walked over, wrapping his arm around me, leaning down to whisper. "He went to talk with the O'Sullivans and Vasquezs. He won't be long." Nodding, I relaxed into his arms. "Did you really leave Wells with a hard-on?" He chuckled.

Smiling, I nodded. "Maybe. I just told him the new rewards and consequences Nicco offered."

"What about me, Beautiful?" Nicco asked, walking over. My breath caught at the sight of him, and I got lost for a few seconds as I stared. All of my husbands were just so yummy.

"Just how you like to incentivize the fighters," I managed to say when I realized the people he'd been talking to earlier were with him.

"Ah, yes, I do have my ways." He grinned, the teasing light hard to miss in his eyes. "Loren, I'd like you to meet the family of one of the fighters I'm considering sponsoring. This is Steel, I mean, Elias' girl-friend, Sawyer, and her other boyfriends, Henry and

Rhett." He winked at me, and I realized what he wanted.

"It's a pleasure to meet you all. I'm excited to see Elias fight now. Nicco is the best at spotting talent and taking care of them, so he'd be in good hands. It's so good that you could all make it to support him. I know how important it is for fighters to have that."

"We're excited to be in Chicago. It worked out that we had another competition as well. Not all of us could make it, but we have our family here to support him," the young woman said. It looked like she physically forced herself to stop before she seemed to lose the battle and blurted something out. "You're not going to say anything about me having multiple boyfriends?" She cringed like she was embarrassed about her outburst.

Laughing, I shook my head. "No, why would I when I have five husbands?"

She stood still for a second before she chuckled, laughing at herself. "Okay, well, I think I like this place even more now. It hasn't been the easiest when traveling and meeting people who don't know us to explain I have seven boyfriends."

My eyes grew wide in surprise. "That has to be a lot of work. But no judgment here. We're all about family and love. It's the Mascro way."

"That's nice to hear," the shorter male said. The other one just stood, staring at us, giving Sax a run for his money on the quiet, stoic front.

"Well, if you need anything or want a tour of the city, let me know. We also have two teenage children, so if we don't know the hip spots, they might."

"Hey, I just turned thirty. I'm still hip!" Nicco protested as we all laughed. Patting his cheek, I kissed him.

"Sure thing, babe."

Monroe and I said our goodbyes as we walked over to the kids. Atticus was sitting with them now, and I relaxed, knowing most of us were here. Nicco would head down before Wells fought to make sure he was ready and walk with him out to the ring since he was acting as his coach. The bond the two had built was solid, and I loved seeing all of my husbands finding their way into each other's hearts.

Atticus looked up as we neared, reaching a hand out for me, but Sax stood and picked me up, sitting me in his lap as he sat. Atticus huffed, but let his friend have his way. Smiling, I patted my giant's arm, feeling safe in them.

"Lor, have you decided where we're going on vacation? I think my presentation was the best," Imogen said.

"New York is too easy," Jude argued, "we should go out west. See the national parks and the Grand Canyon."

Smiling at them both, I debated if I wanted to tell them now or not. "Well, as a matter of fact, for our first vacation, we've decided to go all out and do a tropical location where we can go repelling, snorkeling, shopping, and chill at the same spot."

Their faces brightened as they listened, turning to one another in glee. "Oh, this will be a blast," Jude said. "Could I get an underwater camera to take pictures in the ocean?"

"Of course, that sounds like a great idea."

"I can't wait to go shopping!" Imogen cheered, bouncing in her seat.

"Don't think that since we're on vacation, it means the rules change," Atticus interrupted, staring down the two with his boss face. "No sex allowed."

Their faces both turned red before they burst out laughing. "Oh, Attie, you're so worried about that. We've only kissed. Calm down," Immy said, waving him off.

"You've kissed! Lore, they've already kissed. We need to set up some boundaries immediately," he said, turning to me with panic in his eyes.

Reaching across, I patted his cheek. "Honey, it will be okay. And besides, if Immy gets pregnant, we'll just raise the baby."

His eyes bugged out, and I wondered if I'd given him a heart attack. The rest of the table broke out into laughter as he sputtered, his brain faltering.

"I'm kidding. They're smart kids, and they're almost eighteen. Trust them to make the right decisions for themselves."

His jaw opened and closed as he looked back and forth between the two snickering teenagers at his reaction. "Fine," he managed to say, sitting back in his seat like a sulking child.

Thankfully, the matches began as the announcer came on over the system, announcing the first two fighters. After the third one, Sawyer and her guys stood and walked down to the front area, so I assumed it meant her boyfriend was next. Moving over to the railing, I watched as Steel moved, his steps quick and fluid.

"He's good," I said when I felt arms enclose me.

"Yeah, I think he'll be a good fit for Nicco's team," Monroe agreed.

We watched as he easily defeated his opponent, and I loved watching Sawyer cheer for him. When he stepped down, she ran to him, jumping into his arms and kissing him, and it, for some reason, made me believe in love a little more. I didn't know their story, but I could tell they'd been through something, their bond tight, and I hoped they made it.

"Come on, it's time." Together, we walked down to the floor with the rest of our family. We were all supporting Wells from the front row that Atticus had blocked off for friends and family of fighters, so no one had to search for seats. When we got down there, I bounced on my toes, eager to see Wells and Nicco. It was such a different experience this time as we waited for the fight to start.

For one, we knew Dayton and Darren were gone, and no enemies were lying in wait to strike at us. And secondly, we were all committed together as a unit. When the emcee announced Crash, the crowd went wild, and I loved how many of the Sirens and Mascros were here to support one of their own.

"He looks good," Monroe whispered, and I nodded, realizing how relaxed and confident he was this time.

"He's ready."

The bell rang, but I didn't focus on anything other than Wells as he struck out at his opponent. It was beautiful to watch him move, his muscles bulging and rippling with his kicks and hits. On his chest, his tattoos gleamed under the lights. The arrows and now our family crest. Nicco had given us all one the day we'd realized what we needed to do and join forces. It was the only way forward and a new beginning for both families.

During the third round, Wells' kick landed, and the guy went down, falling to the ground and didn't get up. The referee counted, slapping the floor until he stood, raising Wells' arm into the air, announcing him the victor.

I jumped up and down, the smile spreading across my face as he stared over at me, a hungry look in his eyes. Monroe leaned close, nipping my ear as Sax bent down from the other side.

"I want in on whatever that is," Sax demanded,

clutching my chin to make sure I heard. Laughing, I nodded, kissing the tips of his fingers that were close.

"Of course, we can all celebrate the win together."

That night, Wells showed me how much he liked a little anal, giving me two orgasms before he let anyone else have at me. I couldn't complain, and I didn't even care if I walked funny the following day. It was all worth it.

I knew I would never wish for anything more as I lay in bed with my husbands around me. I didn't need to try to gain more or open the door to something that might bring more pain than joy.

This was it. The life I'd wanted.

"What are you thinking, Bellezza?" Atticus whispered from in front of me. I peered up, not realizing he'd been awake.

"How perfect my life is."

"Oh?" he smiled, smoothing his thumb over my cheek.

"I've made my decision. I don't need the eggs, and the trust can be a college fund for the kids or go toward the center. You guys, the kids, the dogs, my job... It's everything I could want. I'm so happy. So, so, happy." Tears welled in my eyes at the truth in that. "I never thought I could be this free, but I am because of the love you guys give me."

"Are you sure? You don't have to make this decision now."

"I'm sure. It's a reminder of my life before, and I don't need it. I made my peace with it, and it feels weird to not be able to have a kid with each of you. I don't want it to hold me back or always think, what if. It feels too much like a safety blanket, and I don't want that anymore."

"Okay, Bellezza. I'll make the call. And I think the scholarship program sounds like an excellent idea." He kissed away my tears, and I relaxed in his arms, the last weight I'd been carrying around gone.

My perfect life hadn't been married to my high school sweetheart, living in the suburbs with the white picket fence. Turned out that was my nightmare.

No, my happy ending was here, with these men who lived in the darkness and didn't shy away from mine. With the family we made and the life where we got to decide who was in it. We were all broken at one point, hiding behind masks of deception, too scared to look at the truth, until we could no longer hide. I once thought my darkest confession was that I was a fraud, a depressed therapist too scared to live her own life.

Instead, my honest truth was the life and person I wanted to be were there, waiting for me all along. I just had to open my eyes and take a chance. And I took that chance several times, finding love with five men, three kids, two dogs, and a whole heap of friends.

People might never understand my choices, but the great thing was, they didn't have to make sense to others. At the end of the day, the only person whose opinion mattered was my own, and I had finally learned to value it.

EPILOGUE

LOREN

The sun set over the ocean, and I sighed at the beauty. The island we were on was so full of life. It was amazing to see it everywhere I looked. Trees hung with fruit, flowers bloomed over pots, birds cawed, and tiny insects scurried about, not bothered by our invasion. The air was humid, but something about being able to smell the sea on it, to feel the salt on your skin as the day went on, was nice. It made me feel alive in a way I hadn't in a while.

Well, that wasn't true. More like, it contrasted nicely with the barren field I had stared at for so long in my empty and quiet apartment. My life was no longer either of those things, and I loved every second of it. I never thought I'd be one to crave the loud, boisterous noise of a family, but it had become one of the happiest sounds for me.

The kids were building a sandcastle on the beach, having a contest against Nicco, Sax, and, surprisingly,

Atticus. We'd all seen a different side of him here. He'd been slowly dropping his barriers with each passing day after he dealt with his father, and coming here offered him a chance to let them all go. He laughed so much now; it was like he was a different man.

"Hey, Kitten," Wells purred, pulling me back into his chest. I'd been leaning against the patio's railing that led down to the beach.

"Hey, Surly," I purred back, leaning against him. "I can't believe this is our last night here. It's gone by too fast."

He kissed my neck, the feeling sending shivers through me. "It just means we'll have to make Money Bags bring us back. Or better yet, he can buy us this island."

"Oh, is that how it works?" I asked, laughing at the insane game of nicknames the guys had for one another.

"What's funny?" Monroe asked, sidling up to the other side of me.

"Wells said we need to make Atticus buy us this island so we can come back whenever we want."

"That's not a bad idea," Monroe agreed, his face already thinking through the logistics. "I bet I could have a contract outlined and ready before we leave in the morning."

Rolling my eyes, I'd let them have their fantasies. "You two have accepted this new life rather well. Do you miss what your life was like before, though? Do you miss training dogs?"

It was something I worried about, and I was curious about what they would say. I knew they loved me and wanted to be with me, but at the time, it hadn't really been a choice but a matter of survival.

"The dogs were something I did to pass the time, to not feel so alone. I don't need that anymore. I still have Fort and Barkley to train, and Koda and Nova love all the attention they get from the guards. I'm not taking on any new dogs, but I'm okay with it. If I stop fighting, I can look into it some more, but I don't need it like I did."

Wells had finally sold his place, putting his trust in our relationship to succeed and letting go of the one thing he had left. He'd brought the two huskies with him and found they liked having a job and were getting more playtime and attention as guard dogs than they did at the house.

Monroe moved closer, wrapping his arms around me and Wells. "Lo, being part of this family and with you is everything I ever wanted. Levi loves having siblings and all the guards to steal cookies off of. He's never been happier. I get to spend time with you, Wells, and even the rowdy kid. I'm good. I'm so beyond good." He leaned in to kiss me, pressing his lips to mine.

"I know you didn't just call me kid," Nicco yelled, bounding up the stairs next to us. He had a smile on his face as I drew back. He wore only swim trunks, his tattoos on full display, and I found my eyes trailing over them as the water dripped down his abs.

"Fuck," Wells hissed, rubbing his growing erection into me. "I swear, you were sent to torment me."

Nicco winked, sauntering over to the three of us. "Maybe, but oh what fun I have." He leaned forward like he was going to kiss Wells, but pulled Monroe in and kissed him instead. I would say, "Poor Monroe," since he often got pulled between their dominance battles, but I think he liked it.

"You'll pay for that, Tatts," Wells grumbled, but I could feel how hard it made him behind me.

"Oh, I hope so," he teased, pulling back. "I've come to whisk you all away for our last night. Topher and Eric will guard the kiddos so we can have some alone time." He wiggled his eyebrows in excitement.

"Just give me a second to talk to them before we go," I said, kissing all of their cheeks. Atticus and Sax made their way up as I walked down, and I kissed them, telling them I'd be right up.

"Hey Lor," Immy said, smiling at me. Every day she seemed to brighten more and more, and I knew it had to be from knowing that her father was truly gone. She'd debated what to do and worried we'd think less of her if she chose for him to rot, but we all assured her we would understand and support her either way. It took her a few days to decide, and the day after the fight, she finally made up her mind.

I still remembered the conversation we had.

"I THINK I'M READY," *she said over breakfast.* "I'd like to say I could trust that he really is gone, and burying him would make me feel better. But I can't. He's already risen once from the grave, even if it was faked, and I think I need to see that for myself, or I'll never move on. I know it's brutal, but without getting any revenge, it feels empty to not make him suffer. Does that make me a bad person?"

"No, honey. He stole something from you and violated his role as your father. There isn't a rule book on how to get over that. You have the fortunate opportunity to do something about it that most people don't. The only one who knows what they need is you. So, if this is it, then it's not wrong. We'll support you and be there with you for it."

She sighed in relief, and I watched as her whole posture changed.

EACH DAY since she'd become a vibrant version of herself from the girl I first met.

"Hey guys, I just wanted to say goodnight. I guess we're having a date or something. You'll be okay?"

"Yep," the three of them said, giggling.

"Okay, I'm sure you'll be up to some mischief, so be careful and don't be too hard on Topher and Eric."

I hugged and then kissed them all on the cheek before

walking back up the beach. I nodded to Topher and Eric, who stood back, letting the kids have their privacy when they could. We'd relaxed a lot on the guards, but I was guessing that Atticus was taking full precautions since none of us were going to be around.

Stepping into the villa, I looked around, not seeing anyone. I hadn't been gone that long, so I didn't know where they could've run off to. Heading toward our wing of the villa, I found soft petals on the ground as I turned the corner.

Smiling, I had an idea what they were up to, and excitement filled me as I continued down the hallway toward the room I'd been staying in. We didn't spend every night together, so the guys would rotate out who was with me and we'd been able to find a good balance. I got time with them alone and with some double and triple pairing.

We hadn't had a full group activity since the night of the fight, and I'd be lying if I wasn't excited about the prospect of another one.

Pushing open the door, I found all five of my husbands waiting for me.

Wells

Loren walked in, her face beaming, and I wanted to wrap her up in my arms and never let her go. But this wasn't that type of night. I couldn't be selfish. It was hard, and I was still adjusting some days, but I couldn't deny I liked the perks.

"It's our last night here, Bellezza, so we thought it would be best to spend it together."

Loren nodded, trying to take us all in. "I am so on board with this plan," she barely managed to get out the words before Nicco pounced.

"Always the impatient one," Atticus sighed, but you could hear the love he had for his brother.

Sax moved next, pulling them to the bed as they kissed and undressed her. Monroe tugged on my hand and drew me over to the bed, not wanting to miss out on the fun.

While this wasn't our first time together as five, it wasn't the normal situation, so we all looked around for a second, attempting to figure out who went where. Both times before, it was more a heat of the moment thing and hadn't really been coordinated.

"You're overthinking it, Crash," Nicco teased, throwing me a look to come to his side. Monroe followed, putting the three of us on one side and Sax and Atticus on the other. I supposed it made sense; this was our usual groupings, with Sax occasionally joining in when he had his FOMO moments.

Believe it or not, the giant was a softy and needed to know from time to time he wasn't forgotten. I identified with him too much in those moments to deny it.

Monroe pulled my boxers off, reminding me I needed to stop thinking and focus on what was happening. Nicco kissed down Loren's right side, squeezing her breast and tweaking her nipple, and I watched in amazement the sight of his inked hands on her.

Atticus was on her left, kissing her deeply as Sax found his dessert between her legs. A hand snapped out, pulling me closer, and I went voluntarily as Nicco took my hand and wrapped it around his studded cock.

"Don't be shy, lover."

It was all I needed to hear as I began to stroke him, my fingers playing over the studded jewelry. Monroe dropped to his knees, taking my dick between his lips, and I was lost in the sensation for a moment. Nicco moved, pushing me closer to the bed, and I found Loren's waiting lips as I bent down to kiss her. Monroe moved with me, shuffling as he kept my dick in his mouth. When I felt hands on my ass, I knew what Nicco was after.

He bent down a moment later, whispering in my ear, "Good, Crash," at what he'd found.

A shudder ran through me as he traced the outer seam of the plug. I'd hated it at first, but once I let myself relax, I found I craved it from time to time. The dynamics between the three of us were very fluid; though Monroe tended to be the least dominant, it didn't mean he didn't pull it out from time to time. It was a good balance between us to trade-off being top and bottom.

My hands roamed Loren's body as our tongues twisted around one another, and I reached down to find her clit. Sax was already impaling her on his monster dick, so I helped bring her closer to the edge as he pounded into her.

"My turn," Atticus boomed, taking Loren's face from me and kissing her himself. When he was thoroughly satisfied, he placed the head of his dick at her lips, and I watched as she began to lick the tip. Monroe took the new angle to go deeper, and I tugged on his hair, needing a little more from him.

Nicco pushed me down a little as he gently removed his gift to me from months ago and began to lube me and himself up. I lost track of who was doing what, trying to hold on and not spill myself just yet.

Sax let out a roar as he came, falling back to the bed as Loren panted below me. Atticus turned her on her side and began to prep her for himself when I knew what I wanted to do.

"Monroe, move to Loren," I ordered. He snapped up, looking in my eyes, and nodded, letting my cock fall from his mouth. He licked his lips before he moved to the bed and wrapped Loren in his arms as he kissed her, nudging her pussy with his dick.

"Hand me the lube when you're done," I said to Nicco, and he grunted as he began to slide into me. My mind went blank as it always initially did at the feeling of something foreign entering me; once he was past my wall, the pressure lessened, and the pleasure filled me. He stopped, breathing deeply as he handed me the bottle and moved with me closer to the bed.

"You know, you could've just waited until I was positioned on the bed," I said, peeking over my shoulder at Nicco. He smirked, making my insides quiver in such a different way than Roe.

"I know. It's more fun this way. We're like a human jigsaw puzzle."

"You're incorrigible," I teased, laughing. "And I love it. I love you."

Nicco stopped, his eyes going wide. In the past, I would've freaked out, but I just patted his cheek and moved lower to the bed, finding Loren smiling at me.

"That was beautiful," she moaned, as Atticus and Monroe didn't let up, thrusting in unison.

Nicco seemed to come out of his stutter, following me as I prepared Monroe's back door. He was quiet, and I wondered if I'd finally managed to shock the cheeky fucker. Something about that made me smile. I held Monroe's hip as I began to push into him, the tight feeling making my cock weep. As soon as I was in, I let out a sigh, resting my head on his shoulder.

Before I could blink, my head was wrenched back as Nicco peered down into my eyes, a determined look there. "I fucking love you too, asshole." He smashed his lips to mine, stealing all the words from me.

When he pulled back, we both moaned as the force of Monroe and Atticus made us shift as well. Gripping onto Monroe, I managed to move with him and found my own rhythm with Nicco. Sax sat at the foot of the bed, stroking his cock in tandem with our thrusts, looking a little forlorn as the five of us fucked one another.

"Don't even think about it, Sax," Atticus wheezed, making the rest of us chuckle. He pouted a little until Loren wiggled her finger for him to move to the top of the bed. Atticus groaned but moved down so Sax could get near Loren's mouth.

It didn't take long after that, as pleasure raced through my body, tingles running up my spine, and my balls drawing up tight. We all began to come as we crested over the peaks in quick succession, falling into a heap of cum coated bodies.

"That... was... everything... " Loren panted, trying to catch her breath. "I love all of you so much."

"I love you, too," rang out from around the room as we lay in a comfortable pile of bodies, panting for air.

"Okay, I gotta move," Monroe said, starting the

process of detaching ourselves from the giant daisy chain we'd made.

I was spent, so I laid back, not caring my dick was out. A washcloth was tossed onto my chest, so I grabbed it, wiping myself up before I managed to heave myself out of bed and make my way to the bathroom. When I returned, someone had managed to get a tray of drinks and desserts, and a picnic was spread around the bed.

"Nothing's better after great sex than chocolate," Loren said a smile on her face. "I'm so happy I get to do this the rest of my life."

Atticus put on a stupid TV show we'd all gotten into but wouldn't admit it, and we lounged around the massive bed, eating sweets and drinking champagne as we pretended not to laugh.

"Just so you know, I love you other two fuckers, too, just not in the 'I want to suck your dick' way. But you're my bros, and I'm glad to have you in my life," I said, the sentiment surprising even me, but it was true.

"Your loss," Sax grunted, tossing a piece of chocolate in his mouth. We all turned, stunned when he smiled, a laugh bellowing out of him. "Oh, man, your faces. It would be your loss, but I don't want to particularly kiss your face, so let's just keep things how they are."

Loren laughed so hard, she had tears streaming down her face. Nicco and Monroe patted my legs, letting me know they appreciated my vulnerability, and I felt happy that I could be.

When I was younger, I thought wealth was the answer to all my problems, when in reality, it had been the destruction of my dreams. Instead, it was love and these people who made me feel like I mattered and could be any version of myself, and they'd accept it or remind me who I was if I got off track. It was better than any fortune.

My mistakes had been brutal at one time, leaving me desperate and alone, but they somehow brought me to salvation, and that was something I would never regret. backdoor diamond and all.

Have no fear, some of our beloved characters will return in 2023 with a three part Siren series featuring Cami, Nat, and Pixel.
Along with a duet featuring Immy.
Make sure to subscribe so you stay up to date all the news!
Turn the page for a bonus scene.

BONUS

LOREN

"Cake, cake, cake!" the crowd shouted. The staff rolled out the monstrosity as the crowd egged them on.

"Is that a cake or a transformer?" Nicco joked, eyeing the thing. He slung his arm around me as we watched.

"It's the only thing I'd let Nat have control over, and well, I think she went a little overboard," I said, eyeing the five-foot thing as unease sat in my gut.

"She's not like, going to jump out of it, is she?" Wells asked, looking around to spot her.

"You wish," she scoffed, moving into view. The dress she wore was purple and flowed around her. She was trailed by Beau and Byron, who both looked smashing in their tuxedos. Nat placed her hands on her hips, giving me the eye. "You ready?" she asked, and I wasn't sure what I needed to be ready for.

I looked around the yard, spotting all the people I loved. Cami smiled as she danced with Olivia, her rose gold dress swaying in the breeze. Lark and Seb stood hand in hand on one side, with Malek standing on Cami's other, looking at her with pure amazement.

Lily and Levi sat at a table, surrounded by some of the guards, while they played cards for Skittles. Levi had become a shark at the game and was making his way through hustling all the guards.

Jude and Immy smiled at me as I caught their gaze. They were sitting with Marcus at a table, waiting for us to cut the cake. With them sat Pixel and Stacy, who'd become closer since the bachelorette party, and I was glad Pixel seemed to be making a friend.

When I turned back, I found my five husbands waiting at the giant cake for me. Nat walked over, tugging on my arm as she pulled me toward it.

"I swear, you're the most reluctant bride, and you've already been married for months!"

"Nonsense. I'm not reluctant." I rolled my eyes, letting her drag me.

"No? Well, what do you call this?" she asked, stopping to let me answer.

"Happy. Loved. Cherished." I shrugged, smiling ear to ear. "All of this is just the trappings. It's not that I don't care, because I do, but it's more for other people than it's really about me. You'll see one day."

"Yeah, no."

"Now, who's being reluctant?" I teased.

"There's dragging your feet like you've done and just

being smart." She started to pull me toward the cake again, but I stopped her this time.

"I hope you really don't feel that way, Nat. Marriage is one of the most beautiful things you can do. When it's with the right person or people."

She searched my eyes, something on the tip of her tongue before she smiled, linking her arm with mine.

"Another day, okay? Today, it's all about you, friend." She kissed my cheek and shoved me into the waiting arms of my men. Nat turned to the small crowd gathered, only our closest friends and family were here, and it was perfect.

"I think we need to hear that chant again! Levi?"

"Cake, cake, cake!" he shouted, giggling as he and Lily fell out of their chairs in excitement.

"Since Loren wouldn't let me plan anything else for the festivities, I decided to go all out with the cake. Each layer is a different flavor to represent each person in this marriage. First, we have coffee, followed by death by chocolate, strawberry, lemon, red velvet, and finishing with a traditional white wedding cake. And because I'm me, I've started a little bet over to the side where you can make a guess on which cake belongs to which person. Whoever gets the most correct wins a ride with Atticus in his fancy-schmancy car."

"Um, excuse me?" Atticus started until I pulled his face down to kiss.

"That was awfully kind of you," I teased.

"Hmph," he settled on, turning back to Nat.

"Alright, I'm not sure how you guys want to do the cutting," she said, holding up a knife and plate.

Atticus sighed, but walked over and took the two things from her. "Shouldn't we wait until everyone votes, so they don't see which cake we cut?" he asked, eyeing Nat.

"Oh, good call!" Nat exclaimed, turning back to the crowd. "Well, you heard the man. Make your votes now!"

Everyone quickly got up, running over to the table to fill out their ballot card before shoving it into the basket she had out. Laughing at all of their eagerness to ride in Atticus' car, I rested my head on his shoulder as we watched.

"She's a nuisance, but she's got style," Atticus grumbled as we waited for the last of the group to make their guesses. Laughing, I patted his arm, enjoying the activity with our family.

"Alright, well, if you guess death by chocolate for me, you get a point." Atticus cut into the cake, and we both set a small piece onto our forks. Looking into his umber eyes, I relished how remarkable they were as they trained on me.

"Ready, Bellezza?" A slight smirk appeared at the corner of his mouth as he waited for me.

"Always," I said, lifting my fork to his mouth. Together, we both took a bite of cake, and I tried not to laugh as I smeared a little icing on his lips as I placed it in his mouth. His eyes warned that there would be consequences later, but I would gladly welcome them.

Atticus dropped his fork, wrapped an arm around me, and pulled me close so he could kiss me, spreading the icing onto my lips. I willingly accepted his offering, knowing I'd take anything he gave me. The crowd "awwed" behind us as he dipped me before rising and spinning me toward Sax.

Giggling, I fell into my mountain's arms. "Hey, sexy man."

"Hey, Spitfire," he cooed, looking at me with love in his eyes. His thumb rose up, wiping the bit of icing I'd missed from the corner of my mouth, and he raised it to his mouth, licking it slowly off his thumb.

"Okay, next," Nat interrupted, breaking our embrace as she handed us new forks. "Keep it PG," she mumbled, narrowing her eyes at us. Laughing, we stepped apart, walking up to the next layer of cake.

Sax didn't say anything as he cut into the red velvet layer, placing the cake onto the plate. We could hear the crowd make cheers and jeers behind us as they either got it right or wrong.

"Open, Spitfire," Sax ordered, lifting the cake up to my mouth before I could put some onto my fork. Obeying him, I opened my mouth as he delicately placed the cake on my tongue, the flavors spreading across it.

When he stepped back, he had a smug look, like he thought I'd be nice to him.

Taking the cake onto my fork, I wiggled my finger for him to come closer. He smirked, thinking he'd won as he leaned down. Smoothing my hand across his jaw, I tipped forward a little to whisper into his ear and took the piece of cake into my hand instead.

"Nice try," I teased just as I smashed the cake into his cheek as I moved back. Sax laughed, never taking his eyes from me as his tongue reached out, licking some of the icing from his cheek. My breath caught as he continued to lick it, then raised his finger up to wipe the rest, placing it into his mouth.

"Seriously, if you weren't wearing such a nice dress, I'd hose you all down!" Nat griped, stepping in between the two of us. Sax growled as my cheeks heated, forgetting once again that other people were watching us.

"Monroe, you're next. I expect better from you," Nat warned, handing him a fork.

Sax stepped back to make room, but not before he mouthed, "Payback." My face flamed as my clit started to throb from the promise his eyes had just made. Monroe smiled at me, pulling me closer to him. He took out a handkerchief and wiped my hand free of icing.

"Hopefully, I'll avoid that fate," he teased. "Though, I'd love to see you get Wells," he whispered as he leaned over for the knife, sending goosebumps down my arms. Giggling, I kissed his cheek, nodding that I understood.

Monroe turned to the crowd, waving the knife. "Levi, want to come and help?" he asked. Levi wasted no time rushing forward as he wrapped his arms around both of our legs.

"Yes! Can I take a piece for Lily and me back? You're taking too long," he said, looking up.

"Sure, bud. Want to tell everyone which cake is mine?"

"Lemon!" he cheered, placing his hand over Monroe's as they cut into the lemon cake.

"Which kind do you want?" I asked him as I grabbed two empty plates.

"Chocolate and lemon for me, and Lily wants strawberry."

"Okay, you can have these two for now, and then when the strawberry gets cut, you have another piece. Deal?"

"Deal. Thanks, Lommy." He tugged on my hand, pulling me down so he could plant a kiss on my cheek.

Holding the tears back, I rose and straightened the cream silk of my dress. Monroe held the fork with a bite of lemon on it for me, giving me a knowing look.

Together, we fed one another the lemon cake as we smiled, laughing. "Mm, that's really good," I said, figuring out which was my favorite.

"I knew I could count on you, Monroe. Now, you two," Nat said, returning with more cutlery. She eyed Nicco and Wells. The former shrugged, smirking as he watched her, while the latter looked on, bored as he waited his turn. Neither said anything, giving nothing away if they would play by the rules or not.

"Ugh, fine, Nicco, you're first." She handed him the knife and fork, turning to plead with me to keep my libido under control.

Yeah, good luck with that wish.

"Beautiful," Nicco purred, stepping closer. He dipped his head, kissing me briefly as he placed his hands on the small of my back. Nicco peered out at the crowd, smiling at all of our friends.

"There are three flavors left, and guess which is mine?" he asked, winking down at me.

"Vanilla!" someone shouted.

"Coffee," another called out.

"Definitely a trick question. You like chocolate," Beau shouted, making us all laugh.

"Well, the joke is on all of you. My favorite is strawberry. Little cous, you can get your cake now." He nodded to Lily, who ran up, eager to be included. Nicco cut us a piece and then plated one for her, kissing the top of her head as she ran off. Out of all of the guys, I worried he'd miss out on being a dad the most, considering he was the youngest. When he looked back up, the piece of cake ready on his fork, he stopped.

"I love our life, Beautiful. There's nothing more I want." He moved the pink cake toward me, and I nodded, accepting his truth as I opened for the fluffy concoction. As I chewed, I lifted mine, giving him his bite. He smiled, leaning down to kiss me again as we laughed.

"Alright, alright," Nat sighed, trying to break us apart as the crowd "awwed" us again.

"Keep it clean," she said to Wells, handing him the last of the utensils, brandishing the last of her weapons. She huffed as she walked away, mumbling something about being more stressful than she'd anticipated, making me laugh.

"Kitten," Wells purred, stepping into Nicco and me, despite Nat's warning. He leaned over, smashing some icing into Nicco's face before taking my hand and pulling me around to where he could cut his piece of cake. Nicco shrugged, licking the icing as he laughed and joined the others.

"When did you grab some cake?" I asked, curious.

"Secrets," he teased, following Sax's approach and just cutting into the coffee layer without announcing it. A few shouts of glee rang out as they got their guesses right, while others moaned they'd gotten it wrong. Wells ignored all of them, focused only on me.

He took both forks and put a piece of cake on them, handing one to me. "You're my forever, Kitten."

I'd planned to smash the cake into his face, but with such sweet words, I opted not to, smiling at him as I opened my mouth. Wells smirked, and I realized my mistake at the last second as his fork ventured off, spreading the icing all over my face before landing in my mouth.

Sputtering, I laughed, shrugging as I ran my finger through the icing and placed it in my mouth. "Let's all eat some cake!" I shouted, tired of being in the spotlight. Or maybe I was just tired of Nat cockblocking me like a middle school teacher at the end of school dance.

"It's time to dance, Kitten," Wells whispered, taking me into his arms as the music played. I willingly followed him, swaying to the soft music as I laid my head on his chest and listened to his heart. We didn't talk, just happy to be in each other's embrace as we celebrated with our family.

Each of my husbands took their turn, twirling me around the dance floor as Jude took pictures of us all. It was the perfect reception for us, filled with the people we loved, low-key, and nothing but happiness.

Here in our backyard, we weren't Mascros who ruled over Chicago. We were just family. And that was something I'd been searching my whole life for. At times, the path here had been tumultuous, but I couldn't argue where it had ended—complete and utter bliss.

AFTERWORD

Thank you for reading Loren's story. It's hard to believe that it's come to an end. When I first thought about writing, it was Loren's prologue that I first wrote. Or a version of it. Her story is the most vulnerable I've ever been, and it was healing to process some of the things I'd experienced through her. So, thank you to all who have loved her and what she had to say.

If you know me by now, I can't seem to ever let a story go completely, so there will be some novellas along the way and a duet with Imogen. These characters are near and dear to me, so I'm sure you'll see them around more.

As always, I couldn't do this without the fantastic people around me. To my husband, who supports me and my crazy ideas. Thank you for all you do.

To Emma, who I wouldn't know what to do without, thank you. You truly have become my best friend.

To Megan, thank you for jumping on my crazy train and putting up with my ridiculous demands. You and Emma's comments give me life when I don't feel like pushing on. So, thank you.

To my author bestie, Cat, thanks for always giving me feedback and reassuring me that it's not crap.

To Kayla and Lindsay, thank you for being willing to plow through a document whenever I message and helping me make it top-notch. Your feedback is invaluable, and I appreciate you both.

To Michelle and Tory, thank you for being awesome beta readers! I love your comments and feedback, which helped me with the bonus chapter.

To all my arc readers, I appreciate your reviews and the love you have for my books. You're all amazing! I love the support you give on social media. I love your videos and edits!

And to anyone who just happened to pick this up story and fell in love along the way, thank you for giving me a chance to come into your life for a few hours.

Until next time, check out all the great books I have out, and make sure to subscribe to my newsletter to be first in the know of all the amazing books coming this year.

Catch you later, Misfit Penguin.

ALSO BY KRIS BUTLER

The Council Series

(completed series)

Damaged Dreams

Shattered Secrets

Fractured Futures

Bosh Bells & Epic Fails

The Order Duet (Council Spinoff)

Stiletto Sins

Dark Confessions

Dangerous Truths

Dangerous Lies

Dangerous Vows

Reckless (Cami's Novella)

Relentless (Nat's Novella)

Dangerous Love

Tattooed Hearts Duet

Tattooed Hearts Completed Duet

Riddled Deceit (Part 1)

Smudged Lines (Part 2)

Music City Diaries

Beautiful Agony

Vacation Romcom

Vibing

Sinners Fairytales

(standalone)

Pride

ABOUT THE AUTHOR

Kris Butler

Kris Butler writes under a pen name to have some separation from her everyday life. Never expecting to write a book, she was surprised when an author friend encouraged her to give it a try and how much she enjoyed it. Having an extensive background in mental health, Kris hopes to normalize mental health issues and the importance of talking about them with her characters and books. Kris is a southern girl at heart but lives with her husband and adorable furbaby somewhere in the Midwest. Kris is an avid fan of Reverse Harem and hopes to add a quirky and new perspective to the emerging genre. If you enjoyed her book, please consider leaving a review. You can contact her the following ways and follow Kris's journey as a new author on social media.

Join the newsletter

Join my group

Signed books and merch